Praise

Book One – *Shadowkings*

'Cobley's impressively unpleasant first fantasy novel'
AMAZON

'One of the best new fantasy sagas that I have read since
Steven Erikson's *Gardens of the Moon* . . . I want more'
ALIEN ONLINE

'Vigorous, violent fantasy adventure' INTERZONE

'There is a gritty desolate tone in depicting the grime and
horror of conflict; Cobley's skill lies in establishing a sense
of reality unusual in fantasy' TIME OUT

Book Two – *Shadowgod*

'Darkly different . . . writing to rival David Gemmell'
GUARDIAN

'Fantasy doesn't come much better than this' ALIEN
ONLINE

'Resonates with dark magic and violent deeds. Cobley
takes fantasy to new places' INFINITY PLUS

Michael Cobley was born in Leicester in 1959. While studying engineering at Strathclyde University, he DJ'd at the students' union by night, and later wrote an acerbic column of comment for the campus paper. Since 1986 he has had short stories and articles published in several magazines and anthologies, and was responsible for the rambunctious Shark Tactics pamphlet.

Shadowgod is his second novel, continuing the stories and themes begun in *Shadowkings*.

SHADOWGOD

Book Two of
The Shadowkings Trilogy

MICHAEL COBLEY

POCKET
BOOKS

LONDON · SYDNEY · NEW YORK · TORONTO

First published in Great Britain by Earthlight, 2003
An imprint of Simon & Schuster UK Ltd
A Viacom Company

This paperback edition published by Pocket Books, 2004

1 3 5 7 9 8 6 4 2

Simon & Schuster UK Ltd
Africa House
64–78 Kingsway
London WC2B 6AH

www.simonsays.co.uk

Simon & Schuster Australia
Sydney

A CIP catalogue record for this book is available
from the British Library

ISBN 0-7434-1600-7

Typeset by Palimpsest Book Production Limited,
Polmont, Stirlingshire
Printed and bound in Great Britain by
Cox & Wyman Ltd, Reading, Berkshire

This book is for Stewart Robinson, damn fine friend, ace musician and fellow brain pilot.

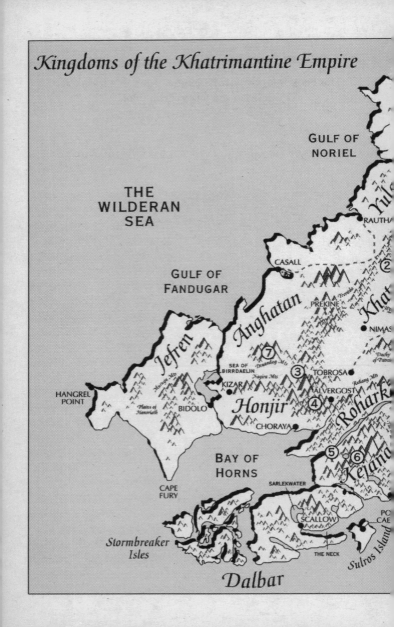

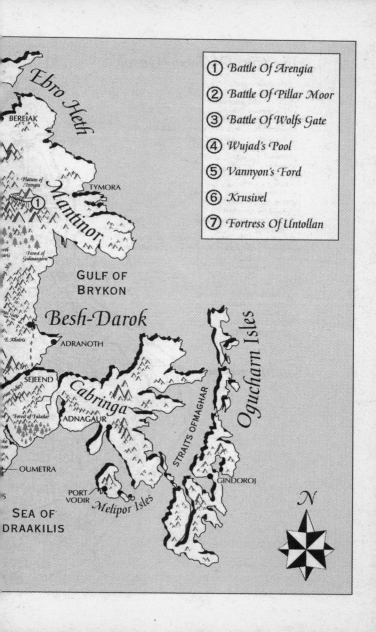

The City Of Besh-Darok

1) The Gallaro Gate
2) The Shield Gate
3) The Gauntlet Gate (sealed)
4) The Imperial Palace
5) Lord's Glade (despoiled)
6) Earthmother Temple Of The Glade (pillaged)
7) The Glade Grove Of Burial (desecrated)
8) Mage Halls (razed to ground)
9) Ironhall Barracks
10) Riverside Barracks
11) Chapel Fort Barracks
12) College Of Hendred's Hall
13) Earthmother Temple at Wybank
14) Five King's Dock
15) Kulberisti Longmarket
16) Four Guilds Merchant College
17) Guildhouse
18) Garrison Of The Order Of The Fathertree (razed)
19) Shrine Of The Rock, Fathertree Temple (demolished)
20) The Long Quays
21) Fishers Quarter

Bridges Of The Olodar (heading upriver):
   a) Knights Bridge
   b) Queens Bridge
   c) Bridge of Hawks
   d) Bridge of Spears
   e) Veterans Bridge

Keshada

Gorla

Prologue

Behold the Cold General –
Mighty and dreadful was he in life.
And in death, more dreadful still.

The Black Saga Of Culri Moal, viii, 4

Across the flat roof of the great drum keep of Rauthaz, with ice underfoot and a chill morn wind, Byrnak walked with a spirit clothed in the flesh of Coireg Mazaret. The inhabiting spirit was known as Crevalcor. According to Thraelor, he was a powerful adept of the Wellsource who had lived at a time when steaming jungles covered much of the continent. That he went hooded and swathed in thick brown garments was no surprise to Byrnak who, scarcely noticing the biting chill, was attired in a long cloak of thin black cloth.

'Were you able to carry out the appointed tasks unobserved?'

'Unobserved, unhindered and uninterrupted, Great Lord.'

'And in your journeying?'

'Unseen, Great Lord. We followed fen-tracks and other little-used ways from our refuge in the Northern Rukangs to the hills around Besh-Darok. None saw us pass.'

Byrnak nodded, inhaling deeply, relishing the iciness in his throat and lungs. 'How went the seedings themselves?'

Crevalcor shivered but his voice remained steady. 'As instructed, we sought out an overgrown location on high ground in the hills north of Besh-Darok. Come the fall of dusk, I performed the first ritual without deviation, or difficulty. Then the yard-deep trench

1

was dug and the bone and blood oblations were made therein before the laying down of the kernel stones . . .' He paused, recollection in his eyes. 'As rough as stone to the touch they were, yet cold as winter's heart and heavier than iron. Once they were laid in the trench, the soil was replaced in layers separated by additional offerings.'

'Keshada,' Byrnak murmured. 'And Gorla?'

'In the hills west of Besh–Darok,' said Crevalcor. 'I enacted the seeding and the rituals as before, then returned to our refuge in the Rukangs. From there we were able to make our way back to Yularia by way of the Arengia foothills.'

Byrnak said nothing as they walked on. The silence stretched till Crevalcor spoke again, a quiver of dread in his voice. 'I did exactly as I was bid, lord. I omitted nothing, I swear it.'

They drew near the waist-high, crenellated battlement which encircled the crown of the massive keep. Byrnak stopped, staring out across the misted city and the sea beyond then turned to face his anxious servant. 'Your progress was noted most carefully, and we were gratified to see that you completed the tasks without error. My brothers Thraelor and Grazaan assure me that the ensorcellments have taken vigorous root, and that the Wellgate will join Rauthaz to Gorla and Keshada in days rather than weeks.' He smiled faintly. 'You are to be congratulated.'

Crevalcor relaxed, relief shining in his face. 'It is an honour to serve the Shadowkings, Great Lord.'

Pity it had to be in such a hazardous manner, Byrnak thought. By the time he discovered that Coireg Mazaret had survived the confusion and failure of Trevada, the Hidden One had excised the spirit imposed on Mazaret by Ystregul, imbuing him with that of Crevalcor who was then set the tasks of seeding by Thraelor. It was Twilight's fortune that Crevalcor returned unharmed; Byrnak could at last find out what was left of Coireg himself.

'Tell me, friend Crevalcor, have you been well-treated since your return?'

'Most certainly, great one.'

'Good, and what of this host – does it meet your needs?'

'Needs, Great Lord?' Crevalcor said thoughtfully. 'It serves well enough. The previous occupant was not overburdened with a sense of caution, and taxed this frame to its limits. But during my expedition it proved sufficiently rugged and agile. And yet . . .' He slipped his hand free of voluminous sleeves, studying them. 'I have never before been in possession of another's body, and there is much to learn.'

'Not least of the original persona,' Byrnak said. 'Does anything of him remain?'

'There is something,' the hooded Crevalcor said. 'In the depths, something is tightly wound in on itself. It does nothing to announce its presence and has remained impervious to my infrequent and admittedly untutored scrutiny.'

'Interesting,' Byrnak said. 'And do you think that your new form of existence has affected your command of the Wellsource?'

'My influence over living things seems much reduced, but my ability to make use of lifeless objects has never been so strong.' Crevalcor smiled. 'Mayhap my own deathliness plays a part.'

'My brothers declared themselves more than satisfied with your talents, and I sense that their confidence is not misplaced.' Byrnak glanced down at the harbour where a four-masted battle-dromond was just leaving the wharf. 'There is a fertile situation far to the south, in a land called Dalbar, one which could be turned to our favour if we plant the right seeds. Of course, this is a task that can only be entrusted to someone with resource and a keen judgement. One such as you, friend Crevalcor.'

The hooded adept bowed. 'I am humbled, Great Lord. I shall not betray your mandate.'

'Excellent.' Byrnak turned as if to walk back the way they had come, then paused. 'Ah, yes, there is something else I would ask of you, a small undertaking which would satisfy my curiosity.'

Crevalcor's eyes were bright with devotion. 'You need only name it, Great Lord.'

'Very well – I wish to speak with the original owner of that body of yours.'

Byrnak watched emotions struggle in the adept's face, shock, duty and every degree of fear.

'Great Lord . . . master, I . . .' Hands tightened on folds of the man's voluminous robe.

'I do not wish you dead, Crevalcor,' Byrnak said. 'All you need do is relax your grip upon your host, yet without releasing it. While you sink into the nethermind, I shall simply call up this buried presence, question it to my satisfaction, then return the body to you.'

'It is an honour to serve,' Crevalcor said shakily, and made a visible effort to stand straighter before closing his eyes.

Byrnak smiled to himself. It was endlessly fascinating to see underlings eagerly submit to his will out of loyalty. Favours and rewards were useful shackles which led to a more efficient obedience than that depending on brute coercion. Byrnak almost preferred Crevalcor's loyalty to that of Obax's – whose devotion was really to the Lord of Twilight – or that of Azurech, whose very mind Byrnak had remade months before.

Azurech was the only one of his Honjir warlords to escape the siege of Choraya. Several armies of hunger-maddened refugees and displaced townsfolk had poured into Honjir from the north and the west about three weeks ago, converging on Choraya, lured by tales of abundant stores of food. The tens of thousands of invaders easily overwhelmed the garrison of five hundred, and few of Byrnak's men escaped. When Azurech arrived in Rauthaz at the head of a ragged band of fighters, Byrnak's pride in the man's intense, unwavering loyalty was undercut by a vague unease. It was almost as if that loyalty itself had come to represent some kind of threat.

Byrnak focused his attention on Crevalcor. Eyes closed, the face had gone slack and the body was swaying a little in the stiffening breeze. With a minor thought Byrnak held him steady, then glided smoothly into the open mind.

The stone chill surroundings of the keep roof drained away into grey silence, the silence of abandonment and wretched sorrow. Byrnak could sense Crevalcor as a shifting, anxious presence off at the margins of this bleak hollowness. For a moment it seemed that there was nothing else, then he became aware of a twisted knot of darkness amid the gloom.

Coireg Mazaret, he whispered to it. *Come forth into the body which is yours once more.*

The knot relaxed slightly and a pale gleam showed. When nothing more occurred, Byrnak felt his patience slipping.

Come forth, Coireg Mazaret, he said. *I command you.*

The pale gleam trembled and flickered, as if an internal struggle was taking place. Seeing this, Byrnak sent claws of thought against the knotted murk to force it apart.

Abruptly, he was back on the cold and windy keep roof with a hooded figure sprawled and sobbing on the flagstone before him.

'Why, why, why, why . . . ?'

'Coireg, gather your senses,' Byrnak said, bending slightly. 'We must speak of your brother!'

'Dreaming . . . I was dreaming a pure dream of birds, and the dream became me and I was flying . . .'

'Forget your dreams! Tell me about your brother!'

From his crouched position Coireg Mazaret looked up suddenly, face distorted with madness.

'I will *fly*!' he cried and sprang up with a wild abruptness that made Byrnak stagger backwards. Startled, he watched Coireg Mazaret's lunge become an upward leap which carried him into the air. Ecstasy animated the man's features and he rose skywards, outstretched arms flapping, loosened garments fluttering as he glided across the keep roof. Byrnak could sense the drain on the Wellsource caused by the man's fancy-driven hysteria, and knew that Crevalcor and his predecessor had inadvertently brought this about. Reaching out with his mind he choked off the flow of that power.

From little more than head-height, Coireg fell with a shriek of terror and arms flailing, landed on his side and tumbled to a halt. Byrnak strode over to the moaning form, bent down to seize a fistful of cloth and hauled him upright by the neck. Fixing Coireg with a black glare, he drew back his other hand as if to strike but instead brought it round to clasp the side of the man's head.

Wincing, lips quivering, Coireg said, 'Who are you that I should fear you so?'

'The sun and the moon,' Byrnak said, moved by a dark lyricism. 'The sea and the stars, the day and the night. For you I am death and life, breath itself.' He relaxed his grip. 'Now tell me about your brother. Tell me what makes him weak.'

He had to know. The Lord Commander was crucial to the alliance which opposed the Shadowkings, the single pin which held all the strands together – which made him more important than Yasgur or those child-heirs. But reliable information about the man was hard to come by. Now that the Crystal Eye was in the hands of the mage Bardow, the only spies who could get into Besh-Darok were low hirelings too powerless or stupid to find out the necessary details.

'Weak?' Coireg uttered a broken laugh. 'What he loves is what makes him weak. It also makes him strong.'

Byrnak shook him once, savagely. 'No riddles.'

The words rushed out. 'The invasion – it wrecked the Empire, which gave him purpose and rank, but his desire to rebuild it gives him strength. And his family . . . they all died, and that woman, the mage who banished the Daemonkind, she died too.' Coireg shook his head. 'Death everywhere, and he survives, getting his armour a little thicker, a little stronger.' A sly look crept into his features. 'Only a ghost could harm him, a ghost corrupted . . .'

'What do you know?' Byrnak said.

Coireg licked his lips. 'Could I not be rewarded for what I know? Might I not receive back my own body?'

Byrnak locked his gaze with Coireg's. 'If you do not tell me what you know, *all of it*, I will gouge it from you.'

Eyes wide, sweating profusely, Coireg Mazaret jerkily shook his head. 'Please, I could be a valuable servant . . .'

'I have many servants.' Byrnak cupped the back of Coireg's head, holding it carefully, then leaned closer and said, 'Now, a ghost corrupted . . .'

Coireg Mazaret trembled, his eyes staring, and choking sounds rose from his throat and turned into words. ' . . . a ghost taken . . . from the mage woman . . . a white ghost, and a second . . . and a third . . .'

The Shadowking Byrnak smiled in recognition and understanding. *Rivenshades* – those Acolytes loyal to Ystregul had pared at least three *rivenshades* from the essence of Suviel Hantika before she died. Yes, a corrupted ghost could be both weapon and trap. He would send a messenger to Trevada at once, someone he could trust, Azurech perhaps. It would also serve to remind the Acolytes of the virtues of obedience.

'. . . ghosts . . .'

There was a feverish light of dementia in Mazaret's eyes, betraying a broken soul.

'. . . everywhere! Ghosts in the sky and the sea and the black chasm of the night . . . surrounded by ghosts, armies and nations of ghosts . . .'

Frowning, Byrnak said, 'Be silent!'

Coireg flinched as if from inner pain but went on. 'World full of ghosts, full to overspilling, hungry enough to eat the flesh of the sky and the bones of the land, leaving nothing, only shadows . . . .'

A deranged energy seemed to pour through him, forcing neck muscles rigid. Byrnak was tempted to end this tirade with a lancing thought but held back, intrigued.

'. . . the world itself is a ghost! . . .' The man's wandering eyes suddenly looked straight at Byrnak. 'Believe me, I beg you! Do you believe me?

'Of course.'

The eyes widened, filling with uncertainty. 'Both of you?'

Byrnak felt a chill go though him. 'What do you mean?' he said, tightening his grip.

'I can see . . . two of you,' Coireg gasped. 'But the other one is saying nothing. Are you real or is he? Ah, now he is smiling at me!'

Byrnak felt a surge of rage. '*I* am real! Only me, you hear? Now drown in silence.'

An emerald aura brightened about him as he reached in and thrust Coireg Mazaret's being down into a dark, unreasoning corner. But even as he began setting the bindings and fetters in place, sinuous shadows shifted at the back of his own thoughts.

Relax your grip, weakling. Sink into the nethermind and be consumed.

Silent for weeks, Byrnak's fragment of the Lord of Twilight had at last spoken.

An image filled his mind's eye, a view of himself drowning in a black, viscous sea, face and struggling hands being slowly pulled under. Byrnak ignored the threat and focused his fury on completing Coireg's imprisonment, refusing to frame a reply, certain that dialogue was futile.

Byrnak set his servant on his feet, steadying him as the spirit of Crevalcor returned. Eyelids fluttered, and a hand rose to massage an aching neck.

'Great Lord,' he said in a hoarse voice. 'Have I slept?'

'You have been gone but moments,' Byrnak said. 'Do you recall anything?'

Crevalcor furrowed his brow. 'Naught but fragments . . . I recall stumbling through a vast hall, perhaps a cathedral . . . the light was like dark copper and there was all manner of debris scattered around . . . and, yes, there were voices roaring at each other in a tongue foreign to me.'

He shrugged apologetically. 'That is all, Great Lord.'

'No matter,' Byrnak said. 'What remains of your host provided me with an intriguing morsel before I returned him to his incarceration. Be assured that he will not trouble you.'

'I am grateful, Great Lord.'

'But now let us return to my map chamber. There is much to prepare for the task which lies ahead.'

Byrnak smiled as he led the way towards the portico entrance which covered the downward stairs. Crevalcor's loyalty was assured now.

Find the exact punishment and the exact reward, he thought, *and you could master anyone.*

His smile widened as he considered the rivenshades of Suviel Hantika.

Even Ikarno Mazaret.

Part One

Chapter One

Soulless hounds and cursed wights,
Groaning shadows with deadly knives,
Tracked the sharp tang of his blood,
From dale to vale to lightless wood.

Gundal, *The Doom Of Gleoras*, Ch. 9, vi

Snow was falling on eastern Khatris. From the topmost spires of
the Rukang Mountains to the Girdle Hills encircling Besh-Darok,
a carpet of large powdery flakes was being laid down, mantling the
fields, softening battlefield scars and debris, masking the blackness
of charred ground and burnt-out farm buildings.

Besh-Darok was becoming a white city. Roofs already icicle-
bearded were growing pale and shrouded, their chimneys and vents
fuming as the mid-morning cooking commenced. Children were
sent out from under busy feet to caper in the streets, laughing and
catcalling as volleys of snowballs flew to and fro. Dogs snapped at
drifting flakes but dray horses just twitched their ears and breathed
out foggy fumes.

Seamstresses and embroiderers were hard at work finishing pen-
nons and bannerets; bakers were carefully packing special orders;
taverners were taking delivery of fresh kegs and new leather
jacks; city wardsmen were salting the icy roads leading down to
the Five Kings Dock; Earthmother priestesses were singing long
canticles from towers scattered across the city; mummers were
cavorting in the squares, while streetsellers hawked their wares
with blandishments and ribald doggerel. For this was the day of the

11

Low Coronation, a day of celebration for commoners, tradesmen, guildsmen, officials, soldiers and sailors, as well as delegations from other towns and cities. It might be that the first true days of winter were upon them, and that terrible enemies still plotted from far to the north, but the roads and lanes were busy with people looking forward to a new Emperor, an event unthinkable just two short months ago.

Other parts of the city utterly lacked this kind of bustling activity. The district which bordered the sawmills, the lairages and the shipyards were full of houses that were as silent and empty as the slipways by the river. But shadows still crept there, and one abandoned street was playing host to a grim drama of blades.

Nerek was passing through a small square in the empty quarter when five men stepped out from doorways surrounding her. They were gaunt, hard-eyed men in shabby, mismatched armour, mostly leather and splint, but their weapons looked well-maintained. Almost at once she cursed herself for not having varied her route. City living had softened the edge of her caution.

'Now,' said one, a fair-haired swordsman in a patched brown cape. 'You'll be coming with us, I think, and peaceably if you please.'

She took in the details of the square in one, quick glance, the broken fountain, the shattered cart half-blocking one of the alleys, the few boarded-up windows and doors.

'Why would I do a thing like that?' she said evenly.

'Well, a merchant of my acquaintance wishes you brought to him, and seeing as I am in the taking and bringing business I offered my services.' He spread his hands and a silken cord swung loose from one. 'Gave him my word that I'd bring you to him.'

Nerek reached for the Wellsource and was surprised to feel its strength and sensual potency rise at her command. But only for a second before it all drained away, leaving her angry and hollow. The man with the cord smiled.

'Seems they were right about your witchery, too.' He nodded at the man nearest her, who moved towards her.

'No,' she said, making her voice quaver. 'Please!' She flung out one hand, palm outwards as if begging for mercy, while the other gripped the barbknife's hilt beneath her long blue robes. The brigand grabbed her outstretched wrist, leering as he pulled her up against him.

'I never had me a witch 'fore,' he began.

She thrust the barbknife into the soft flesh below his ear. Blood spurted forth as she tore the knife free and leaped past his collapsing form. With a chorus of angry shouts at her back she dashed towards a nearby open door. Diving inside, she whirled with both hands on the door, slamming it shut, dropping the hinged latch bar into the iron slot. An instant later someone struck the outside of the door, which shook in its frame but held.

By the time it was kicked open, Nerek was climbing on to the roof and desperately seeking an escape route. Discovering that a lower building adjoined the house, she lowered herself down then leaped across the gap separating it from a flat-roofed stable slippery with snow. A frost-coated, iron ladder led up to a cambered slate roof, the first of an entire row curving up the hill, away from the river.

She heard a shout and looked back to see two men clambering out on to the roof of the last house, while the other two came running into view down in the street, pointing up at her.

The chase was on.

The villa of the merchant Hevrin was hidden by a barrier of snow-laden ankeril trees, behind which was a stone wall. One of the estate wardens had greeted Keren as she rode up from the main road, past busy barns and pens, past labourers in the icy fields and gangs of carpenters putting up new stables. At the gate to the villa grounds, she had to give her horse into the care of the ostlers and hand over her sword to the guard at the gatehouse. Once, such a demand would have provoked her into cold, unbending refusal. But she had learned that a blade was not the only weapon, and surrendered hers without a word.

Beyond the gate were gardens through which a paved path curved to the villa's entrance, twin torwood doors banded with black iron and carved with a simple crest of a ship, a bell and a torch. Even as Keren and the warden climbed the few steps to the porch, the doors opened inwards and a tall, elderly man strode out to greet them, his breath smoking in the chill air.

'Lady Keren – you honour me and my house by your visit. Please enter and be welcome.'

Hevrin had clearly been a man of imposing stature in his youth, and some of that presence remained in his autumn years. It was said that when his first ship had been captured by pirates in the Gulf of Noriel one stormy winter, he had portaged two smaller vessels overland to Rauthaz and led the raid which regained his ship and much else besides. Today, he wore the kind of sturdy, weather-beaten jerkin preferred by working captains, along with plain moleskin breeks tucked into high boots that were well-tooled, almost ostentatious.

'My thanks, ser Hevrin, for your courteous reception,' she said stiffly. 'And your invitation.'

Lady Keren? she thought wryly as the merchant ushered her into a warm, low-ceilinged hall lit by oil lamps. *And here am I in a rider's jerkin and trews, and smelling of horse . . .*

Hevrin ordered one of his servants to bring refreshments, then guided Keren through the hall to a room hung with tapestries and warmed by a log fire. He sat her in a high-backed chair near the hearth then left the room, only to return moments later with a flat box under one arm and a servant following in his footsteps. Once a tray of glasses and delicacies was laid on a table near Keren's elbow, Hevrin dismissed the servant then opened the box and took from it a leather-bound volume.

'The tale that you seek lies within those pages, lady,' he said, offering it to her. 'I've marked it for you with the ribbon.'

The book was a little larger than a pocket journal yet quite thick, and as Keren ran her fingers over the ridges on the spine and the edges of the covers she found herself recalling that terrible journey through the tunnels of the Oshang Dakhal. At the dreadful climax of that struggle in Trevada she had seen how weak they all were in the face of the ancient powers of the world. She knew that if they were to survive the coming clash between the Earthmother and the Shadowkings, they had to have allies, namely the Daemonkind.

When she spoke of this to Bardow he was sceptical, pointing out that they had been the first servants of the Lord of Twilight and were unlikely to risk themselves on behalf of creatures they affected to despise. And then there was the near-insurmountable problem of penetrating the veil between the realms in order to exchange messages with their domain. The Archmage had paused and frowned, then admitted that there was an ancient myth which told of a hero who sang his way to the Daemonkind's realm to solicit their aid. Such bare bones were all he knew, but that was enough to set Keren on a path of questions. Six weeks of asking and begging for entry to private libraries, hunting through rooms of dusty shelves, listening to the random outpourings of market storytellers, questioning the few Earthmother archivists still alive, and finally paying for information from an antiquities chandler who knew of the merchant Hevrin's love for old books.

She opened the cover. The pages were a mixture of parchments, their edges coarsely cut and unevenly matched, and written on the first leaf in Old Mantinor script, were the words:

The Codex Of Northern Sagas, Gathered And Arranged By The Learned Vrasteyn Stulmar And Scribed By His Apprentice, The Humble Edric Of Bereiak, In The Fifteenth Year Of The Reign Of King Tavalir The Second, May His Illustrious Name Live For Ever.

With restrained eagerness, Keren sought the pages marked by a faded green ribbon, opened them wide and peered down at the stanzas of neat script. A moment later, she looked up in confusion.

'Ser Hevrin, what tongue is this?' she said.

The merchant had poured himself a goblet of pungent spirit and was settling into a chair on the other side of the hearth.

'According to scholars more sage than I, Lady Keren, the language is ancient Othazi, conveyed in a mid-Yularian dialect of the time.' He smiled. 'Which, sadly, I cannot read. You see, Stulmar was only interested in authentic renditions of tribal legends, thus his book contains stories written in a score of languages.'

'Do you perchance have a translation of this tale, ser?' she said, feeling increasingly irritated.

'Only of its title, lady – "How Raegal Sang a Road to the Land of the Daemons." When my slightly reputable associate mentioned the details of your enquiry, I knew immediately what you sought and sent my invitation, hopeful that you would also accept this volume as a small token of my goodwill.' He sipped his drink. 'A translation should not be difficult to arrange. The guild colleges employ several scholars of note, most of whom would not be averse to earning a little extra gilt.'

A small token of my goo   . Keren's initial surprise began turning into suspicion.

'Your generosity surprises me, ser. Do you intend to ask something of me in turn?' Her voice was relaxed but her gaze held him cold and level.

The merchant was untroubled. 'No, my lady, it is a gift, nothing more. I expect no token or favour from you, nor would I ask for one. It is enough to have done a small service for one who came face to face with the Earthmother herself.'

Keren studied him for a moment. *He does not have the manner of a zealot,* she thought. *No doubt for some their belief is a deep slow river, while for others it a raging torrent. Perhaps I should keep the details of what happened to myself.*

'It is no small service you have done me, ser, but a great boon.'

'You are kind to say so, Lady Keren. Now—' He finished his drink and stood. 'I must beg your forgiveness for taking my leave, but there are many pressing duties which demand my hand on the tiller. Please stay and enjoy the fire and seclusion for as long as you wish. Will you be attending the Low Coronation?'

'I have been invited, ser.'

'Well, when you are ready to leave, speak to my house warden and your horse will be brought to the gate.'

'You are very kind,' she said.

Hevrin gave a slight but grave bow, then left.

Keren returned the book to its box and waited for a short while before going in search of the house warden. Minutes later she was packing the box away in one of her horse's saddlebags, then hauling herself up into the saddle. She sat there a moment, letting her gaze wander across the frosty buildings and fields of Hevrin's estate, over the wide farmlands to the great, grey fortified walls of Besh-Darok where immense banners hung by the Shield Gate and pale smoke trailed from signal fires all along the battlements.

Somewhere in the city there might be a scholar familiar with ancient Othazi, but could she find one by this evening? That was when she and Gilly and Medwin were due to leave by ship for Sejeend and from there overland to Scallow in Dalbar. 'An undertaking of some importance' Bardow had called it, which probably meant they would encounter trials of unsurpassing horror and peril.

Then she cursed herself and dug her heels into her mount's flanks, startling it into a canter. *If a few hours are all I have, I'm not going to waste them. First the coronation, then the scholars.*

As Keren rode down the track leading back to the main road, she saw a group of riders galloping madly along it towards the city. One of them carried a fluttering standard that she recognised, the tree-and-bull device of Yarram, Mazaret's former deputy and now Acting Lord Commander of the Order of the Knights of the Fathertree. She knew that Yarram had left only days ago with a large contingent of knights to deal with brigands who were raiding villages west of the Rukang Mountains. But what urgency could have brought him haring back to the capital so soon, and with only a small escort?

Keren spurred her horse into a gallop, determined to find out.

Nerek ran through the gloomy, vacant house to the back door, emerged in a courtyard enclosed by high wooden paling and immediately felt trapped. There was a gate on her left and another straight ahead. She chose the latter. It opened on to a rough lane which ran long and straight in either direction.

Which way can I take when each seems as ruinous as the other, and my powers remain as elusive as before . . . ?

She had first noticed a diminishing of her powers three weeks ago. Private discussions with Bardow led to the conjecture that the Shadowkings were exerting their dread influence from somewhere rather closer than Rauthaz and Casall, borne out, Bardow had claimed, by strange tales of ghost children near the Girdle Hills. Only the Lords Regent, Mazaret and Yasgur, and Abbess Halimer of the Earthmother priesthood, were privy to such speculation, fearing that wider public knowledge might lead to panic and worse.

Nerek looked down at her hands, one holding the dagger, the other open and empty. *Keren's hands*, she thought. *Keren's face, Keren's body. Nothing is mine alone. Am I only a hollow thing fashioned for another's purpose?*

Through broken and missing planks she could see the wrecked sheds and overgrown ways of a shipyard, all white from the falling snow. Then a cold fury took hold of her and she clenched her empty hand in a fist, tight and trembling. Her anger cracked the veil within her and there was a rush of familiar power, the acrid emerald taste that awoke new hungers. She grinned at the green fire that sheathed her hand, even as the gap in the inner veil began to close.

Running footsteps drew near, and she switched her dagger to the Sourcefire-wreathed hand, half-turning to conceal it. Just then, one of her pursuers dashed into view, skidding to a halt when he saw her. His face was a mask of malice as he levelled a broadsword at her.

'You'll not get near enough t'use that pigsticker, witch. Give it over, 'r'else.'

'Gladly,' she said, whipping her hidden arm out to hurl the fire-drenched dagger. Hot green flamelets trailed from it as it flew past the man's sluggish parry and thudded into his chest. He cried out and staggered back a step, then his chest caved inwards, his eyes rolled back to show the whites, and he fell dead on the ground.

Nerek, drained of power once more, leaned shakily against the courtyard paling for a moment, senses spinning, her mouth tasting of ash. Then she lurched forward, pried the man's sword from his lifeless hand, and ducked sideways through a gap in the high fence.

Down in the dead shipyards there were no allies and little in the way of a safe refuge, but with any luck she might find a boat.

The snowfall was showing no sign of abating as a shivering Gilly

Cordale trudged along the battlements of the Silver Aggor, the high
inner wall of the Imperial Palace's fortifications. Up ahead were two
unfortunate troopers, one wielding a long broom while the other
scattered handfuls of salt on the flagstones. Gilly, bareheaded, found
himself envying them their leather gauntlets and waxproofed hoods
while cursing himself for ignoring his page's advice and just wearing
a fur-lined short jerkin.

And why did Atroc insist on meeting outside the palace? he thought,
blowing into cupped hands. Why did I agree?

A figure emerged from a guard tower near the Keep of Day. He
was carrying a long object which unfurled to become a large curved
fan. Thus sheltered from the snow Atroc strode towards Gilly.

'You southmen are like children,' the seer said as he approached.
'At the first snow you huddle in mounds of fur.'

'That's because we have blood flowing in our veins,' Gilly
retorted with a smile, 'rather than that fermented dog's milk you
folk drink day and night.'

The old Mogaun gave a gap-toothed grin as he produced an
oval leather bottle from his shabby cloak. 'Mare's milk, mocker.
You wish?'

'I see it as my duty,' Gilly said and took a hefty swig.

As the liquor sent warmth down into his chest and fumes up into
his head, he looked at the old seer.

'So – how may this lackey of the Crown be of service to the
chieftain of the Firespears?'

'Not everything I do is at Prince Yasgur's express command, but
I am always heedful of his interests.'

Gilly stroked his beard. 'You feel those interests are being
thwarted in some way? Yet you would rather talk of this out
here.'

Atroc grimaced. 'Too many mice in this great stone hill, mice
who whisper to bigger mice.' He eyed the two troopers armed
with broom and salt, then shrugged and went on. 'But here is the
knot that grows tighter – the city's regiments, which my prince
commands, are becoming dangerously under strength while at the
same time the Fathertree knights and these other new orders are
overwhelmed by fresh recruits.' The old seer raised a wizened hand,

pointing at Gilly. 'And worse still are those southron soldiers who have been forced to leave the city regiments and join the new Orders by threats made against their families. Many companies, both horse and foot, are now composed solely of Mogaun warriors.'

Gilly sighed a cloudy breath into the snow-filled air. 'I know of this, Atroc, and I know who is behind it, but I'm in no position to voice such suspicions.'

Atros regarded him with narrowed eyes. 'It is the Hunter's Children, yes?'

'Who else could it be? The Mendicant Friars of the Needy?' Gilly gave a hollow laugh. 'They cannot accept that Alael refused the crown, so they've been busy planting little seeds of poison here and there. Ever since the unmasking of Kodel and the Armourer, control of the Hunter's Children seems to have slipped into the hands of an unknown group of officers.'

'I have heard the name Racho mentioned more than once,' Atroc said. 'Can you not lay all this before Lord Regent Mazaret? After all, not only does he command the Office of Papers, he is also—'

'My friend?' Gilly stared out at the cold white woods and fields of the city demesne. 'Since Suviel died, he's been a changed man, cold and distant. After the battle, he assigned me to the Office of Papers, supposedly to help build up a new network of spies. But all that has been done by his own placemen and I've had precious little to do, apart from keeping my eyes and ears open. Mazaret and I have scarcely exchanged a dozen words this last month.

'And even if that were otherwise, from this evening I shall be gone from Besh-Darok and unable to see him when he returns from his latest expedition.'

For the fourth time in six weeks, the Lord Regent had taken two companies of knights out beyond the Girdle Hills and along the Westerly Road to 'seek out the Shadowkings spoor and protect villagers and townsfolk'. But from what Gilly had heard, almost all the inhabitants of central Khatris had fled, leaving behind a vast area of desolate farmlands whose villages and towns were burnt-out charnel houses and where bands of crazed outcasts roamed. And every time Mazaret returned, Gilly could see how the bitter despair had eaten into him a little deeper than before . . .

'I had wondered who was being sent to Dalbar,' Atroc said. 'There are another two accompanying you, I understand. Who might they be?'

Gilly shook his head with mock solemnity. 'Nay, friend Atroc, such information is highly secret.' Then he smiled. 'But since you asked, they are Medwin and Keren.'

'Hmm, a shrewd negotiator, a skilled swordsman, and . . . Ah, why are they sending you, pray tell?'

Mildly affronted, Gilly snatched the leather bottle from the old Mogaun's loose grip and helped himself to a throat-igniting mouthful of the potent drink. 'I'll have you know,' he said hoarsely, 'that my spies and informants in Dalbar are many and talented. Once we reach Scallow, it will be the work of a single morning to . . .'

He trailed away into silence when he realised that Atroc's attention was focused on something beyond the city walls. Gilly followed his gaze and saw a group of riders galloping with all speed along one of the main roads leading to the Shield Gate. One of them carried a standard that Gilly recognised as Yarram's.

'Now why is he back so soon?' he wondered aloud, then glanced at Atroc and caught his breath.

The old man's wrinkled face had gone pale, his mouth hung half-open and his eyes gazed unblinkingly into midair. His lips twitched and he began to speak in a whisper.

'. . . a pale daughter his captor . . . sons born to no wife . . . the hollow father . . .'

He fell silent for a moment, then slowly blinked like a man roused from sleep, moistened his lips with a grey-pink tongue tip, and let out a long, shuddering sigh.

'We seers . . . stand by the Door of Dreams, which opens to the waking eye but rarely.' He fixed Gilly with an implacable stare. 'Pray that it never opens for you, whatever else befalls you.' He turned to leave. 'We shall speak on the matter later. Now, I must be gone.'

Gilly felt a chill of the spirit pass through him as Atroc walked away. Were the old man's vision-words about him, or about Yarram? He recalled the final auguries of Avalti, dying in that razed village – *an iron fox, eyeless to the hunt . . .*

Then he laughed. 'Words, mere words,' he declared aloud. With snow mantling his head and shoulders he hurried off back the way he had come, hoping to catch Yarram as he arrived at the palace and be the first to hear his news.

Chapter Two

O Stallion of the storm,
Let my spear fly true,
May our fields be bountiful,
And our dreams full of joy.

And sharpen our eyes, we pray,
When evil wears your face.

Skyhorse invocation, trans. Antil Fehris

The shipyards were dead but not deserted. As Nerek crept sword in hand past ramshackle sheds and the leaning, mildewed skeletons of half-built keels, she knew she was being watched. The occasional glimpse of a hastily withdrawn head or leg and the faint scrape of a foot told her there was one, maybe two spying on her.

That, however, seemed to be all they were doing as she made a slow way along pathways cluttered with broken timbers and empty crates lying in frozen puddles. She saw no rats but encountered a grey cat sitting at the end of a jutting plank, watching her pass with an unwavering stare. Moving away from the riverbank in search of an easier path, she came to a long hut and, nearing one of its corners, almost walked into her three pursuers. They were standing with their backs to her, swords drawn. Quickly and as quietly as possible, she stepped back out of sight and ducked into a low open door in the hut.

The darkness was total, the icy air dank with decay. She kept still, listening as their footsteps drew near.

23

'. . . don't want you pair splitting up, hear? You're t' move through the yards t'gether, watching for that witch—'

'Why don't we go up ahead, Tavo, 'n' get some of the other lads—'

There was the sound of blow and a stifled cry.

'We don't have time, pigfool. We have to stop her getting t' the coronation. So y'll do what you're told and I'll be up on that bluff, looking down till she shows herself.'

''m sorry, Tavo. Keep 'membering how Olber went and got 'is chest burned out. Horrible it was . . .'

'Well, don't remember and don't think. Just do what I said, and while you're moving along, keep looking up t' me . . .'

There were murmurs of assent, the sound of footsteps receding. Nerek relaxed a little, letting tension ease in her neck and back, but her thoughts were in a spin. *We have to stop her getting to the coronation?* She had been invited to the ceremony as a private citizen, not to carry out any official role. Yet these brigands wanted her kept away from it, for some dark reason. She would have to get to the Five Kings Dock and find out the truth, but without any powers how could she win past these hunters? How much luck was left to her?

Luck is a weapon without hilt or edge, child . . .

Nerek froze. The words were quietly spoken in an old woman's voice from close by yet she could not tell the direction.

Best to employ other sure means – subterfuge and stealth are more useful.

As she turned her head this way and that the voice remained unchanged, and she understood. It was mindspeech that she was hearing.

'Who are you?' she whispered.

A windblown leaf, an empty cave, a forgotten song am I. You may call me Blind Rina. Now, child, look to your left.

Doing so, Nerek saw a vertical crack of dim light appear and widen to reveal a small, indistinct figure who silently beckoned. Her wider senses told her little about this person, but there were no undercurrents of threat so she crossed the hut, half-frozen mud crunching underfoot, and squeezed through the gap. Now she was in a long, narrow space between two sheds, well sheltered from the snow. Her new companion was a small girl with long, tangled hair, muddy clothing and a serious expression.

The girl put out her hand. Uncertain, Nerek did the same and solemnly they shook hands.

'You don't seem blind to me,' Nerek said.

Her name is Peki, and she is my eyes. You can trust her – she will lead you to safety.

'I need a boat,' Nerek said.

That can be arranged.

Peki gave a sharp nod, brought a finger up to her lips then hurried away along the narrow passage, with Nerek close on her heels.

It was a dark and twisting route they followed, sometimes crouching, sometimes dashing across open areas, and sometimes creeping to a halt in the shadows when her two pursuers came close. They were clambering across the decaying clutter of a half-collapsed sawmill when Blind Rina said:

You are unable to draw on the Wellsource, is that so?

Nerek felt a prickle of suspicion. 'For the time being.'

Fear not, child, I intend neither malice nor treachery. After all, one can achieve little enough with the Lesser Power.

'I know nothing of the Lesser Power,' Nerek muttered.

Hmmm. I'm surprised that Bardow has not remedied that for you, considering all the help you have rendered him . . . Oh, what Peki does not see for me in this city I can usually sense in other ways . . .

At length, Peki brought her within sight of a wide, sturdy building just yards from the river. A tangle of old spars, torn sailcloth and bushy foliage concealed their approach (Nerek had already realised that most of the debris which masked their progress had been artfully placed for maximum effect), and a toppled wagon shielded the side door by which they entered.

Inside, a gloomy corridor ran straight to a door on the other side with offices, storerooms and living quarters to left and right, all dark and deserted. Halfway along it Peki paused to listen at a large door for a moment, then tugged it open. Beyond was a walkway overlooking two pairs of cradles where large boats had once rested,

and Nerek followed the litle girl along to a set of downward steps,
Blind Rina spoke in her thoughts.

*Once, river yawls were berthed here, ready to offer aid, to shuttle
passengers and prisoners from ship to shore, and even to save lives. Now
there is only the rot and stink of neglect. But we managed to hold on to
a few treasures.*

Peki had vanished into the shadows beneath the walkway, and
now reappeared dragging something long and narrow, an open
canoe with its paddle loose in the bottom.

*Now you must hurry. Those hunters are drawing near to this place, so
you must pick up this little craft and run down to the water's edge. Now
– go now!*

The urgency of Blind Rina's words stung her into action, and
she lifted the canoe with both hands. There was only time to see
the girl Peki, face still intently serious, give a little wave goodbye
before she rushed forward out of the boathouse. Voices shouted
from along the riverbank but she kept running.

*Ignore them. Get the boat in the water, climb in and start paddling.
Don't worry if you hear them following you – just concentrate on quickly
getting away from the bank.*

Nerek splashed the canoe down and almost leaped in. Then she
began to paddle with furious energy, alternating the strokes from
one side to the other. There were curses behind her and the sloshing
sound of feet trying to run in the shallows, so close she expected to
feel a swordpoint enter her back at any moment.

Then the curses turned to startled cries then to shrieks of pain.
Still paddling she risked a backward glance and saw two figures
flailing in waist-deep water which was rippling all around with small
shapes. One of them stumbled and plunged under the surface which
suddenly boiled with activity, while the other began wading back
to the riverbank.

Ripperfins . . . the ever-hungry, but most dangerous in winter . . .

Blind Rina sounded weary, distant. The escaping man almost
made dry land before slumping face down in the shallows which
were churned into bloody froth by the swarming predators. Meanwhile, up on the bluff overlooking the yards, a solitary figure turned
and dashed out of sight back into the empty quarter.

When next you speak with Bardow, child, ask him about the Lesser Power . . .

Nerek watched the frenzied feeding with cold satisfaction, then nodded and resumed paddling.

Alael shivered and drew her fur-collared cloak tighter as she and her four-man escort followed busy Spinneret Street down to the quayside. The snow had stopped falling but a cold breeze was coming in off the river, nipping ears and noses and bringing a briny sharpness to the air. All around her as she walked Alael saw the poor and down-at-heel of Besh-Darok, their clothes threadbare or patched, their faces made gaunt by hunger and privation. They in turn observed her with sideways glances that held neither adoration nor fear − since the battle, innumerable tales about her and the Earthmother had percolated throughout the city, growing more fabulous with each retelling, regardless of her own patient denials.

On a broad, first-floor balcony some way along Spinneret Street a troupe of choriants from one of the city's academies was singing plainsongs in Old High Mantinoru. Alael understood less than one word in ten but the interweaving voices had a rich, haunting beauty which stirred in her recollections of childhood. Then, near the end of the street, a pair of minstrels with strange, triple-mouthed pipes played an odd, disjointed jig which sounded almost unsettling against the faint voices of the choriants.

Alael and her guards turned with the chattering crowd on to the long, wide quay known as Goldbarrel Wharf, only to find the distance obscured by a staggered series of huge banners hanging from the warehouses' flagpoles. The first one, a long, rose-bordered stretch of blue material, was adorned with the tree-and-bell arms of Besh-Darok itself stitched in gold and silver silk. Others, in shades of green, blue and yellow, bore the devices of Khatrisian noble houses, major and minor, as well as the sigils of guilds and merchant families, with the style of decoration varying from the simple and austere to the riotously intricate. As she walked past the banners Alael saw brightly-coloured kites swaying and bobbing in the air near the quayside, their lines held by people in small boats out on the river. And over the hubbub of the streaming crowd she could just hear the continuous sound of drums coming from the direction of the Five Kings Dock, like far-off thunder.

While following the crowd's winding course along the quayside, Alael caught sight of a small procession coming the other way. Attendants in pale robes and carrying unwieldy standards walked at a steady pace ahead of a strange, horse-drawn carriage on top of which several people stood, holding on to a wooden rail. Other attendants hurried before the bearers to clear the way or push aside the great hanging banners to allow the carriage through unobstructed, and as they drew nearer Alael suddenly recognised the symbol on the standards and one of those riding on the carriage, a man whose right arm was of gleaming metal.

Surprising her escort, Alael moved quickly away from the quay edge, seeking concealment among the crowd and behind the great banners. Her last encounter with Tauric had been hurtful for both of them when she ended their nascent relationship and turned down his desperate offer of marriage, all the time keeping her reasons to herself. For the Earthmother had come to her in a brief, dark dream full of leaves and coiling vines and warned of 'sullying your bloom with barren seed'. Of more importance, however, had been her realisation of Tauric's lack of maturity: he really was little more than a boy forced to shoulder a monarch's burden, with neither natural aptitude nor useful experience to draw on. Ikarno Mazaret, the one man who might have been a good mentor to him, was off pursuing brigands in the wastes of Khatris, and while Mazaret and Yasgur had appointed advisers with the aim of fending off the worst flatterers and schemers, that meant that only the weak and the very cunning could enter the courtly circle, a risky combination.

And now it seemed that her evasive ploy had come to nothing when one of the robed attendants emerged from behind the next banner, approached and bowed.

'Sincerest greetings to the Lady Alael and her retinue. His Imperial Highness is soon to embark upon the next stage of the Low Coronation, and asks if you would care to grace the moment with your presence?'

Her first, quickly suppressed urge was to run. For all that nearly three weeks had passed since their last encounter, the last thing she wanted was an embarassing attempt to impress her before his court followers. Yet refusal might stir up unwanted antagonism between the Hunter's Children and Tauric's supporters, something that the city could well do without.

'I am honoured by His Imperial Highness' invitation,' she said evenly. 'Kindly take us to him.'

The attendant bowed again. As he did so his robe fell open at the neck and a small pendant swung into view. He deftly tucked it away as he straightened but Alael had already seen that it was a bronze amulet in the shape of a horse. Then he turned to lead her and her guards through the crowd.

The carriage had turned off the quay and along a short stone pier where an oar-driven barge was docked. At the end of the pier was a small bell-and-beacon tower, by which the carriage came to a halt. Several people stepped down, except for Tauric who turned to watch Alael as she came to within a few feet of the carriage where she stopped and curtseyed, her face carefully composed. He was wearing dun-coloured rider's breeks and a close-fitting, dark brown doublet with the tree-and-crown device embroidered over the heart and black brocade at the cuffs and the collar, which was open to the third button. And at this distance, she could also tell that there was someone else on the small platform behind him, a woman in a green gown and pale rose mantle who stood facing away.

'It gladdens my heart to see you once more, my lady,' Tauric said. 'Please – come up and see my barge-throne.'

Alael breathed in deep to steady her nerves, indicated to her guards to remain where they were, then climbed the little wood and iron stairway which had been let down. Tauric smiled openly as she stepped up to meet him, and suspicions about his companion began to loom in her thoughts. Was this an adoring sycophant or some other creature of the court whose acquisition he imagined might make her remorseful?

How sad, she thought acidly. *He will be disappointed*. Then she said:

'His Highness is most generous to extend his invitation.'

A slightly puzzled frown creased Tauric's features at her cool formality, but still he pointed down to the vessel tied up at the pier. 'There it is, the craft of my coronation. Somewhat gaudy, I feel.'

Alael frowned a little, and smiled privately. From the palace officials she knew that when the bells began ringing along the river, Tauric would embark on the short journey to the Earthmother temple on the opposite bank. There he would present the Abbess with a carved agathon spear, and she in turn would give him the Flower Crown. Re-embarking, he would then return across the river to Five Kings Dock, where the coronation itself could then proceed.

The ceremonial barge itself was a large, wide boat with a single tier of oars, blue-canopied sterncastle and a raised dais amidships. The barge was adorned with strings of fluttering pennants, small gilt crests and carved figurines, all in stark contrast to the object which lay at its focus. On the dais was a curved, egg-like cage of heavy black iron, within which was a simple, high-backed torwood chair.

'The same barge my . . . father sat in for his coronation,' Tauric said thoughtfully.

'Oh, but Taurici, there's no covering!' said his female companion. 'What happens if it starts to snow again?'

'Then I shall just have to endure the cold, my sweet.' Tauric took her left hand in his metal right, and glanced at Alael. 'Now, I want you to meet a dear friend of mine, the Lady Alael tor-Coulabric. Alael, this is Mila, youngest daughter of the Margrave of Brankenvale.'

Alael was already resting one hand on the platform's wooden railing, but when the woman turned round it suddenly became her only anchor, for looking at the Margrave's daughter was like looking into a mirror.

Somehow she maintained her façade of mannerly calm, said some bland words of greeting then directed her scrutiny at Tauric, expecting to see evidence of malicious intent. But in his stance, his expression and gesture she saw nothing but affection for this Mila who had laid a small, pale hand on the shining steel surface of his arm. Couldn't he see the resemblance? she thought. The narrow features, the long, straight golden hair, the slender build . . . Was he really that oblivious?

Tauric's other companions were boarding the barge, among them members of his White Company, the personal guard founded by several idealistic young men after the Battle of Oumetra. Each was garbed in a white tabard bearing the tree-and-crown, and as she looked closer she could see that each also wore a steel gauntlet on his shield arm. This, together with the appearance of the woman Mila, sent a quiver of unease through her. The Margrave's daughter watched her with nervous eyes and was about to say something when Tauric made a hushing gesture and, smiling, cupped his real hand at his ear.

Still the distant drums pounded from Five Kings Dock, a low insistent undertone to the hubbub of the passing crowd, except that now Alael could hear a faint chime of bells coming from upriver and growing louder. Then the bell on the pier sounded and as she looked up at the tower she saw someone flinging handfuls of petals into the air, a fragrant, many-coloured shower. A joyous cheer went up from the barge in response.

'That is the signal for me to depart, Alael,' said Tauric. 'Will you be attending the final ceremony?'

'Indeed I shall, Your Highness.'

'Good, then perhaps . . .' He faltered for a moment then gave a sad smile. 'Till later.'

With Mila on his arm, he descended from the carriage and strode across the gangway to his barge. Alael watched him go, thinking, *Just a boy, he's just a boy*, but her conviction seemed confused by regret and doubt.

As the couple stepped down on to the deck, the Margrave's daughter glanced back at Alael with a look of unconcealed triumph. Alael was suddenly aware of her prominence alone on the carriage and went over to the little stairway. By the time she was back with her guards, Tauric was but a dim form seated within the iron cage, being borne slowly away across the water.

After nearly colliding with a street-seller's cart for the third time, Gilly decided that the streets were just too busy for an urgent horse ride. He dismounted in front of a coaching inn called the Shaft and Shield and thrust the reins into the hands of a surprised stable lad, saying:

'See she gets fed and watered, and a good rub down too, mind! My name's Cordale—' He flipped a silver halfpiece to the boy. 'And there'll be another of those for your master after the coronation.'

Then he dashed off through the crowd in the direction he last saw Yarram and his men take, themselves likewise on foot.

It had been only a short while since spotting Yarram's galloping approach after that unsettling meeting with Atroc. Despite hurrying down from the battlements, Gilly was too late to catch Yarram's party who, after a brief exchange with the chief ostler concerning the whereabouts of Yasgur, had then taken fresh horses and ridden off towards the docks. Gilly had then faced an argument with the chief ostler before a saddled horse was brought forth and he could begin his pursuit.

Now, as he ducked and swerved through the crowds, craning his neck to stare along snow-whitened side streets and wynds, his frustration grew by the minute. Whatever the nature of Yarram's news, it was sufficiently grave for him to go directly to Yasgur at Five Kings Dock, an act which set Gilly's instincts quivering with dread.

Then he turned a corner to find the way completely blocked by a tight press of townsfolk cheering and clapping along to a troupe of bellwhistlers and jugglers. It was a narrow street with high-walled houses either side and an archway supporting an overhead bridge, full of people standing belly to back.

'Come on, Cordale,' he muttered to himself. 'Think!'

Then he snapped his fingers and looked up at the bridge.

This district of Besh-Darok, known as Highcliffe, had been built on and around rocky spurs of the hill which dominated the southeast of the city. Over the centuries houses, businesses and temples had been hewn from the rock faces while more exclusive residences occupied the higher ground. Bridges spanned the fissures and crevices and passages and stairways had been carved throughout the spurs. Gilly recalled a road which ran the length of Highcliffe District, passing over several bridges before reaching the small park which lay in front of Five Kings Dock. It was sure to be a quieter route than this and – who could tell? – he might even reach the docks before Yarram.

Nearby was a long, winding set of steps called the Envadine Stairs. As Gilly ascended them two at a time he picked up a tail of small boys, chanting and laughing as they pattered along after him. When he paused some way up to catch his breath, they hung back a little, calling out beggar jests.

'You must be fair warm b'now, milor'. Sure y'need that cloak?'

'An' that jerkin – must be right hot for ye—'

'—them shoes'll be pinchin' 'im, an 'all—'

'What about some cups and berries, milor', cups and berries?'

He grinned. The copper half-wen was the lowest value coin of the realm and had an overflowing goblet stamped on its obverse: the wen bore the image of a cluster of berries. But he knew for a fact that all his pouch held was a regal and a few silvers. He faced his followers and tried to look menacing.

'Do your mothers know you're still out . . . talking to dangerous strangers?!'

'Ah, she does, milor', she does.'

'Mine says I'm dangerous enough on me own—'

'—only when ye need a bath, ye mucker!'

Gilly shook his head. *I'd be as well trying to scare off a wolf with a carrot.*

While his juvenile retinue were arguing over who smelled the worst, he decided to resume his climb and dashed up the stairs three at a time. With high-pitched cries rising behind him, he ducked along the first turning he came to, a cobbled street which curved up a steep incline, then slipped down a narrow, dim alley which brought him to an unexpectedly wide and ornate set of stone steps. Whistling a jaunty tune, he sauntered up them and emerged some minutes later on Allutra Parade, the tree-lined thoroughfare which ran the length of Highcliffe.

To his right were a number of large houses in their grounds, their boundaries set by fence or wall, their well-kept gardens laid to winter sleep beneath unbroken mantles of snow. He curled his lip in contempt as he hastened past – there was no evidence here of the deprivations suffered by ordinary folk since the invasion, no signs of impoverishment or self denial. To his left, beyond the gazebos and arbours, the view looked across the artisan district and the abandoned shipyards to the wide, flat expanse of the Olodar River. The river chimes had sounded while he was ahorse so Tauric was probably at the Earthmother temple at Wybank by now, receiving the Flower Crown.

Better you than me, laddie, he thought.

By the time Gilly crossed the third bridge near the end of Allutra Parade, the buildings had become higher and closer and consisted more of ordinary dwelling houses and businesses. Some side roads led further uphill, through the leafy affluence of Highcliffe, while others led off to join the rickety walkways which ran above some of the lower wynds. This part of the artisan district was devoted to textiles and, in the icy cold, the steam from the dye-houses veiled the air with great white plumes and clouds. Outline and details were blurred or completely hidden and to Gilly's eyes the wynds seemed mysterious and deserted. Then out of the fumey haze, on a catwalk running parallel to Allutra Parade, a slender female figure appeared, hurrying along in the direction of the docks. Frowning, Gilly slowed to an amble while staring intently across.

'Nerek?'

That purposeful stride was the same, as was the cropped hair . . . then the woman was gone, engulfed by a billow of steam. Gilly shrugged and was about to pick up the pace again when another figure came into view, a man holding a sword and clearly stalking the woman who had passed before. Suddenly, Gilly was sure that she had been Nerek.

He turned and ran pell-mell back along the avenue a short way to a side alley which led down to the lower district. His rapid footsteps splashed in melted snow and mud then thudded on wood as he charged across a quivering gantry to the catwalk Nerek had been on just moments before. Skidding on icy planks, he slewed round the corner and rushed through damp clouds of steam.

Small decorated banners bearing the names of shops and their craftsmen hung limply on lines strung across the narrow street. Droplets of condensed moisture beaded the wooden handrails of the gantries, and water dripped quietly to the street below. Boards creaked underfoot as Gilly trotted along, sword in hand, senses alert. The overcast daylight was smothered in the chill haze between these buildings and the middle distance was utterly shrouded. Then a sharp gleam penetrated the pale gloom, a hard white radiance coming from the walkway on the other side of the street. There was a choked cry, a woman's voice, and he was running again towards the crossing gantry.

But there were others running the same way directly opposite, small forms heading straight for what Gilly could now see were two figures struggling in a doorway. Coming up fast he could also see that the newcomers were children, mostly young boys it seemed, and a suspicion formed in his mind. But it was forgotten as they closed on the man who had his hand around Nerek's throat . . . while bright, wavering tendrils of power joined his eyes to hers.

There was the flicking sound of a loosed sling and Nerek's attacker let out a cry of anger, turned to confront the boys and was enveloped by a small net. But he ignored it and struck the nearest boy a wild, backhand blow that sent him flying backwards into the handrail, which gave way. The boy screamed as he fell through, arms flailing, but managed to catch hold of the gantry edge. Gilly swore, passed his sword to his other hand, tugged a short throwing dagger from its waist sheath and hurled it. He had aimed at the throat but the man turned suddenly to drag an insensible Nerek to her feet, and the dagger punched into his shoulder.

The man grunted, let go of Nerek and threw himself sideways. Rolling to a crouch, he glanced back at Gilly who was rushing up with sword at the ready. A pitiless, cold look, then the man leaped up and darted out of sight along a steam-fogged alley. Gilly's instinct was to go after him, but a thin cry for help brought him back to the broken railing. He sheathed his blade then reached down and pulled the young boy up to safety. The next thing he knew, the boy had scrambled to his feet and was dashing off into the pale haze. Of the other boys there was no sign.

'Hey!' Gilly cried. 'How about some gratitude, you little wretch?'

For a moment there was silence, then a boy's voice called out:

'Blind Rina thanks you . . .'

'Now who . . .' Gilly began, then a racking cough came from nearby. 'Nerek!'

She was sprawled in the doorway of a candlemaker's, trying to get to her feet. He bent to help her.

'In the Mother's name, woman, rest a while—'

'No . . . *no* . . .' Still coughing and using Gilly for support, she struggled upright and propped herself against the door frame. 'I have to get to the coronation – you *must* help me . . .'

Seeing the state she was in, Gilly felt caught between concern and exasperation. Nerek looked so similar to Keren yet was so different, possessed of an unrelenting quality which occasionally made her seem grim and monstrous. Yet there had been instances when she would do or say something which momentarily revealed a lonely and poignant yearning to understand the world around her. Then there were other times when there was no give in her at all.

'You're in no condition—' he began.

'Listen – they tried to kill me because they don't want me showing up at the coronation,' she said hoarsely, one hand tightly gripping his arm. 'I don't know why, but we have to warn Bardow and the others – if you . . . won't help, I'll crawl to the docks if I have to . . .'

He held up his hands in mock surrender, knowing that she meant every word. 'I bow to your arguments, milady, a shrewd combination of bluntness and coercion.' He took one of her arms across his shoulder while supporting her with an arm about her waist. 'I swear, they should send you to Dalbar instead of me.'

'Did someone say the name "Blind Rina" a few moments ago?' she asked as he helped her along the catwalk.

'Some beggar boys were following me . . .' he said, and related what had happened, including the strange parting thanks. To his surprise, Nerek gave a dry laugh.

'She was right,' she said. 'I *will* have to ask Bardow about learning to use the Lesser Power.'

Chapter Three

In the mirror of souls
Strange things take root

The Book Of Earth And Stone

Kulberisti Longmarket, also known as the City of Stalls, was a canopied street which led from the end of Respil Road to the east side of Five Kings Dock. Archmage Bardow had spent most of the morning in three important meetings, the last of which had involved arguing over tariffs and embargoes with Besh-Darok's richest merchants in Trade Guild offices near the Gauntlet Gate. When the time came to leave for the Low Coronation, Respil Road was the obvious route to take.

But it seemed that everyone else in this quarter had arrived at the same conclusion – Kulberisti Longmarket was one continuous, chattering mass of people shuffling north towards the narrow alleyway bottleneck which was the main way to the docks. On either side of the noisy throng food and drink stalls were doing a roaring trade but that was no comfort to Bardow and his companions who were stuck at the centre of the river of bodies and had scarcely moved in nearly ten minutes.

Serjeant Jamek, the commander of Bardow's small six-man escort, had been surveying the crowds ahead and turned to speak.

'They are making almost no progress, ser Bardow. It also appears that a brawl has now broken out at the far end of the market and the city guards are having trouble reaching it. Perhaps for the safety of yourself and the lady Ffion we should consider making a detour.'

'Through one of those houses?' said Ffion. 'But there are people living there.'

Bardow's red-haired assistant had journeyed from Krusivel soon after the Battle of Besh-Darok, and in resuming her role had shown a welcome aptitude for paperwork. Bardow also found her kindness and warmth a much-needed balance to his daily struggle with city politics.

'All we need is a way through to the back alley, Ffion,' Bardow said reassuringly. 'But we shall only ask, not demand. Serjeant — you and your men clear a way through to those buildings there. Be firm, but try not to break any heads.'

'As you say, ser.'

Jamek was tall and broad shouldered, and had been a Second Rul in the city militia before he was recruited to the Knights Protectorate, one of the four new orders founded by Mazaret. He and his men wore polished leather harness decorated with silver inlay, black iron collarettes, and long, dark blue cloaks. They forged a swift and efficient path through the crowd to the mean, two-storey buildings behind the stalls. The surly, bearded landlord of one dim house soon turned eager and cooperative when Bardow produced a couple of silvers from his moneybelt.

A few moments later they were stepping out into a cold alley where thick snow had gone to grey-brown slush.

'Is there another way to Five Kings Dock from here?' Ffion asked him.

'Indeed there is,' Bardow said.

'Do you have a map?' she asked.

'Indeed I do,' Bardow said, tapping his forehead. 'In here. I grew up in this city, remember. Now, if we head along this way we should find a side street to take us down to the coast road . . .'

He urged them all on at a brisk pace, sensing that another snowfall was imminent. Although Jamek and his men were well-wrapped against the weather, Bardow and Ffion had on thin robes over fine indoor garb. Shivering, he wished they had brought a carriage from the palace.

As they walked, Bardow's thoughts went back to the morning's meetings. The first had been with coronation officials at the palace, a summary of final, unresolved details which were promptly dealt with. The next had taken place in a small room in the Keep of Day: there he spoke to a small gathering of mages, most of whom had been reluctant to attend, and after some intense discussion persuaded them to agree to a further meeting in the next day or two.

For the third meeting, Bardow had left the palace and crossed the city to Gauntlet Square where senior merchants were gathering at the offices of the Trade Guild. There, the arguments had been labyrinthine, a convoluted tangle of specious precedent, dubious legalities and sheer arrogance which all came down to one basic premise – that the merchants of Besh-Darok be allowed to trade whatever goods they liked with whomever they liked, with no tariffs while paying minimal taxes to the Crown. Bardow had listened to all this with a mounting sense of incredulity and the realisation that even after the fall of the Empire and sixteen years of occupation, these greedy men still did not understand the nature of the evil that threatened them all. The world teetered on the brink of an abyss and they thought only of lining their own pockets.

Yet the new government of Besh-Darok needed them, their experience and their webs of contacts. With the prospect of further savage conflict looming in the spring, there was a great need for huge amounts of iron and wood for the weapon forgers, horses for the cavalry, stone for fortifications, textiles for military tailors and sailmakers – the list was near endless and the treasury's funds were finite. So, without making any important concessions, Bardow had to appear sympathetic to the Guildsmen while persuading them to sign a few vital contracts. Bardow had brought with him a personal message from Yasgur (who had dealt with them in previous years), a scroll which he had passed to Serjeant Jamek before entering the conclave hall. Later, while preparing to leave with the signed documents, Bardow had mused on the persuasive effects of a seal- and ribbon-adorned letter full of manly exhortations read aloud by a steely-eyed, six foot four, strikingly attired knight serjeant.

Now, as they hurried along the coast road, buffetted by cold gusts coming in from the bay, a bleak mood stole over the Archmage. Only he and a few others – Medwin, Alael and Terzis and some of the mages – truly understood the threat of the Shadowkings. The Crystal Eye certainly made use of the Lesser Power easier, and stronger in some cases, while serving as a sentinel against Wellsource adepts in and around the city (Nerek it seemed to recognise as an ally). But those who worked with it the most found themselves gaining unsettling insights into the darkness surrounding them. With his perceptions of the sorcerous landscape waxing, he became increasingly aware of the Shadowkings themselves and the sheer scale of the powers at their command. Every so often he had felt the dread weight of their gaze across the hundreds of miles like a black, insidious pressure upon his consciousness. For these brief periods, he had a focus for his purpose, a foe to struggle against, a beguilement to deny. At other times, he threw himself into work on the city's innumerable problems, hoping to evade contemplation's burden of despair.

Yet it seemed unavoidable. Even now, with the sound of thundering drums growing as they neared Five Kings Dock, his attuned senses could feel the faint, patient expectation of distant observers. The fine threads of some malefic intrigue were being drawn together this day and even with the Crystal Eye he had been unable to discern its nature.

Crowds milled around the street level archways that led into Five Kings Dock, but Bardow pointed out a wooden ramp, one of several newly-built ones which led up to the first and second tiers. Snow was swirling about them as they hurried up to the first tier. Pillared walkways ran along the rear and either side of the dock, part of the original stone yard that was built over five hundred years ago. The massive wooden superstructure with its roof was only added a century ago by Emperor Tavalir IX, who had grown weary of conducting ceremonies in the open air.

They were part way along the rearward gallery when Bardow spotted someone familiar among a group of soldiers climbing one of the stairways that went up the outside of the dock to the second tier. It was Yarram, the new Lord Commander of the Knights of the Fathertree. Bardow saw him for only a moment or two but the man's grim demeanour was starkly apparent and the mudstreaks on his battle harness spoke of an urgent purpose. Then he was gone, ascending out of sight.

Frowning, Bardow slowed to a halt. Yarram had come seeking Yasgur, he was sure of it, probably to pass on some dire news. Unease welled within him – was this the opening move in the enemy's intrigue?

'What is wrong, ser?' said Ffion. His companions were regarding him with puzzlement and concern.

With eyes closed, Bardow pinched the bridge of his nose. Even though the din of the drums had subsided to a muted four-stroke rhythm, a dull ache was unfurling behind his eyes. He had been on his way to see the Steward of Ceremonies, but that would have to wait.

'We must go up to the State Chamber,' he told them. 'I have to speak with Lord Regent Yasgur at once. Jamek – lead the way.'

'By your command, Lord Archmage.'

Pushing through tall, layered curtains they emerged in one of the dock's many arbour halls. At any other time, Bardow would have paused to admire the wall hangings, the tiny fragrant garden with its dwarf litrilu blooms, the Cabringan wood carvings, and the roselight lamps, all donations from rich merchants and some of the freed cities. But he hurried them on through a doorway and on to a stone staircase which gave access to all the tiers, and afforded a magnificent view of the entire dock. The banks of seating, the long balconies and the high cupolas were filling with people, while along either side of the dock stood attendants bearing standards or holding lines trailing from the shadowy ceiling. Pale daylight filtered in via high, narrow windows, but scores of torches and lamps burned at every level, providing a suffusing golden glow which struck gleams from the great tree symbols picked out in gold and silver leaf on the gigantic doors at the dock's far end.

As Bardow climbed, thinking thoughts as dark as the waters of the dock itself, he chanced to glance over the balustrade at the citizens pouring down the aisles of the second tier. His gaze passed upwards to the crowded walkway behind the topmost bank of benches, then with uncanny accuracy settled on just one face out of those jostling hundreds, one face which caught his attention and doggedly held on to it.

It was Nerek he saw, with her close-cropped hair and the customary battered leather jerkin, except that she seemed more relaxed than usual, less stiff and reserved. There was even a smile, faint and languorous, and when she turned in her progress through the crowd Bardow saw the line of her jaw and the shape of her ear, and suddenly knew that he was looking at an imposter.

Then she caught sight of something on the other side of the dock, and Bardow felt a trickle of horror at the cold, implacable intent that came over her features as she gripped the handrail and stared out. Swiftly he followed that gaze across, searching the people milling about on the first and second tiers . . . and spotted Keren down on the first in a doorway, nodding and talking with a woman in a flowery headscarf. When he looked back to the other side, the false Nerek was gone and something like panic welled up inside him.

'Down!' he cried to the others, who had clustered around him on the busy stairway. 'We must go back down—'

'But why, Bardow?' Ffion said. 'You don't look well.'

'Be more concerned about Keren,' he said. 'They've sent an assassin after her! Jamek, get us down to the first tier . . .'

And pray that we're not too late.

But even as they started back down the way they had come, bells rang all around and horns brayed as the huge doors of Five Kings Dock began to open outwards. Tauric had returned from the Earthmother temple at Wybank with the Crown of Flowers.

To Keren it was almost as if the woman in the headscarf had her under a spell. She had made the mistake of answering the woman's query about the name Five Kings Dock, that it had been named after five ships that were built here, and that opened the floodgates. Now the woman just would not stop talking, spinning out a long skein of woes and anecdotes about her family and the long journey to Besh-Darok and the state of the roads and the price of food and aren't city folk rude and . . .

Then inspiration struck.

'In the Mother's name!' she cried, pointing. 'Isn't that your husband about to eat a poisonous naqroot?'

As the woman shrieked and looked round, Keren turned and ducked through a nearby curtained archway. Just then bells began to ring and horns blew a fanfare, and there was a rush for the tier seats. Standing by a pillar, Keren avoided being swept down the aisles yet with the phalanx of taller people now standing in front of her she could see nothing but the upper halves of the dock's doors opening outwards.

Deciding to find a way up to the next tier, she hurried along a gallery past several arbour chambers, one where children played around a fountain, or another where two lovers sat kissing beneath a spiraleaf tree, their arms enfolding each other in oblivious passion. One of the main staircases at the rear was in sight when nearby someone uttered her name in an urgent whisper. She turned and was startled to see Nerek standing partly obscured between the folds of closed hall curtains.

'Keren – I need to speak with you in private.'

'Now? But the ceremony will be starting soon.'

A slight nod, half-hidden by the curtains. 'I know, but this won't wait.' Her voice was hoarse and flat. 'There's a small staircase in the next chamber – leads up to a seclusion room. Go there and I'll join you shortly.'

Then she was gone, heavy drapes swaying in her wake. Keren cursed under her breath then stalked along to the adjoining chamber, where several games of Advance lay abandoned, and climbed the narrow spiral staircase in the corner. She came up in a small lamplit room decorated with sumptuous hanging and tapestries, with three quilted settles and thick woven rugs on the tiled floor.

She heard no movement but felt a feathertouch of cold air from a curtain parting at her back. Instinct took over and she went into a turning crouch but a blow still glanced off her temple, sending her staggering sideways to trip over a low table. When she looked up at the face of Nerek, she was ready to unleash a stream of invective . . . until she looked longer into those wide-eyed, unblinking features.

'The mask of the first to kill the second,' the false Nerek said in a deep, rich voice. 'Then the mask of the second will serve the Well.'

A small dagger, scarcely more than a noblewoman's graceknife, came into view and Keren went utterly still when she saw the gleam of moisture along the edges of the blade. *Poison*, she thought. *The merest cut and I am dead . . .*

The false Nerek, still staring eerily, tilted her head to one side and leaned in closer.

'The Well is served,' she said.

She drew the dagger back for a slash at Keren's face, but another hand grabbed her wrist and forced it up and away. Keren gaped to see the real Nerek, her bruised, grazed features snarling with anger and effort. The imposter fought against this intervention, her unwinking gaze flicking from Nerek to Keren and back. As Keren pushed herself away from the dagger, Nerek overcame her imposter and with a cry threw her back on to one of the settles which collapsed under the impact.

There were running footsteps outside, a voice saying 'In here!', and Keren looked up to see Bardow and several cloaked knights enter. Nerek had armed herself with an iron candlestick but the Archmage waved her back. He was about to speak when the imposter sat up on the wrecked settle and raised the poison dagger before her, pointing out.

'The Well shall be served,' she said.

Before anyone could move, the false Nerek slashed the dagger across the palm of her other hand. Then she smeared the bloody wound down one side of her face, and smiled a frozen smile as she toppled backwards, eyes already full of death.

'Nobody touch that dagger, nobody!' Bardow said. 'Or the body either. There is no knowing what traps it carries.'

'Traps, ser?' said one of the knights.

'Fish hooks,' Bardow said. 'Or pins similarly poisoned, or insects, or even slow poison in fine powder. Touch nothing with bare skin.'

As Bardow asked for a pair of gauntlets, Nerek came over and offered a hand to Keren. Getting back on her feet, she muttered her thanks as she dusted herself off.

'Well, now, Keren – that's the second time that Byrnak's failed to have you killed,' said Gilly who was leaning leisurely against a pillar in the corner. 'Mayhap he will tire of the game.'

Keren glared at him. 'This isn't a game.'

'No,' Nerek said, staring down at the dead woman. 'He will never stop. Never.'

On the great balcony which overlooked Five Kings Dock, Yasgur stood to the left of the throne dressed in full furred cloak and ceremonial armour which spoke as much of his Mogaun heritage as it did of his adopted home. A roar of cheering, stamping and clapping came from the citizens who crowded the tiers and enclosures in their thousands. The chants of the choriants could hardly be heard and when the Imperial barge floated in past the open doors the thunderous din rose still further and clouds of petals began drifting down from the rafters.

On the other side of the podium stood Abbess Halimer, now recognised as High Priestess of the Earthmother faith. Yasgur glanced over at her – she was a tall, matronly woman with a steady yet imposing presence, which almost compelled others to be equally calm and even-tempered. He wondered what the Abbess thought of the many rumours about the Earthmother, that she had appeared in the Spire during the height of the battle to take back the spirits of the dead. He wondered if it were true. His own patron god was Vaarut, Lord of the Hunt, and there had never been tales of him stepping forth from the sagas to speak with mortals, apart from the delusions of the weak-minded. Perhaps he should convert, offer up oblations to a goddess who actually took a hand in the affairs of mortals.

Then Yasgur thought of what his senior officers might say and do, and smiled sardonically. Perhaps not. He was already walking a thin line with regard to the feelings and loyalties of the Firespear clan, especially since the start of these cowardly beatings meted out to a growing number of his warriors by masked ambushers. Murmurs of discontent were passing around, along with the notion that the Firespears had been tainted by this alliance with their former vassals. But their ingrained distrust of the other clans and tribes, coupled with the terrible dishonour committed against the spirit of Hegroun by the Shadowkings, was sufficient to maintain their discipline and loyalty to Yasgur. For now.

The crowd kept up its full-throated roar as the ceremonial barge let down its gantry and Tauric, wearing a long, pale blue cloak, crossed to the flagstoned wharf. Two men and a woman, known as the Keepers of Anointment, approached and bowed. Yasgur had gone over the rituals of the Low Coronation with the stewards, but some of the details had been unclear.

'In times past, my lord, it was a senior priest of the Rootpower faith who stood to the left of the throne,' one had told him. 'Under the circumstances, it seems appropriate for one of the Lords Regent to assume this role. So we thought.'

'What ritual words must I speak?' he had asked.

'None,' was the answer. 'Only the heir speaks, once the coronation has taken place and then only to the citizens.'

As Yasgur watched, Tauric lowered his head and the woman stepped forward to place a seashell amulet around his neck. Tauric straightened and handed her a coronet woven of flowers, then the two men came forward, one giving him an iron lantern, the other a polished bull's horn.

Yasgur frowned. Many signs and tokens were sacred to the Mogaun, and he knew that the iron lamp was a symbol of the Lord of Twilight while the bull's horn was that of Orrohn, Lord of the Forest. The seashell, too, was familiar but beyond recollection for the moment. Not for the first time this afternoon, he wished he had ignored the palace advisers and brought Atroc with him.

Led by the three Keepers, and followed by his retinue, Tauric walked towards the stairs that rose in two flights to the great balcony. Red, yellow and blue petals lay like a fall of leaves over everything and very long, thin banners of a fine, gauzy material had unfurled slowly from the ceiling and were floating and undulating on the warm updrafts rising from the still-cheering crowds.

The small procession finally reached the foot of the podium where Tauric bowed to Abbess Halimer and gave her the bull's horn, then bowed to Yasgur and gave him the iron lamp. The young man's metal arm shone in the rich golden light of a hundred torches and Yasgur stared at the lamp in surprise for a moment, then remembered his next part in the ritual and went down on one knee. The female Keeper placed the Flower Crown on his head, and when he stood it was Tauric's turn to kneel at the foot of the podium. All the Keepers moved to the rear of the balcony as two smaller figures stepped forward, a boy and a girl aged about ten, who climbed nervously up to the throne on which a large wooden crown lay. It looked dark and finely grained and had the dull sheen of something that had been through many hands over many years.

By now the noise of the crowds had diminished to a subdued rhythmic chant as the children carefully carried the crown between them down the steps. Tauric's face was calm, almost serene as he bowed to each in turn, and when he straightened Yasgur noticed a small pendant protruding from the buttoned seam of his dark brown velvet doublet. It was only visible for a moment before it slipped back inside but Yasgur saw that it was a rearing horse cast in bronze.

Then the children were lowering the wooden crown on to Tauric's head to an accompanying mass roar from the crowd. As the young heir turned to face the exulting thousands, Yasgur reflected wryly that in sixteen years they had never once cheered like that for him.

Tauric stepped up to the balustrade of the great balcony and raised his arms, one metal, one flesh and bone. Flanked by blazing pole-cressets and framed by heraldic banners, Tauric truly had the bearing of a monarch. After a moment or two the clamour subsided and he began to speak. This was the cue for Yasgur and the Abbess, and the others, to retreat to the shadowy rear of the balcony. Once there, Yasgur slipped between the dark, heavy drapes and emerged into a long, low chamber.

He was passing the Flower Crown and the iron lamp to an Earthmother priestess when there was a touch on his shoulder. It was Ghazrek, his friend and First Captain, looking sombre as he bowed smartly.

'My prince – Lord Commander Yarram has returned unexpectedly. He has disturbing news.'

Yasgur snorted. 'Disturbing enough to bother me with, eh? Why isn't he at the palace, talking to Mazaret's second?'

'It is do to with Mazaret, my prince.'

Ghazrek's face was grave, which made Yasgur stop and consider.

'Very well. Take me to him.'

In a small room off the main state conclave chamber, Yarram was standing by an arched window, peering through meshwork shutters at the city outside. As he turned, Yasgur could see the strain etched in his features, as well as the dust and grime that marred his clothing.

Yarram bowed. 'Milord Regent.'

'Lord Commander,' Yasgur said. 'What brings you back to Besh-Darok with such haste?'

'Lord Regent Yasgur, my men and I have for the last four days been harrying the brigands responsible for the many raids on either side of the Girdle Hills. Yesterday, we came face to face with their leader.' Yarram gazed levelly at Yasgur. 'Milord, I am not a man given to flights of fanciful rumination, so please accept that there is no embroidering in what I am about to relate.'

'Your honesty is known to us, Lord Commander. Continue.'

'We followed the brigands into the Girdle Hills southwest of Besh-Darok. Our pursuit brought us to the ford of a river swollen by the snow and rain, but we arrived to find that the brigands had wrecked the bridge and were waiting to defy us. As we approached, their leader emerged on horseback – from where we were I could see that it was a woman, garbed in a winding gown as pale and hueless as her face and hair. She rode slowly out on to a flat boulder and said "Who commands?"'

'I said nothing but urged my mount forward to the grassy bank of the spated river. Only when I halted by the river's edge was I able to discern the woman's features.' Yarram paused. 'I am certain that you never met Suviel Hantika, the lady mage who was my Lord Mazaret's beloved. I, on the other hand, saw her on many occasions—'

'The woman is dead,' Yasgur said bluntly. 'Or so that turncoat sorceress Nerek insisted. But you saw her alive and leading our enemies, is that what you're saying?'

Yarram nodded. 'She looked more wraith than living flesh, but it was her face that I saw and her voice that I heard speak, I am certain.'

Yasgur inhaled deeply, thinking, *Atroc, you should be here to advise me . . .*

'What else did she say?'

'She said, "Tell your masters that Death has many doors and they cannot lock them all. And tell Ikarno that I shall await him at Blueaxe Ridge." Then she and her followers turned and rode off.'

Yasgur felt the hairs on his neck stir, and a chill go through him. In the Mogaun sagas there were many tales of the power of the words of the dead. *The Shadowkings are close to us, stretching out their hands, sending forth their creatures to taunt us. And those words were meant for Mazaret — what will he do when he hears them?*

He clenched his fists, burning with the need to act. 'There is little sense in waiting here,' he said. 'Let us return to the palace with all speed, and I shall call the High Conclave to meet—'

'An excellent idea, my lord,' came a voice at his back. 'I have already sent several people ahead to prepare for just such a gathering.'

It was Bardow, his eyes bright with purpose, his mouth curved in a small, hard smile.

'Greetings, my Lord Regent, Lord Commander, and my apologies for intruding, but I bring word of unsettling developments within the city itself.'

'A timely interruption, ser Archmage, as I have just received a disturbing report from the Lord Commander here. I suggest that we hasten to the palace and share around each other's dread news as we travel.'

'Mayhap one will cancel out the other, my lord,' said Ghazrek, grinning darkly as he went to open the door.

Bardow uttered a dry laugh. 'An unlikely event, captain.'

Chapter Four

The roots of meaning and memory,
Are a deep, dark tangle,
Which holds love and hate,
In eternal, unbreakable bonds.

Avalti, *Augronac's Lament*

In the sharp, grey cold of dawn, Ikarno Mazaret sat on a wide rock on a snowy hillside overlooking the former Duchy of Patrein, thinking of the two occasions on which he had slain the Warlord Azurech.

Or at least of the blows he had struck the man, blows that would have killed any *ordinary* warrior. The first time had been in the burnt-out ruins of Tobrosa during a rainstorm, hunting Azurech and his guards through black, wet streets. Catching him unawares and alone, Mazaret had beat aside his sword and dealt him a thrust of such fury and might that his blade had punched through the man's mailed shirt near the heart and impaled him from front to back. Mazaret remembered how he wrenched his dripping sword free, and how Azurech had swayed then retreated but a single step before collapsing to the ground, apparently dead. With shouts coming near through the hissing rain, Mazaret had taken to his heels, seeking concealment in a wrecked taphouse from where he looked back.

And stifled a curse when he saw Azurech's form stir and sit upright, then shout for his men.

The second time was by sunset at the Kings Gate Pass, when Mazaret and his knights were returning to Besh-Darok. They had just cleared the pass when the Warlord's warriors fell upon them from either side. Battle was furiously joined and Mazaret was forcing his way through the press of men and horse, slashing to left and right with his battleaxe, when he found himself confronting Azurech himself.

Clad in ornate black armour and a snarling wolf's-head helm, the Warlord blocked Mazaret's first blow with a night black shield from which a circle of curved spikes protruded. Then he swung a serrated broadsword which Mazaret only just managed to parry before spurring his horse up against Azurech's mount. He pushed his own shield into Azurech's face, at the same moment bringing his axe down on the man's lightly armoured thigh. His hold on the axe was white-fist tight and the blade edge bit through mailed leather and flesh, jarring as it clove the bone. The Warlord's horse screamed as its flank took a cut, and reared away from Mazaret but not before he saw what he had done. Azurech's leg was hanging by scraps of flesh and leather, with blood gouting forth, a blood that was black.

The ambushers had broken off the attack, retreating back through the Kings Gate Pass to the wastes of central Khatris. Mazaret had conducted a search of the bodies afterwards but Azurech's was not among them. It had seemed that the Warlord could only have ridden off to die, but three weeks ago word came that he had returned to Khatris with the avowed intention of dragging Mazaret all the way to Rauthaz in chains. In response Mazaret sent out more spies and consulted with Bardow but although the Archmage was able to see further with the Crystal Eye, the Shadowkings and the more powerful of their servants remained hidden. However, it transpired that a band of slavers was abducting refugees from the ruined citadel of Alvergost and selling them on to Azurech. Mazaret listened closely and laid his plans accordingly.

From where he sat on that bleak hillside he had a panoramic view of the white emptiness of southern Khatris. To the south, the deserted city of Tobrosa – its towers now blackened and gutted hollows – was just visible as a dark blotch on the horizon while to the east the Rukang Mountains presented an ashen barrier of unscaleable peaks and ridges. The surrounding plains looked near-featureless beneath the recent snowfall; this had once been rich farm land but the whiteness hid a multitude of ravages and ruins.

Mazaret's knights were encamped at the foot of the hill, in a small gully behind a copse of leafless, skeletal trees, but his gaze was fixed on the slight figure standing by a drystone pen down and off to his left. Terzis Kommyn had incurred Bardow's anger by volunteering to accompany Mazaret on his forays, but she had proven her worth so convincingly that the Archmage had relented. Now, she was using her talents to scry movements in the distance and the unseen aspects of the great arena they would soon enter.

A dark dot in the grey sky slowly grew until it was seen to be a small bird winging madly towards the hillside. At the end of its flight it swooped down to alight perfectly on Terzis' upraised hands. She drew it close and bent her head, remaining thus for several moments before tossing it into the air where it darted off into the east. Wiping her hands on her woollen cloak, Terzis then began climbing towards Mazaret.

'So,' he said. 'Where is he?'

The female mage gave a half-smile as she came and sat beside him on the wide rock. 'I know what route Azurech is following, but I did not see him – my little spy would not go anywhere near his procession. But by my reckoning, he should cross the Westerly Way late in the afternoon, perhaps an hour before sunset.'

'And our allies?'

'Domas and his men left their hideaway an hour ago,' she said. 'They should reach the meeting place by mid-morning.'

Mazaret had been wary on receiving Domas' offer of alliance over a fortnight ago; Keren's account of the man's deeds as a mercenary in Alvergost were still fresh in his mind. In his missive, Domas had claimed that an argument had led to a fight in which the mercenary captain and his main supporters were slain. After that, the mercenary company elected Domas their leader and took on the role of protecting the refugees from the Red Priests and the slavers who appeared to be working together. For a short time they had been successful, driving off several raids and protecting a train of supply wagons sent secretly by farmers in the eastern dales. Then, about a month ago, the slavers had launched an attack on Alvergost, supported by skilled, well-armed troops that Domas had never seen before. So ferocious was the attack that Domas and his men abandoned their camp and fled east into the dark ravines of the Rukang Mountains. It was soon after this that Domas made his offer, which Mazaret had accepted only after a face-to-face encounter with the man on a hilltop near the Kings Gate.

Mazaret stood and stretched, surveying the land before them and the sky above, and breathing in the cold air.

'Time we were leaving,' he said. 'It would not do for the knights of Besh-Darok to be tardy in such an undertaking.'

Together they descended the snowclad hillside, crunching through clumps of frost-laden grass and stepping carefully across iced-over streamlets. As they approached the encampment, Mazaret beckoned over his Captain of the March and ordered the camp struck. A short time later everyone was on their mounts and when the handlers strapped the last baggage to its pack horse, Mazaret led the column at a steady trot up from the gully and out from behind the cover of the copse. As they rode out into the wintry plain, Mazaret tugged off one of his leather gauntlets then felt beneath his tied cloak and inside his jerkin. He found the flat, palm-sized square of ivory which he kept there and brought it out. It was a single leaf from what would have been a small bound book, and on it was inscribed:

> Oft times in dreams, my love,
> It seems that you lie beside me.
> Yet with the waking day,
> My soul's desire becomes but a dream,
> And it seems the day will never end.

He had found the ivory leaf two months ago, in the mud near a razed farmhouse east of Tobrosa, and since then reading it once a day had become a private ritual, his own silent keening.

'Suviel,' he whispered as he slipped the leaf back into its inner pocket, then, with a raised hand and a cavalryman's cry, urged the column into a swift canter across the snows.

The meeting place was the great Rootpower temple at the market crossroads town of Nimas. Its builders had burrowed deep into the side of a rocky outcrop overlooking the town, using that sheer mass of stone to help support soaring pillars, high walls and an immense arched roof. But fire had burnt out the temple's heart, pulled in its roof and shattered the walls, leaving only the part that was hewn from the rock. Since the pillage of Khatris, and the slaughter of the chieftains at the Battle of Besh-Darok, most of the population had fled and now Nimas was utterly abandoned, its sad vacant houses looking dark and choked with snow and ice.

From doors and windows some of Domas' men regarded the knights' approach along the main street. Mazaret saw that they had quartered their mounts in the shell of a granary near the cross. Those of the mounts that he caught sight of were brown, shaggy ponies but there was also a mixture of sway-backed mares and underfed plough horses. More men gathered to watch, darkly ragged figures, all with the hard-bitten look that spoke of many battles. In all, Mazaret reckoned they numbered little more than two score.

At the cross Domas himself emerged from a half-demolished inn. Mazaret dismounted and the two leaders clasped hands in the warriors' grip.

'Well met, lord of Besh-Darok,' Domas said. He was a rangy man, almost as tall as Mazaret, with black hair and full beard and pale eyes which gave the newcomers a quick appraisal. 'Your knights are finely attired and well armed, my lord. I look forward to seeing them fight.'

'Have no doubts, Domas. My men will not be found wanting.'

Mazaret nodded to his Captain of the March, who gave the order to dismount, then passed his horse's reins to one of the handlers before walking with Domas up towards the temple.

'My mage tells me that Azurech will reach the Westerly Way by late afternoon,' Mazaret said.

'Sooner,' said Domas. 'The dog has changed his course in the last hour, turning on to the Sunplain Road which take him close to Prekine.' Domas spat on the ground. 'Two hundred captives he has in those wagons, more than half of them children.'

At this, Mazaret felt a cold anger. He had heard many rumours and tales about what the Acolytes had done to children in Trevada before the Daemonkind Orgraaleshenoth clashed with them in the High Basilica. Now it appeared that they had resumed their vile atrocities.

'This is ill news,' he said. 'Can we catch them?'

'It is possible,' Domas said, beckoning a short, hooded figure over to join them. 'This is Qael – he is one of my eyes in the wilderness, and has just returned from tracking Azurech's caravan. Qael, tell the Lord Regent of our enemy's strength.'

The spy was a short, wiry man swathed in a grubby brown cloak. From within a tattered cowl birdlike features smiled and glittering eyes regarded Mazaret for a moment before he spoke. 'Of the Gidreg slavers there are no more than thirty, half ahorse, half with the wagons. There are also two dozen riders like the ones that fell upon us at Alvergost, each one with a little lamp hanging from his saddle. But those following Deathless number more than six score, all mounted and well armed. A pair of those Mogaun shamen also ride with him.'

Mazaret frowned. 'Deathless?'

'We have heard of your own encounters with the dog, so one of my captains coined that for him,' Domas said. 'Then we found out from an escaped captive that he has the same nickname among his own men.' The former mercenary sent Qael off with a few murmured words, then gave Mazaret a wry grin. 'So now the odds are laid bare – daunting, are they not?'

There was a challenge in his words, and the hint of a taunt, and Mazaret gave him a sidelong glance as they strode between tumbledown buildings.

'And I say again – can we still catch them?'

'They may have altered their route, but they're escorting slow wagons and have to keep to the road.' He paused by a fallen piece of masonry and quickly sketched lines on its flat, frosted surface. 'There is the Tobrosa Road, which we thought Deathless was going to take, and here is the Sunplain Road. There is one place along it which is perfect for an ambush, a long shallow gully between rocky slopes impassable to wagons . . .'

'Which we attack from either end after they enter it,' Mazaret said.

'Just so. The night's cold will be rising by then so we may be lucky enough to have the falling snow to mask our approach. I will take my men and follow them up the Sunplain Road, while you and your knights ride round to come at them from the north. Qael will be your guide, if that is agreeable.'

'It is a simple strategy, and surprise should help even the odds,' Mazaret said. 'But what are your thoughts on those shamen?'

Domas shrugged. 'How good is this mage of yours?'

Mazaret gave him a sharp look. 'Every one of us would trust Terzis with his life. I shall tell her who we face – she will know what is required.'

They were almost at the Rootpower temple, ascending wide shallow steps that were once shaded by trees now reduced to hacked and charred trunks. Mazaret's knights had gathered at the foot of the slope with their mounts, who were enjoying a well-earned feed and watering.

'Time is against us, my lord,' said Domas. 'We should depart as soon as possible. In the meantime I thought you would like to visit the temple's sanctoral.'

They had reached the head of the steps, from where a broad path led to the temple's once-massive doors. But the doors were long gone and a knee-high line of broken stone was all that remained of the mighty east-facing wall. The tiled expanse of the temple floor was open to the sky and wet with foot-stamped slush. Snow lay atop the shattered stumps of pillars and, at the west wall, the wide chalern dais, the place of holy discourse. Mazaret knew that there would be steps leading down into the sanctoral, a deep, long recess in the top of the chalern. There would be wall-carvings, floor tiles covered in symbolic patterns, and three altars near the west wall where a living tree should be growing up from the hidden earth, up the wall and out of the carefully constructed roof.

But from where he stood he could see the black charring which ran all the way up the wall like a scar, and knew that the sanctoral was nothing but a shell. He turned to Domas.

'Why did you think I would want to come here?'

Domas was taken aback. 'But your knights are of the Fathertree order—'

'And the Fathertree and its spirit died,' Mazaret said bluntly. 'And the Rootpower too was destroyed. There is nothing to pray to here,

Domas, nothing to honour or contemplate. The mysteries are dead and there is no hope of intercession.'

Domas' surprise had given way to resentment. 'Yet you have not changed the order's name, my lord.'

'Most of the knights do not share my views, and that I must respect. But there is nothing for me in this place – I will not pay homage to the memory of what was.' Mazaret turned to retrace his path. 'Send your man Qael to me, Domas. We shall be ready to leave soon.'

But as he descended the steps, his thoughts were in a turmoil of self-reproach. *Liar! Hypocrite! What else is that ivory book leaf but a worship of what is dead?*

Suviel was dead, and the Fathertree was dead, while a host of abominations lived on. Like Deathless Azurech.

Deathless, he thought grimly. *I shall turn that name into a black jest.*

A short time later Mazaret was in the saddle once more, leading his knights past the temple, the scout, Qael, to his left, riding one of the shaggy-maned hill ponies. Terzis rode on his right, her tense features betraying an inner trepidation. When he had outlined the enemy's strength and the presence of two shamen, she went pale. Now, as he observed her with a sidelong glance, Mazaret's own doubts began to gnaw at him.

Then he grew angry. Why burden himself with ghostly what-ifs? Terzis had promised that she would devise a way to counter the shamen, and he trusted that promise.

For the next two hours they rode swiftly across the low, rolling whiteness of central Khatris, guided by Qael. On horseback the icy air nipped at exposed skin and most of the knights fixed flaps of their cloaks across their faces below the eyes. But still the aching cold seeped into every extremity.

Through a world of white fields, skeletal woods and ice-capped ponds they rode with wary purpose. Qael was careful to avoid towns and villages, and even roadside guardposts, no matter how deserted they seemed. Occasionally they would draw near low hills, or a wooded dale, and the hooded scout would dart on ahead to spy out the land, then return to show the way. They were starting along a long and gentle hogback ridge when Mazaret saw darker clouds in the middle distance and snowfall advancing like a wide grey wall across the plains towards them.

'Our veil,' said the scout Qael with a feral smile. 'We shall be the unseen.'

'Where is the gully?' Mazaret said, voice raised above the drumming of the hooves.

Qael grinned. 'Beyond it.'

Not long after, the first white motes came fluttering down. Moments later the snowfall proper swept over them on a rising wind that drove large icy flakes into their faces as they rode. At first Mazaret was pleased, almost exhilarated at the snow's arrival but then the blasting chill of it increased. The visible distance was growing steadily shorter and he realised that their ability to fight on horseback would become severely hampered.

At the far end of the ridge the trail dipped into a long depression in the terrain which ended with a path that rose and curved along the flank of a steep hill. Qael brought them to an abrupt halt here. Mazaret felt a stab of foreboding at the confusion in the man's face.

'There should be scouts here to greet us and say when the enemy will arrive,' Qael said.

'Did Domas send them ahead from Nimas to observe,' Mazaret said, 'or was he going to wait till he was in position?'

Qael was sombre. 'He intended to wait.'

'Then he has been waylaid, or has suffered some other misfortune. We may have to follow the route back—'

Then sounds came to them through the rushing snow, cries and the clash of weapons. Qael immediately leaped from his horse and dashed up the hill, falling to hand and knees to crawl the last yard or two. Mazaret was close behind and heard the man curse before reaching his side.

'Poor fool,' Qael muttered.

Mazaret was filled with dread at what he saw. From the dozens of corpses, human and horse, that lay scattered across the gully it appeared that the enemy had caught the advance party in the open. After a bloody battle only two of Domas' men were still alive, one prone and bleeding on the ground while the other stood over him with a quarterstaff and weakening visibly as he held off his terrible assailants.

Four figures surrounded him, and not one among the living. Gore dripped from the cloven head of one, entrails from the midriff of another, while the others had been horribly hacked. All could stand and swing a weapon, and all moved to the will of the two shamen who watched from their horses a few yards away.

'I have seen the dead walk and kill before now,' Qael said through gritted teeth. 'We must act or those men shall surely die.'

'But look at all those other bodies,' said Terzis, who had joined them. 'If we attack, we would be facing more than just four.'

'We have to get in close enough to kill those shamen,' Mazaret growled. The hand-to-hand fight with the waking dead in Oumetra was still fresh in his memory. 'Yet we must conceal the move, or fight an army of corpses.' He looked at Terzis. 'Could you create the illusion of, say, a dozen men on horseback with myself in the lead?'

'Yes, my lord, I can.'

'Can you maintain four such illusions at the same time?'

Her eyes widened. 'My lord, I'm . . . not sure—'

Mazaret frowned. 'And if I order you to do so?'

The lady mage was still a moment, then nodded sharply. 'By your command, my lord.'

'Good,' Mazaret said. 'Then this is what we'll do . . .'

Minutes later, Mazaret and twelve of his knights were galloping along behind the hill to a notch which led into the north of the gully. At the gap they slowed to a halt at a point he was sure was visible from the crest of the hill. A moment passed, then an image of Mazaret on his horse began to appear, wavering as if seen through water. Then details grew sharp, and he was startled at the sight of a grey-haired man past middle-age, garbed in mailed armour and heavy furs, his face lined and weathered, his pale eyes both intense and sorrowful.

Is this really how I am? he wondered. *Or is this how Terzis sees me?*

The rest of his knights were also present in mirror image, patiently waiting as a second group quivered out of nothing and grew solid, then a third and a fourth. Mazaret could hear his men muttering fearfully among themselves and felt a ripple of primitive dread when all his likenesses looked directly at him. Reaching for his blade, he had to grip it hard and tight to quell the trembling that threatened to unman him. Then he raised his sword aloft before lowering it to point at the enemy.

'The Tree and the Crown!' he cried and spurred his horse into a plunging gallop.

Following him, his men took up the battlecry. Then two of the ghostly bands moved to overtake them, led by mirage Mazarets who gestured with their blades and bellowed war shouts in perfect, silent mimicry. A freezing blast of wind tore at their cloaks as they came out from the lee, and dense swirls of snow scoured them with icy claws. The deep moan of the storm seemed to fill the gully like a song and in the eery madness of the moment he imagined that his horse was his fear, which he was riding into the razored heart of peril.

A shriek went up from the snow-blurred shamen on their horses as they caught sight of the charge. The lone fighter still held off the walking dead, but he was staggering now. Then there was a second figure at his side, slashing and kicking to hold back the abominable attackers – it was Qael.

Up ahead Mazaret saw a few carcasses stir beneath their mantles of snow, but they slumped back into stillness when the shamen realised what they were facing. As the leading group of mirages were dispelled, another rode past Mazaret to his left while yet another appeared on his right. Amid their shielding phalanx of illusions Mazaret and his men held to their grim course. They were close enough now to see the shamen's faces, the bones in their tangled hair, their ritual scars, their hungry malice. And beyond them, way along the gully, Mazaret could just make out figures and shapes approaching through the blurring snowfall . . .

Then suddenly there were no ghostly images between himself and the nearest shaman. Across the rapidly diminishing yards the Mogaun looked into Mazaret's eyes and saw the promise of doom, but before he could do more than began the first mouthings of a cantrip Mazaret's hurtling blade took his head off with a single blow.

As the lifeless body toppled from its saddle, Mazaret let out a shout of triumph and reined his horse round in search of the other shaman. The four corpse warriors were sinking down into the snow, and beyond them he saw the remaining Mogaun riding madly up the north slope of the gully. Then movement and noise surged into his awareness as the dim shapes he had seen before were finally upon him, riders armed with spears and poleaxes, wagons full of weeping children and adults, and swordsmen and bowmen on foot running and stumbling as they tried to keep up. Mazaret's knights fought to control their mounts amid the pandemonium while Mazaret watched for any sign of Domas himself.

'My lord . . .'

He turned at the shout to see Qael tending to several of the arriving wounded and urging them to stay on the wagons.

'What's happening?' Mazaret said.

The scout wiped blood from his cheek and looked up. 'Domas and his men were discovered and had to attack the caravan,' he said. 'He is fighting a rearguard action with the bulk of his men, trying to give time for the wagons to escape . . . Wait, that's them now . . .' He began helping and prodding his charges back into the nearest wagon. 'Go – go now!'

Riders were emerging from the veiled distance, less than a dozen in addition to a couple of riderless steeds. Mazaret bellowed a rallying call to the nearest of his serjeants then turned to signal Kance who he knew was waiting up on the crest of the hill. When he gave the field gesture for a flank attack, the lone figure on the hill waved once then vanished. When Mazaret looked back the survivors of Domas' warband were arriving, bloody, battered and angry. Domas himself was helmless with a raw graze down one side of his face and a wound on his shield hand. He allowed one of his men to tie a bandage before shaking him off and turning his dark and bitter gaze on Mazaret.

'Where are your fine knights now, my lord?'

'Waiting and ready, good ser.' With a tilt of the head he indicated the gully wall to their left, and Domas nodded slowly.

Snow rushed all about them, growing heavier by the minute. As the wagons rumbled off to the rear, the all-too-few riders and warriors formed a thin line across the gully. Down the far end, at the edge of visibility, a dark mass of horsemen was approaching at an almost leisurely canter.

'Deathless has a great appetite,' Domas said. 'And he hungers yet.'

'Then let us stick in his craw,' Mazaret said, turning to shout, 'Ready spears and bows if you have them . . . Wait for my order . . .'

He glanced along the line. Faces were grim and staring or exhausted and beyond fear, but there was no give in them as Azurech's troops came onwards at the gallop. Snow sprayed from beneath hammering hooves, white breath gushed from horse nostrils and harness clinked and jingled.

'Wait . . .' he said.

Azurech's riders looked well-armoured, with most wearing concealing helms and small bannerets that fluttered from shoulders and backs.

'Wait . . . and – LOOSE!'

A wave of spears and arrows leaped towards their targets. Some missed entirely, others rebounded from shields and body armour, a few struck riders who cried out and fell, or horses which shrieked and lunged to the side. But the rest never paused. They came straight on. Mazaret stared at the dark and thundering wall of enemies for a moment, then roared the charge and spurred his mount forward.

The two forces met with a din of battlecries and clashing metal. Amid the barbed and armoured tumult, two horsemen, one with a sword, the other with a spear, rode towards Mazaret. He deflected the spearpoint with his shield and landed a well-aimed boot on the man's hip, sending him spinning from his saddle. At the same time he leaned away from the swordsman's slashing blade, slipped past and found himself facing another enemy who he outfought and despatched.

Then the high voice of horn sounded above the battle's raw clangour, and Mazaret glanced round to see Captain Kance leading the rest of his men down the side of the gully. The galloping wedge of knights held their formation even as they struck the flank of Azurech's column, splitting it in two. Divided and caught, the enemy's ranks dissolved into uncoordinated knots and pairs yet still fought on resolutely.

There was another hornblast and a long line of mounted knights came into view on the opposite rise, while half a dozen charged in from behind the original line. At this, Azurech's men broke and an attempt to retreat back along the gully turned into a chaotic rout. Unnoticed, the knights up on the rise faded away.

Terzis, Mazaret thought with a grim smile.

The victors were pursuing and riding down the vanquished, yet a few still managed to escape. Blood drenched the cold ground and the bodies of men and horses littered the gully, growing pale beneath the falling snow. Those mortally wounded were quickly despatched while surrendered prisoners were being disarmed and forced to leave on foot. Now dismounted, Mazaret strode over to where some score of his and Domas' men stood gathered around something. A few saw him approach, their faces anxious as they stepped aside to let him through to stand over the enemy he had already beaten twice.

Azurech was a tall, lantern-jawed man but now he measured his length on the ground, propped against the neck of a dead horse. His wounds were ghastly – one leg was shattered and lay bent in implausible places with bone shards visible; one arm was handless while the other was missing entirely from the shoulder.

Yet still he lived. Black blood soaked his armour and the ground below and around him but the wounds seemed to have staunched themselves. And still he lived and breathed. Within the black iron frame of his helm his face was a waxy white mask, its hollows and wrinkles tinged with a grey-pink hue. Red-rimmed eyes full of burning vitality looked up at Mazaret and the thin-lipped mouth smiled.

'Your thoughts write themselves in the pages of your eyes, my Lord Regent,' said Azurech in a voice unexpectedly deep and articulate. 'Thoughts like "How can this be?", and "Can he be killed?", and even "Should I take him back for judgement?"'

'Only the third part of your maunderings has any bearing on my purpose,' Mazaret said. 'You will return with us and answer for your foul acts.'

Azurech gave him an amused look through half-closed eyes. 'Hmm, Besh-Darok – a sizeable city by all accounts. Were you to take me there, you might have cause to wish you had done otherwise.'

In a single, swift movement Mazaret unsheathed his sword and levelled it at the Warlord's throat.

'Or I could end your life here,' he said. 'One thrust, and no more Deathless.'

There were nodding heads and murmurs of approval from the gathered soldiers. Mazaret noticed Domas watching from the side, agreeing with the rest.

Azurech just sneered.

'My master is the great Shadowking Byrnak, fool, and he has promised me life unending. You have no conception of the powers that you face. Slay me and my master will call my spirit back from the feeble bonds of the Earthmother's realm and attire me in new flesh. Then we shall resume our joust, you and I.'

The onlookers muttered fearfully and made warding gestures, but now it was Mazaret's turn to smile.

'There are other prisons, ' he said. 'The mine and well-dungeons of Roharka, for example – one of those might suit you, in that broken body of yours.'

Azurech's gaze grew hard with hate. 'There are ways and ways. I may have no talent for sorcery, but my master's will can reach out to touch the deepest pit and the highest peak. I shall not remain captive for long.'

'How sad,' Mazaret said to the gathered men. 'Witless as well as deathless. Have one of the wagons brought so that we might transport our *luckless* guest—'

A sound penetrated the muffling moan of the snowstorm, a brazen cry that shivered down from the sky. Fearful eyes peered into the blurred distance. Mazaret tightened his grip on his sword and was about to ask for Terzis when the sound came again, louder and closer and quickly followed by an answering cry from another quarter. Both climbed the scale into tearing shrieks that grew ever nearer . . .

'Deliverance,' murmured Azurech, just as a great winged form emerged from the grey veils of the snowstorm. Spines ridged its back, whiplike tendrils flailed from its wingtips and sharp cusps jutted from the joints of its lower legs and the knuckles of its clawed forearms. The narrow, armoured head possessed wide jaws filled with serrated teeth and a slender black tongue, but below it, in the upper chest between the clutching claws, was a second mouth, its thin lips gaping to reveal rows of incurving fangs.

'Spears and bows!' Mazaret roared, but most of the men broke and ran in the face of the screaming, onrushing horror. The remaining few were readying their weapons when someone behind Mazaret yelled in fright . . . and something struck the back of his head, hurling him to the ground. There was a numb pain in the back of his head and a dizzy nausea as he struggled to regain his feet. Then he realised that someone was dragging him away, trying to get him to stand. As he did, he caught sight of a second monster, a long serpentine shape of armoured segments with two pairs of wings keeping it aloft.

Nighthunters, he thought hazily. *But how . . . ?*

Then, with faster wingbeats, it began to rise into the air, followed by the double-jawed one which was carrying a limp form in its foreclaws.

Azurech.

'Flee, Lord Commander,' came that mocking voice. 'Take your rabble and flee back to your hovel city, and to your bride . . .'

Pain throbbed in Mazaret's head, and a sudden fury took him.

'To the horses!' he cried, lurching upright. 'We . . . hunt him . . . now . . .'

But his legs shook and he would have fallen had other hands not grabbed him in time.

'My lord, you're badly wounded,' said Captain Kance, his face as blurred as the sound of his voice. Next to him was Terzis and Domas, and Mazaret was about to speak when pain stabbed in his head.

'Half your scalp is flayed,' Terzis said. 'You must rest . . . that I can heal you . . .'

Yes, you are right, he wanted to say but his eyes felt like caves that he was falling backwards into, caves that swallowed him in dark oblivion.

Chapter Five

Up rocky stairs,
From the black halls of death,
Came cold, fierce spirits,
With our fate in their hands.

Calabos, *Beneath The Towers*, Act 3, ii, 12

It was the second night since the Low Coronation, and in secluded chambers near the Earthmother shrine in the Keep of Day, Alael slept. And in sleeping, she dreamed.

Soothed by a warm cup of mulled wine, she had drifted effortlessly away into misty slumber which gave way to vivid reverie. She dreamed that she was standing in a pillared room in the Keep of Day, talking with Abbess Halimer. Bright sunlight poured in through an open window to flood the room with gold while sweet scents spread from bowls of flowers hung from the pillars.

Why are you so sad, child? said Abbess Halimer, but Alael was trying to hear what someone was singing in the garden below the window, a song about rings and crowns and winter . . .

You must bind up your sorrow, the Abbess said behind her. *You have much to do.*

Alael turned, ready to deny any feelings of sadness, but froze in silence when she saw that the Abbess had been talking to Tauric, not her. The young Emperor kissed the Abbess' hand, bowed solemnly to her then crossed to an open door, pausing on the threshold to give Alael a single, brief look of longing. He was attired in a black doublet over a sky-blue shirt, and wore on his head a slender silver circlet adorned with small red stones. Her heart leaped at the sight but before she could speak he was gone, the door closing behind him.

Ignoring the Abbess' pleas, she ran to the door, wrenched it open and rushed through . . .

Into a dim, entangling undergrowth redolent of fertility and decay. As she pushed her way through, a dusty silver radiance settled over her surroundings, making every sprig and leaf and tendril look shining and dark, like polished iron beaded with moisture. Then the enclosing foliage thinned and she stepped out on to tilled earth.

Behold the vale of unburdening, daughter . . . all souls and essences journey along it . . .

Alael caught her breath in surprise. Since the Battle of Besh-Darok she had heard the Earthmother speaking in her dreams many times, but always as if from far away – this was the first time she had been spoken to directly. With the goddess' words sounding in her head like a great bell struck softly, Alael looked all around her. She stood at the edge of an immense valley, its sheer sides made from towering peaks and jagged ridges, its floor a wide, flat expanse of evenly-turned dark brown earth. Pale, tenuous human forms were sweeping past in their dozens, scores, hundreds, bobbing and flailing, dipping in and out of the soil as though in the grip of an invisible river whose currents rushed them along. Then she noticed, here and there, solitary figures fighting against the flow, grasping at clumps of weeds or protruding rocks . . .

Those who will not shed their burdens . . .

As she watched, a bright green mote flashed down from above and struck one of the struggling spirits. Immediately, it ceased all movement and rose into the air in a smooth, vertical ascent that Alael followed until it vanished in the black, empty vault of the sky.

Still they violate my realm, knowing that I will not retaliate . . . How I long for revenge against the Lord of Twilight, that arch-murderer, that thief of eternity . . . They think to keep him divided and thus keep their pathetic powers . . . Soon all their schemes will come to naught and you will be my blade upon his neck . . .

'I . . . I do not wish to do that,' Alael whispered.

The way is set and the masquers have their appointed goals . . . Daughter, *you* shall be my blade . . .

Then the ground opened under her feet and down she plunged into darkness. Somehow she went from falling to running along a low, narrow tunnel and then to climbing a rope ladder up a constricting hole which came out in the rotting bole stump of a tree. Clambering out she found herself in a forest clearing where Tauric stood on a mound, peering through a gap in the foliage. Following his gaze, she saw Besh-Darok from afar, its walls and towers ablaze and belching smoke.

'Save them!' she cried to him. 'You must save them!'

But Tauric turned and ran down the mound to a tall, brown stallion. Only when he had mounted up did Alael notice that both his arms were metal, but as he rode past her, away from the city, his glance was full of sad yearning.

Alael dashed up the mound for a clearer view, and found on the grassy crown a winged helm, a spear and a round shield. Hastily, she donned the helm and shield, picked up the spear and started down the slope towards Besh-Darok. But something was stopping her, grasping her, shaking her—

Awake to look up at the worried faces of Abbess Halimer and Keren Asherol.

'Was it a bad dream, Alael?' said the Abbess.

She nodded, then said, 'Was it hard to wake me?'

Keren gave a wry smile. 'Yes . . .'

'She spoke to me,' Alael said abruptly.

'I see,' the Abbess said. 'Would you like to tell us about your dream?'

Keren brought over a couple of chairs as Alael related all that had happened, leaving out nothing. The Abbess' demeanour was relaxed and composed but her eyes never left Alael as the tale was told. Alael thought she saw a certain hunger in the woman's gaze, as well as an intense interest, but when the account was done the Abbess sat back, looking pensive.

'There was a time, before the invasion,' she said after a moment or two, 'when those sisters who underwent true visions numbered perhaps one in every fifty. For the Rootpower priests such mystic experiences were much more frequent, almost as if the Fathertree himself was overflowing with the need to reach out to his followers. We sisters of the temple pretended to look down on the brothers of the tree, while secretly envying them their talkative god.

'But now, when I think of all that has happened and hear you speak of your dreams, I find my envy balanced by fear. She sounds so . . . cruel and pitiless. Does she even hear our prayers for mercy and compassion and peace?'

'I do not know,' Alael said quietly.

Sighing, the Abbess got to her feet. 'And knowledge is not faith. All we senior sisters can be sure of, in terms of knowledge, is the fact of the Goddess' Gift.' She opened one hand, palm upwards, and a pure white flamelet flickered and shone there. Instinctively, Alael knew that the tiny shred of magical fire came from the Earthmother's power. She could almost taste it.

The hand closed, snuffing out the tiny argent blaze.

'A rare and secret thing among the sisters of the temple,' Abbess Halimer said. 'I would be grateful if you refrained from speaking openly about this.'

Alael and Keren murmured their assent.

'Now, Alael – rise and dress. The farewell gathering is being held in the ground floor conclave chamber in an hour. So, till then.'

Recollection struck Alael as the Abbess made a graceful exit. Of course, the delegation to Dalbar was leaving today, Gilly, Medwin and . . .

'You forgot, didn't you, little sister?' Keren, arms crossed, was giving her the single arched eyebrow look of mock disapproval, which quickly dissolved into an open smile.

'Not forgotten, peerless big sister!' Alael said. 'Merely distracted.'

'Hmm, yes.' Keren said, standing up. 'Come on – I'll help you choose a gown fit to distract our boy-Emperor.'

Alael tried to look outraged but failed – Keren's wit was at once sharp and on target.

The two women had been introduced soon after Alael recovered from the terrifying possession of the battle, and was surprised and a little wary to discover that Keren's ordeal had been so similar to her own. Sharing her experiences, and learning about what it felt like to be a Daemonkind, brought them together in a fast-deepening friendship.

Wearing a brown and red dress more demure than the one Keren had picked out, Alael hurried with her companion down a minor stairwell whose wall tiles bore patterns and forms of sea creatures. As they walked, Alael asked Keren if anything more had been uncovered about the attempt on her life.

'Nothing of significance. The woman who tried to kill me was a player who had gone missing from one of the beggar troupes over a week ago. Bardow is sure that someone used the Lesser Power to weave a compulsion into her mind, possibly the same person who attacked Nerek in the Artisan Quarter.'

'Did none of the senior mages sense such goings-on?'

They were passing through a small courtyard busy with carters unloading their wares, and Keren lowered her voice.

'Not one. Bardow thinks that the person behind all this may be masking his use of the Lesser Power by tainting it with another . . .'

'The Wellsource?' Alael whispered in dread.

Keren shrugged. 'It would be the obvious choice . . .'

From a bright outer corridor they entered the ground floor conclave chamber, a vaguely triangular room with benches and high-backed seating arrayed before a dais at its narrow end. And when Keren left Alael's side to join Medwin and Gilly who waited near the luggage piled on the dais, it finally sunk in that her friend was leaving. Others were already there, sitting on the benches, familiar faces like the Lord Regent Yasgur with his advisers, Atroc and Ghazrek; Nerek, looking pale and impassive; red-haired Ffion and a few of her fellow mages; Yarram, Lord Commander of the Fathertree Knights, sitting with the commanders of the new orders, the Knights Protectorate, the Knights of the Moon and Stars, the Knights of Keys, and the Knights of the Bell. And Tauric with three of his White Companions.

It was a brief farewell ceremony, yet full of warmth and regard. Abbess Halimer and two Temple sisters sang a soft, wordless cantion as Bardow said a few words about the three travellers and their desti-nation. Then Yasgur gave Medwin a flat leather case of documents and spoke quietly to all three, before departing with his retinue.

Sitting near Ffion and the other mages, Alael did her best to avoid looking in Tauric's direction and was relieved when the ceremony was over. After exchanging a few words with Gilly, Tauric and his followers left straight away. The three delegates then moved towards the doors which led out to the coaching stables. Alael began hurrying after them but slowed and held back when she saw Nerek and Keren walking side by side, speaking close and serious. Keren carried a pair of saddlebags over her shoulder and was reaching into one when she noticed Alael.

'There she is.'

The two look-alike women exchanged words of farewell and clasped hands, then Nerek gave Alael a brief nod on her way towards the door.

'What a hasty leavetaking,' Keren said as she fumbled in her saddlebag. 'I was afraid we might not have a chance to speak . . . Ah, here it is . . .'

She produced a thick, leather-bound volume and gave it to Alael. 'This is a rare book called *The Codex of Northern Sagas* . . .' She indicated a fringed cloth bookmark protruding from the pages. 'That marks the place of a very old sagasong called "How Raegal Sang a Road to the Land of the Daemons" which, unfortunately, is written in an ancient Othazi dialect. While I am away, could you make enquiries among the scholars of the city to see if anyone is able to translate it?'

'Why, I would be happy to.'

Keren smiled. 'Oh, thank you. I'm taking a copy with me, in case I encounter someone capable of translating it, but it is good to know that another will be pursuing the mystery. If you speak with Bardow he will know which of the colleges to approach, and when I return we can compare notes, eh?' She laid a hand on Alael's arm. 'Take care in your dreams, little sister. And don't be too afraid of looking Tauric in the eye.'

From a balcony off the conclave chamber, Alael held on to the book firmly and watched the delegates' coach clatter away from the palace, heading off towards the harbour. There, they were due to board a fast galley to take them to Sejeend where a barge would carry them along Gronanvel to the northern end of the Red

Way. From there, they would travel south on horseback to Dalbar's capital, Scallow. As the coach receded, she uttered an inner prayer for their safety.

'Ah, I see she gave you that collection of, ah, doggerel.'

It was Archmage Bardow, regarding her with a humorous gaze.

'Oh, ser Bardow, I am to ask you about which colleges . . .'

'Indeed, translations and so forth. I can offer a few recommendations, but I would prefer to deal with that later since there is another more pressing problem at hand. I have been meaning to discuss certain matters with Nerek and yourself, and this assassination business has made it all the more urgent. I shall be meeting Nerek in the mage hall shortly – if you join us now, we can make a start. Is that agreeable? And we can talk about that translation after.'

Alael thought a moment, picturing Nerek in her mind, and knew that she needed to know more about Keren's sorcerous twin.

'I would most happy to help,' she said.

'Excellent, then let us be on our way. Time is of the essence – Lord Regent Mazaret will be at the gates in only a few hours . . .'

It was late afternoon when Mazaret and his knights escorted the wagons of wounded and refugees through the Gallaro Gate. City wardens were already waiting, alerted by the message bird he had sent from the fort at Shekaruk Pass. There would be food and drink and warm shelter, remedy for the sick and care for the anguished.

The first watch-brands were being lit along the city walls as Mazaret and the others rode their weary horses up the Shaska Road. Snow and sleet had come down in icy, needling showers during the return journey, but now the sky was a dark blue, star-strewn canopy where scraps and rags of cloud rushed from horizon to horizon. It was dry but the wind that blew in from the bay was bitterly cold and made all of Mazaret's wounds ache just that little bit more. The slash at the back of his head, however, was a constant source of pain. Terzis had successfully cleaned the laceration and healed its edges, but the shock, concussion and bruising had combined to make him feel every one of his fifty-two years.

When they neared the Ironhall Barracks, Mazaret and Captain Kance shook hands before the Fathertree Knights turned away to their new quarters. Mazaret and Terzis urged their mounts along the other road, splashing through pools of slush before they reached the main palace gate. Once through, they dismounted and let the ostlers lead the horses away, then walked an ache-filled walk across the torch-lit yard to the northern vestibule. There, a court steward was waiting.

'Welcome back, Lord Regent. Lady Terzis, I am to inform you that the magehall steward wishes to speak with you upon your arrival.'

'My thanks, ser,' Terzis said, turning to Mazaret. 'My lord, if your wounds offer great discomfort, please send for me without delay.'

'I am grateful for your concern, lady.'

When Terzis was gone, the steward spoke again.

'My lord, the honourable Archmage Bardow presents his warmest greetings and respectfully requests your attendance at an urgent dialogue soon to commence in the fourth-floor library.'

'And how urgent would that be?'

'The moment you entered the palace, my lord.'

Mazaret massaged a taut ache in his neck, and tried to think through his exhaustion. Then he sighed.

'Inform the Archmage that I shall attend, once I have been to my chambers to change into fresh garments.'

'As you wish, my lord.'

A short while later, he was descending the warden steps from his rooms on the fifth floor, feeling somewhat less dusty and grimy but still longing for a hot bath, not to mention food and a warm bed. Mazaret was following the spiral stairwell down, soft-soled boots making scarcely a sound, when he heard voices talking. Something in the voices made him slow till he saw a narrow archway leading off to one of the outer balconies. Curious, he stopped and listened.

'. . . four new orders but did not offer to create one for you?' said one voice, that of a young man. 'We already number more than forty, and every one of us has pledged his service. I can even suggest a title for us – the Knights of the Order of Companions—'

'Hmm, I like that,' said another. 'It's got the ring of nobility to it.'

'And we could swear a solemn oath to the Emperor,' said the first.

'No,' said a third man that Mazaret immediately recognised as Tauric. 'The ideals of such a brotherhood should reach further than the body of the Emperor. They should be dedicated to something higher and purer . . .'

'You mean like the—'

'Yes, but that brings us back to the same problem as before,' Tauric said. 'The lack of a consecrated shrine.'

'*He* might know where to find one . . .'

What am I doing? Mazaret thought suddenly. *I don't have time for this eavesdropping . . .*

He tiptoed back up several steps then came down again with noisy footfalls and a cough or two thrown in for good measure as he carried on past the archway, apparently oblivious. But he could not help wondering about the reference to a shrine, and who this *He* might be? Did they mean Bardow? Perhaps he would mention it to the Archmage before retiring to bed.

The fourth-floor library was really an annexe to the main library on the second floor which occupied fully half of that level. The annexe was narrow and had been refashioned into two tiers to make greater use of possible shelf space. As Mazaret entered, he was assailed by the peculiar smells of parchment and old leather, laced with the tang of burnt lamp oil. It was an oddly comforting meld of odours, reminding him of the library in his father's house many years ago, when he still lived in Besh-Darok.

An elderly but spry-looking man came forward.

'Ah, m'Lord Regent – I am Custodian Felwe. The honourable Archmage and his companions await you at the great table at the far end, near the chart drawers. Please forgive this apparent disarray – we are currently storing most of the contents of the tenth-floor reading room while it undergoes refurbishment.'

Mazaret thanked him and walked on past piles of boxes and drawers, and bound bundles of scrolls. *Tenth floor?* he thought. *That would be where Tauric encountered the stone apparition of Argatil, Korregan's archmage . . .*

No lamps burned on the upper tier and the shadows seemed dark and enfolding. At a well-lit, good-sized table in the last alcove heads turned at his approach and chairlegs scraped as they rose to greet him. As well as Bardow, Mazaret saw Yasgur, his adviser Atroc, and Yarram, successor to the Lord Commandership of the Fathertree Order. They all looked strangely sombre and quiet as he sat down beside them.

'My sincerest thanks for joining us, my lord,' Bardow said. 'We understand how weary you must be after such a hazardous foray, but there are certain matters which must be discussed now rather than the morrow.'

'Did the coronation go as planned?' Mazaret said, suddenly worried. 'I would have been present, had it been at all possible.'

Atroc snorted, and Yasgur grinned. 'The boy's crowning passed well enough, but the spectacle was only an arena for hidden treachery,' the Mogaun prince said. 'It was sheer good fortune that our enemy's plot went awry, else our delegation to Dalbar would have ended in disaster.'

'Lord Regent Yasgur is entirely correct,' said Bardow, who went on to give Mazaret an account of the events leading up to the suicide of the false Nerek. Mazaret listened closely, mind made clear and alert by this dread news.

'This woman,' he said when the Archmage was done. 'The streetplayer – was anything more learned about her, and who she might have been involved with?'

Bardow shook his head. 'I questioned her companions myself, and had our guilemen ask and listen around that quarter. Nothing was uncovered. She vanished off the streets a week ago, and no one saw her with anyone or remembers anyone asking after her.'

'It occurs to me,' Mazaret said, 'that if our enemies are prepared to set such a scheme in motion, its failure will not prevent them from trying again.'

'Precisely so, my lord,' Bardow said evenly. 'Fortunately, our delegation departed for Dalbar this morning without incident, but with a stronger escort. Ah, Gilly asked me to pass on his regards.'

'I had hoped to be here in time for their leavetaking,' Mazaret said. 'But—'

The seer Atroc leaned forward and said, 'I am told you defeated the one called Deathless.'

Mazaret gave him a small, hard smile. 'How did you come by that name, ser Atroc? I didn't mention it in my message from the pass fort.'

'We seers live night and day by the Door of Dreams,' Atroc said bluntly. 'In sleep we hear many things both clear and uncertain.'

'We are all eager to hear you speak of this encounter, my lord,' Yasgur said, glaring at his adviser, who merely chuckled.

Mazaret cleared his throat and related all that had happened from the point where he met Domas at the abandoned town of Nimas. Gazes grew grim at mention of walking corpses, then shocked at the description of Azurech's injuries and his evil pronouncements. Only Atroc seemed unsurprised and nodded on hearing of Azurech's rescue by two nighthunters.

'Domas and the survivors of his band elected to return to Alvergost,' Mazaret concluded. 'To offer protection to any who remain there, Domas said, but he is clearly reluctant to place himself and his men under our command.' He rubbed his forehead. The dull pain was rising again. 'So, how are we to counter these threats?'

'Before we consider that, my lord, there is one more report to hear,' Bardow said. 'Lord Command Yarram, if you will . . .'

At the other end of the table, Yarram got to his feet, clasped his hands behind his back and began. Mazaret heard of the brigands who had been raiding from beyond the Girdle Hills, and how Yarram and his men pursued them and their leader deep into the hilly ravines. How the brigands had crossed a rain-swollen river by way of a bridge which they wrecked before the pursuers reached it, and how their leader, a woman, had come forward on her horse to speak . . .

Yarram paused and gave Mazaret a troubled look. 'My lord, you know me, and you know that I place great store by truth and accuracy.'

'That is so,' Mazaret said. 'Say on.'

'Well, my lord, the brigand leader came to the edge of the riverbank, by the rushing waters, so I rode down to our side to confront her – my lord, her winding cloak and everything about her was palest grey, and her face was that of Suviel Hantika . . .'

In the shocked silence, Mazaret stared at him while a numb, dislocating sensation swept through him.

'No,' he said. 'That cannot be . . .'

Yarram looked wretched. 'My lord—'

'You *must* be mistaken.'

'My lord, I was as close to her as I am to ser Bardow there, and I swear to you that it was *her*.'

Mazaret pushed himself shakily up from the table, pain pounding in his head. 'I cannot listen to any more of this—'

Bardow laid a firm hand on his shoulder. 'You must, my friend. You must hear it all.'

After a moment Mazaret sank back into his chair and nodded wordlessly. Yarram seemed to gather his determination before continuing.

'She looked at me with bone-white eyes and said, "Tell your masters that Death has many doors and they cannot lock them all. And tell Ikarno that I shall await him at Blueaxe Ridge."'

There was utter quiet for a second or two, then Mazaret said:

'Where is Blueaxe Ridge?'

'Southwest of the city,' Yasgur said thoughtfully. 'A stone track follows a long slope up to it. It is a good lookout point, and easily defended. Be wary of the words of the dead, my friend. Once uttered, they are like hooks in your soul.'

'My lord,' Bardow said. 'Think carefully. It would be a fool-hardy act—'

'How did this happen, Archmage?' Mazaret said, voice made raw by grief. 'What did they do to her?'

Bardow met his gaze. 'The Lord of Twilight's followers have a ritual which can pare away a person's spirit to create images of the original called *rivenshades*. Sometimes they can even clothe them in flesh.'

'The Acolytes did this to her in Trevada?'

'Yes.'

Mazaret could feel his heart thudding in his chest. 'You said *images* of the original, Bardow. Could they have made more than one of these things.'

Bardow let out a long sigh. 'Nerek thinks it almost certain that they would.'

Mazaret nodded slowly. Now the horror was complete. The pain in his head had become a kind of strength now, and he stood up, steady and unwavering.

'They did this to her,' he said in an iron voice. 'The Acolytes, sitting in their stolen towers, dripping evil into the veins of our lands. But their towers are only of stone, and they bleed when cut . . .'

'You cannot propose an assault on Trevada, my lord,' said Bardow. 'It's practically a fortress—'

'If I did,' Mazaret snapped. 'No one would question the just-ness of it!'

Bardow sat back. 'Regardless, you and all who went with you would die,' he said quietly.

Mazaret paused and bowed his head, striving to master his anger. 'I do not propose such a course of action, my lords. But the time may come soon when we will have to move against our enemies with all our might.'

'Till then,' Yasgur said. 'We should plan and train and build.'

'I shall redouble our efforts to corner these brigands, my lord,' said Yarram. 'Soon they will have nowhere to hide.'

'Thank you for your wise counsel and concern, my lords,' Mazaret said, his fury reined in. 'Now, by your leave, I shall retire to my chambers and a much-needed rest.'

'And try to put Blueaxe Ridge out of your mind, my lord,' Bardow said as Mazaret turned towards the door.

If only I could, he thought grimly, walking off through the shadows. *But the reckoning has to begin somewhere.*

Shrouded in the shadows of the library annexe's upper tier, Tauric listened with mounting alarm to Bardow's account of the attempt on Keren's life, then to that of Mazaret's foray into central Khatris. Certain details of the first were new to him, like the attack on Nerek and the use of tainted Lesser Power, and the grotesque horror of the second made him feel pure despair.

A situation like this demanded a real leader, one with wisdom, battle experience, authority and, above all, sorcerous power. Instead, they had himself, a powerless boy-Emperor who felt himself grow more superfluous with each passing day.

Then Tauric heard Yarram tell of the brigand leader who looked like the dead mage, Suviel Hantika, and her doom-laden message. When Mazaret reacted with disbelief and anger, Tauric could feel the man's pain. His own anger kindled as he listened, and when Mazaret all but vowed revenge upon the Acolytes of Twilight it sparked a decision.

He crept back along the darkened tier to a false panel between two sets of shelves. He had learned of the secret tunnel from a seldom-visited section of the main library, an archive collected by Korregan's father and his grandfather, Emperor Varros the Third. A stub of candle burned in a clay holder sitting on the floor just inside the hinged panel, and after closing it behind him he picked up the lamp and followed a low, narrow passage round a short curve. At its end a steep set of steps in the stone went up to bring him out behind a statue of one of the palace's architects. He squeezed out of the small square hole, fitted the stone-tiled wooden cover over it, then straightened to gaze out over Besh-Darok. He was back on the outer balcony.

His two Companions, Aygil and Dogar, gave expectant smiles as he emerged from behind the statue. Both wore blue sashes over heavy white tabards and carried sheathed long knives at their waists but only Aygil had a standard bearer's hook on his belt.

'A gainful experience, majesty?' said Aygil.

'A sobering one,' Tauric said. 'And one that I would discuss with our *guest* – straight away.'

The Companions' eyes widened.

'After that,' he went on, 'I shall ask *him* how to look for a shrine. But let us be on our way back to the Keep of Night. The sooner we get there the sooner we can find out what *he* knows.'

Flanked by the two youths, Tauric followed the warden stairs down to the second floor where a covered gantry led from the side of the High Spire over to a stone walkway halfway down the sheer inner face of the Silver Aggor. The walkway afforded a wide view of the Courts of the Morning and as they strode along Tauric could just make out the last labourers leaving an almost-complete stone dais down near the base of the Spire. Upon it would sit a statue of Gunderlek, the tragic rebel leader. Tauric had argued passionately that the man should be honoured, and had been surprised when both Lord Regent and the Archmage agreed. It was also suggested that smaller statues of him be commissioned for public squares, the Hall of the City Fathers, and Five Kings Dock.

Watch-brands flared in recesses to either side of a large door in the wall of the Keep of Night. Guards saluted and stood aside as Tauric and the two Companions passed through. A short passage led into the third floor, most of which had been given over to Tauric and his retinue as temporary accommodation while the upper levels of the Spire were being rebuilt. Inside, they hurried along corridors to a square room where half a dozen Companions sat or lounged on settles. All stood when Tauric entered but he gestured them to take their ease as he and the others crossed to a curtained arch. Beyond was a small anteroom and two Companions guarding a plain wooden door. The guards stood to attention as Aygil opened the door and led the way in.

It was a small room, dim inside with the only light coming from a pair of tiny bronze oil lamps burning on an altar in the corner. A hunched figure knelt on a mat before it, muttering in a low monotone, so Tauric and the other waited respectfully. At last, the man stopped, uttered a long sigh then said:

'Divine Skyhorse, behold these three who don the burden of valour in your name. Bless their tasks, O Stallion of the Storm, that soon all the people shall raise up their voices in praise of you. By plain and sky . . .'

'By plain and sky,' Tauric and his Companions repeated, each with a hand lifted to grasp the horse amulet that he wore about his neck.

There was a protracted moment, then the man, still on his knees, said, 'You honour this poor priest with your visit, majesty. Does new knowledge trouble you?'

Tauric shivered at this demonstration of prevision but accepted it. 'Greetings to you, priestly one. I have indeed learned many unsettling things today . . .' And he proceeded to give a brief retelling of all he had overheard in the library.

'Evil is a sprouting poison that can take root in any soil,' said the shadowy priest.

'And we seem almost powerless to stop it,' Tauric said.

'Hmm . . . don't you mean "I" rather than "we", majesty?'

Tauric's shoulders slumped. 'Yes,' he said. 'All around, people I know are risking their lives and their very spirits in this veiled battle, while I sit with empty hands, powerless.' He clenched his fists. 'Surely now is the time to awaken the Skyhorse to a land desperate for his protection, if only we knew where to find a shrine or a place of power—'

The priest sighed again. 'After the battle, in the days and weeks during which I crawled along the shore with my shattered leg, many things passed through my mind, faces, images and patterns that scoured me out, purifying my essence before I was permitted my first vision of the divine Skyhorse, Great Mane of the World . . . and in my time here in this sanctuary, some of those wild seeings rear up from memory now and again, as did one in the midst of your account, majesty. Pray tell, what was the name of the town where the lord Mazaret met his allies?'

'Why . . . it was Nimas . . .'

There was a sharp intake of breath and the priest struggled to his feet with the aid of a staff. 'Nimas . . . where once, in ages past, there was a great temple dedicated to the divine Skyhorse . . .'

Then he turned to face them. Bald and ageing, his long-jawed features showing the strain of his crippled leg, the Armourer regarded Tauric with bright, fervent eyes.

'Nimas, majesty,' he said. 'There you will find the power you need.'

Tauric felt on fire with exultation. 'When shall we leave? How soon?'

'Soon, but not too soon, majesty. We must wait for a sign and we must be ready, and therefore we must prepare.' He smiled, revealing broken teeth. 'Yes, in this, preparation is everything.'

Chapter Six

Fear my hand,
Which will crack thy walls,
And make a thousand armies,
Out of sand.

Calabos, *The City Of Dreams*, Act 2, ii, 8

In pale green light, deep below the deepest dungeons of the citadel of Rauthaz, Byrnak stood by the wall of a vast, silent cavern, gazing across a restless lake of bodies. The Wellgate had made this possible, hollowing out a great emptiness that was twin to the one beneath Casall, a huge workshop fit for the fashioning of the Host of Twilight. The cold, damp air held a rank odour of iron, or perhaps rust. The enfolding green glow emanated from the opaque, smooth walls and ceiling, adding to the silver–grey radiance that filtered up between the still bodies. The lake seemed to ripple and lap, yet it was made not of water but of souls, a shimmering, silently writhing expanse of souls. Crouching down by the brink, Byrnak could see tenuous, distended forms crammed together, sliding and struggling for possession of the flesh that floated upon them . . .

Leap in, worm . . . join with the mindless . . .

Byrnak rose and stepped back from the edge.

Consider it a moment – were you to relinquish this form, you could very quickly seize another, once its owner was dealt with . . . you would be free of me . . .

Byrnak laughed with unconcealed contempt. *I can think of at least half a dozen possible outcomes to such a scheme,* he thought. *None of them favourable to me.*

An image flashed into his mind, a giant in a horned helm turning slowly to grin at him, with black glints for eyes – **There will be no peace for you, no rest** – and one huge hand reaching towards him—

He blinked, saw the cavern once more, and gritted his teeth in a stifled snarl.

'Keeping our guest amused, brother?' said an approaching voice.

Grazaan was striding along the lakeside path, followed by three shaven-headed Acolytes. He wore his habitual battered leather harness and trews, and over that a great, dark red cloak adorned with spiders and scorpions, its folds lifting slightly as he walked. He also appeared to be weaponless, while behind him the Acolytes carried coils of rope.

'Greetings, brother,' Byrnak said. 'He certainly seems to need no sleep. Unfortunately, I do.'

Nodding, Grazaan came to a halt a few feet away. 'Night before last I made the mistake of falling into a drowse unprepared. Woke to find my left hand around one of my servant's throat, having choked him to death. Which is why I've thought to devise a precaution.' With a tilt of the head he indicated the accompanying Acolytes.

'At least our minds remain inviolate,' Byrnak said.

Grazaan frowned. 'How did our brother Thraelor seem when you and he last conversed?'

'Tired – of course – and somewhat distracted. That was in mindspeech this morning.'

'I spoke with him yesterday, using the Wellmirror,' Grazaan said. 'I could scarcely get any sense out of him, and the last thing he said was, "Is he the mask or am I?"'

A dark ripple of unease passed through Byrnak, and he thought he heard a harsh inner laughter, faintly as if coming from afar.

'We shall have to keep him under watch,' Grazaan said. 'In the meantime, I assume that you are here to observe our progress and pester us to do more in less time.'

'Several intrigues will soon come to fruition, brother,' said Byrnak. 'Some time in the next day or two we may need to move a force of at least ten thousand down the Great Aisle, all armed and provisioned.'

'So the Aisle is complete.'

'The Wellgate finished the bore a short while ago,' Byrnak said, enjoying the satisfaction. 'Should we wish, we could ride from here to Besh-Darok in less than a day.'

'With this strategic superiority,' Grazaan said, 'why do you continue to indulge in these minor ploys and schemes?'

'We face the imponderable, brother,' Byrnak said. 'What is the Earthmother's purpose and will she act when we begin our campaign? When that moment arrives, all resistance must collapse like an eggshell. Then, with the Crystal Eye and the Motherseed in our hands—'

'We may at last be able to deal with our lord and master,' Grazaan said with a wintry smile.

Byrnak nodded. The fragments of the Lord of Twilight that each of them carried were hungry for union, whatever the cost to their hosts. One of their number, Ystregul the Black Priest, had already succumbed to insanity instigated by his own shard of the Lord of Twilight, and was held ensorcelled and enchained in Trevada.

'Just so,' Byrnak said. 'And time is not on our side.'

Across the cavern, a group of Acolytes was helping several naked people out of the lake of souls. At that moment, a shriek cut through the liquid silence, a sound full of madness and despair. Some way along, Byrnak could see the figure of a man crouching amid the prone bodies, one hand clasping his head while crying out wordlessly and trying to wake those around him.

'Occasionally, a quelled host awakes while one of the harvested souls is trying to take possession,' Grazaan said. 'The shock is usually enough to repel the incursion and destroy any lingering sanity.'

As a pair of Acolytes, walking on green footholds in the air, seized the weeping, babbling host, Byrnak looked thoughtfully at the other Shadowking. 'How often does this happen, and what do you do with them?'

'We get four, perhaps five of them a day,' Grazaan said. 'We put them out in the garth-yards behind the curtain walls. Helps feed the eaterbeasts, brother.'

Together, they laughed.

'And just how many warriors *can* you provide me with?' Byrnak said.

'Assuming that the supply of hosts does not falter, both caverns could produce between two and three thousand a day,' Grazaan said.

'Excellent,' Byrnak said. 'Now I must take my leave of you — there is much I have to discuss with our brother Kodel.'

'Have a care with that one,' Grazaan muttered. 'There are nothing but self-serving plans behind those eyes.'

Byrnak grinned savagely. 'I'd be almost disappointed if there weren't. Till later.'

'Till then.'

There were passages leading up to the lowest underlevels of Rauthaz Citadel, but for Byrnak it was the minimum of effort to summon a side portal of the Wellgate. A slender dark opening widened before him in the air, and with an image of his destination in mind he stepped through.

The Hall of Forging had once been a vast temple dedicated to the Fathertree and the Rootpower. Now, soot and grime blackened the patterned windows, the fluted columns and carven stonework, and sixteen huge forges occupied the entire ground floor, eight on each side. Massive flues jutted from the rears of the great furnaces and passed through the temple walls, carrying most of the spark-laden fumes outside. But a permanent smoky veil still hung in the air while gangs of sweating smiths and stokers worked with manic fervour down in the fiery golden light.

'Ah, brother Byrnak. How very timely — I was about to send forth for you . . .'

Byrnak's use of the Wellgate had brought him to a long, low chamber, one end of which was an open balcony that looked out over the Hall of Forging. The other end was divided into large rooms devoted to templating, assaying and proving, with a wide corridor passing by them on its way to Kodel's private chambers. Kodel himself stood by one of several cluttered drafting tables. His hair was shorter now, though still top-knotted, giving him a feral look, and the coat he wore was a long affair of rough brown leather marred by many scorch marks.

'So,' Byrnak said. 'Why did you wish to see me? To tell me that the production of armour and weaponry proceeds apace?'

Kodel gave a sly smile. 'That was to be a salient issue, but then something else caught my attention. Come with me, brother, if you will.'

Irritated, Byrnak nevertheless followed him along the broad corridor to a junction where Kodel opened the left hand door and stepped through. A short dim passage led out on to the flat stone roof of an adjoining temple building. It had been swept of the early morning fall of snow but a thin white layer had come down since and an icy breeze was cutting in from the east. A few spidery metal frames stood on either side of the roof, each with an intricate, wire-bound array of lenses aimed at the late morning sky, and all bearing fringes of icicles. But it was the hexagonal wooden canopy near the centre that Kodel was heading towards. Beneath it a figure lay unmoving on a trestle table, and as they drew near Byrnak could see crude bandages around terrible injuries before being able to make out the man's features.

'Azurech,' he murmured.

At the sound of his name, the former Warlord's head tipped over on to one side to look, and a dull fear settled over his features.

'Master, forgive me – I've failed you . . .'

Under the six-sided canopy it was warmer, quieter. Some glamour put in place by Kodel kept out coldness and the unceasing din of the forges. Byrnak made no reply but instead looked to Kodel for an explanation.

Kodel shrugged. 'He was rescued from a battlefield in Khatris two days ago by a pair of nighthunters who carried him to our stronghold in the Gorodar Mountains west of here. They then refused to take him any further, so the commander bound his wounds and sent him on in a wagon. When he arrived a short while ago I had one of our nighthunters bring him up here.'

'Failed . . . failed you, master . . .' Azurech mumbled.

'How did this happen, Azurech?' Byrnak said. 'Who were you fighting?'

'Mazaret, that . . . grey-haired old dullard . . .'

'Again, eh?'

'Send me back, master, I beg you! Make me strong and fast and I'll bring back his head . . .'

Byrnak leaned closer. 'I shall send you forth once more, Azurech, but my plans for Ikarno Mazaret do not involve his death at your hands.'

'Ah, the white woman.'

Byrnak called up the power of the Wellsource and shaped its bright emerald fire into skeins of fine tendrils and serrated whips which he folded around the wounded man.

'Prepare yourself,' he said. 'There will be pain.'

Azurech uttered a single, throat-tearing scream before lapsing into unconsciousness. As his will directed the Sourcefire, Byrnak glanced at Kodel who was watching in fascination.

'What news from your spy in Besh-Darok?'

Without so much as a blink, Kodel said, 'Which one?'

Byrnak smiled. 'Somehow, you enveigled your servant back into the boy Tauric's favour and now he's secreted somewhere in the palace . . .'

'The boy thinks that the Armourer has become a Skyhorse priest,' Kodel said testily. 'And he is so desperate for power of his own that he and his closest followers have taken to Skyhorse worship.'

'The empty in pursuit of the futile,' Byrnak mused aloud, regarding Kodel. 'So we can have their boy-Eemperor slain whenever we wish – good.'

'What I had in mind was getting him out of the city and into our hands at a time that suits us,' Kodel said. 'He would follow the Armourer almost anywhere.'

'Yes . . . I can see the advantages of having the boy in our power . . .' Byrnak paused and gazed down at the form on the table. Nodding, he let the meshes of power dissipate and woke his servant. 'It is done. Sit up.'

Gingerly, Azurech levered himself into a sitting position and as he examined and prodded his renewed arms and legs, Byrnak admired his own handiwork. For Azurech now had Byrnak's face.

Nearby, Kodel chuckled and produced a small mirror from a wisp of Wellsource power, and held it up for Azurech's inspection. The man looked and gasped.

'You still have your height and build, so only the ignorant would mistake you for me,' Byrnak said. 'But this will suffice for the tasks I shall set you, and for the first you will travel down the Great Aisle to Gorla.'

Azurech knelt before him and gazed up, eyes shining.

'To hear is to obey, oh Great Lord.'

Chapter Seven

Neither blade nor song nor graven duty,
Could break the chains of her dread beauty.

Avalti, *Song of the Queen's Regard*

The College of Hendred's Hall lay north of the Chapel Fort barracks, on the hillside near a lakelet, overlooking a district full of narrow streets and old, dilapidated buildings. The college, one of several in the old town, was the second-oldest in Besh-Darok and had a Chamber of Parlance the equal of any in the western domains. These were the few details Alael had learned from Bardow earlier that morning but as the horse-drawn carriage passed through the ornate gates she was surprised at how forbidding it seemed. While not much wider than a large city villa, its grey walls were high and featureless and its four corner towers were square-built with small, peaked roofs. In contrast, the grounds were the epitome of nature's grace, their clusters of perennial bushes gathered about the college, softening its severity, enhancing its dignity.

Snowmelt from the last fall lay thickly on the lawns and leaves, now hard and glittering from the deep frost that had settled overnight. But the sloping, cobbled drive was clear as Alael's carriage rattled up to the pillared entrance. Wrapped in a dark violet cloak she descended from the carriage, thanked her driver and hurried up to the already open main doors.

'Welcome to Hendred's Hall, milady,' said the elderly steward waiting there, black cap in hand.

'My thanks for your hospitality, ser,' Alael said as the great doors swung shut and the warmth of the interior enfolded her. The college lobby was a small but luxuriously marbled hall hung with pictures and tapestries, its floor tiled in red, blue and black patterns with mosaics of the Fathertree and the Earthmother at the centre. A great fire roared in the hearth and each wall had an archway leading off.

'We received the message from the palace, milady, telling us to expect you.'

'Ah, yes . . . I have my confirmation here.' She took a rolled parchment from an inner pocket and passed it to him. He examined it for a moment or two, then nodded.

'From the hand of the Archmage himself, and bearing his seal. Lady Alael, we are honoured by your visit. Kindly follow me.'

The steward led her through the left-hand archway and along a narrow corridor lined with painted panels and floored with wooden tiles which clicked underfoot, past several lecture rooms and a scullery, then up a stone spiral staircase. After climbing some way, the steward halted to open a side door into a small L-shaped room where he bade her wait and left by another door. A moment later he reappeared and beckoned her over.

'Ser Melgro Onsivar, Master of Parlance, will see you now,' he said, pushing the door wide open.

Alael entered a high chamber seemingly dominated by bookshelves, both freestanding and wall-mounted. Following an aisle between the shelves she came to the other half of the room, which was large and long and well furnished for an scholar's needs. An oval table sat to one side, cluttered with tables and maps, while a large, elaborately-carved desk occupied much of the remaining space. A few chairs were scattered around this part of the room, beyond which was a raised section bounded by a wooden balustrade with a few steps leading up to it.

'Over here, ah . . . young lady, yes . . .'

Ser Melgro Onsivar, Master of Parlance, was a gaunt man of advanced years, with a head of fine white hair grown sparse enough for the curve of his skull to be perfectly visible. Dressed in a pale grey gown edged with yellow and blue, he sat in a tall chair with a wide, paper-busy desk before him and a west-facing glass window behind

him. Scarcely glancing up from a small white book, he gestured at
a wooden stool on to which Alael climbed while trying very hard
not to think of him as a large grey bird sitting on his perch . . .

Onsivar closed his book and laid it carefully on the desk. 'So . . .
young Bardow sent you, did he? Said you had some passage or other
that requires translating.'

'Yes, Master Onsivar,' Alael said, taking out the book Keren had
given to her, opening it at the relevant page. 'A friend of mine asked
me if I could have this examined by a scholar such as yourself. Other
than that, I know nothing more about it.'

So saying, she passed the book to him. Onsivar took it readily
but he was studying her as he did so.

'Southern Cabringa,' he murmured. 'Probably Adnagaur, yet
there are sidetones of Mantinor to your articulation – am I correct?'

Impressed, Alael nodded. 'I was raised in Adnagaur, although my
mother was from Tymora on the Mantinoren coast.'

The Master of Parlance gave a satisfied sniff and turned his
attention to Alael's book. 'Now, let me see what we have here.
Hmm – it appears to be in ancient Othazi but the dialect is uncertain,
possibly northern, possibly also misconstrued. Yet the hand . . .' He
stroked his chin, then looked up at Alael. 'Am I right to assume
that this is an original?'

'I do not know,' Alael said.

Onsivar frowned, made a drawn-out hum and glanced down
at the open book with unconcealed irritation. As the silence
lengthened, Alael felt her patience fraying till she could no longer
keep silent.

'So, Master Onsivar, is the piece translatable?'

'Yes, my lady, though I'd much prefer to consult the original . . .'
He tapped the open pages. 'This is a copy, I am afraid.'

'Will that affect your abilities, ser?'

Bristling eyebrows raised above piercing eyes. 'Not in the least,
although I shall need to keep this here – if you have no objections,
my lady.'

'I've already had a copy of the sagasong made,' she said. 'So you
may indeed retain the book for the time being. How long will your
efforts take?'

'Four, perhaps five days,' Onsivar said. 'The Othazi lexicae we have here refer only to the tongue's main orthodoxy, thus I shall have to send borrowing requests to two private libraries in Besh-Darok in the hope that either possesses the dialect gradus I need. If I have to write to libraries outwith the city, it may take a ten-day or more.' He closed the book of songs, and picked up his small white book again. 'Be assured, my lady, that I shall keep you informed of my progress in this matter.' Then he reopened his book.

Aware that she had been dismissed, Alael held on to her temper and slid off the hard stool.

'Then good day, Master Onsivar. I look forward to your first repor . . .'

Her voice trailed off as she caught sight of a body of riders cantering down the road from the Chapel Fort barracks. The College of Hendred's Hall sat near the crest of the ridge that joined the fort hill and a steep-sided knoll set aside as a small park. The Master of Parlance's chamber was high enough to look out across the snowy road which sloped down from the baracks, curving away and around the west flank out of sight.

The band of riders, numbering perhaps twenty, were all attired in cold weather cloaks and their mounts were large and healthy-looking. But it was their leader who caught her attention, a tall grey-haired man who rode straight-backed in the saddle. As she peered across at him, a familiar prickling sensation raced through her and cold sharp tastes bloomed in her mouth. The odour of rich leaves, sweet berries, pure mountain water ice, all the tangs and scents of the Earthmother's realm drenching her senses as the goddess herself rose up from within and stared out of her own eyes. The intervening distance fell away and the lead rider's face was abruptly closer and instantly recognisable as Ikarno Mazaret.

A wordless satisfaction passed through her and a moment later that ineffable presence was gone, leaving her weak and dizzy. With a shaky hand she leaned on the wooden balustrade and strove to calm her whirling thoughts.

Four days had now elapsed since the Lord Regent Mazaret's return from Khatris with a caravan of refugees. In the taverns and inns the dramatic tale of a battle against walking corpses and winged monsters had been supplanted by a dark rumour that the queen of some Mogaun hell had marked Mazaret for death. Having heard the truth from Bardow, Alael could only speculate upon his riding forth while hoping that it signalled some unremarkable task . . .

'Lady Alael? Are you unwell?'

She breathed in deep the dusty, bookish smells of her surroundings and forced a smile. 'Nay, Master Onsivar. Merely a brief dizzy spell, nothing more.'

'I see. Well, if you return to the antechamber, my steward will see you out.'

Alael gritted her teeth. 'My profound thanks, ser,' she said and hurried out, wondering how quickly her carriage could negotiate a route back to the palace.

'Now, you should sense the Lesser Power as a kind of pressure in your chest, almost a tightness.'

Tense with anxiety, Nerek had been feeling it for the last five minutes as she sat on the cold stone seat with her gauntleted hands clasped in her lap. She gave a brief nod and Blind Rina smiled. She was a short, dumpy woman whose headscarf, shapeless brown robes and scarred walking stick implied that she might be a market-stall owner. But her opaque eyes suggested otherwise.

'Ah well,' she said, as if perceiving Nerek's discomfort. 'If you'd come to me as a seven year-old, it would be rather less, hmm, testing.'

'I never had the luxury of being seven,' Nerek said curtly. 'May we continue?'

'Maintain the rhythm of your breathing for a little longer, a smooth, natural ebb and flow . . . that's right.'

The air poured into her, then out, as if she was a vessel filling and emptying. A certain calmness began to emerge yet seemed to be apart from her body and waiting to enter. She kept breathing. Blind Rina sat beside her on this polished stone seat worked into the side buttress of one of the main supports of the Queen's Bridge. Directly behind them, a narrow wooden walkway passed along the side of the bridge, providing a safe crossing for those on foot. From where she sat she could look north along the gentle curve of the Olodar river to the Bridge of Hawks and the timber- and stone-yards that occupied the west bank right up to the Bridge of Spears.

'Think of the Lesser Power as a slow, surging lake,' said Blind Rina. 'So unlike the raging torrent of the Wellsource.'

Two days ago Blind Rina had proposed, via one of her messengers, that she teach Nerek the fundamentals of the Lesser Power and when Nerek asked Bardow for his permission he surprised her by consenting almost at once.

'Yes,' he had said. 'She would be a good tutor for you.'

'You know of her? But she is not one of your mages, is she?'

The Archmage snorted. 'She would be a bad pupil, for me. Her talents are . . . minor, in some respects, and lie in a strange direction.' He frowned. 'You see, Rina has a curious affinity for this city, much as her family has had for several generations. I would rather she was a secret guardian than have her trying to cope with palace politics.'

Grey river-frost coated the stonework of the bridge's side buttress. Nerek's pale breath feathered away in the light breeze and her chest ached with every chill inhalation. Part of her wanted to shiver, except that a faint tingling sensation was spreading across her back and through her vitals . . .

'Good, now it comes,' Blind Rina said.

Nerek could not see her, but somehow felt her give a single, pleased nod.

'We use loops of symbols, known as cantos, to shape and direct the Lesser Power,' Rina went on. 'These symbols are individual to each of us, little scraps that have meaning, memories, images, tokens of one sort or another. At the same time, there are many symbols that mean the same things for nearly everyone, and for the Lesser Power. But rather than explain this more, you and I shall attempt a little demonstration.'

From a deep pocket, the elderly woman produced a small model of an army standard, a thumb-sized square of parchment stitched to a piece of thin dowel which was stuck into a block of damp clay. She placed it on the waist-high wall which enclosed their seat.

'We shall use the thought-canto Waft to raise a slight breeze and knock over our little flag,' Rina said. 'Firstly, I want you to picture in your thoughts a bird's feather.'

'What kind of bird?' Nerek said.

'Any bird you're familiar with, one of the river birds, the galley tezzig, say. Their feathers are grey and white and they taper nicely. Can you see it?'

To her surprise, she could, a slate-grey feather with pale patches, a darker tip and fine tufts at the base of the quill. It was so full of featherness that a suspicion formed at the edge of her thoughts . . . and was swiftly answered.

'Yes, Nerek,' Blind Rina said. 'I am giving you a little help with your envisioning, for now. Later, you'll find yourself noticing things like feathers or seashells or leaves, noticing them for the details which make them what they are, and which fix their meaning in your mind.

'In the meantime, we need another two elements to complete the thought-canto. For the next one, keep the feather in view and try to imagine a blazing torch – good. Now make it shrink to the single flame of a candle . . .'

Nerek could feel perspiration prickling under her clothes, on her back and from her neck down between her breasts. At first it had seemed quite easy to keep the two objects clearly in her mind's eye but the demands on her grew as Blind Rina reduced her contribution to the effort. But she did it, kept the images of feather and candle steady in her thoughts, to the near-exclusion of her surroundings.

'Well done. The strength of your focus is quite . . . enviable. Now, the third and final part of the thought-canto—'

The woman's voice paused and Nerek could feel that attentive gaze shift in another direction.

'Interesting . . . What purpose have we here?'

Feather and candle blurred sideways, and suddenly Nerek was seeing her surroundings but from Rina's perspective where every-thing was hazy and shadowy as if veiled in dusk. Yet colours were subtler and touched with a delicate metallic sheen that made wooden bridge supports coppery, dipped trees and bushes in verdigris, and sent mother-of-pearl ripples across the river. To the north, on the

Bridge of Hawks, were the objects of Blind Rina's regard, a line of riders crossing over from the Old Town.

Abruptly, the viewpoint leapt forward like an arrow from a bow, towards a small shape perched on one of the bridge's upper columns. In the next instant, Nerek felt vertigo clutch at her innards as she became airborne, her field of view wavering in time with the wingbeat. Then the wings spread in gliding flight, curving round to swoop past the front riders. There, clearly recognisable despite the bird's distorted vision, was the Lord Regent Mazaret, garbed in mailed armour and furs, his long lined face showing no expression as he led the column of knights towards Ironhall Barracks.

A flickering blur filled Nerek's eyes, dizziness swirled through her and she gasped as her surroundings sprang back into focus. The cold hardness of the seat, Blind Rina watching her, smiling, her gauntleted hands locked together, the little flag sitting on the wall . . .

'Hmm, perhaps a little early to experience Beasteye,' Blind Rina said. 'Still, it was a useful excursion—'

'That was Ikarno Mazaret at the head of those knights,' Nerek said.

'Knights of the Order of the Bell,' Blind Rina said thoughtfully.

Nerek watched her, wondering how much she knew. 'He could be returning to central Khatris,' she said.

Rina shook her head. 'No packhorses or supply wagons. It may be that he merely intends to conduct training manoeuvres, but it would be wise to keep the Archmage informed, I feel . . .' Her voice trailed off and she became utterly still. A moment or two later she stirred, chuckling under her breath. 'He *was* surprised. Grateful, too.'

'I should return to the palace,' Nerek said, starting to rise, but Blind Rina leaned forward to gently push her back down and pat her arm.

'No need,' she said. 'Bardow asked that you remain with me and finish this lesson. He was quite insistent.'

Nerek let her shoulders slump as dejected frustration settled over her.

'You have doubts about your usefulness,' Blind Rina suggested.

'It is not doubt. I know that I am of little usefulness.'

'If that were so,' said Blind Rina, 'Bardow would be unconcerned about you, and you would be sitting here on your own, talking to the birds!' She leaned a little closer. 'You have achieved much, thrown off the shackles of your own delusions, and there is much more you can yet do.'

Nerek sat straighter at the sharp tone in her voice, suddenly angry at herself. *I have a duty to fulfil,* she thought. *Bardow and Alael are relying on me.*

'Shall we continue?' said Rina.

'Yes,' she said.

'Good. Now, we have the feather and the flame, to which is added the final element, a snowflake . . .'

Up on the broom-swept roof of the Keep of Night, Tauric and a dozen of his Companions stood before the cowled priest who listened closely while they chanted Skyhorse prayers in unison. At the priest's behest they had all doffed their heavy cloaks and padded jerkins, even Tauric, and were kneeling on the cold flagstones as they spoke in firm but low voices, not wishing to attract any attention.

Tauric was shivering constantly and the icy chill had crept up his legs and was sinking into fingers and toes and still deeper into his bones. Yet he felt a sense of peace and purpose, something he had been lacking for a long time, and his fears and doubts seemed more subdued . . .

He glanced up from his clasped hands at the Skyhorse priest, who had once been known as the Armourer, and saw that the hooded man was looking sideways to the west, regarding something down near the western wall. The priest uttered a quiet grunt of satisfaction then turned back.

'Please, all may rise now and garb yourselves again.'

Despite the tranquility of the moment, Tauric was thankful to get back on his feet. While others coughed, he fought off a surge of dizziness and hurriedly slipped back into his heavy shirt and jerkin. Then, wrapped and shivering in his cloak, he went over to where the Skyhorse priest was leaning on the wall, looking out once more.

'Ser priest,' he began, 'were our devotions sufficiently reverent?'

'Majesty,' the priest said. 'I could find no fault in your orisons – truly, you are on the path to enlightenment and power.'

Tauric nodded, elated, then glanced outwards, following the priest's gaze. A column of mounted knights was riding at a light canter away from the Shield Gate, with a tree-and-crossed-sceptres standard flying at its head.

'Is that not the Lord Regent's standard?' he said.

'I understand that the Lord Regent Mazaret has despatched a number of knights to patrol the southwestern approaches, majesty,' the priest said smoothly.

'But why send his own banner with them?' Tauric said.

'Merely a minor sleight meant to deter petty brigands, majesty,' the priest said. 'In this, as in all things, fate shall be served. Now, I feel it is time to see if all of you have been practising the Solemn Supplication of the Flame Everlasting . . .'

Tauric suppressed a groan and took off his cloak again.

The column of knights was half an hour out from Besh-Darok, trotting southwest along the great tree-lined Torrillen Way when the Captain of the March brought news of pursuit to Mazaret's ears.

'Single rider approaching, my lord.'

Mazaret nodded. 'Bring him to me.'

Ahead, he could see how yesterday's snowfall had turned the Torrillen Way into a straight white avenue leading through the skeletal trees of the Peldari woods, and was musing on the frozen slush of the highway when the newcomer arrived at the gallop, slowing to ride alongside Mazaret. Swathed in tattered brown robes, it was Yasgur's elderly seer and adviser.

'Greetings, Atroc,' he said. 'Are you here at your master's behest, or merely lost?'

'Nay, my lord. I am hunting truth, having been driven forth by faint hints, the lightest rumour that the honoured Lord Regent had gone in search of his doom. Could this be true, lord?'

'What doom do you speak of?' Mazaret said, even as the self-doubt which for days had been a growing whisper became a chorus in his thoughts.

Atroc leaned in closer. 'The white woman, my lord,' he said. 'In the stews and taprooms of the city, there is talk of a Mogaun queen of torment who has marked you for a dark fate.' The older man snorted derisively. 'But it is her words which have drawn you out, words meant only for you, hooks fashioned to drag you towards an unknown peril.'

No, not hooks, Mazaret thought grimly. *Like deadly arrows those words pierced my heart with a poison that eats at my soul. My beloved suffered a terrible evil at their hands – how can I do nothing?*

But he kept these thoughts to himself and shook his head. 'There is villainy afoot within sight of Besh-Darok, ser. Farms are being raided, houses put to the torch and innocents killed. We are riding out to bring this pillaging to an end . . . I am here to assuage the ravages of my soul. I seek the truth, ser Atroc, not my doom.'

Dark eyes regarded him from within a coarse, tattered hood. 'Forgive my saying so, my lord, but I do not believe you.'

'I care not what you believe,' Mazaret said sharply. 'However harsh my own grief may be, I am not about to throw my life away. It has been a long hard struggle to get to where we are and the greater battle is yet to come. I shall be there to draw my sword, I promise you.'

'Hmm – in a battle you think is already lost?' Atroc said.

'*What?*' Mazaret cried, his sudden anger so unsettling his mount that he had to calm it with soothing murmurs and one hand stroking and patting its neck.

Atroc shrugged. 'Who could blame you? We face an evil power that will neither cease in its brutal campaign nor stay its hand for the sake of the defenceless. Hope? – The vanity of the blind and the ignorant.'

Mazaret gritted his teeth. *I will not be goaded by such as you.* He took a calming breath, then spoke again. 'Since you are so convinced that all is lost, you must be keen to leave me to my folly. Perhaps I should detail a few of my knights to escort you back to the city, or even as far as the docks. I'm sure there will be one or two long-haul traders bound for Keremenchool and willing to take on paying passengers.'

Atroc smiled a bright and wolfish smile. 'Ach, your company

is not so bad, my lord. I fancy I shall ride along with you a little way yet.'

With an effort Mazaret bit back the retort that came to his lips and in brittle silence they rode on.

The Torillen Way was a nine-mile-long avenue which ran from Magsar, a shrine village just outside Besh-Darok, southwest to Lake Jontos which was fed by many streams coming out of the Girdle Hills. The road was wide and built of alternating sections of cobbles, flagstones and patterned ironwood blocks, mostly obscured by the snow and the half-frozen slush. Branch roads and turn-offs were common along its length and, being a well-made thoroughfare leading right to Besh-Darok, it was in continual use by farmers and traders, messengers and local patrols, and the displaced.

Today, in the early ice-cold afternoon, the traffic was light yet the knights rode along two abreast. The winter sun was just past its zenith but high, thin cloud filtered out its strength and the light was white without warmth. On either side mist clung to the leafless trees and the column of knights, wreathed in the grey fuming breath of men and horses, seemed almost funereal. Riding at its head, Mazaret was certainly in a sombre mood. Atroc had slipped back to ride beside Barik, Mazaret's Captain of the March, and was regaling him with some of the old city tales that Mazaret had learned at his mother's knee. Barik was a blacksmith's son from eastern Cabringa and would thus have been new to the lore of the Imperial city. Then Mazaret's heart sank as the old seer began to relate the origin of the Torillen Way itself.

'Three hundred years ago, the lands of the Crown were ruled by the Emperor Hasil. He was only nineteen when he came to the throne, and soon after his coronation he met and fell in love with the beautiful Torilli, daughter of one of the city barons. She was younger than the Emperor and nearly two years short of her majority, but Hasil pledged himself soul and flesh to their future bond. Then he commanded his architects to design and build a great avenue for their already-arranged marriage pageant, with a celestial pavilion at its far end . . .'

Mazaret knew the rest of the story well. Hasil's bride-to-be died of a fever just weeks before the day of her majority and the pavilion was turned into Torilli's mausoleum. Overcome with grief, the young Emperor abandoned his chambers at the palace to sleep on the pavilion's tiled floor by the tomb of his beloved. Hasil's vigil of mourning was to last nearly ten years during which he steadily relinquished most of his prerogatives to a circle of court officials whose infighting with the noble Conclave of Rods brought the Empire to its knees. Only his abdication in favour of his younger brother prevented the horrors of civil war.

A parable, he thought sourly. *A neat little tale meant to illustrate my folly and somehow shame me into turning tail back to the city. No, master bard, not I . . .*

Standing in his stirrups, Mazaret raised one hand and called out, 'To the canter!'

Behind him, Captain Barik repeated the order and the entire column picked up the pace. It was not long before the faint silveriness of Lake Jontos emerged from the white misty distance. As it grew clearer, Mazaret could just make out the conical white roof of the mausoleum nestled among trees at the foot of the snow-streaked Girdle Hills.

They were less than a mile from the lake when a horse and rider emerged from the dense trees in the middle distance. The rider was hunched over with head bowed as if wounded, while the horse merely trotted along aimlessly. Mazaret was about to order Barik to ride ahead to investigate when two more riders appeared and galloped leisurely after the first. No details of their garb were visible so far off, but it seemed that they might be going to the wounded man's aid until one of them raised a bow and sent an arrow into his back.

'In the Mother's name!' Mazaret cried as the wounded man fell from his horse. 'Barik – all with me!'

Then he spurred his mount into a gallop, with his knights thundering after him. Up ahead the two pursuers had vanished back into the woods, and some travellers on the road had rushed over to help the stricken horseman. But by the time Mazaret dismounted and joined them it was too late.

'Poor man,' an elderly peasant woman said in a north Kejana accent. 'He said some things I did not understand, then he wept and the life just went out of him.'

The dead man wore the brown livery and red shoulder-badge of the Crown Rangers. There was an ugly torn-out wound in his side and the stump of an arrow protruding from his shoulder.

'I understood him,' said a younger woman in a hooded shawl. 'He said, "The Queen of death, white she was, so white, so white . . ." And that was all.'

'May the Mother guide him,' murmured someone and the prayer went round all the onlookers.

Mazaret straightened, his anger feeling hot and sharp. 'Captain Barik, have a serjeant and two men take the body back to the city and inform the Master of Rangers. Then have your best tracker find those killers' trail—'

'No need to bring out a cub, my lord, when a wolf is at hand.'

Mazaret turned a harsh eye on Atroc the seer.

'You can find this witch and her vermin?'

Atroc closed his eyes, breathed in deep, and repugnance settled in his features. 'I can already taste her cursed spoor.' His eyes snapped open and fixed Mazaret with a piercing stare. 'Is it your will to do this?'

'It is.'

The old seer nodded and sighed. 'Then we should go now. If we are quick and cunning enough, we may yet dodge fate's black hand.'

So the hunt was on. Atroc led the way into the woods along a heavily-trampled, slush-choked trail. A short while later Mazaret's nose caught the taint of smoke and Atroc quickened his mount's pace. Soon the track widened on to a small village bordered on two sides by orchard groves. Bodies lay scattered between the buildings, some with womenfolk keening by them. Mazaret had six knights of the Bell stay behind to lend aid, then told Atroc to resume.

The trail curved north and they were just entering an area of craggy outcrops and marshy gullies when a hunting horn sounded up ahead and several birds burst from cover off to the right. Immediately sensing a trap, Mazaret roared the order to wheel left and charged off the trail. Arrows came whirring through the gaunt, icy trees, most of them deflected by branches, then another flight came arcing down from on high. There were some shouts of pain when a few of the knights were hit, but none seriously. Mazaret began to panic as he realised that the uneven terrain with its rocky ledges and sudden ravines was scattering his men across a wide area of dense, trackless woods.

With Mazaret were Atroc and three knights, two of the Bell, one of the Fathertree. In an attempt to see further they rode up the first clear rise they came to, negotiating boulders and a fallen tree. This higher ground proved to be the first of a group of hillocks near the lower slopes of the Girdle Hills, but the view from it was unrewarding. The mist was rising as the sun dipped and all that was visible were grey, ghostly woods surrounding the hillocks and filling the shadowy dales between them. The air was bitterly cold and a muffling silence reigned.

'Can you not track my men?' Mazaret said to Atroc impatiently. 'You were bold enough when it was the enemy we were after.'

'The emanations of an evil spirit are harsher by far than those of ordinary men,' the seer said. 'Some of your men are wandering east of here, perhaps half a mile distant. Our enemy, though, is . . . close.' Then his eyes widened as he peered downslope at the way they had come. 'Riders,' he said.

But Mazaret's attention had been snagged by faint but strange noises coming up from the mist-shrouded dale directly west of their hillock. Whispers, the creak of branches, the low rush of a breeze through leaves despite the lack of foliage. Drawn by this susurration, he strained to make out any words or even number of voices and at first there were only those sighs and purls interweaving at the edge of audibility. Then through it all, low, quiet and clear, came a voice he had never thought to hear again.

'*Ikarno . . .*'

Across the dale the mist parted to reveal the near slope of another hillock and a pale figure on horseback, one hand out-stretched.

'*. . . my love . . .*'

He was not aware of having urged his horse forward until he felt a hand pulling at his arm and heard an urgent voice cutting through his dulled thoughts.

'Do you hear me, my lord?' Atroc was repeating. 'It was only the enemy's trap, a net of imaginings sent to tangle up your mind, nothing more.'

Coming to his senses, Mazaret realised that he was halfway down the other side of the rise, and reined in his mount. As well as Atroc and the three knights, there were two newcomers, both Crown Rangers whose looks of concern were shared by all. He was about to assure Atroc that his mind was his own when the sound of hoofs drew all eyes north to the bare top of a low hill wreathed in mist. A line of seven or eight horsemen came up out of the grey veil, over the hill and down the other side. The last rider, garbed in white, halted her skittish mount at the crest for a moment before following the others.

'You see, ser?' Mazaret said to Atroc. 'No imaginings but a real enemy.' Before the seer could answer he turned to the rangers. 'Good sers, what landmarks are those to the north and west of that bare hill?'

'Nearest is the scree slopes of the southern face of the Quern, my lord,' said one, a freckled, sandy-haired youth. 'A perilous hill, that one, full of rock falls and loose ground. Further by half a mile is Greylok Hill and between them is Blueaxe Ridge.'

Despite the chill that went through him, Mazaret looked at a grim-faced Atroc who shook his head. 'Fate's black hand, my lord.'

'We are close,' Mazaret said, 'and I would pursue them. I must confront this evil shade, Atroc. I must look it in the face and see it and know it for what it is. Perhaps then my soul would find a measure of peace.'

The seer's face was unforgiving. 'Some faces are best left unseen. Listen to me, my lord—'

Mazaret silenced him with a raised hand and a glare, then addressed the rangers. 'Sers, ride to the woods east of here, gather together the rest of my knights and guide them to the foot of Blueaxe Ridge where I shall be.'

'By your command, my lord,' the rangers said and swiftly departed. Mazaret glanced at his three remaining knights, saw their sombre readiness then looked at Atroc.

'My course is set, seer,' he said. 'You may accompany us if you wish.'

'I would rather you followed my counsel, my lord.'

'Mayhap your quick cunning will suffice.'

The elderly seer gave him a hooded look and chuckled softly. 'Truly, you know how to lead men, my lord. But into folly?'

Mazaret was resolute. 'Be sure to give Prince Yasgur a full account on your return.'

'I shall, my lord,' Atroc said. 'After witnessing this skirmish in its entirety.'

Feeling curiously reassured, Mazaret replied with a sharp nod then tugged his horse's nose round to the north. A brief dig with the heels and he was off at the gallop with the others following.

As he rode he could smell the moist iciness of the slow-moving mist, but there was something else in the air, a faint odour like dry earth but dustier, sharper. When they came to the slope where the enemy had been a short while ago, he noticed that the snow lay only in a few diminishing patches and that light wisps of vapour were rising from the ground. At the crest of the hillock there was no snow at all and the winter-bleached clumps of grass were gleaming with dew.

Atroc dismounted and knelt to lay his hand on the earth. 'Warm,' was all he would say as he climbed back into the saddle.

Mazaret urged his mount on down the other side of the hillock. To their left reared the stony promontory of the Quern with Blueaxe Ridge coming off its shoulder, a sheer dark wall that stretched for more than quarter of a mile before merging into the more rounded Greylok Hill. At the foot of the ridge was a wide, shallow bowl bounded by the flanks of the hills at either end. The ground looked marshy and Mazaret could see several meltwater rivulets running towards the centre while the steam coming off the ground made the mist heavy and damp.

As they entered the bowl at a slower canter, Mazaret could just see at the other side a solitary figure descending from a notch in the flank of Greylok Hill. A brief survey of their surroundings revealed no sign of enemies lying in wait but mist such as this could conceal a multitude of foes. The figure walked along the foot of the ridge towards the midpoint and stopped to watch the knights' approach. Mazaret frowned and when they reached what he hazarded was the centre of the muddy depression he called a halt.

'Now sers, I want you to remain here while I ride over to discover what I can from the one who waits,' he said. 'If I need your aid I will hold my sword aloft.'

'If you need our aid, my lord,' Atroc said drily, 'most likely we'll be in need of it ourselves.'

'You shall be my eyes,' Mazaret went on. 'If any enemy attackers appear, give a loud, repeated whistle.'

The seer's face was full of flinty-eyed disapproval but Mazaret ignored it and turned to ride on alone. He knew he could only do this on his own. By now he could see that the lone figure was wrapped in white robes and had a womanly appearance, but was it truly Suviel or some corrupt fragment of her spirit? If it were the latter, would he be able to bear such knowledge?

Then he remembered something she was fond of saying – 'They cannot corrupt everything because they cannot reach everything.' The memory warmed him until, a few moments later, the cold, luring voice from before slipped again into his thoughts.

'*I knew you would come.*'

Longing and fear shuddered through him but still he rode on.

'*Soon you will be by my side, never to leave . . .*'

He halted his horse some yards away, calmly dismounted and hung the reins on his saddle before facing the woman who in every detail resembled Suviel Hantika. Steeling himself, he walked up to her and stopped two paces from her, close enough for scrutiny, far enough away for safety.

'*How is Gilly?*' she said. '*And Bardow – how does he cope with that old seer Yasgur keeps around?*'

He studied the line of the nose and mouth, the movement of the lips, the shape of the ears, the form of cheekbone and chin, and found no fault, nothing out of place.

'*And how is Tauric? The Emperor's crown must be a great burden for such a young man. Does he speak of me?*'

The hair was long and fine and utterly white, but it was the eyes that told all. Icy-grey they were, cruel, staring and soulless. He turned and moved towards his horse.

'*Wait! Beloved, remember our last night together? It can be so again—*'

He came round angrily. 'You are not her!' he said. 'She would never deliver up her closest friends to our deadliest foes. There is *nothing* of her in you!' He could not keep the force of his loathing hidden and the rivenshade recoiled slightly. 'I don't know what you are, something caught in a mirror perhaps, made to strut and mouth your masters' foulness. You are naught but a hollow—'

The rivenshade snarled in hate. '*I meant what I said about you never leaving!*'

The damp grassy earth under his feet trembled. A black dread came over him and he turned to run but before he could reach his startled horse the ground juddered violently, making him stumble and fall. His horse panicked and leaped away at a mad gallop. As he tried to regain his feet he could see Atroc and the other knights struggling to control their mounts as they likewise tore away.

A rumbling, grinding sound came from the ground under Mazaret as the chill voice of the Suviel-rivenshade whispered on and on. Endearments and coaxings mingled senselessly with malefic curses while the bones of the hills gave forth a ghastly groaning fit to unbalance the mind.

'*We have come with knives to cut away the old land and all of its useless past. The world will have a new face . . .*'

Another giant spasm shook the ground and Mazaret turned to see the pale rivenshade floating no more than a foot in the air, facing the ridge with her sinuous hands outflung. His hate cut through his fear and he grasped the hilt of his sword, determined to cut her down. But before he could rise fully from his knees, sharp snapping sounds came from all around and in horror he saw large cracks spreading up and across the looming face of Blueaxe Ridge. He cried out as massive, moss-covered pieces of rocks tilted away and fell, turning over and over. Massive shards split off, wide sections slipped and shattered, and clouds of pulverised grit and dust poured down. The catastrophic cascade was happening along the entire length of the ridge, and even the hills at either end seemed to be breaking apart.

A huge spear of stone slammed into the ground only feet from Mazaret. He was about to try and scramble away on hands and knees when he saw an immense piece the size of a house tumbling through the air towards him. With the first words of a prayer to the Earthmother on his lips, he could only watch the hurtling approach of his inescapable doom . . .

And stare as the great fragment, whose every ragged, broken detail he could see, suddenly slewed aside and rushed past him to bound across the rubble-littered ground.

'*No death for you, beloved,*' came that voice. '*No darkened depths, no flowing tribulations in the Earthmother's realm. A new dream awaits.*'

She smiled down at him from where she hung in the air, arms lifted wide, the windings and folds of her pale robes floating gently on otherworldly zephyrs. Sprawled and half-sitting amid the roaring chaos, Mazaret saw a succession of jagged chunks of stone diverted away from himself and the Suviel-rivenshade, heart hammering in his chest at each one. Yet despite this precarious safety, he noticed that something was emerging from the ruptured face of Blueaxe Ridge, something sheer bearing vertical grooves and striations . . .

With a shock he realised that it was a wall surmounted by battlements whose tapered merlons curved outwards like claws. The dark barrier was becoming gradually visible all along the ridge and when Mazaret looked to the southern end he could see massive pieces of the Quern calving away as the unmistakable shape of a fortified tower slowly thrust up from the hill's interior. To the north a second tower was turning Greylok Hill into rubble.

More fortifications were grinding their way up out of the ground, a wide curving wall punctuated by turrets and enclosing most of the shallow bowl. Beyond it to the east, a solitary rider watched from the crest of a hillock and some shred of intuition told Mazaret that it was Atroc, paying witness to this monstrous calamity.

The terrible, rasping roar took on a deep drone which began to climb in pitch and strength till Mazaret could feel his scalp itch and his teeth ache. A spidery crawling sensation attacked his skin and a needling irritation made his eyes water. The air in his lungs vibrated and in panic he clamped his hands over his ears and closed his eyes.

After long moments the droning suddenly faded away into a strange, reverberant silence. Breathing heavily Mazaret lowered

his hands and opened his eyes to more surprise. The shattered
remains of the ridge which had formed heaps below were gone,
and the muddy, mossy ground had been stripped away to reveal
a wide courtyard of interlocking flagstones enclosed by the curved
battlements. But what dominated the transformed landscape was the
vast structure which now reared up behind the wall before him. It
resembled a drum keep but built on a prodigious scale from a pale,
almost translucent green stone. An eldritch, pearly aura surrounded
it, slightly blurring the details of the relief carvings which encircled
it in great bands.

'Behold the glory of Gorla.'

The rivenshade's words were icy intrusions upon the utter quiet.
She was now standing several yards away and directly in front of
towering double doors which were slowly beginning to open. Each
door must have been thirty feet wide and a hundred high, and
hung on a spindle hinge that made a rolling iron sound as it swung
outwards. Within was a canyon of shadow, a high-sided passage
beyond which Mazaret could see the softly-radiant bottom levels
of the keep called Gorla. And marching ranks of soldiers, chariots
and cavalry.

Mazaret's own composure in the face of this naked might pleased
him in a way. His fear seemed to have dissolved in the corrosive
knowledge of his vulnerability and now all that he had left was
to decide how to die. Then he saw a tall figure emerge from
the shadows, a man in black-stained leather armour who walked
with a certain swagger and carried a heavy broadsword at his hip.
He had a full head of curly black hair and a trimmed beard, while
his eyes brimmed with hate and a gleeful intensity. He halted beside
the Suviel-rivenshade who put her arms about his neck and pulled
him lower for a long, lascivious kiss. When he straightened there
was blood on his lip.

'I always knew we'd meet again, my lord.'

The rich, expressive voice instantly struck a chord in Mazaret's
memory and as recognition came to him, a cold voice spoke.

'Truly, he is the Deathless one.'

A pale figure in a fawn leather bodice and kirtle, and bearing a
spear, stepped from the blackness of the gate, and anger kindled

in Mazaret's thoughts – it was a second Suviel-rivenshade. Then a third came out, garbed in chainmail and carrying over one shoulder a long-handled woodcutter axe.

'*What joy it will be to fight at your side,*' the one with the spear said.

'Never,' Mazaret said.

'Ah, but you shall be with us,' Azurech said with his new mouth. 'I promise.'

'And I will make you break that oath,' Mazaret said, drawing his sword and charging.

Azurech brought out his own blade swiftly enough to parry Mazaret's incoming blow. Mazaret then ducked under the backswing and swept on past the warlord, running with sword raised towards his true target, the rivenshade with the spear. If he could slay just one, it would be a kind of vengeance.

As he beat aside her spear he cried out, 'Suviel, forgive me!'

But the rivenshade shrieked with laughter and the shadows flowed out to engulf him.

From the hillock, Atroc had watched the breaking of the hills and the battlements which they birthed and the vast keep which rose up out of the earth. The titanic din was like the roaring of a thousand beasts heralding the sight of a legend made real.

Gorla. The oldest sagas of the Mogaun told of the Lord of Twilight's banishment by the Fathertree and the Earthmother after a great battle at the world's dawn. Of all his fierce bastions, only two of the lesser ones – Gorla and Keshada – did they allow him to shift into the Realm of Dusk.

And what a place for this ancient fortress to appear, on Besh-Darok's front doorstep!

With eaglesight, an old talent learned in his long-gone youth from a forest crone a continent away, Atroc was able to see all that transpired before the huge gaping doors. When the Shadowking Byrnak came striding out he uttered a black oath, then a moment later frowned. Despite the man's astonishing resemblance, he was tall and gaunt where Byrnak was shorter, broader and bearlike. And when Mazaret unsheathed his blade, Atroc felt a sense of

bleak approval for the man's determination to die like a warri-
or.

Then he was startled to see the Fathertree knight swerve past his
foe and rush at one of the rivenshades. For a moment it seemed he
would overcome her until a mass of guards wielding clubs and nets
swarmed out of the shadows and overpowered him by sheer force
of numbers.

As they dragged the sad, bound form off into darkness, Atroc
grimly tugged his horse round and dug in his heels, urging the
animal into a gallop. He had to return to the city with all speed
and find out if Gorla's sister citadel, Keshada, had also appeared. If
it had, then Besh–Darok faced a tidal onslaught of violence and evil
not seen in these lands since the world's dawn.

He lashed his mount faster through the misty trees, as if trying to
outride what he still saw in his imagination, Gorla's huge courtyard
athrong with hosts of men and horrors.

Part Two

Chapter Eight

Empty and hungering, Winter comes,
With white chimes and chains,
And a pale embrace for the unwary.

Jedhessa Gant, *The Lords Desolate*, Act 2, ii, 18

Inside the swaying boxwagon, warmed by the bolted-down brazier, Gilly sat on an unsteady, padded stool while striving to restring the eight-string kulesti he had bought early that afternoon. The varnish was chipped and scored in many places and one of the ivory tuning pegs had been replaced with a wooden one, but he had noticed that the neck had a metal, perhaps bronze, chine, a clear indication of quality. Its former owner was a sorrowful mother of three clearly driven by hunger and desperation to sell the instrument. A twinge of pity had made him give her an extra half-regal on top of the asking price. Now, as he struggled to thread one of the tuning pegs with a catgut string while the wagon lurched along, he could feel his patience starting to fray.

'If you wait till we stop to make camp, you might find that less challenging.'

Gilly glanced over at the shell-like wicker chair in which Keren sat, legs drawn up as she lounged amid an abundance of garishly-coloured cushions. Various cutting remarks suggested themselves, but instead he put on a smile that was almost a leer.

'Ah, but I enjoy a challenge, dear lady.'

Keren regarded him coolly from within the wicker chair as it shifted and creaked on its four short legs. 'That must be why you were sent with us.'

'Hmm, you really need more practice with the barbed insults, you know. That one barely made sense—'

At this Medwin sat up in the boxbunk fixed to the front of the wagon's interior, a look of exasperation on his face. 'I don't know which will drive me mad first – your bickering or this monstrous decoration!'

Gilly looked around him at the crimson-and-gold wall hangings, the curlicue-carved woodwork (painted bright blue), the array of torn and peeling paper masks pinned to one wall, the tinkling clusters of charms, the bronze openwork tallow lamp swinging from the roof, and the moth-eaten, heavy purple drapes that hung across the rear door. It was gloriously hideous.

Gilly stroked his chin, smiling. 'I find it quite soothing.'

'Compared to your incessant sparring, it may well be,' Medwin said sharply. 'But for the time being, kindly confine your conversations to pleasantries and necessary matter. Agreed?'

Gilly and Keren looked at each other but before either could speak the wagon lurched to a halt and knuckles rapped urgently on the slatted shutter on Gilly's side of the wagon.

'Ser Medwin,' came a voice from without.

Gilly stood quickly, flipped the latch on the big square shutter then opened it and leaned out into the cold night. The commander of their escort, a city militia captain called Redrigh, sat on horseback before him while beyond the riverbank and all the towering cliffs and slopes of Gronanvel looked dark and ghostly pale in their shrouds of snow.

'What news, captain?' Gilly said.

'Ser Cordale,' Redrigh said. 'We're within sight of Vannyon's Ford but I can see fires burning on its opposite bank—'

'And fighting too, captain,' came Medwin's voice from the roof of the wagon where a skylight afforded a higher view. 'How long till we reach the town?'

'At least another hour, ser. Two, most like.'

Gilly stared along the dark, high-sided valley, squinting to make out details from the far-off yellow glows. He was fairly sure that it was buildings that were ablaze but all else was lost in the distance or obscured by the sheer cliffs that hemmed in the great valley of Gronanvel between here and the mouth of the waters beyond Vannyon's Ford. At this point, though, the road passed between the frozen shoreline and steep, densely-wooded slopes but would soon curve south and climb into hilly uplands before joining the gulley that would bring them to Vannyon's Ford.

A finger prodded him in the shoulder. Sighing, he moved back from the open window and gave a mock-graceful sweep of the arm to Keren. She sniffed haughtily and stepped over to take his place.

Medwin was standing four steps up on a green-painted, flaking ladder attached by hinges to the edge of the skylight, discussing the situation with Captain Redrigh. Gilly smiled to himself. After being ambushed on the outskirts of Sejeend, the captain had insisted that the three delegates continued the journey under safer conditions. Gilly had sent forth word of their need through a few local contacts and later that day they found themselves looking over the gaudy carriage. Medwin and Keren had been unenthusiastic, but for Captain Redrigh it was enough that its sides and roof were solid wood and the purchase was duly made.

Gilly returned to his padded stool, retrieved the kulesti from a heaped woollen blanket and was about to resume the restringing when he heard a slight scratching. He frowned. It seemed to be coming from the wall opposite Keren . . . then he saw it, the dark iron tip of a blade probing between shutter and frame for the latch. Quick and quiet, Gilly wrapped the kulesti in its blanket, stowed it in the nearby corner, then drew forth his broadsword, muffling it on the heavy cotton of his trews leg.

On careful feet he went over to the window and quietly placed his sword point in the gap below the probing dagger. Then with all his might he thrust his blade through the gap, felt it strike home and heard a shriek of agony.

'Ware — ambush!' he roared. Wrenching his sword back, he whirled to grab Medwin's arm and drag him down from the skylight. Gilly heard shouts outside and the thud of feet landing on the wagon's roof, then a snarling, tangle-haired man appeared in the square opening and leaned down with a cocked and loaded crossbow. Keren, having rolled away from the other window, jumped up with a small, studded shield which she threw at his face edge-on.

The brigand yelled as blood spurted from his smashed nose. In shock he let go of the crossbow, clasped hands to his wrecked features and rolled away from the skylight, bellowing and cursing. Before another could take his place, Keren leaped up the ladder, pulled the cover shut and twisted the dog latches, locking it in place.

'This is the third ambush we've had to endure,' Medwin said, angrily pushing up his sleeves.

Gilly nodded. 'Once might be chance and twice a coincidence, but three times is just bad manners . . .'

Something began hammering on the ceiling above them. Glancing up, Gilly saw splinters fly as an axeblade bit through the wood. At the same time, a thudding came from the door at the rear while sounds of fighting filtered in from outside.

Keren, who had retrieved her own sword as well as the blood-spattered shield, looked across at them: 'Sers, we have visitors.'

'Methinks it time for a hearty welcome,' Gilly said with a grin.

He unlatched the door, threw it open and leaped out into the fray. Torches burning atop the wagon cast a fitful ochre glow on knots of struggling figures. The ambushers looked to have outnumbered the escort but Redrigh's men were giving a good account of themselves. Gilly took on a quilt-armoured man wielding a club and a rapier and found himself fending off a frantic barrage of blows. The brigand had bronze Ebroan charms woven into his braided beard and uttered a string of curses in Hethardic as he fought. Backing away Gilly flashed a grin and replied with a couple of choice insults he had come by in Bereiak a few months before.

The Ebroan warrior glared and spat as his face went red with rage, then he lashed out madly just as Gilly had hoped he would. Ducking the club arm's wild swing, he dodged past and hooked the man's feet from under him. The Ebroan pitched forward on to his face and Gilly finished him with two savage blows to the neck.

Straightening and catching his breath, he saw Medwin subduing one of the brigands with a cold, blue nimbus while elsewhere

Redrigh's men were gaining the upper hand. Then he heard Keren shout his name and whirled to see her empty handed and running from a pair of determined ambushers. Gilly threw himself after them, but felt something snag his ankle. He went down, gasping as he hit the snowy ground and his sword spun off to the side. Looking back he saw a badly-wounded brigand crawling towards him with a bloody axe in his hand and an evil grin on his face.

'I don't have time to play!' Gilly snarled, snatching up a handful of wet snow and flinging it in the axeman's face. Then he rolled to his feet, aimed a kick at the man's head, then snatched up his sword and resumed the chase.

Away from the wagon's torches the night was ashen. He could hear snapping twigs and footfalls moving back from the shore, and could just make out a pale, snow-patched trail winding off into the encroaching blackness of the forest. Without hesitation he dashed along it, but before long the trail petered out to leave him stumbling among the trees. The depths of the night seemed to flow through the leafless, icy undergrowth, masking the thorns and roots that plucked at his garments or sought to trip him as he followed the faint sounds of pursuit. The enfolding shadows roused his fears which began to people the formless darkness with a legion of horrors. In mind the clicks and rustles of tiny creatures became the slight movements of enemies poised to take his life, their hands tightening on sword hilts, pitiless eyes sighting along arrows, cruel talons jutting from crooked fingers on hands barely human—

A man's scream shattered it all, an agonised sound that ended abruptly. Gilly felt a rush of exaltation, certain that Keren had despatched one of her pursuers. The scream had come from directly ahead, perhaps fifty yards away past the solid black flank of what seemed to be a small hill. Then he heard the second brigand call out fearfully for his companion, his shouts turning to ugly promises of what he would do to Keren when he caught her. Then he fell silent, but not before Gilly was able to judge that he was skirting the hill from the right.

Should have kept your mouth shut, my lad, Gilly thought as he started up the hill.

He had taken no more than a dozen steps when a sick dizziness assailed him. Further on his stomach threatened rebellion, forcing him to pause. Was it something that he ate earlier, or some poisonous miasma welling up from the night-drenched ground? Whatever it was, he was determined in his course so he breathed in deep, swallowed hard anger and pushed on up the slope.

A few steps more and he felt as if he was dying, with the air creaking in his chest and his limbs quivering as the strength drained out of him. He staggered against a broad tree in the dark, pressing his face to the damp roughness of its bark, inhaling the cold, moist odours of wood and moss. Then his grip slipped and he fell . . .

And found himself crouched at the edge of a strange, softly illuminated clearing. Pearly radiance came from the flowers of small bushes scattered plentifully around and between a wide circle of standing stones. His feelings of illness were almost gone, and his senses were soothed by the very faint sound of many voices holding the same note, a sound which swirled and flowed through the air. Yet with his returning vigour came a growing unease.

The hill was actually a flattened rise amid the steep hills banking on to Gronanvel. Everything outside the clearing was plunged in an impenetrable darkness, while at the centre of the stone circle was the lightning-blasted stump of a once-majestic tree, with but a single branch still growing from it. Nearby was a small pool whose waters shimmered with golds and blues. The slight, brown-robed figure of an old woman stood over it, sunk in contemplation. Gilly slipped behind one of the standing stones to observe, brushing against one of the light-bearing bushes as he did so. Immediately, its flowers released a flock of radiant motes into the still air, each emanating a tiny, pure ringing which faded away as they did.

The old woman seemed not to notice, concentrating instead on the slow-turning mass of mist that was rising from the pool. Gilly stared, Keren and her pursuer forgotten. A low note crept into the muted ghostly chorus as the old woman raised her arms before the swirling opacity.

'Great Mane of the World – hear thy servant, Valysia!' she declaimed in a cracked voice. 'Show me the dark mysteries, unveil to me the secret paths and seeds of power, give to me the ancient words of making and unmaking—'

Suddenly she uttered a shocked cry as light brightened within the misty vortex, a burning core which threw off threads and tendrils. Gilly felt rooted to the spot as he watched in fearful fascination. The old woman raised one trembling hand and spoke a string of incomprehensible words then stepped back. The glowing vortex slowed and began to thicken in places, coalescing into a definite shape, something with four legs that set it taller at the shoulder than a man. To Gilly it looked very horse-like as the details grew stronger, except that the ears were rounder and a pair of short, ridged horns protruded at the top of the head . . .

A thrill of recognition passed through him as he realised that it was a witchhorse.

Pale and restless, the apparition reared with a strange shout of despair then leaped from the pool and began to canter angrily round the clearing. Tenuous wisps of its form trailed behind it and its eyes glowed white hot.

'Who has done this?' it raged. 'Who has wrenched me to this place so foolishly and left no way of returning . . .'

'T'was I, Valysia, O mighty Skyhorse,' the old woman said through tears of joy. 'I spoke the words taught me by my father, as they had been passed down generations of priests of the faith . . .'

'But you closed the way, careless one!' the witchhorse said, trotting over to her. 'If the Acolytes or their agents discover my presence, they will not rest until we few survivors are slain, all my herdsisters and brothers, all my children.' The opaque creature towered menacingly over the now-cowering woman. 'Enemies are everywhere, even over there behind that stone.'

Hearing this, Gilly stepped into view, empty hands half-raised. 'Wait, I'm no friend of the Acolytes—'

The witchhorse swung its head to look at him and cried, 'Betrayer!'

'What?' Gilly said. 'No—'

'I have seen you lead armies of darkness,' the witchhorse said. 'Our final refuge hangs between the veils of the Void where fragments of past and future rain ceaselessly all around us. Your face I have seen before.'

'Impossible,' Gilly said, shaken and fearful. 'I would never betray my friends and all I've worked and fought for . . .'

'Only if you remember these things,' the witchhorse said. 'But you will forget—'

'Gilly!'

Across the level rise he saw Keren fall to her hands and knees, retching and coughing. He ducked past the witchhorse and ran across, weaving between the stones. The old woman Valysia glared at him and flung out an accusatory, pointing hand.

'Trespasser! You defile this sacred place with your profane acts.'

Gilly ignored the wizened Skyhorse priestess and rushed to Keren's side, helping her into a sitting position.

'Mother's name,' she gasped, wiping her mouth. 'What is this place?' Then she looked up, eyes widening as they saw the witchhorse which was trotting back to the pool, fury in its every movement.

'Now *two* intruders have seen me, fool, and soon others shall follow them here. You must open a sending door for me – now!'

'I do not know how,' said the aged Valysia, quailing miserably. 'I was never taught.'

'I cannot remain here!' the witchhorse shrieked. 'I must not! The glamour you set upon this place will fade with the morning, and when it does I shall be revealed to every sorcerous eye and spy from here to the Rukang Mountains.'

'There are caves nearby,' Valysia said. 'You could hide—'

'There are no caves deep enough in all this land,' the witchhorse said grimly. 'You must perform a banishment.'

Old Valysia was aghast. 'You would be lost in the Void – I can't . . .'

'You must. You will! Use this tree as your focus.' The creature nudged her with its head. 'Do it!'

Trembling, she complied.

Gilly watched the unfolding ritual with an outward calm, but a kind of numbed panic was quivering at the core of his thoughts. The words of the witchhorse kept repeating in his mind – 'I have seen you lead armies of darkness . . . you will forget' – intermingled with Avalti's pain-drenched foretelling, 'an iron fox, eyeless to the hunt . . .'

A helpless feeling gripped him. *I have been chained by the words of others*, he thought, *and now these words ride me like chattering ghosts.*

Across the clearing a faint aura flickered around the tree, and sharp gleams came and went in the lightning-charred gouge that ran up its length. Valysia, hunched over with one arm outstretched, shook her head and let her hand fall. Panting breath wheezed in her small frame.

'I . . . cannot find the . . . strength,' she said. 'It needs more . . . than I have to . . . give . . .'

'I understand,' the witchhorse said. 'And I am grateful for your sacrifice.'

'Oh no . . .' Keren whispered next to him as the witchhorse pushed Valysia into the gap in the tree. The old priestess was too weak to resist and the start of her scream was cut off when the witchhorse lunged and tore out her throat. The frail figure convulsed for a moment before death took her, and as her blood poured into the tree its surrounding aura flared. In the blood-soaked gap brightness appeared like a long, widening crack.

The witchhorse turned to regard Gilly and Keren with fiery eyes. Gore dripped from its jaws as it spoke.

'With this act I have darkened my spirit, yet yours will become as dark as the womb of the night. I would have made you the sacrifice but I cannot be sure of our places in Time's river, thus you live. I pray that when your end comes it will be full of savage irony and extravagant torment. May you die badly.'

So saying, the witchhorse leaped over the old woman's corpse and straight into the radiant opening in the tree. As soon as it was through and the feathery end of its tail was swallowed by the dazzle, the long gap snapped shut and flames burst from the trunk. The soft glow of the bushes went out like snuffed candles and wind and darkness rushed in from all sides, held back a little by the burning tree. Gilly somehow mastered his shock and tugged Keren to her feet.

'We should wait next to the fire,' he said.

She nodded, shivering in the sudden cold, and followed him over.

When Captain Redrigh and half a dozen of his troopers found them, Gilly was sitting by the pool and watching the flame eat into the heart of the tree stump. In that comforting heat it was an effort to drag his gaze away and focus on Redrigh.

'Are you wounded, ser Cordale?' the captain said.

Only by words, he wanted to say. *Only by my fate . . .*

'We are weary, captain,' Keren said. 'How is Medwin? Is it safe to return to the wagon?'

Redrigh was a young man with old, experienced eyes. A foe's blood stained one side of his mailed harness and he wiped at a cluster of shallow scores on his cheek.

'We killed most of them and drove the rest off, my lady. A lone brigand came at us on the path to this place but I slew him myself.' Redrigh glanced at his sabre, holding each face to the flames. Gilly saw gold light ripple down the blade while a frown crossed the captain's face.

'Medwin is unharmed, but he was seized by a peculiar trance as we were putting the surviving brigands to flight. When he came back to himself he looked stricken, as if by grave tidings . . .'

Suddenly, Gilly was not listening as a robed figure came stalking out of the darkness towards the tree's fluttering flames. It was Medwin, his expression sombre. All eyes were on him as he joined the group.

'A short time ago I conversed with Archmage Bardow,' he said. 'There have been grim happenings near Besh-Darok in the last day . . .' He paused to rub his forehead. 'The unimaginable has come to pass – in the Girdle Hills west and north of the city, where once there were only rocky, grassy slopes, there now sit two evil fortresses, each having thrust itself up from beneath the very hills themselves!'

A stunned silence greeted this news, broken only by the crackling of the burning tree. A sense of foreboding threaded through Gilly's mind and he made himself get to his feet as Medwin continued.

'Thousands of people are fleeing the towns and villages within the compass of the Girdle Hills. There has been no sign or declaration from whatever power is behind this dire invasion, but Bardow has little doubt that the Shadowkings are responsible. No force has yet issued forth from either citadel to challenge the Emperor's rule, yet we have already suffered a terrible loss. Lord Regent Mazaret and several dozen knights were in the hills to the west when the ruinous eruptions took place. A witness saw him subdued and taken captive.'

This is how they will ensure our defeat, Gilly thought emptily. *Taking the strongest of us one by one . . .*

'Will we be returning to Besh-Darok?' Keren said.

'The Archmage insisted that we continue on to Scallow,' Medwin said. 'Now that the blow has finally fallen, our task in Dalbar has become even more urgent.'

Keren looked about her. 'Then we had best be on our way.'

Severed branches from nearby trees were lit from the blazing stump to serve as torches. As Captain Redrigh led his men back down to the shore, Gilly stood gazing at the diminishing flames and the fading ruby embers in the tree's heart, wondering why Mazaret would have been at such a place at that moment.

Was it unavoidable fate, Ikarno, or did your grief lead you into folly? If chance wills it, perhaps we shall talk of this over some good wine one day. But if death comes for you, my friend, we will burn their towers in your memory, I swear it!

Turning, he walked over to where Keren stood waiting, torch in hand. Behind him the burnt-through stump split with a soft crack and a thud but he hurried on without a backward glance.

Chapter Nine

From his great hands came
Ships, laws and a mighty city.
Vessels all to sail the oceans
Of Peace, War and Fate.

Jurad's *Life Of Orosiada*, Bk 8

Not till Bardow reached the third floor of the High Spire did he realise
how weary he was. His legs trembled and a hollow weakness in his
stomach reminded him that he had not eaten for several hours, since
mid-afternoon in fact. He stumbled over to a wooden bench near the
head of the steps and sank gratefully down on to it, letting his heavy
leather document wallet fall beside him. The past day and a half since
the appearance of the citadels had been a non-stop round of the city's
nobles and merchants, reassuring them and downplaying the enemy's
strength, or if that failed to work, indulging in good old-fashioned
bombastic bluster. Those who would not be swayed even by this
were allowed to leave Besh-Darok however they wished.

Which gave rise to other problems.

Two palace guards on night patrol emerged from a side corridor further along, saw the Archmage seated with head bowed
and hurried over. He looked up at the sound of their footsteps.

'Gentle sers, I am well,' Bardow said, forestalling any queries.
'Just a little tired.'

'Forgive my asking, ser,' said the younger of the two, who was
carrying a lantern. 'We heard vague news of ships colliding at the

129

Molembra wharf, and I was wondering if you knew aught of this. I have a cousin who works there.'

'I have just come from the Long Quays,' Bardow said. 'There was a collision but it took place out in the harbour, so no one ashore was in danger. Now, sers, the mage council should be meeting in the assembly chambers on this floor. Am I correct or have the proctors rearranged it to another place?'

'Nay, ser,' said the older guard, a smile twitching at his lips. 'It has not been moved.'

'Good, then I shall not detain you any further,' Bardow said, ignoring the ache in his back as he stood. The guards gave a quick bow then continued on their way while Bardow headed in the other direction.

The high corridor followed the curve of the tower's outer wall and was lit at intervals by ornate copper lamps hanging from adjustable ropes. The walls on this floor were faced with pale grey and light brown stone, a smooth unadorned expanse broken by just a few tall, narrow windows. Each one that he passed had its iron-gridded shutters firmly fastened shut except for one which stood open, admitting a flow of freezing night air. When Bardow went over to close it he saw that it looked north, across the clustering lights of Besh-Darok and the farms and darkened estates beyond to the Girdle Hills, their flanks no more than a degree of darkness in the indivisible night.

But faint lines and strings of bright pinpoints told of the sorcerous battlements which now lay across those slopes. At the centre of these fortifications was the citadel Keshada, an immense cylindrical tower whose pale aura carried across the miles like a beacon promising only death and ruin. Bardow stared at the distant bastion for a moment, striving to master the cloud of doubts which stirred at the back of his thoughts. Then he determinedly closed the shutters, tugged the levers which locked the sliding bars top and bottom, and walked on.

The large, plain doors to the assembly chamber were further along the corridor. As he pushed them open a hubbub of conversation from within faded abruptly.

'At last,' said a tall woman in black known as the Nightrook. 'We were getting a little concerned.'

'My apologies to you all,' he said, walking down the inclined aisle to the great hexagonal table where most of those he had summoned were gathered, less than a score it seemed. Tiers of empty seats faced inwards in a great semicircle, and the few lit lamps were augmented by the large fire burning in the long straight wall's hooded hearth. That entire wall was a single, vast stone-carved mural depicting Orosiada's various triumphs and his later founding of both the mage halls of Trevada and the building of the Imperial Palace at Besh-Darok.

As Bardow descended the gently sloping wooden steps, he noticed that Alael and Nerek were standing off to one side. Both appeared a little ill at ease, and he realised that bringing them into the company of other mages would be more difficult than he had first anticipated.

'Friends and colleagues,' he said as he drew near the table. 'Please accept my sincerest gratitude for coming here at such short notice, and for your patience. I have just returned from the Long Quays where I was assisting Lord Sedderil's harbourmasters. There was a collision between a departing passenger carrack and an arriving cargo vessel, and they needed help finding survivors in the dark.'

Blind Rina stepped into the firelight. 'Are many dead?'

'The pilot captain wasn't sure. He and his men rescued about two dozen from the waters, but the carrack was carrying at least two hundred.'

Rina put her hand to her mouth and turned away. In the darkness behind her Bardow noticed Terzis perched on the edge of a trestle to one side of the hearth, her features silent and sorrowful.

'Could it have been arranged?' said a tall, black-cloaked mage named Cruadin. 'Someone working for the Shadowkings, per-haps?'

'One of those Mogaun, I'll warrant!' said the Nightrook bitterly.

'Don't be foolish,' came a dry, scornful voice. 'It was a stupid accident caused by stupid people who wouldn't wait for dawn, nothing more.'

The speaker limped into view with the aid of a stick, an old man whose face bore terrible burn scars on the left side. The left hand was missing two fingers but held the stick's crook handle tightly, while a single, fervent eye regarded Bardow with an unkind intensity.

'Amral,' Bardow said to the others, 'is, as always, succinct while avoiding the burdens of tact.'

Some smiled, or stifled their laughter while one or two chuckled openly. Amral ignored the mockery and kept his singular gaze fixed on Bardow.

'In the shadow of ancient evil, tact is for weak minds,' he said. 'I don't think you brought us here to be tactful, Archmage, or to spare our feelings about the dread might that we face.'

Bardow spread his hands in a sombre gesture. 'You are right, Amral – the situation is grim. Only if we were suddenly deprived of the Crystal Eye could things be worse. The fields and houses for miles around are standing empty, while yet more refugees choke the roads south. Panic and fear stalk the wintry streets and the docks are crowded with people so determined to leave that not even tonight's ghastly disaster will deter them. And all the time our enemies sit and watch from their parapets as Besh-Darok's will starts to crack before even a single skirmish has been fought—'

'Yes, I have seen this,' Amral said testily.

Bardow leaned towards him, not disguising his anger. 'But isn't that what you wanted to hear, Amral? Does it satisfy your hunger for gloom and despond to know that darkness is coming and the light of day is bleeding away—'

'Enough!' the old mage cried. 'I will not listen to this poison—'

'But you foster futility with your bleak remarks,' Bardow said. 'Mindless optimism is not the only alternative to defeat. Not one of us here is blind to the terrible realities of who and what we all face, yet we must deny all temptations to despair and betrayal, and hold on to hope.'

He was addressing the entire gathering now. 'The future is *not* written, whatever the seers may say. It is the masters of those baleful towers who work to forge a doom for us. It is they who seek to be the architects of the future, and it may well be that all our efforts and suffering *shall* be for nothing! But equally, it might just suffice in the end. You and I do not know what the future holds, and neither do they, so I will stand against the Shadowkings and fight them at every turn until the last breath is driven from my body . . .' He paused a moment, suddenly aware of the vigorous resolve coursing through his senses, and the rapt attention of his audience.

'Yet we shall not stand alone,' he went on, turning back to the crippled mage. 'Cavalry reinforcements have already arrived from Sejeend and eastern Cabringa, and a steady stream of cargo boats has begun unloading at the docks. All the peoples and cities of the south are ready to come to our aid, so if we can hold the city we shall become stronger with every passing day. But if the city falls—'

Bardow left the unfinished sentence hanging. Amral stiffened his stance and looked up to meet Bardow's gaze.

'Forgive my earlier words, Archmage,' he said levelly. 'I have lived with personal bitterness for so long that hoping for the benign providence of the unforeseen seems like a childish act of faith, and still does . . .' There were angry mutters at this but he went on. 'Yet I have left my hillside home to come here and fight these lordlings of foulness and their slave creatures. When my turn to stand in the breach comes, Bardow, rest assured that I shall not break.'

The others murmured agreement and Bardow felt at once elated and humbled.

'I am gladdened beyond words,' he said, staring up at the tall image of Orosiada on the wall above the fireplace. 'Together we reaffirm the courage and responsibilities of the mage council as it was at its foundation. Soon we shall debate how best to deploy our various strengths and talents in the coming struggle, but firstly there is another matter.

'The High Conclave is divided on how to respond to the appearance of Gorla and Keshada. All three of the City Fathers and a third of the lords want to despatch some kind of spearhead host as a show of strength to our unwelcome guests, and to bolster the city's morale.'

'The plan of an idiot,' said the Nightrook, her eyes dark with contempt.

'That was my initial counterargument,' Bardow said drily. 'Although I phrased it a little differently. Neither Emperor Tauric nor Lord Regent Yasgur ventured a preference, seeking instead to wait for this council to present its advice.' He paused to glance round the table. 'Such advice, of course, would not be binding on the High Conclave but I am certain that Tauric is yet to make up his mind.'

'What of Yasgur?' said Cruadin. 'Wants to sit tight, I'll wager.'

Bardow regarded the dark-cloaked man. Like most of those gathered at the table, Trandil Cruadin had been a mage of the order before the invasion sixteen years ago. He had fought as a senior mage at the Battle of Pillar Moor which put him well into his middle years, but to Bardow's eye he had somehow retained the look of a man in his early thirties. His views on the Mogaun, however, had the inflexibility of his true age.

'I know that the Lord Regent's advisers are opposed to any such sortie,' Bardow said. 'But it seems that he himself is in favour of it.'

'It would surely be extremely rash to send any size of army against such unknown odds,' said a portly mage called Zanser. 'Even after an entire day we know next to nothing about those fortresses.'

Bardow sighed. 'I was hoping that Creld and his birds might have helped us arrive at some kind of map, but he's not here, is he?'

'He left on a merchantman bound for Gindoroj,' said Luri, one of the Anghatani twins. She exchanged a look with her sister, Rilu, and together they produced from within identical blue, hooded coats several sheets of parchment covered in detailed drawings and notes.

'It was not easy using insects,' Rilu said as Bardow peered wonderingly at the intricate plans, which had been delineated in fine silverpoint. 'They kept getting eaten by birds and other vermin, but we were able to sketch all the main fortifications and guard towers, as well as the outlines of the citadels.'

'These are excellent,' Bardow said. 'I'll have the scribes make copies.'

There were murmurs of agreement from the others as they pored over the fine plans, but the twins looked nervously at each other.

'Sadly, our maps are no longer accurate, Archmage,' Luri said. 'You see, the enemy's walls are growing.'

All fell silent at this, and Bardow frowned in puzzlement.

'You sound very certain of this,' he said.

Rilu nodded. 'Through the eyes of insects we have seen entire walls gradually pushing up out of the hills like ice rising from muddy ground, although the further from either citadel the slower the growth.'

'But the walls appear to be extending along a curve which will eventually enclose the city,' said Luri.

'Like a trap,' said Rilu.

'Well that puts a different cast on it,' said Cruadin. 'Should those walls reach the sea, everything we need will have to come in by ship. And how do we know that these walls won't continue on into the sea and completely surround the city?'

'Ah, panicking, forgetful youth,' Amral said. 'The sea is a place of primal and subtle powers, all of which have historically been inimical to the Wellsource.'

Cruadin gave the old man a dark look. 'What has the historical record got to do with this terrible crisis? I'll tell you – nothing. We are facing—'

'The same evil that has harried this continent for centuries,' Amral said, rapping his stick on the floor. 'We ignore the past at our peril . . .'

'Sers,' Bardow said sternly. 'We have strayed from the matter most urgently at hand. The High Conclave is due to reconvene soon after dawn and will be looking for this council, such as it is, to offer sage advice on the question of sending forth troops.'

'The consequences of doing so could be disastrous,' said the barrel-chested Zanser. 'But the consequences of doing nothing . . .' He shrugged. 'Imponderable, now that we know about those walls.'

'If we sent a sizeable host against, say, Keshada, then we might force their hand,' said Cruadin, flattening one of the maps on the table. 'Or if we sent the troops up the coast on barges, we might gain an element of surprise and rather than having to fight their way back they just return to the boats.'

'A mage would have to accompany such an army,' said the Nightrook. 'Naturally, I volunteer for the post . . .'

As argument and counterargument took hold, Bardow stepped back from the table and beckoned Alael over.

'Would you do something for me?' he said. 'A small errand.'

'Of course, ser Bardow.'

'Good. Take the main stair down to the second floor and walk left until you find the scriptory – you'll know it by the quill device over the door – and ask one of the scribes to return here with you. By my command, of course.'

'I understand, ser.'

He gave her a narrow look and in a quieter voice said, 'What do you think of this gathering of mine?'

Alael frowned. 'They are very . . . self-admiring,' she murmured then bit her lip.

Bardow smiled. 'Vainglory is part and parcel of magehood, I'm afraid. But without them, the city could not withstand even a single assault on the walls. That's the truth of it.' He straightened. 'Now hurry on your way.'

She nodded sharply and made for the door while Bardow turned back to the table and the heated discussion raging across it. Nerek was still sitting off to the side, watching the proceedings with disapproval plain on her lean features. He smiled at this for a moment, then silenced the rancorous exchange with upraised hands.

'Sers, be gentle to my ears,' he said, bringing his hands together. 'Clearly our advice needs to satisfy both caution and boldness, hard things to reconcile, I know. I have listened to your arguments, and what I propose is this – that the High Conclave sends two or three companies of infantry out to the ruined fort on the old smugglers' ridge, accompanied by carpenters and stonemasons and wagons of building materials. Once there, they would set about shoring up and repairing the defences and erecting a mast from which the commander will fly a truce flag.'

'You don't seriously believe that the enemy will accept the offer of a truce,' Cruadin said abruptly.

'I don't know what they'll do,' Bardow said. 'But they might consider their own position so strong that toying with us in a truce would afford them some amusement. And if we use such a face-to-face encounter with wise cunning, we could buy ourselves more time.'

A slow smile spread across Amral's scarred face. 'Aah, I see –

"Are they merely insanely rash or do they harbour some unknown power?"'

'Exactly,' Bardow said.

There was a chorus of approval from the rest, except for Trandil Cruadin who folded his arms and glowered. He was about to speak when a rapid string of oddly harmonised musical notes sounded above the babble. Bardow noticed that Blind Rina was the only one smiling at this interruption, then glanced over to where Nerek had twisted in her seat to look behind her. A few tiers back a gaunt, red-haired figure sat with his feet on the chairback in front while balancing upon his chest a curved silvery instrument consisting of a row of bulbous chambers sprouting slender musical pipes. Bardow almost laughed out loud – Osper Trawm was the last person he had expected to see here.

'Ser Trawm,' he said. 'How surprising. What brings you to Besh-Darok and indeed to this meeting?'

'Greetings, Archmage. I confess that while my natural instincts, as ever, are those of the observer, I could not refuse the plea of an old friend.' He stood, a tall and lanky man dressed like an artisan, and climbed down over the seating, pausing to wink at a haughty Nerek before striding over to Blind Rina where he raised one of her hands to his lips. She shook her head and smiled before turning her sightless eyes to the Archmage.

'You see, Bardow, I was having little success in tracking down the man who tried to kill Nerek and decided that I needed help. I remembered Osper and he came at my request.'

Bardow regarded the red-headed man with a fixed smile. Osper Trawm had been a highly talented yet feckless student of the Rootpower up to the invasion. Although he was one of the few to survive its destruction, he fled the conflict and slipped into the life of an itinerant bard wandering the isles and backwaters from Ogucharn to Dalbar. Seven years ago, purely by chance, Bardow encountered him briefly on the dockside of Port Caeleg on the island of Sulros, since when he seemed to have scarcely changed. The gleaming musical instrument that hung from his neck was new, however.

'It pleases me to have you join our common effort,' Bardow

said guardedly. 'How soon can you begin working with Blind Rina?'

An edgy eagerness shone from Trawm's eyes. 'I have already begun, Archmage,' he said, fingering the instrument's pipes. 'And I have tracked down the would-be assassin's movements, some of them at least.'

'We found no trail,' said Luri. 'No trail at all.'

'We searched very carefully,' said her twin, Rilu. 'There was no trace of the sorcery he used anywhere. How could you succeed where we did not?'

Trawm grinned widely. 'By breathing the air, fair ladies. By employing this, my ventyle.'

Heads craned forward, eyes narrowed to peer at the musical instrument hanging about his neck, Bardow included.

'It looks like a glorified syrena,' said the Nightrook.

'That's what I modelled it on,' said Trawm. He pointed at the row of bulbous chambers. 'In any or all of these I can instigate the thought-canto Zephyr which then produces sweet notes according to whichever keys and pipes I use. Or I can use Cadence as well to add a voice-like quality.'

'What then is the purpose of that mouth tube?' Amral said.

'A little fakery,' Trawm said. 'Making it seem that my own lungs are doing the work.'

'And how does this aid our search for Nerek's attacker?' Bardow said.

'By subtly changing the Zephyr canto, I can turn my ventyle into a retort for distilling odours from the air! Blind Rina took me to those places where Nerek and her foe clashed and despite the lapse of time I have been able to sift out the man's very personal redolence.'

'How unpleasant,' murmured the Nightrook.

'Yet effective,' Trawm countered. 'With Rina's help I have found faint traces of his spoor in several locations, including the vicinity of the Imperial Palace.'

There was an uneasy silence at this news, and Bardow immediately sensed a change in the tone of the gathering.

Why would he come here, he thought, *if not to make another attempt on Nerek's life? Or could he have contacted someone within the walls? By the Void, this could have us flinching at our own shadows! But how undo this . . . ?*

'Can you tell how long ago this was?' Bardow said evenly.

'Roughly two days ago,' Trawm said. 'There are no more recent hints of him so he may have gone to ground.'

Bardow nodded sagely, keeping his features composed while his thoughts raced. *I'll have to nip this in the bud or everyone in this palace will be watching each other . . .*

He gave Trawm a condescending smile. 'Well, it certainly sounds like an interesting exercise,' he said, 'and those pipes are quite ingenious—'

'You don't believe him,' Blind Rina said suddenly. 'You think that all our searching has been a waste of time.'

'That's not what I said,' Bardow replied. 'I just need some genuinely convincing proof before bringing such conclusions to the attention of the High Conclave. Perhaps Osper should spend another day or two tracking down these odours, then see what the outcome is.'

Blind Rina shook her head. 'How can you be so short-sighted, *you* of all people?'

'We are short of everything we need, Rina, including time,' Bardow said testily. 'You will both have to do more to persuade me—'

Suddenly Trawm broke away from the gathering and hurried towards the door. Blind Rina faced Bardow with wordless reproach then followed the bard out, almost colliding with Alael as she arrived with a bleary-eyed scribe.

Gods, Bardow thought dismally. *What will it take to smooth those ruffled feathers? If only she and Osper had come to me privately, then I wouldn't have had to put them through such public humiliation. But we can't afford mass internal suspicion right now . . .*

'Archmage, it occurs to me that no one has mentioned the Dalbar crisis,' said Zanser. 'Or the Jefren involvement.'

'That, my friend, is because the High Conclave has already taken the necessary measures.'

'Necessary measures?' Zanser retorted. 'Despatching three negotiators, not one of whom is from the aristocracy, and a mere troop of riders? Why, that makes it look as if we've already written off Dalbar as a lost cause.'

Bardow gave him a sharp smile. 'Yes, I expect it would. Perhaps our enemies will come to the same conclusion, eh?'

Zanser stared back at him with vacant puzzlement for a moment until the light of comprehension dawned in his eyes.

Bardow turned to Alael and the scribe she had brought with her, a shaven-headed young man in a plain brown tabard, carrying a resting board under his arm and his writing materials in an oval leather case strapped around his waist.

'Jarl, isn't it?' Bardow said to him.

'Yes, m'lord'

'Good. Firstly, there are these—' He patted the twins' finely-drawn maps. 'I want you to start transcribing these in your blackest ink, two copies of each as well. You can undertake this here, for we shall have another document for you to commit within the hour. Understood?'

Wide-eyed, the young scribe nodded.

'Excellent.' Bardow surveyed the expectant faces at the table. 'Now sers, let us apply our minds to the wording of this proposal – there are several persons to be swayed, including the Emperor himself, so let our phrasing be clear and direct.'

And later, he thought, *I shall have to be coaxing and manipulative in order to persuade Rina and Trawm to continue their search for our skulker, and to do it in secret.*

And after that . . . I just might find time for sleep.

Byrnak led the two Mogaun chieftains along the ornate gallery at a leisurely pace, pointing out this detail and that as they progressed. Small glass oil lamps hung high shed a low, yellow light but much of the stonework here was black marble or polished granite so the effect was one of a gleaming dimness, with soft glitters reflecting from a multitude of carved intricacies. A common motif of this corridor was that of horses, in spirals around pillars, in narrow relief panels running the length of a wall, or as pairs of life-size statues set on plinths flanking a few archways and doors, rearing in frozen wildness. He paused before one of them, indicating its expression to his guests.

'Regard those eyes, my friends, the way they gaze down with an unassailable disdain. In fact, both of these statues are looking down at us, not at each other, as if trying to intimidate anyone looking up.' He glanced at the two chieftains. 'Why do you think that is?'

The taller of the two, Welgarak, shook his head slowly.

'I don't know, Great Lord.'

'Of course, you wouldn't know,' Byrnak said. 'The story goes that the chief architect of this, Rauthaz Fortress, was an initiate of a secret Skyhorse cult. Unfortunately, his employer, King Tynhor, was High Priest at the temple of the Nightbear, the official creed of Yularia at the time. When Tynhor discovered that his pet architect was a devotee of the despised Skyhorse, he had the man slain in his home before his family. Then he turned the adornment of the remaining chambers and passageways over to an architect who was an avowed Nightbear follower. But it transpired that he was an inferior craftsman, so nowhere else in the fortress but here is there the feeling of being observed by a godhead.'

Except within your own skull, wretch.

He almost snarled at this interruption from from his inner mind, but steeled himself against it, refusing to be distracted by the god-fragment he carried. Instead he forced himself to remain calm before the brutish servants he had ordered brought to him.

The disastrous battle at Besh-Darok and the aftermath of pogroms and executions had drastically reduced the numbers of the Mogaun host, and killed off most of their chiefs. A few tribes had turned renegade but most of the remaining warriors had obeyed the Acolytes' command to pledge their allegiance to Welgarak and Gordag. With most of the Mogaun shamans dead, insane or fled, there was little stomach for mass rebellion. But Byrnak had taken it upon himself to examine these two more closely and determine the strength of their loyalty and their fitness for the battle ahead.

'How would you feel,' he said to them, 'if such statues were made of you? If it came to be that you inspired this kind of veneration?'

Welgarak blinked but his frown remained grim. The other, Gordag, whose once-stout frame was now gaunt, seemed stupefied by the suggestion for a long moment. Then he gave a hesitant smile.

'I . . . I don't know, Great Lord,' he said. 'Happy, I suppose.'

'When all our battles are won,' Byrnak said, pitching his voice low, almost as if he were confiding in equals, 'there will be a mountain of treasure to be divided, and land, titles and power. All for the brave and the loyal.'

Saying no more, he made a small beckoning gesture and led them further along to where the corridor turned left, stopping before a massive mirror. Its frame was intricately carved to resemble one continuous tree entwined with leaves and vines and sprigs of berries, with creatures, faces and people scattered along every side, hiding within or peering out from the foliage. Every time he passed it by, Byrnak fancied that he saw something new among the profusion of images.

The mirror stretched from floor to more than twice a man's height, perfectly reflecting the rest of the corridor and the three figures standing before it. Byrnak's attire was that of upper nobility, a neat-fitting midnight blue doublet with silver embroidery on the sleeves and the high collar.

In contrast the chieftains looked dishevelled and unwashed, with their shirts and breeks bearing rips and grime, theirs furs as matted as their hair, and the sheaths on their belts empty of all blades. Fingers twitched for hilts surrendered to the fortress stewards while eyes scowled at their reflections.

'Now as it might be,' Byrnak said and swept his arms across the mirror.

Its surface shivered and there were twin intakes of breath, then muttered oaths of awe. In the mirror Welgarak wore burnished iron armour inlaid with his clan's black moon totem in gold and pearlshell. His silver hair was long and combed straight and his beard was forked into three with the tips dyed red. Beside him, Gordag was garbed in a bronzed breastplate, gleaming mail, and a red-horned helm over dark, finely-braided hair. Both carried iron-hafted war axes and both seemed taller, straighter, their stares fierce and proud.

Byrnak regarded the chieftains with a sidelong glance, and smiled at their mesmerised stillness.

'There is much to be gained,' he said smoothly. 'By those of unshakeable loyalty and courage.'

'I am for you, Great Lord,' said Gordag, unable to look away from the mirror.

'I too, my lord,' Welgarak said, his voice slack. 'What would you have us do in your service?'

'Gather together all the tribes and warriors you can in the Forest of Gulmaegorn in northern Khatris. In just a few days I will come to you both with orders that will change this world for ever.'

With an effort Welgarak then Gordag looked round at him and he was pleased to see that there was something new and hungry in their eyes.

'As you will it, Great Lord,' Welgarak said. 'So shall it be.' Gordag gave a sharp nod of agreement.

'Good. Now go forth and do my bidding.'

The figures in the mirror reverted to a true reflection and although pangs of longing crossed the cheiftains' faces, that glittering desire was still there. As they bowed and left it was with a purposeful swagger utterly different to how they were earlier, subdued and sullen, like whipped dogs.

Byrnak smiled as they receded along the corridor. This was a subtle sorcery using the mirror to bind them not to himself but to the half-illusions of their greatest desires. From now on, every time despair or doubt crept into their minds this enchantment would blot out such frailties with those shining visions of themselves. The need to attain them would seal their loyalty.

They will still betray you, fool.

Your concern is so touching, he thought mockingly. *Such a pity that you didn't see fit to warn us about Ystregul.*

Crush their wills, I say, chain them to us, grasp every one of their lives in your hand like a leash . . .

Byrnak laughed out loud, despite the harsh voice ranting away within his head. At times like this in the past he had feared that this inescapable torment would eventually drag him down into insanity, but he had found one solution – drowning out the hated, grating tones with a louder sound.

So it was that he caused the mouth of every carven face, mask, horse and creatures on the walls and pillars to utter a wordless, full-throated song. The dark interweaving chorus of hundreds of voices filled the air, shook paintings and mirrors on their nails and echoed down the side passages. Most important of all, it became the only thing that Byrnak could hear as he walked the length of that beautiful black corridor.

Chapter Ten

Then to the King's Masks he said:
'The meagre justice you niggardly portion out is but a
loosening of the strings that tie us to your unjust hands.
If ever true justice awoke in this nightbound kingdom,
I would tear off your masks!'

Momas Gobryn, *The Trial of Aetheon*, Pt 4

Under a grey afternoon sky eight days after departing Besh-Darok,
the three delegates and their escort arrived in Scallow aboard
a two-masted barkan. A cold breeze clawed at their hair and
cloaks, and as they descended the icy gantry the first thing Keren
noticed was the frantic activity on the dockside. Every available
foot of quay and pier was occupied and a small forest of masts
and furled sails swayed to and fro all the way along the low
wooden wharf.

Winter had come to Dalbar but this far south the snow had yet
to fall heavily enough to settle, with only a few grey patches and
streaks seen at the edges of the loading area. As Keren set foot on
the worn planks of the quay she caught a whiff of rotting fish that
made her eyes water. With a hand raised to her nose she looked
around for the source.

'Ah, the delightful aroma of Scallow docks,' said Gilly as he
followed her onto solid ground. 'Once savoured, never forgotten.'

'Mother's name,' she muttered. 'It was bad enough spending
over a day on that stinking tub . . .' She paused as she noticed

seabirds dropping down behind a wall of crates stacked across the quay by the next berth where a shabby-looking netting ketch with a triangular sail was tied up.The crates failed to completely hide a large wet mound of fish heads and innards being added to by a swiftly gutting team of fishermen. Keren held a fold of her cloak to her mouth and nose and stepped away, trying to get out of the fish-tainted wind.

The wharf backed on to a long strip of muddy, rutted ground utterly lacking any kind of storehouses or godowns. Instead, dozens of carts and wagons were being loaded with goods from the docked vessels then hauled off by horse, though a few small ones were drawn by gaunt-looking men. Packs of hooded urchins did most of the lifting and carrying apart from the adult gangers who bore the truly heavy loads. Beyond the busy loading ground was a long ditch and beyond that were a mixture of timber yards and mean, single-storey houses. It was a bleak sight.

Leaving Gilly by the ship, Keren found a spot by a fencepost away from the odour of fish and leaned there for a moment. Beneath her cowled cloak, belted to her waist, was her old straight-edged sword, just about the last of the weapons she had carried away from Byrnak's camp months ago. By touch she could feel its leather-wound hilt and the tear she had always meant to have stitched, the solid curved tangs of the crosspiece and the triangular pommel with its inlaid faces. A comforting blade, one that had seen her through several fights, although in the past she had preferred the lighter cavalry sword which let her employ swifter, more precise methods. But that one lay twisted and melted in a tunnel beneath the Oshang Dakhal, along with the certainties of another life.

Also beneath her cloak, tucked into a small leather satchel slung under one arm and pressing into her side, was the parchment copy of the Raegal sagasong from the codex book, which seemed to hint at a ritual by which a gateway to the realm of the Daemonkind might be opened. She had accepted the merchant's gift in gratitude and passed the book into Alael's keeping before leaving Besh-Darok. At the time she had been full of certainty that the song about Raegal, once translated, would provide the evidence and clues she needed but now she was less sure. The ambush by the banks east of Vannyon's Ford and the astonishing appearance of a witchhorse suggested a possible alternative in her search for allies. However, such a course of action would present a similar set of problems: from what the witchhorse said, he and others had found a sorcerous hiding place between the realms from which he had been dragged by an ancient Skyhorse incantation, but where would she find someone with the arcane knowledge of a defunct creed? She sighed, putting these enigmas aside for the moment as she gazed out at the wider view of this southern cityport.

Scallow lay at the bottleneck between a long inlet and Sarlekwater, a curved inland sea. The Sarlekwater's distant northern shore fed into the Bay of Horns via a river canal down which Keren and the others had sailed after buying passage on a cramped and smelly barkan. The wharf where they had docked was on the western side of the bottleneck and during the approach to Scallow Keren had noticed on the eastern shore a series of larger, more elaborate quays made from heavy piles and massive masonry. Many of the buildings over there were built on or around several small hills, the highest of which was occupied by a squat castle, whereas the eastern shore was fairly flat.

This was her first visit to Scallow and she knew little of the city beyond its talents at shipbuilding and sea warfare. Gilly had mentioned a place called Wracktown, supposedly the surviving vessels of a defeated Anghatan fleet that had been lashed and nailed together between a cluster of small islands, their decks and cabins turned into homes, taverns and workshop. But all Keren had seen as they arrived were some densely overbuilt bridges spanning the rocky islands in the strait.

She was watching a long, oar-driven Honjiran galley approach from the north when Gilly came over to join her. Instantly, the fishy odour returned.

'Fine fellows, those fishermen,' he said. 'Very welcoming and gossipy.'

'How welcoming?' she said, wrinkling her nose.

'Well, shook hands once or twice . . .' Frowning, he paused

and sniffed his fingers, then shrugged. 'At least I found out a few things . . .'

Before Keren could make an acerbic observation, Medwin came stalking over with a face like thunder.

'What a lying, swindling reptile,' he said between gritted teeth, clearly straining to keep his voice down.

'Ah, our noble captain,' said Gilly.

'What is wrong?' Keren said.

'He refuses to allow the horses off,' Medwin said. 'He claims that two of them were not hobbled properly, and that they panicked and kicked out their stall doors. He wants to take me down and show me, but I had to come over here and let you know what is transpiring.' He breathed deeply. 'And to calm myself . . . Ah, there he is. I shall return as soon as I find out just what the truth is . . .'

With that he strode off back to the dockside where the captain, a tall, lanky man, waited with some of his crew. Gilly snorted in amusement.

'I'm afraid that the only truth Medwin will discover is that all barkan captains are insidious rogues,' he said.

The mage and the captain went back on board and descended into the hold, reappearing a few minutes later accompanied by Redrigh, their escort captain who stayed on deck while Medwin returned to Gilly and Keren.

'So – how much extra did he want?' Gilly said.

'One and a half regals,' Medwin said. 'When he showed me the so-called damage I almost laughed in his face. Certainly the doors were lying in pieces, yet even I could tell that they could be easily reassembled and hung again.'

'No doubt as easily as they were disassembled,' Keren said.

'Just so.' His anger now fading, Medwin shook his head. 'There was a moment when I was tempted to use the Lesser Power, even with his crew nearby, but I decided against it and paid the money instead.'

'Very wise,' Gilly said. 'News of such an incident would travel fast, and the rebel septs would seize upon it with glee.'

'I know,' said the mage, glancing round as Captain Redrigh joined them, his face dark and angry.

'Ser Medwin, I fear it may take another half an hour for these oafs to move the mounts ashore,' he said. 'Will you wait or find a wagon to take you across to the east shore?'

'Such a pity we couldn't bring the wagon with us, eh?' said Gilly.

Medwin arched an eyebrow and Keren coughed.

'Before we boarded the good captain's manure boat,' the mage said acidly. 'I despatched a message bird to the Crown representatives here, informing them of our progress. But we were delayed on the way, so they may have been here earlier and departed . . .'

Keren looked past him to the Bridges district, a jumble of houses and angular roofs that extended over the water and further down the western embankments where they merged with the shorebound houses and yards. A pair of two-wheeled, horse-drawn traps had emerged from a wooden archway and were following a stilt road round to where it met solid ground. One of the trap drivers waved as he approached, and Keren pointed him out to Medwin. Looking relieved, Medwin turned to murmur to Captain Redrigh who nodded and hurried off towards the ship once more.

Some moments later the small carriages, each with a tattered, cane-frame leather canopy, rolled to a halt in the mud before them. The leading driver, a pale young man wearing a long hooded coat of some coarse green and brown weave, climbed down and bowed.

'Ser Medwin, ser Cordale, Lady Asherol, greetings,' he began. 'My name is Astalen and my fellow driver is Broen. I am honoured to be Trader Golwyth's secretary and it pleases me greatly to see that you have arrived safely. Normally I would take time to enquire about your journey and your well-being but I fear that we must proceed to Eastbank with all speed.'

'Is there some kind of emergency, Astalen?' Medwin said as the young secretary guided them to the horse carriages. 'Are we in danger?'

'I would give a qualified yes to both your questions, ser mage,' Astalen said. 'You see, every year at winter—'

'Ah, the bodush,' Gilly said suddenly. 'Is it the bodush tourney? I know it can get a bit rough at times . . .'

Astalen was shaking his head. 'When did you last visit Scallow, ser Cordale?'

'A little over ten years ago,' he admitted.

'I'm afraid the game's character, shall we say, has changed for the worst since then.' So saying he ushered them into the carriages, Keren and Medwin riding with Astalen and Gilly by himself in the second. Astalen flicked the reins, the carriage jolted into movement and he steered it round and back along the muddy road. Keren noticed a number of sullen glances turned their way, openly resentful faces watching them leave. She felt a quiver of relief as the wharf slipped out of sight.

Once the low docks were behind them, they passed by a succession of warehouses and timber yards bearing merchant sigils and guarded by nervous-looking swordsmen and spearmen. At a fork further on Astalen turned left towards the Bridges district and as the carriages passed on to the wooden stilt road the wheels began to rumble loudly. Then it was up a curved incline and along a level stretch before dipping down and round a curve with black water lapping only feet away. Wooden buildings rose to either side, connected by a maze of walkways and gantries, each one a strange amalgam of styles and shapes with some balconies and floors appearing have to have been added as afterthoughts. A few looked to be tilting dangerously and had been shored up with heavy supporting beams, some of which had themselves been strengthened with iron strapping. There was also a low, incessant chorus of creaks as if the entire timber town shifted with wind and tide.

The stilted road sloped up and became a narrow bridge across a small area of open water between the crammed, shadowy buildings. To the right a row of four evenly-spaced poles jutted up from the waters. Wide cartwheels had been lashed to the tops as platforms and on the first three Keren could make out fleshless, sun-bleached bones. On the fourth was a body being torn at by a full-grown crownhawk while a few small birds circled overhead.

'A Mogaun of the Stoneheart tribe, which is apparently in control of Choraya,' Astalen said, slowing the carriage. 'They sent a raiding party across the Bay of Horns and our mounted *altasti* only caught up with them after they'd pillaged and raped their way through several northern villages.'

'I'm surprised not to have seen more like that one,' Keren said, remembering some of the towns they had passed through on their journey, especially the ones that had suffered badly under the Mogaun. Their retribution had been openly savage.

Astalen glanced over his shoulder. 'That is because those we took prisoner were drowned, my lady.' He looked forward once more. 'Ceremonially, of course.'

Of course, Keren thought wryly. *But who is this meant to warn — Scallow's enemies or its citizens?*

There were some people out on foot, but they were staying away from the main streets and mostly using the narrow dogwalks that clung to upper storeys or curved across from eave to eave. Keren noticed that there was more activity down on the water channels which passed beneath them, coming into view now and then. She saw laden canalboats being poled along by hard-eyed boatmen or being unloaded at tiny landing stages jutting from the barnacled waterlines of great buildings which creaked on their submerged supports.

A succession of smells spoke of crafts and artisans — the rich yeastiness of a brewer's, the woody smoke of a fish-curer, the aroma of freshly-baked bread. But all these were whipped away on an icy wind as the carriages came out from among the dense buildings and up on to a small, stone wharf on one side of a open canal. On the other side a stout wooden drawbridge stood up almost straight, held there by thick, taut ropes wound through a train of gears and winches manned by nervous-looking wharfers. A blunt-bowed barge was slowly passing through the channel, its crewmen using heavy staves to steer it clear of the sides while four guards with crossbows kept a tense watch on deck.

'Wonder what their cargo is?' Gilly muttered from the other carriage.

Keren would have answered but for an odd sensation that flickered through her, like some faint sound or the slight hint of an odour, there in one instant and gone the next. Frown-ing, she turned to look along the canal and as her gaze came round a figure on the towpath opposite quickly stepped back out of sight.

'Interesting,' she murmured.

'Indeed, my lady,' said Astalen. 'Was that person watching the barge or us?'

'I expect we'll know soon enough,' Medwin said evenly, staring across the white-capped waves of the Sarlekwater, north to hidden lands.

Once the barge was through, the suspended bridge came down on its creaking hawsers and once a few people had hurried over on foot either way, the carriages continued across. Astalen kept them to an open road which crossed a number of short bridges and another larger swing bridge before finally reaching the solid ground of Eastbank. Throughout this eastward journey Keren noticed the growing prosperity, the better houses, the bigger, busier wharves, and the more frequent guard patrols. As the carriages rattled side by side along a cobbled street away from the ship-crowded main docks, Gilly asked Astalen how life was in Wracktown.

'Difficult,' was the reply. 'Many good people have moved away while all manner of villains and brutes have made their lairs there. The submerged hulls of some of the ancient ships have rotted through and their lower decks have flooded. It is said that new, lethal kinds of fish and eel are breeding in the darkness down there, but I have seen no evidence of this.'

Gilly sighed. 'A great pity. Wracktown had such character and life when I was there last.'

At a junction, Astalen steered towards a narrow street, forcing Gilly's driver, Broen, to fall back into single file. The buildings here were straight and well-made and beyond several courtyard walls Keren spied small, luxurious gardens, ornate gazebos and balconies and pillared cloisters. All of which was in stark contrast to the outer façades of these residences with their plain stone walls, few windows and unremarkable front doors. So different, she thought, to the timber buildings of the Bridges district.

'Astalen,' she said. 'Did we pass through Wracktown on our way here?'

'No, m'lady, Wracktown is the westerly part of South Bridges – it would be instantly recognisable from its dilapidated appearance, the roving gangs of feral children, and the reek of decaying refuse.'

Keren exchanged an amused glance with Medwin and whispered, 'So it's not on our itinerary, then . . .'

Medwin coughed and said aloud, 'Friend Astalen, am I right in thinking that talks between the Moon Council and the rebel septs are due to take place very soon?'

'That is so, ser mage. As a matter of fact, the discussions were almost abandoned since some of the rebels wanted to fight now and talk later. Then the Hevrin announced that he would attend and the others followed in his wake.'

Keren looked up, frowning. 'The Hevrin.'

'Well, his given name is Rikketh Cul-Hevrin, but as the High Chief of Hevrin Sept he is simply referred to as the Hevrin.'

'I see,' she said, feeling the hard outline of the codex in its satchel under her arm. 'Before leaving Besh-Darok, I met a merchant named Yared Hevrin. I wonder if there could be any connection.'

Astalen glanced round with new respect in his eyes. 'Yared Hevrin is well-known and much-respected in Scallow, m'lady, and happens to be a half-cousin to the Hevrin himself. However, because he supports the Moon Council he is a figure of loathing and contempt for Hevrin Sept and its allies.'

'No blood is as bad as that between warring relatives,' Medwin said. 'Is that likely to have a bearing on the talks?'

'Without a doubt, ser Medwin,' said Astalen. 'Yared Hevrin is expected to arrive sometime tomorrow, and is bound to have his say.'

A cold wind blew in from the north with a light rain that pattered on the carriage's leather canopy. Keren shivered, thinking on all that Astalen had said and wondering if her part in this task was really necessary. She knew nothing of Dalbar or Scallow and its politics, and her confidence in her own fighting prowess was not what it once was. As for her sorcerous abilities, they seemed little more than vestigial to her for all the optimism expressed by Bardow and Medwin. The Archmage was convinced of her potential, and at intervals during their journey Medwin had devoted several hours to teaching her the rudiments of Lesser Power cantos. Yet a part of her still yearned for that absent power, the ancient, implacable might of the Daemonkind, a part of her that would always play traitor to her loyalties.

The rain was coming down in gusts as they drove through a market square. All around the townsfolk were laughing and ducking under stall covers or stepping into doorways for shelter as the hail came down with a hissing, rattling din that sounded especially loud under Keren and Medwin's carriage canopy. They were almost at the other side of the square when a group of bedraggled men wearing green sashes and carrying sticks came running out of an alley to the right, Keren's side. The leader made straight for the carriage, leaped on to the running board and leaned in close enough for Keren to smell ale on his breath.

He was young with coal-black beard and rain-matted hair, his face full of a casual hostility that faded when Keren pushed aside her cloak and half-slid her sword from its scabbard. Astalen was cursing him and ordering him off, but he ignored the tirade, sneered and banged his stick once against the side of the carriage, then uttered an odd howl before jumping lightly off. Other, different sounding calls went up behind them as Astalen began lashing the horse into a swift canter.

'It will be safer if we hurry,' he shouted above the racket of the wheels on the cobbles. 'The bodush factions will soon hold all of this district.'

'What about Gilly?' Keren said, but Medwin was already turning to pull aside a cotton flap in the rear of the canopy. Together they squinted through the gap, and Keren gasped to see Gilly's carriage brought to a halt by a crowd of rain-soaked people wearing red sashes. An argument between the crowd's leaders and Gilly's driver, Broen, led to him being dragged down from his seat under a hail of fists.

'Mother's name,' Keren said, angry at this brutality and wishing vainly that they had waited for Redrigh and his men.

Then she almost cheered when Gilly climbed over into the driver's seat and grabbed the reins, stamped on the fingers of a man trying to get on board then lashed the horse into motion. Members of yet another bodush faction, in white sashes gone grey in the rain, had emerged from a side street to taunt the red sash faction while blocking the road behind Astalen's carriage. Gilly yelled at his horse, yanking on the reins to turn its head and move off to the side, still hemmed in by howling, stick-brandishing bodush players.

'Astalen,' Keren cried. 'Gilly's in trouble.'

'So are we.'

She just had time to see a mob in yellow sashes hurrying along a muddy alley towards them before the carriage suddenly leaped forward, throwing Medwin and her back into their seats.

'Greatest apologies,' Astalen called out. 'We will have to go by another route, and with some haste.'

Buildings sped past, windows and doors a blur. Dogs ran yapping in short-lived pursuit and startled townsfolk shrieked curses and shook fists in their wake. The carriage swayed and rattled as it hurtled along, sometimes giving a banging jolt as it ran over a hole or a jutting cobble in the road. Keren had not thought Astalen capable of such skilful charioteering but the way he took them round several narrow corners made her revise her opinion.

They managed to leave behind most of the yellow faction mob in the first five minutes, apart from a few dogged individuals who knew the back roads and alleys well enough to keep the carriage in sight for another ten minutes before being outdistanced. Astalen slowed the pace, following streets which curved around the southern flank of the hill occupied by Scallow Castle. Keren's tense alertness was just starting to ease when they rolled to halt before the tall, iron-banded gates of Golwyth's compound a short while later. Astalen called up to someone in the guard tower and as the gates began to open he turned to Medwin and Keren.

'Once Trader Golwyth learns what has befallen Ser Cordale and Broen he will send some of his guards out to find them.'

Medwin nodded wordlessly, as if resigned, but Keren could feel her anger rekindling.

'Tell your master that I have to go with them,' she said.

The carriage moved through the inward-swinging gates. The trader's compound was a high-walled enclosure with several store-sheds along one wall, stabling and a barrack hut opposite, and a larger two-storey building against the far wall. Before the building was a long, weather-beaten table around which were gathered a dozen leather-armoured men, all laughing uproariously. As the carriage came to a halt nearby, a familiar grinning figure stood up from amongst them and toasted Keren and Medwin with a sloshing cup of ale.

'Have I got a story to tell you,' said Gilly Cordale, making his way through his audience.

Stepping down from the carriage Keren tried to substitute sternness for relief but failed. 'What happened? How did you escape that mob, and just *how* did you get here before us?'

Gilly shrugged. 'Sometimes the dice roll for you, sometimes you roll for the dice.' He took a hefty gulp of ale. 'Did you see how they dragged Broen off his perch? Aye, well, I quickly took his place, seized the reins and beat that horse into action again. Because the road ahead was blocked by the whites I couldn't drive after you. So, I tried to force a way across the square while punching and kicking any green rogues who attempted to board me.'

By now he was recounting the tale to Golwyth's men as well as Keren and Medwin, his gestures wide and dramatic. 'But I didn't get far. A squad of greens charged at my carriage and tipped it over. The whites came in hard, then sticks cracked heads and a merry old brawl got into full swing all about me as I crawled out from the wrecked carriage. Back on my feet I made a run for a street leading off the square and down towards the docks. I was part way down it when there was a shout and I looked round to see a gang of yellows coming for me, with an ugly intent in their eyes. I ran as if the Grey Lord himself was after me, ducked along an alley and on to the waterfront. But my pursuers weren't to be lost so easily, so I kept along the wharf and up a crowded side street full of stalls . . .' He held out his empty cup and it was swiftly refilled.

'But, my friends, this street was so busy with townsfolk and hawkers that I couldn't get through. I was filled with panic and fear, then a hand grabbed my arm and pulled me into the dimness of one of the stalls. Naturally, I reached for my sword but then suddenly a small, dwarfish figure dressed in a shroud and sporting a beard swooped down to hang before me. "Hold, brave stranger," it said in an odd voice. "Put up thy blade for we offer you sanctuary."'

Everyone present was suddenly engrossed by this strange turn of the story.

'I was struck with fear at this apparition, but for only as long as it took me to notice the strings holding it up. For you see, I was standing behind the wings of a puppet theatre, and it was the puppet master,' he winked at the guards, 'and his beautiful daughter—' There was a chorus of jeers and ribald remarks at this. '—who saved me from a yellow-handed beating. They took me out a back door to a narrow wynd leading back up the main streets of Eastbank. Where, as fortune would have it, I encountered the valiant Captain Redrigh and a couple of his men who brought me here to Golwyth's refuge with all speed.' He drained the last of his ale. 'And then my good friends here arrived in time to hear this amazing saga.'

He bowed as Keren and everyone applauded, including Captain Redrigh and his men who had emerged from the stables midway through the performance.

'Well told, ser Cordale,' came a deep voice.

As the applause subsided, the guards made way for a tall, well-built man wearing a plain doublet and trews in rich grey leather edged with red, and a dark blue cloak fastened at the shoulder with a bronze wheel brooch. Keren guessed this to be Golwyth, the trader appointed by the High Conclave as their representative in Scallow. The man clearly possessed that charismatic air of purpose and experience that she had seen in all great leaders, among whom she incuded Mazaret and Yasgur. Golwyth, however, had something extra in his eyes, a mingling of wisdom and delight which countered the abundant silver in his neatly-clipped hair and beard. Once he and Gilly had shaken hands, Astalen came forward to introduce him to Medwin and Keren. When she met that dark, warm gaze a small, pleasurable shiver went through her.

Then he stepped back a little to survey all three for a moment.

'Survival in these bleak times requires strength,' he said. 'But to survive and force back the tide of evil demands both strength and a rare courage. I have heard many reliable tales of the great struggle for Besh-Darok, and I am honoured to make you guests under my roof. I am just sorry that thus far you've only seen the worst that this city has to offer.'

'All cities have their dark byways, honoured Golwyth,' Medwin said. 'Yet your gracious welcome gives light to our arrival and makes us glad to be in Scallow.'

As both men bowed slightly, Keren exchanged an amused look with Gilly, then spoke to the trader.

'Ser Golwyth – what reason would these bodush factions have for chasing us through the streets? Might there be a sinister motive at the back of it?'

Golwyth gave her a knowing smile and strode towards the rear of their carriage. 'I think I can answer that quite easily, Lady Keren . . . Ah, yes . . .' He bent down, reached out and straightened with a long strip of white cloth in his hand, much to the puzzlement of Keren and Medwin.

'I regret to announce that you have been unwitting players in this year's game of bodush,' Golwyth said, holding out the cloth strip. 'This is a *box* of the White Faction, one of five scattered around the city by the tourney assessors.'

'But, ser Trader,' said Gilly, who had doffed his jerkin to examine it. 'I find no trace of such a flag upon my person.'

Golwyth smiled. 'During this annual stampede misunderstandings are the rule, ser Cordale, not the exception. But hopefully my men shall soon return with your driver, Broen, and then we may learn more. Till then, let me show all three of you to your quarters while the cook prepares the table for us.'

As the trader led the way with Medwin at his side, Gilly hung back a little and murmured to Keren, 'I just hope there's no misunderstanding about how hungry I am!'

Then he laughed, shrugged on his jerkin and hurried after Golwyth and Medwin, exchanging a word or a handclasp with a few of the dispersing guards. Watching him, Keren smiled, then shook her head and followed.

Chapter Eleven

Behold with thine unsleeping eyes,
The blind ambition and petty vengeance,
Of cutthroats and kings.

Calabos, *The Black Shrine*, Ch. 2, iii

The next morning, Medwin appeared at Gilly's door to offer advice as to his choice of clothing.

'Golwyth is taking us up to the High House of Keels to meet senior members of the Council of Moons, ' he said. 'Now, bear in mind that it is a place with a long history and thus has rigid views on the propriety of dress.'

'You mean they're antiquated traditionalists obsessed with absurdities.'

Medwin winced. 'I mean that observing such customs would be a minor concession to the vital business we must conduct here.'

Gilly was wearing a long shirt and baggy trews as he lay sprawled in his small room's cramped boxbed. He sighed theatrically.

'And these customs are?'

'Sober and dignified garments with the minimum of adornments; sturdy and unembellished footwear—'

'And I was so looking forward to wearing my jewelled mountain clogs.'

'—and no cloaks or capacious gowns.' Medwin went on, glaring. 'Sigils of the Earthmother or Fathertree are permitted, so long as they are Dalbari depictions. Also, wearing the colour red within the walls of the High House is utterly forbidden. On pain of death.'

Gilly was wide-eyed. 'Red?'

'About two hundred years ago a pirate armada, supposedly from some legendary western isles across the Eventide Ocean, attacked Scallow, burnt half of it to the ground and slew two thirds of the populace. The pirates flew red flags and wore red clothing, hence the ban.'

'Interesting,' Gilly said. 'Oddly enough, the new Jefren regime's banner is mostly red too, or so my informants back in Besh-Darok claimed.'

Looking suddenly anxious, Medwin made a hushing gesture with one hand. 'Don't speak of that too openly. For the moment it is as well that no-one knows what we know.'

'But we don't really know very much,' Gilly said, fighting the urge to grin.

Medwin nodded. 'And it's my job to let others think that we do. In the meantime, I'm more interested in what you can find out about the rebel chiefs and their not-so-secret allies before the first convocal at the High House, or at least by dusk. How soon can you make contact with your, ah, talebearers?'

Gilly grinned at that. 'My snooping taprats? Well, I have the names and addresses of two members of the Southern Cabal here in Scallow, but I've no idea how out of date they might be.'

'You should pursue them anyway, once this meeting with the councilmen is done.'

'Is my presence really necessary?' Gilly said. 'I'm sure that the High House of Keels is a fascinating place but I think that my time could be better spent.'

Medwin shook his head. 'Officially you and Keren are my personal advisers so they will be expecting all three of us. Once the formal meeting and its dialogue are over, I'll be able to dismiss the two of you on some pretext or other.'

'Then the real discussion starts, eh?'

'Quite. Now, Golwyth's cook is laying out our breakfast so – enough lazing about, ser! Time you were up and getting dressed!'

Gilly gaped at this but before he could frame a suitable retort, the smiling mage was gone and the door was swinging shut. He stared at the door for a moment, wondering if he had brought any clothing of a suitably shrieking red with him, but a brief rummage through his haversack confirmed that he had not.

A short while later he followed the stone sidestairs down into Golwyth's low-beamed dining hall, earning a hearty welcome from the master trader, a wry smile from Keren and an approving nod from Medwin. Gilly wore a plain, high-necked doublet of light brown kidskin which he had brought with him, and hedge-green twill leggings selected from garments offered by Golwyth. On his head was a close-fitting, dark-blue cap edged with light-blue embroidering, his boots were low and plain, and in one hand he carried his old slate-grey riding gloves.

Breakfast consisted of exquisite, freshly-baked herb rolls, sharp-flavoured cheese and bowls of sprigs and corn, all washed down with beakers of sweetened spring water. When the meal was done, Golwyth led them out to a waiting two-horse carriage, ordered his guards to open the gates, and they were away.

The journey from the compound up to the High House of Keels was brief and uneventful. With the dark battlements of Scallow Castle looming ahead, Gilly saw before it a tall peaked roof adorned with massive beams, then a turn in the road revealed the rest of the building. The massive beams resembled ship keels, their prows curving claw-like over the roof's peak while their sterns reached down to plunge into the ground on either side. The walls were high and straight with a pillared gallery along beneath the eaves, and as they drew nearer Gilly could see that the great council building's rear wall actually abutted against the castle's outer bulwark.

A gravelled drive led past small, patterned gardens to a spacious coach and stable courtyard next to the High House. Leaving the carriage and horses in the care of the ostlers, Golwyth took them down a pathway that ran alongside the building beneath the great keel beams. At the front entrance, a few long steps led up to arched doors that opened into a square lobby. The lobby walls were high and to left and right was frail-looking wood scaffolding that reached up to the ceiling, with artisans at every level working to restore the expanses of stone relief carvings. Heavy sailcloth hid most of the details and light from the artisans' oil-lamps cast their own crouched or squatting forms on to the drapes, providing a strange lanternshow for any watchers below. Yet despite the steady stream of people entering or leaving, Gilly and Keren were the only ones pausing to look up.

An elderly, balding man in a blue short-sleeved, knee-length surcoat came forward from the well-guarded inner doors, Smiling he extended a hand to Golwyth who accepted the clasp and then introduced him to Medwin as Aftmaster Yeddro. Bows were exchanged and Medwin in turn introduced Gilly and Keren as 'my personal advisers'.

'Greetings to you all, and welcome,' said Yeddro. 'Cordmaster Doreth awaits you in the Chart Chamber. If you'll follow me . . .'

Flanked by Medwin and Golwyth, he led them through a side door and up three flights of broad stone steps. The stonework all around was solid and plain yet the corridor they emerged in was noticeably more elaborate. Floor tiles bore a repeating anchor motif and black and ochre while spaced along the left wall were bow-curved columns that gave the semblance of a vessel's ribs. Between them hung the wooden name-crests of ships and the coats-of-arms of captains and nobles, many of them looking cracked and weathered.

The right wall sloped up in a gentle curve, with windows all along it affording a view of the long, busy gathering hall below. Aftmaster Yeddro had just commenced a commentary on the heraldic crests when Keren stumbled and paused to lean against one of the sloping wooden supports, then sat on a protruding stonework ledge and covered her face with her hands.

Quickly Gilly was at her side. 'What's wrong?'

'I'm not . . .' She let her hands fall and shook her head, confusion in her eyes. 'I felt dizzy and cold all at once.'

'Can you go on with us?' asked Medwin.

Keren breathed in deeply and blinked once slowly. 'It's passing now. I can continue.'

She pushed herself upright and resumed walking. Gilly frowned but resisted the impulse to point out her pallor and the trembling in her hands.

Then something down in the hall caught his attention as he walked along the gallery. The long hall was really a series of seated chambers divided by head-height stone walls and lit by oil lamps hung overhead. Some were like formal meeting rooms, others were serving up ale or hot dishes. There were no doors so anyone could pass all the way through from one end to the other. Various groups had gathered in this or that chamber, most looking like townsfolk while others wore garments more suited to shipboard life and rough weather.

There was one man walking confidently from chamber to chamber, a short, stocky man in a baggy, dark green tunic and breeches. No details of his face were visible from this vantage, but the more Gilly studied him the more he felt a nagging sense of familiarity so, largely ignoring Yeddro's voice, he followed the man's progress.

When the man reached the doorway to a busy room at the far end he paused for a moment, then sidled into the crowd. Just at the moment Gilly felt a hand on his shoulder. Startled he glanced round to see the aged Yeddro at his side.

'Ah, ser Cordale, you espy the very crux of our grand predicament,' the Aftmaster said, pointing a bony finger at a group of bearded men sitting in a corner of the chamber. One of them was almost bear-like in stature and had long grey hair and a short but bushy beard. Gilly noticed him almost in passing as he surveyed the crowded, ill-lit chamber but of his quarry there was no sign.

'Yes, see there,' Yeddro went on. 'Flanked by his captains sits the Hevrin, leader of the ship-clans of the Stormbreaker Isles and source of all our strife. Yet without his will, there would be no talks this day . . .'

Gilly was only half-listening as he peered down at the busy corner chamber, most of which was blocked by nearside walls, trying to distinguish the backs of heads from each other. Suddenly there was his quarry, slipping between those grim-looking bearded captains and bending to speak in the Hevrin's ear. The great chieftain said something in response and the man laughed, nodded, then straightened, giving Gilly a full view of his face for the first time.

'In the Mother's name,' he said. 'It can't be . . .'

From memories of Krusivel, back before all this began, Gilly remembered him. It was Ikarno Mazaret's brother, Coireg.

'Gilly, Cordmaster Doreth is waiting for us,' Medwin said testily from across the corridor.

'One moment, ser Medwin, I pray,' Gilly said.

Yeddro murmured something to Golwyth who smiled and shrugged while Keren, looking better, came over to Gilly.

'What are you doing?' she muttered.

'You see the bare-armed man, down there?' He pointed. 'There, just coming out of the end room . . . Look closely. Recognise him?'

She stared for a moment, then her eyes widened. 'Coireg Mazaret . . . but didn't Nerek say something about him being possessed?'

'Yes, and this possessing spirit just might know what's been done with Ikarno,' he said in a hard voice. Then he made up his mind. 'I'm going to follow him – tell Medwin . . .'

Then he was off at a run, ignoring the shouts behind him. His sudden anger gave him vigour and alertness as he reached the stairs and dashed down them two at a time. Rounding the corner of the next landing he just managed to avoid colliding with a servant carrying a small keg on either shoulder. Both did a swift dodging dance of sidesteps, then Gilly was past him and descending the next flight. He stumbled halfway down and had to leap the rest of the steps, landing on both feet with a mighty thud. He laughed shakily at the luck of it then raced down the last flight and rushed through the busy lobby, drawing cries from the door masters and whistles from the workmen on their gantries.

Once outside in the full light of day, he slowed to a walk, surveying the vicinity of the High House of Keels, the road and its three-storey residences and the openings of side streets. There were a few passers-by visible, as well as the trickle of arrivals to the High House itself, but of Coireg Mazaret there seemed no sign. Then he saw a small horse trap with a single passenger turning south along one of the side streets, and a quiver of instinct convinced him to follow.

Several one- and two-seat carriages were lined up at the gates to the High House precincts. Gilly leaped into the nearest, patted the driver's shoulder and pointed at the receding trap.

'Quickly – after that rig!'

The driver, a bibulous-looking man in a bulky coat and a decrepit hat, regarded him with suspicion.

'Is this some bodush playout? If it is, I want no part of it, hear?'

'It isn't, I swear,' Gilly said. 'Do you see any tokens on me?'

'Hmph. That don't mean nought to some o' them. Not like it were in my day . . .'

Yet he tightened his grip on the reins, cracked his whip lightly over his horse's ears and the cart jerked into motion, turning a wide curve in the street. As the wheels rattled over the cobbles, Gilly looked back at the High House of Keels and wondered what Medwin was thinking or saying at that moment.

Something deeply guilt-provoking, no doubt, he thought. *That man could harvest remorse from a Jefren executioner.*

Gilly and his driver trailed the other carriage down through Scallow's narrow streets. When asked to keep a good distance from their quarry, the driver grunted, clamped his hat more firmly on his head and did as he was bid. Before long it became clear that Coireg Mazaret was heading for the Bridges district. A light rain was falling by the time Gilly's carriage crossed from the shore on to a wooden stilt road which passed between storehouses and odd travellers inns with their own small jetties, over bridges whose underspans were crowded with a ramshackle array of homes, taverns and workshops.

Gilly wiped raindrops from his face and ran fingers through his damp, greying hair. The rain had eased off to a scattering of droplets but the sky remained a rush of sullen cloudracks all the way to the horizon, a sure sign of more bad weather to follow.

As the carriage lurched and rumbled along, Gilly imagined himself cornering the possessed Coireg, somehow forcing him to disclose where the Shadowkings were holding Ikarno and what they were doing to him, and from this devising a plan of rescue . . .

A fool's plan, he thought suddenly. *A bout of rashness and folly, that's what this chase is. What am I doing here? Who knows what dark powers this sorcerer has at his command . . .*

He was on the point of telling the driver to turn round when the carriage came to a halt.

'As far as I go, good ser,' said the driver over his shoulder.

They were sitting on a raised planked area overlooking a darker district from which reared what appeared to be the sharp corner of a tilted building. Gilly realised that it was a ship's stern with a weather-beaten roof atop it. Visible in the shadows further along was a row of supporting beams, clearly shoring up one side of the leaning vessel, while heavy, mildewed hawsers ran straight and taut from holes in the rotting hull to rusting iron stanchions. Beyond this mouldering ship Gilly could see the lines of others, some almost vague beneath encrustations of makeshift huts and buildings and gantries and smoke flues and balconies and pigeon lofts . . .

Wracktown. It was set lower than the rest of the Bridges district, its shadowy rubbish-strewn wharfs and walkways raised little more than a foot or two above the waters. From where Gilly's driver had stopped, a long ramp sloped down to a cluttered dockside: halfway along it was Coireg's carriage, moving further away.

'Why have you stopped here?' Gilly said.

'Sorry ser, but I don't go inter Wracktown for anyone's money, beggin' yer pardon. Ain't safe.'

Gilly snorted. 'Between my blade and your whip, we can surely see off any cutpurses or petty rogues.'

The driver shook his head. 'Far worse than them down there, ser. I'll not be going.'

Seeing that he was adamant, Gilly shrugged, climbed out and paid him a generous quarter-crown. The driver gave a bleak smile and tipped his disreputable hat.

'Mind yer step in there, ser,' he said. 'And be wary of the waters.'

The horse and trap wheeled round and headed back towards Eastbank. Gilly turned and trotted down the ramp, careful to avoid a hole in the heavy planking at the foot of the slope, an arm's-length gap from which a watery sloshing and a rank seaweed stench emanated.

The other carriage had slipped out of sight but he determined to follow in any case and headed towards where he had last espied it. This took him along a wharfside caught in perpetual shadow between the jumble of ancient, refashioned ships and the high wall of wood and stone that marked the main boundary between Wracktown and the rest of the Bridges district. Along the bottom of the great wall was a variety of shacks and lean-tos, a few being oddly elaborate with tiny upper floors, windows and flues. Most, however, were merely rough and squalid, their inhabitants looking starving and broken.

Mother's name! he thought. *There was none of this when I was last here . . .*

Between a couple of sturdier hovels someone had built a shrine out of crates, a shabby wooden alcove with shelves that were cluttered with little carvings of animals, symbols scrawled on scraps of parchment, ivory leaves inscribed with prayers and hymns, and the puddled remains of votive candles. But since it was open to the sky, everything was wet from the rain, including a solitary statuette of the Earthmother carved from pale draelwood. It was about two feet tall, showing the goddess as the sorrowful soother of pain. Someone had painted red tears leaking from her eyes, and someone else had tried to scrub them out. But the ink had soaked too far into the wood for that, and to Gilly a figurine of the Earthmother weeping bloody tears seemed somehow grimly apt to this place.

'Buy lights for t'Lady, milord?'

A hunched and ragged beggar proffered a tray bearing a handful of green, stubby candles. The beggar smiled fixedly through an unkempt beard while his pungent, unwashed odour assailed Gilly's nose.

'Not at the moment,' he replied. 'But I might have a couple later, if you're still here.'

At this the beggar gave a cackling laugh which quickly turned into a raw moist cough that made Gilly wince.

'Y'should buy 'em now, m'lord,' he said. 'You might not come back this way . . .'

Chuckling, the candleseller shuffled off into into one of the dim hovels. Gilly shook his head and strode on, glancing warily about him.

Soon he came to a good-sized opening between two of the ancient hulks. Most of the gaps he had seen were narrow, sometimes no more than a cramped doorway leading into some enclosed warren of stuffy passages and odd-shaped rooms. This opening was formed by a large gantry linking the two ships, and was easily wide enough for the carriage that stood empty and motionless some distance along the boardwalk.

He passed a few locals as he strolled along: washerwomen, some old fathers gathered around a copper flagon steaming over a brazier, a yawning stall owner, and a few hard-faced youths lounging by the way. All watched him pass by, cold eyes taking in the details of his fine garments, but he stared back with a sneering half-smile that brought uncertainty to their features. Unhindered, he walked on.

At the abandoned carriage, two children were feeding oats and roots to the horse still waiting in harness, but when he seemed about to speak to them they dashed off past him. To the left was the near-vertical hull of a large vessel, a former cargo dromond perhaps, its planks gone green and black with mould, gaps and holes sprouting weeds and seedlings. To the right was the half-sunken ruin of a smaller ship, canted noticeably away from the boardwalk with a gantry sloping up to a dark doorway cut crudely into the hull's curve. Since the broadwalk ended several yards further on, broken and slanting into the water, the gantry seemed the most likely route to take. Drawing his sword, he started up it.

Beyond the door was a narrow companionway stretching off into pitch black on either side while before him a wooden ladder led up to an open hatch and grey sky. He sheathed his blade, put one foot on the bottom rung then froze, breath held as he listened to the darkness.

A faint scratching came to him, like rat claws. A thud, a gasp, a heavy splash from what seemed to be further down. A dread chill went through Gilly and he quickly climbed towards daylight.

His fingertips found the woodwork damp and gritty to the touch as he pulled himself up on to a sloping deck, bared his sword again and looked around him. There seemed to be no trace of anyone, just the empty deck with its shattered stump of a mast and a ravaged bridge house amidships. There were signs that other buildings, huts or the like, had once sat on this deck but they had been ripped up and discarded quite recently. Smashed timbers, rotting rope and other debris had gathered along the foot of the slanted deck and swathes of twisted netting hung over the side.

'Greetings,' said a calm voice from somewhere behind him. 'You appear to be lost.'

Tense readiness rushed through him as he turned and stepped up to the bulwark. Across on the next ship was Coireg Mazaret, standing barefoot on the raised prow and regarding Gilly with icy interest.

'Nay, ser,' Gilly said. 'I believe that I have arrived at the right place.'

'By following me, it would appear.' The other man shrugged. 'No matter . . .'

Then to Gilly's astonishment, he sprang into the air in a long leap that carried him across the intervening distance in an arc of effortless ease. He landed lightly and perfectly on the hulk's raised peak, legs slightly bent, arms loose at his sides, and Gilly noticed that a faint green nimbus clung to him.

Gilly grimaced. *More than a hint of sorcery to this one*, he thought. On impulse, he resheathed his sword and sauntered casually along to the bows. Pausing a few feet away from the prow, he leaned against the bulwark, folded his arms and looked up.

'Pray tell me, good ser,' he said. 'Just who are you?'

The face of Coireg Mazaret, every pore and crease tinged with vibrant emerald, stared down, the eyes full of a usurping presence. Gilly ignored the penetrating gaze and went on.

'You see, I recognise your form and face, but I know that another's thoughts move behind those eyes. You are not Coireg Mazaret, thus I am curious to know who you are.'

The possessed man uttered a quiet laugh. 'Such boldness should not go unrewarded. Very well, child of earth, know that my name is Crevalcor of the First-Woken.'

'The First-Woken.'

A nod. 'After the Lord of Twilight raised up the Daemonkind from the Great Lake of the Night, he knew that he would need other servants to aid him in the coming struggle against the other two gods, the forsworn ones. Dawn-Eagle and Sun-Tiger were their aspects then and all the tribes across this land and others bowed down before them. Only among outcasts and dissenters did the Prince of Dusk find those who would listen, those like myself.'

A melancholy note crept into his voice. 'He woke us to the presence of the Wellsource and opened our minds to its powers. By his hand he taught us, rewarded us, and even punished us, and to us fell the same tasks when others turned to his banner. We helped in the construction of fortresses to which Gorla and Keshada were no more than outposts, and commanded armies vaster than all the Khatrimantine Empire's combined.'

'I can only assume that this was a very long time ago.'

'Several ages have come and gone since then,' Crevalcor said. 'What was land now lies below the waves, and farms and forests garb ancient seabeds. And who is to say that such tumult may not occur again?'

'Indeed,' Gilly said, wrinkling his nose at the reek of decay that seeped up from the wreck. 'Sadly my curiosity is scarcely whetted, ser Crevalcor. You were one of the Lord of Twilight's generals in that long-past age, yet here you are prowling alone through these rotting ships. I wonder why . . .'

'For the fulfilment of a long-held purpose,' said Crevalcor, his eyes shining. 'I saw the many-towered citadel of Jagreag topple and crash, and the Dusktide phalanxes falter before the For-swearers' horde on the Plains of Kogil. I fought and wept and fought for days on those fields of slaughter till at last I too fell. For a timeless time my spirit wandered in the jungles of the Earthmother's under-realm and drifted down its limitless rivers, but I could never be washed clean of my devotion and purpose.

'Then came the moment for which I had hopelessly wished down long eras, the obliteration of the Fathertree and the destruction of the Rootpower. That mighty death reverberated throughout the Earthmother's realm, and her cry of grief was pleasing to hear. It seemed quite soon after that the Shadowkings sought out my spirit and raised me up into this useful vessel.' He glanced down at his body and smiled.

Gilly listened and shivered in the stinking, deepening cold, knowing that he faced ancient, implacable sorcery. *I could make a run for the hatch*, he thought, letting his hand slip down to grasp his sword's hilt. *Or dive over the side . . .*

'A futile plan,' Crevalcor said. 'For I do not prowl alone . . .'

All Gilly heard was a faint creak from behind him but it was enough. He leaped forward onto his left foot while swiftly drawing his sword, then swung it to the right and round in a savage disembowelling slash. The blade hacked into the side of his assailant and lodged there. Gilly's fury at this turned instantly to horror as he beheld the creature he fought.

He had listened to Alael speak of the walking dead they fought in the battle in Oumetra, and had heard a few of Mazaret's men whisper tales of unquiet graves in the wastes of Khatris. Neither could have prepared him for this. Standing in rivulets of water, the cadaver still wore flesh and garments in places, dripping, rotten coverings encrusted with sand and broken shells. Skeletal hands twitched at its sides while a sickly hot green radiance flickered around exposed joints and in the vacant eye sockets.

Gilly wrenched his sword free and retreated down the sloping deck. The cadaver watched him then turned to Crevalcor, ruined throat straining to form words.

'. . . drown him . . . for you . . . drink from him . . .'

'No, captain, I want him taken prisoner to keep your brothers under control.'

Other mouldering revenants were emerging from the hatches, pulling themselves up on to the deck or lurching out from the bridge, some carrying ropes. As he watched the dead converge Gilly heard splashing in the water and looked over the side to see more of them clambering up the seaweed-choked nets.

Gilly dashed madly back up the deck, kicked the legs from under one pursuer who came too close and hewed the arm from another. He reached the bulwark and even had one leg slung over it before a thrown rope mesh tangled itself about head and arms, and bony hands hauled him back. His blade was torn from his grasp and once he was firmly bound he was dragged over to sprawl at the feet of Crevalcor. The sodden rope of the mesh had rasped across Gilly's mouth, pushing past his lips until he turned his head aside. The taste was vile.

The ancient sorcerer smiled at him. 'My Source-sense knows of you, so I am sure that you will have much to tell me.'

'Might be less than you think,' Gilly said, despair honing his wit. 'A few songs about the ladies of Choraya and a recipe for Falador game stew, that's about it.'

'Yes, I'm sure you will amuse me greatly before we have it all.' He turned to the cadaverous captain. 'Soon the warblood will be spilled and we shall cast off. Do those we leave behind know what to do?'

'Yes, my lor'. . .'

The captain turned to his crew and grunted wordless orders at them. As most of them descended the sloping deck and climbed over the side, Crevalcor spoke to Gilly.

'Most of them were sailors on these broken ships. It was little effort to wake them from their watery tombs.'

A deep groan came from within the vessel and the deck under Gilly shuddered. The sound of splitting wood came from the stern. He felt the entire hulk lurch as it began to right itself. Struggling into a half-sitting position he saw the ramshackle structures and roofs on either side sliding sternwards. They were heading out to the inlet that led to the sea.

Without oars or sails, Gilly thought dizzily. *And a hull punched with more holes than my socks . . .*

Shouts came from the decrepit jetty as onlookers gathered, but their voices soon faded. Other sounds reached Gilly's ears, a thrashing surging din that emanated from a nearby cargo hatch, and in his mind's eye he pictured torrents of water gushing through splinter-edged gaps in the hull . . .

A ship of the damned, he thought with grim relish.

'A ship of sorcery, child of earth,' Crevalcor said. 'Driven by my will, my unwavering purpose.' He turned to look ahead with a breeze ruffling his hair and an emerald aura shifting about him.

'A ship of twilight!'

Chapter Twelve

Fever dreams full of fire,
Crash on to the shores of sleep,
And seep steadily out,
To set the day ablaze.

Jedhessa Gant, *Dreams In The Red Chamber*, 2, vi

Even as the ravaged wreck was carrying Gilly Cordale out to sea, the Archmage Bardow was standing on a frosty balcony near the top of the High Spire, watching a group of horsemen ride away from the Shield Gate and the snow-shrouded walls of the city. From the great audience chamber through the arch behind him came the sound of hammer chisels but his thoughts were wholly on the meeting that would shortly take place out at the rebuilt fort. As soon as Yasgur arrived.

The stratagem offered up by the Mage Council had been accepted by the High Conclave with surprisingly little resistance, almost as if everyone knew that launching an attack would be as hazardous as inaction. Bardow had spent most of that day advising on the gathering of materials and volunteers, and the assigning of knights from the Order of the Fathertree under Yarram. The small caravan had then set out in the icy late afternoon to arrive at the old smugglers' ridge by sundown. By evening, he knew, a flagpole would have been erected along with several tents before work began on the ruined fortifications by torchlight and continued through the night.

The early morning brought a steady snowfall and a masked

messenger from one of the enemy bastions to propose a meeting of the opposing commanders before noon.

'And to converse with the honoured Archmage Bardow too,' the messenger had said. 'Such is my master's request.'

'I shall convey your words to my Lord Regent,' had been Yarram's stiff reply.

Recalling the verbal report brought by one of Yarram's serjeants, Bardow smiled bleakly. *The enemy are so eager to learn what lies behind our apparent confidence, that they're almost daring me to meet them face to face*, he thought. *Which, of course, is out of the question.*

Instead, the Shadowkings or their underlings would have to deal with Yasgur, with Atroc and Yarram on hand as useful distractions. Without any mages to take the measure of, the enemy would be forced to speculate on the nature and scale of the powers ranged against them. And in the light of the Earthmother's intervention during the last battle, the Shadowkings might be inclined to be more cautious.

At least we can hope they will, he thought. *We need more time . . .*

There were footsteps behind him and he looked round to see Tauric, alone and garbed in a long, mauve fur-collared cloak.

'Greetings, majesty,' he said with a slight bow.

'Archmage,' was Tauric's taciturn reply.

Warily silent, Bardow watched as the young Emperor came out on to the balcony and rested gloved hands on the wooden balustrade.

After a moment, Bardow said, 'How is your metal arm, majesty? I see that you're wearing a leather sleeve over it – does the cold affect it at all?'

Tauric frowned and his left hand went to his right elbow. 'Sometimes it aches at the join,' he said. 'And I have to unstrap it for a short while.' He gave Bardow a sharp look. 'But it is only a minor discomfort, not unlike the everyday nuisances that any knight or soldier has to endure.'

Bardow resisted the impulse to sigh heavily. When Yarram's officer had brought the news of the enemy's meeting offer, Tauric staged a dramatic confrontation with Bardow and Yasgur, while accompanied by about a dozen of his White Companions. He had demanded that he and some of his Companions be allowed to ride out with Yasgur to the rebuilt fort. It was his right as Emperor, he insisted, to defy those who had brought death and violation to his realm. It was his duty, he went on, to see and know the faces of those who would eventually be brought to account for their vile deeds. All this was proclaimed passionately while his Companions provided a boisterous supporting chorus which quickly wore away Yasgur's already frayed patience. Voices were raised, which Bardow only subdued by persuading Yasgur to wait in the next chamber.

Unfortunately, Tauric was a youth forced into the mould of a man, forced to adopt the outward appearance of a man while still lacking the experience and pragmatic good sense that made an effective ruler. And as he regarded Tauric now, still brooding over that earlier humiliating blow to his pride and what he saw as his duty, Bardow braced himself for another outburst of anger and frustration. Yet the outburst never came. The young Emperor turned his morose features away from Bardow to stare out over the white-blanketed lands beyond the city walls. The ringing of the stonemasons' hammers from within had ceased and a chill stillness held sway.

'I feel useless,' Tauric murmured. 'Useless and caged.'

'I've felt that way for most of the last sixteen years,' Bardow said. 'And I feel little different now, if truth be told.'

Tauric looked shocked. 'You? Useless? How could that be?'

'Because we are weak and vulnerable, majesty. All that we have gained has been a consequence of divisions among the Shadowkings and the Earthmother's unforeseen manifestation.' The Archmage leaned on the balustrade. 'Our goddess, however, seems to follow her own whim in these matters. Neither the appearance of Gorla and Keshada, nor Mazaret's capture, have provoked the slightest response from her. No visions in the temple, not a dream, not a whisper nor the vaguest omen. Meanwhile, our enemies carry their plans forward with deadly precision and the only things holding them back are the Crystal Eye and this precarious stratagem on which we've embarked.'

Tauric swallowed, his expression full of dismay. 'You make our situation sound desperate.'

Bardow paused and reined in his thoughts, suddenly aware of how angry and unguarded he had been.

'Desperate, yes,' he admitted. 'But not hopeless. You are a living source of hope for this city and all the lands that we liberated. Strength comes from the knowledge that you are alive and well – it was your father's death combined with the destruction of the Rootpower that so quickly broke the Empire. If he had lived, events might have turned out differently.'

Tauric looked back out at the wintry fields with burning, determined eyes. 'I've been thinking about abdicating the throne,' he said evenly. 'I would then be free to take up arms and play a part in the struggle.'

Bardow regarded him a moment, suddenly fearful. 'Alael would never accept the crown,' he said.

'I know, and I know that I could never relinquish my responsibilities so easily.' He looked down at his hands. 'But if only there were some way for me . . . Tell me, are you certain that the Rootpower is completely gone?'

Bardow gave a hollow laugh. 'I can assure you, majesty, that it is utterly extinguished.'

Tauric clasped his hand. 'I have heard it said that the Rootpower still exists, that only the gateway to it through the Fathertree has been closed to us. Could that be possible?'

'A fanciful notion, your majesty, nothing more,' Bardow said, curious at this line of query. 'There is no evidence that would support such an idea.' *And where, I wonder, did you hear of it?*

Sighing, the young Emperor ran his real fingers through his hair. 'And thus no explanations,' he said 'A great pity. I have such strange and uneasy dreams – sometimes, I am back in Oumetra, riding through deserted streets, searching for Alael and Lord Mazaret, but there's no one there and the sun gradually turns black, plunging everything into night.' He turned to Bardow with anguished eyes. 'Sometimes I am climbing a vast tree whose every trunk and branch is composed of the bodies of people, all hard and grey, yet I can feel their pain with every handhold as I climb and search, for what I'm not certain.'

Bardow smiled faintly. 'That one requires little interpretation, your majesty. Duty cannot be measured with rule or scale but it has a very real weight.'

'Exactly, Archmage,' Tauric said, straightening. 'I have responsibilities to shoulder and a duty to fulfil.' He stared out at the enemy's citadels. 'In whatever way I can.'

He turned to leave, pausing in the archway. 'Would you inform me when Yasgur returns?'

'Indeed I shall, majesty.'

'And tell me, do any of the palace stewards own a big black dog?'

'Not to my knowledge, sire,' Bardow said. 'Why do you ask?'

Tauric shrugged. 'I've seen one prowling through the gardens these last few nights, and thought I saw it in the great hall early this morning.'

Bardow shook his head. 'I know that a couple of the coachmen and one of the ostlers have dogs, but they're all brown shorthairs from the same brood. But I shall make enquiries on this matter, majesty.'

'My thanks, Archmage. Till later.'

And he was gone, leaving Bardow still wondering what Tauric meant by 'a duty to fulfil'.

Upon a wooden platform behind a partly rebuilt wall, Atroc huddled in his skins against the knifing cold. Shivering beneath this cruel grey sky while waiting for Yasgur was, he thought, the duty for a younger man. About two hundred yards north of the ridge, ten riders from the direction of Gorla had camped on a wooded knoll near a fire-gutted farmhouse. He stared gloomily out at them but at this distance all he could tell was that all wore dark, hooded cloaks, and one held a large, draped banner braced against a stump. This, he knew, would be a covered battle standard of some sort. Brought to truce talks, it was nothing more than a gesture of arrogance by the side that believed itself certain of victory.

He snorted. *Then why are you not already in Besh-Darok, O children of fear?* he thought. *Or have your own fears become our allies?*

Beside him stood Yarram, the new Lord Commander of the knights of the Fathertree Order, as dour and unbending a warrior as any Atroc had encountered in his life. He knew that the man's grimness was in part due to the loss of Lord Regent Mazaret, but he could not resist testing that impassive exterior to see what lay beneath.

'Have you always been a warrior, friend Yarram?' he said.

The wiry, grey-haired knight glanced darkly at him. 'Is this more of your impolite badgering, ser? Perhaps you should forage in someone else's thoughts.'

Atroc shrugged. 'Hmph. Impolite, eh? Nay, ser, curiosity goads me into asking such questions, the desire to know what twists and turns of fate have brought you to this cold and dangerous place.'

'It is none of your business, ser.'

'This is so.'

Yarram breathed in deeply and cleared his throat. 'My family were originally from Sejeend and my mother and father were both weavers. I would have been one too, but my parents died in a loomhouse fire and I decided to join the Imperial militia.'

'Ah, a weaver,' Atroc said. 'A noble trade. Perhaps you could make some nice socks for my cold feet, eh?'

A thin smile cracked Yarram's reserve. 'Should we live through this, ser, I'll make you a damned shirt and trews. And what of you? Have you always been a seer?'

'Always.'

'Could you have ever been anything else, something productive perhaps?'

Atroc smiled at the jibe, pleased by Yarram's table-turning. 'From birth it was written on my skull that my eyes would see more than others – "We sleep by the Door of Dreams/We hold to the old ways/Blood cast into fire puts fire in the blood. . ."' He nodded to himself, recalling the ancient words, then looked at a confused Yarram. 'We are the blood, Yarram,' he said. 'You and I and Bardow and Yasgur and our young Emperor, everyone under our banners – we shall all soon be cast into the fire—'

He broke off as a commotion came from the other side of the half-made fort, the thud of horses hoofs drawing near. Yasgur had arrived.

By the time Atroc and Yarram had descended from the crude

parapet, Yasgur and his officers had dismounted and were entering the fort. The Lord Regent wore a long black cloak edged with bear fur, over a silvered breastplate chased with the tree-and-crown device of Besh-Darok. His curly black hair had been trimmed and oiled, and on his forehead was a bronze circlet adorned with a single blue stone.

As he approached he looked at Atroc.

'So, are we in the fire yet, old one?'

Atroc grinned. 'Not yet, my prince, but the flames grow hot.'

Yasgur smiled and as he turned to Yarram, a lookout shouted, ''Ware riders!'

'I want both of you by my side,' Yasgur said to Atroc and Yarram. 'I may wish either or both of you to play a part – you will know when.'

An open-fronted tent had been been rigged against one of the fort's original walls, and Atroc and Yarram exchanged a look as they followed the Lord Regent under its shelter. The opening faced along the length of the old smugglers' ridge and Atroc curled his lip in contempt as the ten hooded riders came into view, urging their mounts up the slope's long, narrow trail. Once up on the rise they drew to a halt some way along, four of them dismounting. One of these spoke to the standard bearer, then all four walked across the icy ground, faces still hidden by their cowls. At the tent three waited outside while the fourth, who was the tallest, stepped under the canopy and threw back his hood. Atroc gaped, and heard Yasgur take a swift intake of breath.

Byrnak! – Here? were his first thoughts. Then realisation struck. This was the man who had emerged from Gorla to confront Mazaret mere days ago . . .

'I am named Azurech,' the man said to Yasgur. His black hair was long and braided, his teeth were even and stained red, and the white vapour of his breath fumed about him. 'Once chieftain of the Whiteclaw clan, but now the voice of the Shadowking Byrnak. With his likeness I offer greetings and friendship to all who would pledge their allegiance to the Shadowkings. I also bring the promise of destruction and unrelenting slaughter to all who oppose us. Think on this with care.'

'By what right do your masters invade this domain?' Yasgur said abruptly.

'By the most ancient right of the Lord of Twilight who with his bride ruled all these lands and others in the dawn of the world, before the usurper came. But now a new crown shall rule and a new nobility shall know glory and the fruits of loyalty.'

Yasgur glanced at Atroc who smiled and cleared his throat.

'Whiteclaw clan, eh?' he said. 'Weren't they settled in northern Honjir?'

But Azurech ignored him. 'Yasgur, I bear a message from your fellow chieftains, Welgarak and Gordag. They say, "Why have you betrayed your people, Yasgur Firespear? Return to the Host, friend. Repudiate these worshippers of a dead god for it is not yet too late. The clans are waiting to rally to the son of Hegroun's banner and sweep away the past."' Azurech's smile was like a dagger aimed at Yasgur. 'Do you have an answer?'

'Only this – in the last battle for my city, the clans lost a great throng of warriors as well as many chieftains.' Yasgur stared back. 'I don't believe that you have the army which can take those walls.'

Azurech met the Lord Regent's gaze with open amusement.

'Your ignorance is profound, Yasgur. The people of Yularia and Anghatan flock joyously to my masters' banners. Their armies swell by the day and shall soon be sufficient to darken all this countryside with their numbers.'

'Then why, I wonder, were you buying slaves stolen from refugee camps in southern Khatris?' Atroc said. 'Perhaps this flocking is not joyous, eh?'

For the first time Azurech looked at Atroc, who felt satisfaction at the fury that shone from those eyes.

'I had hoped to confer with the Archmage Bardow,' he said. 'I do not need to waste my time with a petty dowser.'

'You honour me,' Atroc said. 'I shall wear your contempt like a scar of honour.'

The man with Byrnak's face turned back to Yasgur. 'We do not require your answer now. Take stock of your situation, ponder the consequences of your actions, and if by dawn tomorrow you agree to our demands, fly this from your topmost tower.'

From within his grey robe he took a folded wad of cloth. A flick of the wrist and it unfurled into a large square banner of vivid green, its device a rayed golden sun impaled on an upturned black sword set. Carefully, Azurech hung the banner over a crook in the tent's central pole then turned to the three hooded figures still waiting outside.

'If you will not listen to my words,' he said, beckoning two of them into the tent. 'Then heed some more familiar voices.'

Atroc steeled himself as two cowls were pushed back to reveal the faces of Ikarno Mazaret and the woman he had confronted at the gates of Gorla, the one named Suviel.

They were only rivenshades of the original people, one captured and one dead, but knowing that did not make this sight any easier to bear. Their skin and hair were a chalky white and their eyes were pale grey, calm and unblinking. Their breath came in streams of vapour so thin it was as if they were themselves cold to the bone.

'You should listen to him,' said the Suviel rivenshade. 'Whatever weapons you have, be they sorcerous or iron and wood, they just will not be enough.'

'It's true,' said the one with Mazaret's face. 'I have been inside both of the citadels and seen the armies quartered there. Valour and skill would be of little use against such a host,'

There was curious hollowness in their voices and as Atroc listened he understood the aim of this puppet show. Rather than trying to persuade, it was saying, 'Look – this is what we have done to your best and bravest. What hope is there for the rest of you?'

'A great change is coming,' the Suviel rivenshade said.

'All the realms will flow into one another,' said the Mazaret, 'and from it will arise a world of enchantment and unsurpassable beauty.'

'You could decide to be part of what is to come,' the Suviel said. 'Or . . .'

She shrugged and glanced at Azurech who nodded at her, smiling. An icy draught passed through the tent and, as the rivenshades pulled their hoods back up, Azurech looked to Yasgur and the others with a malign satisfaction. But before he could open his mouth, Yasgur suddenly spoke.

'You will not take Besh-Darok easily – every yard of ground, every building, every street will be watered with the blood of your troops should you come against us,' he said.

'This we know,' Azurech said. 'From our encompassing walls to the shoreline, these miles of fields and farmlands shall become a floodplain of death and havoc if we ride to the attack. But you can prevent that happening, Yasgur Firespear.'

Turning, he stepped outside and laid one hand on the shoulder of the fourth and thus far unhooded member of the group.

'I leave you with this final argument,' he said, then he and the two rivenshades were walking away, returning to their horses, watched by every soldier and officer in the fort. The fourth person stood unmoving, cowled head slightly bowed, arms crossed with hands buried in long sleeves. Atroc frowned and approached the stranger who, he realised, was just visibly trembling.

'Who are you?' he said warily, aware of Azurech and his companions, now remounted and trotting down the path from the ridge. Then Atroc noticed something about the silent stranger which made his skin prickle.

'Has he said anything, old man?' said Yasgur, emerging from the tent with Yarram at his side.

'Wait, my prince!' Atroc flung out one hand to the Lord Regent who halted abruptly. 'There is black evil afoot here . . .'

Everyone froze, still upon the ground, and every eye was fixed on Atroc as he reached out and pushed back the stranger's hood.

It was a man, his head utterly hairless. He stared fearfully at something unseen and his scalp and face were beaded with perspiration. His head was quivering and Atroc watched the sweat trickle down from brow to jaw to chin, there forming droplets.

'What is your name, ser?' Atroc said quietly. 'Where are you from?'

The man's head jerked up, burning eyes regarding Atroc.

'Search . . . Domas said search for . . . Deathless . . .' The gaze drifted, as if seeing memories. 'Caught me, though . . . no longer Qael . . . I am . . . I am . . .' Veins stood out on his skull as he drew a deep breath and bellowed, 'Warblood!'

One hand came out from the enveloping sleeves bearing a

wickedly curved knife. Atroc cried out and lurched away, lost
his footing and sprawled on the ground, yet the knife went up
to the man's own throat. The cut was swift and unerring but it
was not blood that gushed forth, but liquid, silver fire.

It poured down his chest and immediately the front of his robes
was ablaze. There were curses and gasps of horror from all who
watched, and Atroc stared, dumbfounded, as the fiery blood kept
coming and enveloped the man in a raging shroud of flame.

Yet he seemed unharmed – his skin did not blister and crack, nor
were his eyes seared from their sockets. He just stood and stared and
shook violently as if in the grip of a terrible ague. Then he sank to
his knees with a web of bright lines spreading across his head and
face like fractures. Atroc began to back away as the man raised his
pain-wracked face to the sky with an agonised moan coming from
between clenched teeth.

Then, unexpectedly, Yarram stepped forward with sword bared
and before Atroc could speak, he hacked the man's head off with
a single blow. The fiery body went out like a snuffed candle and
toppled over to lie motionless. The still-burning head Yarram neatly
flipped away with the tip of his sword, and to everyone's surprise it
split open in a flaming coruscation even as it spun through the air.

'Friend Yarram,' Atroc said hoarsely, getting to his feet. 'What
made you act? How did you know—'

'I knew nothing, seer.' The Lord Commander's face was a picture
of anger and tiredness. 'I found it . . . hard to bear seeing my Lord
Mazaret and his lady dishonoured so by that filth Azurech. Then
they left this poor wretch behind to die before our eyes . . . I had
to put him out of his misery.'

'Your heart is good, ser,' said Yasgur who came to stand near the
smoking, headless corpse. 'You've kept some of us from death this
day.' He looked at Atroc. 'Are you familiar with this, old man? Is
it an artifice of war from some bygone age?'

Atroc shook his head. 'No, my prince. This is a newly-made
weapon.'

Yasgur glared down at the charred body. 'I had feared as much.
Which leads me to wonder how many others like him are already
in the city.'

Atroc met his master's uneasy gaze with growing alarm as the implications began to dawn.

In an elevated alcove overlooking the broad, ceremonial corridor, Keren sat with the mage Medwin and Cordmaster Doreth, watching the main body of delegates file into the Keelcourt. The majority of them were anxious, worried-looking Scallowmen while the rest were angry or sullen Islesmen captains from the rebel ship-clans, plainly resentful at being here. Only the High Chief Hevrin seemed at ease, his steady gaze surveying the passageway and the balconies to either side. For a moment his eyes met hers, startling her out of her preoccupied thought. Then he was past, striding through the main doors.

As the last of them crossed the threshold, a pair of aftmasters pulled on the heavy, ponderous doors which swung shut with a solid thud.

'He's late,' Medwin murmured, voice low and tense.

'Patience, good ser,' said Cordmaster Doreth, a pudgy man in his forties. 'He will be here.'

It was the merchant Yared Hevrin they referred to, but Keren's thoughts were centred on Gilly. It was over an hour since he had gone haring off after someone who might have been Ikarno Mazaret's brother. At the time she had recounted Gilly's suspicions to Medwin and Golwyth, and the master trader offered to send some of his men off in search of the hunter and his quarry, and Medwin gratefully accepted. But thus far there had been no sign of either Golwyth or Gilly, nor any news.

Apart from some muffled voices filtering through from the Keelcourt, the high-walled corridor was strangely peaceful. Keren could just hear the sound of flutes from down in the main hall as she watched a House attendant on the opposite balcony carefully refilling one of the ceiling oil lamps. On either side a series of banded poles were bolted to massive roof beams and the oil lamps moved to and fro on intricate runners.

Approaching footsteps broke into her reverie and she turned. What she had taken to be a wall hanging at one end of the balcony was bunched over to one side, revealing an open archway. The newcomer came into the light and leaned on the table where they sat. It was Yared Hevrin.

'My profoundest apologies, sers!' he said with a rueful smile. 'I was forced to take a different route to the High House and once here decided to seek you out via the Foremasters' office.'

Grinning, Medwin clasped hand, with him. 'Well met, ser Hevrin. And was the overland passage fortuitous?'

'It was, ser mage. Without a doubt.'

Medwin nodded and sat back, seeming to Keren both satisfied and relieved. Hevrin smiled at Doreth and exchanged greetings, then looked straight at Keren. 'Your gown is most comely, Lady Keren – you wear it as naturally as a rider's garb.'

'You are most kind,' Keren said, annoyed at feeling a rush of heat to her face.

'Have you had that sagasong translated since we last spoke?' he went on.

'I brought a copy of it with me, ser,' she said. 'But have not been able to have such a task undertaken, as yet. I did leave the book with a friend in Besh-Darok before leaving – perhaps she has been more fortunate than I.'

Hevrin frowned slightly. 'I see. I also took a copy of it before gifting it to you, and purely by chance we encountered during our journey to Dalbar a party of scholars returning to Oumetra. One was a Master of Parlance who very kindly rendered it into Khatrian for me, and pointed out some oddities. It makes for interesting . . .' He smiled. 'But we can talk on that at length later, once we've seen this anger-and-thunder performance through.'

Everyone rose and followed him along to the archway. Keren paused to look back down at the corridor but saw no one, and went with the rest.

Beyond the curtained entrance was a curved, narrow passage between the main outer wall of the Keelcourt and the high clothscreen back of the tiered seating. Hevrin showed them to a balustraded staircase which sloped up to the rearmost seats.

'That is where guests and visitors can sit and watch,' he told Keren and Medwin quietly. 'While you find yourselves places, I must enter the Court by another door. Till later.'

Hevrin and Cordmaster Doreth continued along the passage and out of sight round the curve. Keren followed Medwin up carpeted steps to find seats on a long, hard bench from where she could survey the entire Keelcourt. The chamber itself was oval-shaped but the tiers of seats were arranged in two long, curved blocks facing each other with a small third block set at one end. In front of that was a dais with an elaborate carven pedestal from where speakers could address the assembly.

All of which contributed to the appearance of a great open ship. At the other end, standing over the court's double doors, was a large stone statue of a bearded, bare-chested man holding a gnarled staff in one hand and a cluster of sea creatures in the other. Keren wondered if it was meant to be a representation of the Fathertree, perhaps in his sea-dwelling aspect. She would ask Yared Hevrin later, once the matter of Gilly was resolved.

The atmosphere in the packed chamber was very tense. There were other conversations and arguments going on around the tiers, and the man speaking from the dais was being constantly interrupted from all sides. There seemed to be different factions among the representatives but from where Keren sat, at the top halfway along one of the side tiers, the only clearly-defined one consisted of the Islesmen and their leader, the Hevrin. He sat on one of the bottom benches near the dais, seemingly motionless, his feet planted apart, his big hands resting on his knees.

A roar went up when Yared Hevrin entered by the ceremonial door in the corner by the rear of the dais. He acknowledged the welcome and shook a few hands before assuming a seat almost directly opposite his cousin, the chieftain. The speaker tried to continue but a rising tide of barracking forced him to conclude and surrender the floor of the Keelcourt. There were more cheers as Yared Hevrin rose and stepped up to the pedestal. The din faded into silence as he sombrely surveyed the ranks of faces on either side.

He began to speak, hearkening back to the foundation of Scallow more than a thousand years before when the tyrant King Dahorg was toppled by a coalition of ship clans. Yared went on to speak of the sixteen-year-long oppression at the hands of the Mogaun and

the sorcerous Acolytes of Twilight, and how a dauntless alliance of
knights and forest fighters blessed by the Earthmother had routed
the enemy horde.

'Yet the dread Shadowkings have not been defeated,' he said.
'Even as I speak, their forces gather around the city of Besh-Darok,
their sorcery darker and more deadly, their warriors as numerous
as grains of sand upon the beach. We should be at the side of the
defenders, ready to fight, but instead our ships sit at anchor, waiting
for the ship-clans of the Isles to come against us. We should cease
this wasteful and pointless conflict . . .'

Keren did not see any signal given, but suddenly the Hevrin's
captains began rising one by one from their seats and walking calmly
out of the chamber. Angry voices were raised at such a stark affront
and Yared Hevrin faltered in his delivery.

'Medwin,' she said. 'Why are they doing this?'

'I'm not sure,' he said, grim-faced. 'These staged interruptions
are usually planned in advance, but why would the Hevrin agree
to come here only to walk out?'

Eventually Yared fell silent, his face full of anger and confusion,
and as the last dissenter strode from the Keelcourt, the Hevrin
himself got to his feet. Leisurely, he crossed the dais and halted
about an arm's length from Yared Hevrin. For a moment, the
cousins glared at each other.

'Why have you sent your men away?' Yared said. 'Call them
back that we can continue this—'

'You kept your name.'

The statement stopped Yared in mid-sentence.

'My . . . name?'

'The family name which came down from our fathers' father,
Agandrik, who was the Hevrin of Hevrin Sept in his day. When
you broke with the sept years ago and went to live in another
land, little was thought of it. But after the Mogaun were eradicated
from these shores you began writing to many chiefs and notables,
advocating the elevation of the so-called land- and trader-clans to
seats in this hallowed chamber. And every letter you signed with
my grandfather's family name, sullying it.'

Yared's gaze was cold. 'Now I see – you want me to give up

the name of my line. That is a custom long out of use, and I will
not bow to it.'

The chieftain glanced around the chamber, at all the faces
watching, and Keren saw him smile and turn back.

'I am the Hevrin of Hevrin Sept and I command you to either
recant all the poison you have uttered and rejoin the Sept under
burden of penance, or give up the name Hevrin for ever.'

Unyielding, Yared folded his arms. ' I shall do neither.'

At this, the Hevrin turned to face the five Cordmasters in their
ornate chairs overlooking the speaker's dais.

'As High Chieftain of Hevrin Sept, I demand restitution for
wounds inflicted by this man, who refuses to renounce my sept
name. Do any here deny me this right?'

As the Cordmasters leaned closer to consider, a hubbub of
disbelief and anger filled the Keelcourt and Keren could see that
Yared looked worried.

'What does that mean?' she asked Medwin.

The mage shrugged. 'Money or belongings, or some form of
servitude, perhaps . . .'

The Cordmasters seemed to reach a decision and the whole
Keelcourt fell silent as their spokesman looked down at the Hevrin
Chieftain and nodded once.

'State the manner of your restitution.'

What happened next took place so quickly that Keren almost
missed it. Off to the side, Yared Hevrin had turned to beckon
to someone on the front benches and never saw the chieftain's
savage lunge. A powerful left arm snaked round Yared, across his
chest to grasp his right shoulder while the other hand took hold
of his head. There was a wrenching twist, the body turning one
way and the head the other . . . then there was only a lifeless,
broken-necked body slumping on to the dais with roars of fury
filling the chamber like a storm. The Hevrin just stood there,
smiling down at his cousin's corpse while outraged members leaped
up from their seats.

At that very moment, the doors of the Keelcourt were thrown
open and the Hevrin's men marched in, every one bearing a blade.
The din of shouting faded abruptly, apart from a couple of voices

which continued to rant and rave from high up in the tiers. Someone further down was weeping amid the sickening silence as the Hevrin stepped down lightly from the dais and, without a backward glance, strode out of the chamber flanked by his captains.

Keren found that she was on her feet and holding on to Medwin's arm with both hands. A few people were gathering around Yared Hevrin's body but everyone else seemed to be shocked and aimless, unable or unwilling to disperse. Keren was about to suggest that they descend when a man came running and stumbling into the chamber.

'The ships . . . in the harbour,' he gasped, chest heaving, 'All the ships are sinking!'

Chapter Thirteen

Seeds of fire and iron and pain,
Sprout within the captive throng,
Whilst deep down in the lifeless dark,
Gapes the very throat of war.

Ralgar Morth, *The Empire Of Night*, Canto xvi

Byrnak strolled slowly around the cavernous audience chamber of
Keshada Citadel, admiring the dark intricacy of its adornments.
While doing so, he listened to Azurech deliver a report from the
foot of the stepped throne dais where he waited in the company
of the commanders of Gorla and Keshada, amongst others.

'. . . and when our rivenshades spoke to Yasgur and his seer,
the fear in their eyes was their spirit fear. Already they are half-
defeated.'

Byrnak trailed his fingers over the interlocking serpent tracery
of a black iron screen which spanned the distance between two
pearl-opaque pillars. The pillars were roughly five yards apart and
the screen was half the chamber's height, about fifty yards. There
were a score of such screens spaced around the chamber, each with
its own motif, and with lamps on the pillars casting pattern shadows
in towards the throne.

'And then?' he said.

'We left the warblood sacrifice behind and rode away to watch
from a distance. They were unsuspecting almost to the end when
an officer beheaded the sacrifice. Another moment and Yasgur and
his pet would have been smoking meat.'

'A minor disappointment,' Byrnak said, gazing up at the immense relief carving in green stone of a snarling nighthunter which dominated the entire wall above the throne, and the grey-and-black floor tiles that mirrored its outline exactly. Byrnak's tour had at last brought him back to the throne dais where his own honour guard of mailed axemen waited, along with his standard bearer. He climbed only two of the dais' ten steps and considered the upturned expectant faces for a moment, then beckoned to the commanders of Gorla and Keshada. One was tall and cloak-clad, the other burly and garbed in a mismatch of leather and battered armour – both came forward and in silence went down on one knee before him.

'Is it true that you are both of the First-Woken?' Byrnak said.

'Aye, my lord.'

'Then you will know the name Crevalcor.'

'One of our brothers, Great Lord, and a potent warrior,' said the tall commander of Gorla. 'He helped build mighty Jagreag and stood against the Forswearers till the uttermost end.'

'And how does Keshada, or Gorla for that matter, compare to Jagreag? In essence, are we ready for the assault on Besh-Darok?'

The commanders exchanged a look and the burly master of Keshada gazed up with a devoted smile. 'Oh Great Lord, these citadels of ours would have been no more than meagre turrets next to the grandeur of Jagreag. Yet for this struggle they will more than suffice – Besh-Darok's walls are stout and well made and will hold us back for less than a day. Our warriors will be a raging sea tearing them down.'

The hard, confident purpose of his words sent a thrill of satisfaction through Byrnak. He turned to Azurech.

'So you have given them until dawn tomorrow to decide,' he said.

'Just so, my master.'

'Tomorrow at sunset would have been better,' Byrnak said. 'As it is, you will let the deadline approach and pass without incident until the onset of dusk, then give the warblood sign.'

Azurech's face – which was Byrnak's face – was alive with eagerness. 'Is that when we unleash our armies, master?'

'No,' he said, smiling as the eagerness changed to disappointment.

'No, for there are still unexplored dangers to be delved, too many uncertainties to be made clear.' He turned to stare across the massive chamber, seeing beyond the masonry and the thickness of the walls, southwards to the mile-distant battlements of Besh-Darok. Even this far away, he could sense the Crystal Eye, could feel the *force* of its watchfulness, like the heat of a fire or a dancing light, yet not. Information from inside the city was scant, with nothing coming from Kodel's man in nearly three days, yet Byrnak's deepest instincts told him that there was something . . . *waiting* there for him and the other Shadowkings, some kind of deadly fate.

He knew that Bardow and those other crippled mages possessed the Motherseed too, but that would provide little cause for this undersensed danger. Legends, and even reports from the revenant First-Woken, mentioned a third artefact of great power. Some called it the Staff of the Void, while others said it was the Song of the Void. Other sources pointed to the ancient verses on the Fires of Old, claiming that 'the fire that sleeps' was the third artefact. *But if those enfeebled mages were in possession of this lost talisman, surely they would be using it against us even now*, he thought. *Assuming that they would know how to use it.*

He glanced at the patiently waiting group. 'We have to know what hazards may lurk beyond those walls. Once the warblood sign is given and havoc begins to grow, our new friends will have a part to play.'

Smiling, he beckoned to the pale-skinned rivenshades who stood a little apart from the rest. The woman came forward first and Byrnak descended the steps, hand outstretched which she took gracefully. Firmly he raised her hand to his lips and gave the cold flesh a lingering kiss. She seemed, he thought, only faintly appreciative while her companion, the Mazaret rivenshade, looked on with detached amusement. Byrnak could sense the emptiness in both of them, the vacancy beneath the outer shell. The rivenshade ritual was an ancient method of creating assassins, usually from the essence of the unsuspecting victim, and while this situation was a little different, they were still the perfect vessels for his purpose.

'While confusion reigns in Besh-Darok, both of you, and all your brothers and sisters, shall ride forth from Gorla and Keshada at the head of raiding parties. There yet remain occupied villages near the city so from there you will spread the tide of terror. Also, harry those fleeing south so that word of our dominion may travel to other regions.'

A sly look came over the Suviel rivenshade's features. 'What mercy do we extend, lord? What quarter?'

'None for any taking arms against you,' he said. 'Make sure some refugees escape with their lives and the memory of your faces.'

The rivenshades exchanged a satisfied look.

'As you have said,' the Mazaret said. 'So it shall be.'

Byrnak then turned to the rest. 'Be assured that we shall put forth all of our strength and sweep our enemies into the pale memory of oblivion, but that time is not yet.'

Audience at an end, Byrnak descended the dais steps and nodded to the captain of his honour guard. They followed in his wake as he crossed the shadow-embellished floor to tall, arched doors of red granite which opened inwards at his approach. Beyond was a high corridor along which he walked, past narrow open windows that stretched from floor to ceiling. He paused at one and gazed out at the snow-covered fields and meadows and estates, an abandoned territory of whiteness turning pale and blue beneath the encroaching dusk.

As time passes, he thought, *the landscape of this struggle becomes harder to understand, not easier. The nearer we come to the core of it, the less certain its outlines . . .*

Then he laughed to himself. Even the deathly inner presence of the Lord of Twilight had fallen silent, as if in satisfaction at the pace of events.

Are you hoping to draw some cold strategem together? he thought inwardly. *Some play of dream and deception? If so, it will avail you naught for I have seen through every illusion in your arsenal, every bluff and pretence and threat. We shall subdue you, my brothers and I.*

There was no response, no sense of any presence deep within the veiled parts of his mind, only a hollowness . . . and an involuntary suggestion suddenly coalesced that he and the other Shadowkings were little more than elaborate rivenshades being driven like everyone else towards the forge of fate by a force unseen . . .

He recoiled from the dread notion, turned sharply and strode along the corridor, his demeanour full of smouldering anger. A door full of glinting haze took him down ten floors to a wide walkway overlooking one of Keshada's great storage vaults. Groups of officers and artisans, surprised by his appearance, bowed or saluted but he ignored them as he watched the noisy, vigorous activity below. Several teams of horses flanked a wide square opening in the dusty wooden floor, straining on pulley-wound clusters of hawsers, hauling up from some ways down a cross-joisted rack piled with crates and bundles of supplies. There were another three loading bays across the huge floor, each surrounded by horses and labourers all made small by the vault's massive scale.

Wordlessly, Byrnak continued along the balcony, still followed by guards and standard bearers, and passed through another glittering archway. Beyond it he emerged in a long curved gallery, the inner wall being of sheer, polished ash-grey marble and marred only by a line of niches, each containing a metallic head murmuring verse in an ancient language. The outer wall was of rough brown stone broken by large triangular openings through which he could look across the dry, rocky desolation of the Realm of Dusk.

For although Gorla and Keshada were now able to exist in the mountains around Besh-Darok by virtue of the spells laid down by Crevalcor, their true foundations remained in the Lord of Twilight's own realm. It was from there that the powers of the Wellsource fed both the citadels' requirement such that any force that reached these walls would face its raw power in addition to numberless defenders.

But still uncertainty nagged, prompted by the emerging fragments of that shattering war at the ages-past dawn of the world. What if the mages were in possession of all three artefacts, and they were playing the waiting game with unbending cunning? What if they were biding their time until it was right to unleash it all in a single, devastating thrust?

With a clenched fist he struck his thigh in frustration. He had to know more, and Kodel was the one who held the threads along which rumour flowed. And since Kodel was currently visiting the Acolytes' stronghold, that was where he would go.

As he continued along the corridor, he studied the lesser strongholds clustered near Keshada's walls out in the Realm of Dusk. A
rambling castle, diminutive next to Keshada, stood wall to wall with
a square-built keep, a primitive conical tower, and what seemed
to be a fortified temple. Sentries were visible on the dilapidated
parapets, and gazing off to one side Byrnak could see the edge of the
silver-grey Skeletal Forest, hazed by wind-driven curtains of ochre
dust. Looking the other way he could just make out one shoulder
of the hollow stone colossus, half-buried in the shifting searing
sands. Straight ahead the ground sloped down to a great parched
plain dominated by the gaping, jagged immensity of the Hewn
Mountain at whose centre was, he knew, the pillared chamber
of the Wellsource.

He had visited it several times since that first meeting with the
Acolyte adept, Obax, months ago. More recently, he had found his
powers strong enough to go there unaccompanied, albeit briefly. On
each occasion he had stared into the flickering emerald ghost of the
Source's ever-changing form, striving to discern the secrets at its
heart. But no two appearances ever seemed the same, although a few
times he thought he glimpsed thin black webs amidst the ceaseless
turmoil. But he dismissed this as evidence of a weariness in the eyes.

He walked on, seeking another glittering doorway and pondering
the apparent ease with which the Acolytes were able to enter and
linger in the Realm of Dusk.

The next traversing door took Byrnak and his retinue down
to a pillared walkway overlooking a vast enclosed hall divided
into several drill grounds and innumerable training pens and pits.
Thousands of warriors sent up a cacophony of grunts and shouts as
drillmasters put them through exacting exercises. Knots of officers
and scribes and runners paused when he passed, some bowing
heads, others prostrating themselves on the warm stone. Byrnak
spoke to none, only nodding gravely as he strode towards another
doorway.

Again the slow-swirling glitter stroked his face with icy tendrils
and he stepped through to a stuffy dimness reeking of horse manure,
harness leather and sweat. Extensive stabling took up almost all of
Keshada's underground level, its chambers and stalls built of heavy

wood beams and planking and heated by sorcerous braziers. Oil
lamps burned in grilled wall cressets, shedding a grimy yellow light.
More bowing and saluting greeted his arrival, and Byrnak left the
ordering of readied mounts to his subordinates. One spirited brown
stallion reared and almost broke free as it was brought for him, but
he subdued it with a single glance before climbing smoothly into
the saddle. Moments later he and his retinue rode slowly out to a
long, low-roofed chamber busy with troops of cavalry, caravans of
pack animals and strings of new mounts. Three large gates led to
upward-sloping stone passages, one straight ahead, the other curving
off to left and right. Across from them was a single wide opening and
a downward ramp of hoof-stamped gravel and dirt towards which
Byrnak led his group.

Shouts and applause erupted from the riders passing through as
Byrnak and his banner were recognised. Some of his attendants
were affronted at this disrespectful display but he shook his head
at them then bestowed a wintry smile on the cheering crowd as
they passed by. This raucous praise was a welcome change from the
submissive obeisance he had experienced elsewhere, and brought
back memories from that long-gone time in Honjir.

The downward ramp brought them into a torch-lit, rough-hewn
stone cave which opened out to become the entrance to the
Great Aisle. Chipped and broken rock melted into the Aisle's
smooth, grey-green wall from which a muted, silver-green radiance
emanated. Created and sustained by the Wellsource, the Great
Aisle was a wide, oval tunnel that stretched away in a long,
gently upward curve at whose other end, a mere day's march
hence, lay the caverns beneath Rauthaz. The first time Byrnak
saw it, soon after the Wellgate completed the bore, it looked to
his eyes like a gigantic gullet. Now, as he led his followers into it,
he imagined it growing and widening into a maw fit to swallow
cities, mountains, nations . . .

They rode at a canter past several long columns of marching
troops before reaching the point where their branch of the Great
Aisle met that coming from the citadel of Gorla. Here Byrnak
paused and instructed the captain of his honour guard to continue
on to Rauthaz, and as they resumed at a steady gallop, he faced the

wall of the Aisle. At his first thought of need, the Wellsource was there. He reached through it for the Wellgate, a self-perpetuating spell which he and Kodel had devised, and called up a side-portal. A tall oval depression appeared in the wall of the Aisle and sunk quickly inwards, a dark, round-edged door. Byrnak fixed firmly in his mind his destination and urged his nervous mount forward—

—and emerged in the stone chamber beneath Trevada where Ystregul, the fifth Shadowking, was imprisoned. In the iron casket, suspended on heavy chains, he was still held fast, his head and shoulders visible, his every grimace and head movement slowed by the enchantment laid upon him by the other Shadowkings. In the months since the cataclysmic battle for Besh-Darok, less than a day had passed for him.

Small lamps burned on stands in the chamber's corners but most of the light came from the grooved patterns scored into the flagstones below the prisoner, ancient symbols glowing with iridescent green power. Emerald radiance mingled with oil-lamp-golden highlights across the swirls and strings of glyphs that wound around Ystregul's casket.

It was hot. As Byrnak dismounted, a figure in short-sleeved black garments rose from a cross-legged pose in one corner, his clean-shaven, narrow features creased by a dark smile as he regarded the casket and its contents. Still smiling, Kodel then glanced at Byrnak.

'Our brother has had a visitor,' he said. 'Quite recently . . .'

Before Byrnak could reply, another figure stepped into view, his robes long and green, his hair grey and braided, his eyes a milky white. It was Obax, Byrnak's former guide and now the High Master of the Acolytes at Trevada.

'Greetings, Great Lord. Are you well?'

Byrnak's grin was savage. 'I am in admirable health, friend Obax, and in full possession of my destiny.'

The priest nodded sagely. 'Truly, your thriving fitness is an inspiration to us all, most puissant lord, and helps to sooth our sorrow that such vigour is not shared by all the Shadowkings.'

Byrnak glanced at Kodel who offered naught but an amused shrug.

'Hard work, mastery and cunning will in the end overcome such hindrances,' he said, voice hardening. 'But tell me about the new rite for the Weaving of Souls – am I correct in thinking that you and your adepts are making progress?'

'Ah, 'tis a difficult task, Great Lord,' Obax said. 'Somehow we must abstract the five-fold essence without causing harm to yourself or your brothers, then weave these shards of the Godhead together within a new host strong enough to serve.' He sighed. 'A monumental task, yet progress is being made.'

Byrnak met that white gaze, thinking, *Yes, as slowly as possible.*

'All your efforts shall be rewarded,' he said evenly. 'In the meantime, my very good friend, kindly see to my horse.' So saying, he held out the stallion's reins.

For a moment Obax stood stock still, his pale-eyed face an expressionless mask. Then, smiling thinly, he accepted the reins.

'As you wish, Great Lord,' he said. 'I shall see that it is well fed.'

Then the senior Acolyte turned and led the creature out of the chamber. As the heavy doors thudded shut behind him, Kodel laughed.

'I didn't realise it before, brother,' he said. 'But the man hates you, and with a passion. Might he not present a problem for us?'

'We shall attend to the matter of the Nightbrothers once Besh-Darok is broken,' Byrnak said, wiping a patina of sweat from his brow.

'I understand that all is in place,' Kodel said, returning to the low stool where he had been sitting. 'Why do you delay the attack? Still worrying about this third artefact?'

Byrnak grunted. 'They're hiding something, Bardow and those weakling mages, and hiding it from their own general, that turn-coat Yasgur. I have to know what it is before I commit our armies.'

Kodel squinted at the suspended Ystregul through a spider-wire arrangement of glowing lenses. 'I take it that you've been hearing some tales of the battle of Kogil, the fall of Jagreag and so forth.'

'Too many, and most of them have the ring of truth.' He stabbed a forefinger at Kodel. 'Which is why I want to know what your spies have been saying.'

The other Shadowking blew dust from an amber four-sided gem before fitting it into the gold-wire assemblage. 'I last heard from my secret eyes in Besh-Darok nearly two days ago – all he had to tell me was that some kind of strange activity in Sejeend's boatyards had ceased abruptly several days before, that food riots had stopped after cargo ships arrived from Cabringa, and barring the unforeseen, the boy-Emperor is ripe for the picking as and when we desire. Of the mages' activities he knows little, except that they've started looking for him.'

'That is still of little help to me,' Byrnak said.

'Then bide your time, brother. Let the armies wax while we bring together the strands and tails of rumour. There is much else afoot, most importantly the Dalbar plan. Once Crevalcor has dealt with the High House of Keels, the way will be clear for Jefren ships to start raiding all along that southern coast.'

Byrnak frowned. The Theocracy of Jefren had taken root soon after the defeat of the Empire as a Twilight sect which established itself in the Hanoriath Hills in west Jefren. With the passing years, they gradually extended their harsh rule across the whole of the former Kingdom of Jefren, and tested the resolve of neighbouring rulers. As Warlord of Northern Honjir, Byrnak had repulsed their exploratory raids on more than one occasion.

'Our Jefren allies!' he sneered. 'Every time I meet one of those masked priests, I get the impression that he thinks himself greater than I.'

'There is a delegation of them currently in Trevada,' Kodel said, getting to his feet and picking out a wooden tripod from several leaning against the wall. 'Apparently they are asking for aid against a small army of rebels who have entrenched themselves in some old fortress high in the Druandag Mountains. The Acolytes' response so far has been to insist that most of the nighthunters died during the battle with the Daemonkind, and that the few survivors are not sufficiently strong for both a mountain assault and the coming campaign.'

'Is this true?'

Kodel nodded. 'I believe so.' He affixed the intricate object of wire and jewels to the top of the tripod and stooped to peer into it. 'We still have eaterbeasts on hand, of course. The tinemasters, both here and and at Casall, have had to dig out new pits and lairs to accommodate recent brood spawning. But all this is just a side issue – there's another problem brewing which we may have to be ready to deal with at short notice, namely our brother, Thraelor.'

Byrnak's frown deepened and he crossed his arms. 'Go on.'

'He only communicates via the Wellmirror now, and in conversations over the last three days he has been growing noticeably . . . erratic. I spoke to him earlier today, and there were several moments when I *knew* that it wasn't him behind that face.'

The two Shadowkings regarded each other with mutual unease.

'Have you heard aught from our dark passenger recently?' Byrnak said.

'Not for a day or two,' Kodel admitted.

'Nor I.' Byrnak glanced at the imprisoned Ystregul and gritted his teeth. 'Should we start preparing another casket in the event that Thraelor succumbs?'

Kodel was likewise studying the captive Shadowking though his glittering device once more. 'It might be prudent, but it may no longer be as unassailable as we thought.' He straightened, his smile crooked. 'You see, someone has been tampering with the spells we wove around our brother here.'

Byrnak went over to stand next to the device on its tripod but deigned to look through it. 'Are you certain?'

Kodel nodded. 'I've imbued the elements of this little artifice with Wellsource power, and I can see how the web of spells has been altered.' He stroked his chin. 'Perhaps not so much tampered with as tested.'

'There can only be a few capable of this,' Byrnak said, his thoughts flying. 'I doubt that it would be in Grazaan's interest, but what of Thraelor?'

'He's hardly strayed out of the Red Tower in Casall this last month,' Kodel said. 'And I'm sure I'd have known if he'd come here.'

'What of our loyal Acolytes?'

Kodel laughed aloud. 'The likeliest candidates, although I cannot fathom how the Black Priest's release could serve their cause.'

A cause dedicated to the ascendancy of the Lord of Twilight, Byrnak knew, and inevitable oblivion for the Shadowkings.

'The spells will have to be strengthened,' he said. 'Maybe we could include some painful surprises for any meddlers, yes? And when I return to Rauthaz, I'll have a second casket made secretly.'

The two Shadowkings exchanged cruel smiles then turned to face the captive Ystregul, their hands aflame with emerald power.

Aboard the ancient and decaying vessel, lashed to the shattered mast, Gilly had sunk to sitting on the damp deck and was trying to loosen the bonds on his wrists. The day was almost done, the chilling tide of night was rising and the ship was at rest after its spell-driven departure from Scallow. This was Sulros Island, and the vessel now lay beached on a pebbly strand not far from Port Caeleg, an independent city-port which had a reputation for intrigue and all manner of illegalities. A sickly green nimbus flickered about every part of the sea-rotted hulk but the greater part of Gilly's attention was fixed on the dread-inspiring spectacle taking place on the forward deck.

Crevalcor, the revenant sorcerer, was kneeling on the rough planking while before him a small fire with a blue heart burned and threw off sullen, spark-laden coils of smoke that drifted upwards. To his left, also kneeling, was the brawny, bearded figure of the Hevrin, chieftain of the rebellious Islesmen. His slumped posture, however, spoke of the compulsion laid upon him by Crevalcor, invisible shackles that rendered him subservient. Yet when he had come aboard a short while ago, Gilly had espied a look of murderous hate flash across the man's face when the sorcerer turned his back.

Sitting cross-legged to Crevalcor's right was a Jefren warrior-priest, his face hidden by a full mask. The quality of the mask, carved in black ironwood, and the red richness of his cloak, confirmed Gilly's suspicion that this was a high-ranking officer of the Theocracy.

I'll wager a wagonload of pearls that there's a Jefren fleet anchored off the coast near here, he had thought when the man came aboard from a ceremonial pinnace.

The masked priest had assisted Crevalcor in preparing the foundations of his ritual, then sat in silence as the other began intoning a guttural incantation. The air above the fuming fire had twisted, tendrils of smoke had swirled inward for a moment or two, then a curious radiance had emerged from the centre, a darkling red mingled with glassy green. This lurid light swirled sluggishly along invisible curves and edges, scribing boundaries, and gradually above the fire a huge head took form, its features man-like and narrow, the eyes almond-shaped and unwinking, the full-lipped mouth wearing a cruel smile.

'Hail and praise to thee, Great Lord Thraelor,' Crevalcor cried out.

The apparition of the Shadowking Thraelor gazed down, studying each of the three crouched beneath him. A strange disjointed exchange then ensued, sometimes spoken in common Mantinorian but at other times Crevalcor and Thraelor switched to a harsh, throaty tongue incomprehensible to Gilly. And whenever this happened, the face contorted briefly and black and silver streamed through it only to ebb away moments later when the speech became recognisable once more.

Finally, the ghastly ceremony came to an end and the Shadowking's distorted features faded away. After a brief murmured discussion, the Jefren priest rose to leave, turning his masked face in Gilly's direction just once before climbing over the bulwark and descending out of sight.

There was a faint hiss as Crevalcor poured a beaker of something, wine perhaps, over the ritual fire. As a gout of steam and smoke floated away across the shadowy deck, he got to his feet and walked lightly over to Gilly. By the weak glow of the ensorcelled vessel, his face looked dark and sweat-beaded, his eyes pale and full of vitality.

'I wonder if you've understood the least part of what's been agreed this night,' Crevalcor said.

Gilly smiled. His wrists were rubbed raw, some of his fingertips were icily numb, he could feel a chilly ague working its way into his chest and vitals, and he ached with weariness. But still he would respond to his captor.

'Hmm, let me see . . . Ah, I know, you and your Shadowking masters have decided to depart our lands for ever and sail back to the northern shores, but before that you're going to hold a gigantic farewell banquet and invite many honoured guests, myself included . . .'

Crevalcor chuckled, crouched down before Gilly and reached out to pat his cheek. 'By the Well, I believe you could be up to your waist in an eaterbeast's gullet and still spout like a buffoon. This is good – strong enemies make for effective servants.'

Gilly uttered a hoarse laugh. 'Never.'

The sorcerer ignored him. 'This day a hidden pact has been forged. The efforts of the Acolytes and the Jefren priesthood will combine to ensure the ascension of the Lord of Twilight, despite the reluctance and stratagems of the Shadowkings. Their obsession with the overthrow of those petty rebels and outlaws will be their undoing – while their attention is elsewhere, we shall strike. This is how you will prove to be useful to us.'

He got to his feet and gazed sternwards, out at the Sea of Drakkilis.

'Your friend Mazaret has become an excellent servant to the wider cause,' he went on. 'Did you know that?'

'You lie,' Gilly said, knowing with a sudden, cold certainty that it was true.

'The mage Suviel, too. She helped draw Mazaret out from Besh-Darok.'

'But . . . she died at Trevada.'

'She was held in the Acolytes' spell chambers for days before the unfortunate battle with the Daemonkind.' Crevalcor turned to look down at him. 'They know how to make good servants, and everything that they know I knew first.'

He smiled at Gilly's confusion.

'I think that five of you will suffice.'

Chapter Fourteen

A cruel hand reached out,
From the deep and sonorous gloom
And made a wreck
Of bright and true dreams.

Calabos, *The City Of Dreams*

Alael received the message from the College of Hendred's Hall late on in the evening. It said simply:

Lady Alael,
The translation which you requested is now complete and awaits your collection. However, further study of the codex has brought to light some material which may merit the attention of a higher authority. Personal infirmity confines me to my chambers, therefore I would be obliged if you would come directly to the college this eve and without delay.
In anticipation of your arrival, I remain —

Ser Melgro Onsivar, Master of Parlance

Straight away she took the message up to the Archmage's chambers and, after gaining admittance and exchanging greetings, showed it to him. Sat in a high-backed chair of polished, dark red torwood, Archmage Bardow stroked his beardless chin as he read.

'It certainly has the cast of Melgro's thoughts,' he said, 'and appears to be genuine, as well as urgent. Very well, I shall allow this but you will travel on horseback and accompanied. Agreed?'

She was quick to accept his conditions and a short while later was departing the palace by the Belling Gate, a high but narrow passage running crookedly from within the Silver Aggor to the Imperial Barracks outwith the Golden Aggor. Her escort comprised six knights of the Protectorate Order, yet their commander was Ghazrek, one of Prince Yasgur's senior banner-captains. She wondered if there was any friction between he and they, but to her eyes they all looked so grim and forbidding that she decided against any querying, however mild.

The night was dark and blustery as they rode out of the gates of the Imperial Barracks. Like her escort she was heavily clad against the icy weather, but the chill nonetheless cut through her garments. No snow was falling yet the sky was a slow-moving mantle of broken cloud, tattered gaps giving glimpses of star-strewn blackness.

The streets along which they cantered, hoofs clattering, were littered with heaps and pools of dirty snow and were mostly deserted. Lamplight showed through many a tightly-shuttered window and a deadening silence held sway, almost as if the city was pulling in on itself after all the crises of previous days. True, swinging lanterns burned outside the occasional tavern they passed, and raucous din sounded from within, but that only served to emphasise the widespread sense of sombre isolation. Somewhere nearby, a dog barked and was answered by a mournful howling off in the night.

The route led east to a crossroads then north towards the river. As they rode, Alael felt her own mood of anticipation gradually change to one of dejection and gloom. The nearest bridge across the Olodar lay straight ahead but immediately to their right the buildings suddenly gave way to a wide, square depression littered with broken masonry and bordered by the tumbled remains of walls. For some reason, little snow lay here. Everything within the walls was blackened and a faint charred smell reached Alael as she slowed her horse to a walk. A heavy sadness seemed to well up from this place, tomblike and continual until a cracked, anguished voice called from the nearby ruined walls.

'Let the dead things be!'

A cowled figure half-slumped by the masonry flung out a bony hand as if to fend off the riders, and the warning was repeated, more hoarsely this time. Appalled, Alael reined her horse round to approach the figure but one of her escorting knights stopped her.

'Please, milady, nothing can be done for her.'

'Her?'

The knight nodded. 'I've seen her in the day when I've passed by before. She's a lamenter, milady, and refuses to leave these ruins. Some say that when the halls burned down she must have lost someone close and the grief has driven her mad.'

Alael stared into the blackened ruins, hearing the old woman moving around, and felt a stinging pity. 'What is this place?'

'It was the old mage halls,' said Ghazrek suddenly. 'If it pleases my lady, we should continue on our way – it is not safe to linger in the one place after nightfall.'

His manner was stern in a way that brooked no dissent and as she rode on amid her escort Alael found herself beginning to understand Tauric's fierce feelings of duty towards the people of this city. A terrible enemy was building its forces higher and higher outside while tides of despair and futility ebbed and flowed within. Tauric's impulse was to press again and again for a place in the fighting, yet Alael felt that if she were in his position she would be more involved in trying to set right some of the hardships faced by ordinary people.

Then she imagined how impatient her Uncle Volyn would have been at such a desire on her part, and smiled sadly.

When they crossed the Royal Knights Bridge at a canter, the horses' hoofs sent up a thunderous din. Passing over into the Old Town, Ghazrek led the way east along a wide thoroughfare which curved around to the north. The breeze was stiffer now, hurling occasional scatterings of icy droplets into Alael's face, and when she glanced up at the Chapel Fort she could see two great watchfires burning, ragged, bright yellow tongues of flames flapping wildly in the wind.

Before long they were riding up the road that Alael had last travelled by carriage. At the half-overgrown college gates her escorts slowed and they all trotted up the gravelled way to the college itself, startling a large, black dog which sprang up and dashed off into the shadows. By night the building was a shapeless mass set amidst the gloomy darkness of the surrounding gardens, dim and grey apart from the bright torches flaring either side of the main entrance. As they dismounted, the door swung open and the aged steward emerged.

'Greetings, Lady Alael,' he said as she hurried up to him. 'Master Onsivar is expecting you.'

She nodded and looked to Ghazrek as they both entered the small hallway. 'I should not be very long, ser captain. I may need to ask a few questions of the Master of Parlance, and I do not know if he'll wish to answer them.'

Ghazrek gave her a brief appraisal with his dark, hawkish eyes. 'Is this place safe, my lady? I could send a guard with you . . .'

'It is a college, captain, a place of learning,' she said. 'Anyone wishing me harm would have to fight their way past you and your men, a hard task I'd warrant.'

'As you will, my lady,' he said. 'But I would send one of the men to make certain of your wellbeing every quarter hour.'

She agreed, then turned to the old steward who led the way out of a side door. It was colder and darker than before along the passageways, and the quiet of empty classrooms was almost strangely peaceful. Up the lamp-lit winding stairs and through to the door of the Master of Parlance's study she followed the college steward. A precise rap on the door, and a voice called out 'Enter!', and Alael was ushered in.

There was a candle inside, just by the door, casting a small halo of illumination on nearby bookshelves, and the only other source in the dark pit of a room was an oil lamp over on Onsivar's desk. He was there as before but now he sat in a soft chair with enclosing back and sides. By the lamp's warm amber light he did not look at all well, and wore a heavy, swaddling gown while on his desk a beaker of something hot gave off wisps of vapour.

'Ah, Lady Alael – please join me. Forgive my infirmity but the weakness of this poor frame is a constant burden . . .'

Carefully she picked her way through the shadows, up the three steps to his raised platform and seated herself before him. Keren's book lay open on the desk before him, but she kept silent, waiting for him to begin.

'Yes, hmm . . . m'lady, the humble Edric's transcription of Stulmar's disorganised scholarship, specifically the sagasong concerning Raegal . . .' He pressed the pages flat with one spidery hand and held up a single sheet of parchment with the other while glancing between the two. 'I did have to send forth for an Othazi gradus in the end, from the College of Guilds, and was thus able to complete the translation with no great difficulty.'

The candle over by the door suddenly flickered and went out and an icy draft brushed over Alael's face, but her attention was wholly on the Master of Parlance.

'Does it say how Raegal crossed into the Daemonkind's realm?' she asked.

'Yes . . . yes, there is mention of him borrowing something called the Voidsong, a strange term which – assuming translation from the pre-Othazi Ebrun tongue – can be recast as "the Staff of the Void". Which, if memory serves, is one of the Nightcat's gifts to the Sun-Tiger in ancient Yulari mythology. Whatever it was, he later returned it, once his adventure was done. The fascinating thing about this document is that it is a palimpsest . . .'

That's it! she thought. *It has to be* . . .

'Is there any clue to where it can be found?'

'Oh yes, milady – there are quite accurate directions . . .' He paused to unearth a tattered map of the continent of Toluveraz from a pile of papers behind him. He laid the faded, wine-stained chart atop Keren's book, swept a pointing finger over the north-west coast and brought it down squarely on a stretch of open water labelled 'the Gulf of Fandugar'. 'Yes, about a hundred miles north of Jefren.'

Her heart sank. 'Out to sea?'

'Once, many ages ago, the lands of Anghatan and Yularia extended much further north. But a terrible convulsion dragged that entire region beneath the waves, leaving the northern coastline as it is today.' He tugged his gown tighter and tapped the map. 'So if Raegal did return this Staff of the Void, it may well be at the bottom of the ocean and thus utterly beyond reach.'

'Excellent,' said a man's voice from the darkness behind Alael. 'Now give me that parchment.'

Scarcely daring to look round she jerked in fear as a hand

grasped her shoulder and pushed her sideways out of her seat. She shrank back against the book-shelved wall as the newcomer came into view.

The man looked very ill, cadaverous features blotched and shiny with sweat while the bones of his skull seemed overly defined. His lank hair was missing in patches and a swelling under one side of his jaw made his face lopsided. Yet his eyes blazed with strength and purpose, and for all that his clothes were torn and stinking, the misshapen hand that he held out was calm and unwavering.

'The parchment, old man – now.'

Melgro Onsivar, to Alael's surprise, stiffened in his seat, tossed the sheet of translation on to the desk and glared at the intruder. 'Take it then. The knowledge yet remains with me.'

Alael had a sense of foreboding as the man grinned unpleasantly.

'Yes,' he drawled, picking up the parchment. 'I know . . .'

He raised his other hand and it was wreathed in flame, an unnatural writhing gauntlet of fire. The flames were a mingling of bright corrosive green and dazzling argent, flickering, clinging to the skin of hand and fingers. Alael could feel the impossibility of it, this interweaving of the Lesser Power and the Wellsource, and her frozen shock began turning into anger and a bitter craving for the Earthmother's gift.

The man gave a sidelong, contemptuous glance. 'Where's the goddess now, eh?'

Even as the bolt of green and white lanced out at the Master of Parlance, Alael let out an incoherent cry of rage and lunged at the man. Onsivar's cry of pain cut through everything and spurred her on, heedless of her own safety. The nameless man, unprepared for such ferocity, staggered sideways into the bannister that surrounded Onsivar's dais, uttering a bellow of fury. Alael struggled with him, trying to snatch back the parchment, but the man's speed and strength quickly told against her. With an elbow he thrust her off him then dealt her a buffet to the head with the back of his hand. Alael managed to turn away from the oncoming blow but still it had force enough to hurl her back against a low, padded settle.

The eldritch glow of his burning hand cast strange glints of green and white across his form and face. Staring down at her he clenched the hand into a fist and seemed about to strike at her with the mingled power when the door flew open with a thunderous crash.

First into the room was Nerek who jumped up on to a cluttered table, stared at the tattered man for the merest second and said:

'You!'

The man sneered. 'So you remember our brief encounter before the coronation, mirrorchild? I see you have no street urchins to aid you this time. Well, you had best be ready for I am now stronger than before.'

'So am I,' said Nerek who flung out one hand. A pale web of power left her fingertips and sprang across the room at the man's throat. He fumbled with it for a moment or two before it dissipated but by then Blind Rina and Osper Traum were in the room, their hands aglow with the Lesser Power. He uttered a chilling laugh of derision, and Alael all but cried out for the Earthmother to aid her. The only response was an aching emptiness, so she hauled herself upright with the intention of throwing herself at him again. But before she could a trembling hand reached up from behind Onsivar's desk, seized the lantern that sat there and hurled it at the intruder.

Glass broke, oil splashed and suddenly the man's back was a flaring sheet of flame. By the lurid light of his blazing form, Alael saw Nerek come vaulting over the bannister to attack him with her bare hands. He on the other hand was desparately trying to shuck off his burning clothes when a leather-clad forearm elbowed him in the chest. He staggered back but recovered quickly and swiped at her with his green-wreathed hand. Nerek stepped in close and hammered her gauntleted fist into his face.

Alael heard a crack as the blow sent the man flying backwards across a low bookshelf and, with a brittle shattering, through one of the mullioned windows. Later, Alael remembered perfectly that his hair was on fire and that just before he fell out of sight, his skull-like face was grinning.

For a moment the room was plunged into a shout-filled darkness, then a bright glow bloomed between Blind Rina's hands, revealing the presence of Captain Ghazrek and three of his knights.

'Downstairs, captain,' Alael said, gasping. 'One of the enemy's agents . . . fell out of the window – see if he yet lives.'

Ghazrek gave a sharp nod and hurried out.

Alael went over to aid the Master of Parlance. His upper clothing was scorched, his eyebrows and some hair was gone and the skin on one side of his face was red and blistered. As she helped him into his chair, his breathing was shallow and he seemed close to collapse yet still trying to speak. Calming him, she looked round to see Blind Rina examining Nerek's bare hand while a slowly twisting skein of light floated over her head. Halfway across the room, the mage-minstrel Osper Traum looked on with troubled eyes, his hands fingering the silvery instrument at his chest.

Blind Rina came over and crouched beside Alael.

'Is he in much pain?' she said.

'Such a . . . foolish question,' the old scholar said hoarsely. 'Lady Alael, I must . . .'

'You must rest yourself, Master Onsivar, while I tend to these burns,' Blind Rina said.

The Master of Parlance rallied at this. 'My good woman, you may carry out such ministrations as you are able . . . but there are matters that I must make clear to the Lady Alael now.'

Blind Rina smiled with ironic brightness. 'As you wish, ser.'

'Hmph, very good . . . Now, my lady, listen well. As I began to explain a short while ago, the Raegal manuscript is a palimpsest – an older piece of writing was scraped from the surface of the parchment, allowing it to be used again.

'By various means, I was able to discern those older lines and found to my astonishment that it was a page from an ancient work of philosophy called *The Teaching of Korrul*. The last copy was thought to have been in the great library of Alvergost when it was sacked after the fall of the Brusartan throne . . .'

Alael interrupted him. 'Master Onsivar, what do these ancient words say?'

'They give instructions, very detailed, on the making of weapons, my lady,' he said. 'Weapons made from a mingling of powers, spears, daggers and swords, with not an ounce of iron or wood.' Exhausted, he slumped back in his chair. 'There is . . . a sheet of translation in your book – please, show it to the Archmage.'

'I will, this very night.'

Then the door opened and Ghazrek entered, looking grim, and Alael knew.

'Is he there, captain?'

The Mogaun captain's frustration was plain. 'No body, my lady. By torchlight we could see where he landed and we found some burnt scraps of clothing and a few bloody footprints, but they disappeared in the bushes.'

'After all that, he's still able to run off,' Blind Rina said. 'A tough one.'

And now he's out there, Alael thought. *Wounded but still full of hate and power.*

'I'll have to leave you here,' Alael said to Blind Rina and Nerek. Standing up she checked that the translation was in the old book of sagas then closed it and tucked it under her arm. 'I'll have to take this to Bardow now. You can see why.'

As Blind Rina nodded, there was a discreet cough from across the room.

'I, on the other hand, will be quite happy to remain here,' said Osper Traum.

'I won't,' said Nerek shortly. 'I shall return with you.'

The lean woman smiled coldly as she tugged her gauntlets back on. Alael knew there would be no point in argument.

'Very well,' she said, coming down from the dais. 'Captain Ghazrek – we shall depart as soon as I've spoken with the old steward.'

But Ghazrek shook his head. 'Sorry my lady, he's dead. Strangled. Found his body in a room on the floor below.'

Alael clamped down on her sense of grief. She put one hand to her eyes for a moment and breathed deeply. *Death, death and more death . . .*

Then she let her hand fall and wordlessly gestured Ghazrek to leave. Before they reached the door, Blind Rina spoke.

'Alael, you must also tell Bardow that one of the enemy's agents now knows that we don't have the Staff of the Void,' she said. 'Tell him the moment you see him.'

'I don't imagine he'll be pleased to hear it,' Alael said.

Blind Rina gave a quiet laugh, which Alael echoed as she left, closely followed by Nerek who laughed not at all.

Chapter Fifteen

Now comes the hour of trial,
When ghosts and dead souls rise,
Hollow and howling,
And hungering for ruin.

Vosada Boroal, *The Fall Of Hallebron*, Bk V, 7, 11

The attack on Scallow began just before sunrise.

In the grey light of pre-dawn, Keren was in Trader Golwyth's stables, rechecking her mount's harnessing when she heard the stir of voices from the yard. Stepping outside she saw Captain Redrigh and a few of Golwyth's men gathered round a runner, listening closely. A moment later the messenger was dashing out of the gates while Redrigh and the others hurried over to the stables, faces eager and alive.

'Word from the Grand Marshals' tower,' Redrigh told her. 'Coastal rider scouts have reported a fleet sailing up the Neck. Huge battle dromonds, apparently, bristling with war machines.'

'Are we still patrolling the west bank?' she said.

He smiled sardonically. 'The Marshals have decided that we'd be of greatest use over on South Bridges.'

Keren shook her head. 'They really don't understand cavalry, do they?'

The young captain shrugged, then turned to bellow last directions and warnings to his company. Keren pulled on the heavy, non-too fresh-smelling rider's jerkin loaned to her by Golwyth's chief stablemaster, but as she fastened hooks and eyelets down the front she found herself missing Gilly's presence. He would have made some revolting comment on the origin of the jerkin's odour and caused her to defend its sturdiness.

Where are you? she thought as she patted her horse's neck then hauled herself into the saddle. *What kind of peril have you got yourself into?*

The scant investigations she had been able to make the day before had cast up few shreds of information about Gilly's movements after leaving the High House of Keels. Down in Wracktown a couple of sullen youths said they saw him board one of the old hulks which then broke loose and sank, taking him with it. Others claimed that it sailed away along the misty Neck, crewed by the dead. If there had been more time, she might have uncovered more but Medwin had commanded her attendance at a conclave called in the aftermath of Yared Hevrin's killing and the subsequent escape of the Chieftain Hevrin and his captains.

It had not been an even-tempered meeting. Junior floorsmen had levelled charges of gross negligence at the Grand Marshals, three grey-haired, hard-eyed men, who responded by pointing out that one of the conditions for the Hevrin's participation at the High House had been the removal of Scallowan troops from its immediate vicinity. They also pointed out that their opposition to such a condition had been overruled, then went on to say that indulging in blame-laying while the enemy was preparing to strike was the folly of cretins. After that, Medwin was asked to conduct the conclave which he did with relish.

Which is why I'm riding in this makeshift mobile reserve concocted by Medwin out of Redrigh's men and half of Golwyth's. Just to show that the Crown Renewed is playing its part . . .

In addition, Medwin had promised the Grand Marshals that aid from Besh-Darok would be arriving very soon but would not be drawn on the specifics. Keren did not know what to make of this, although at one point in the hours following the assassination she did spy Medwin deep in conversation with two men who, she later learned, had been Yared Hevrin's advisers.

As she spurred her horse out of the gates of the compound, she found herself smiling at the pull of the jerkin and her mailshirt on her shoulders, the bulk of the small shield slung over one shoulder and the solid weight of her sword on her left hip. Along with the smell of her horse, it was a combination of sensations and pressures which her body remembered well, and which made her feel protected and ready for anything. The Daemonkind Orgraaleshenoth's assault on her flesh and spirit a few months ago suddenly seemed a world and an age away.

This early the streets of Scallow were icy, cold and grey, but not deserted. Word of the impending attack had spread quickly through the town and as Redrigh's riders trotted down towards the river, they passed groups of women and children trudging the other way. Some would be going up to the castle for shelter and safety while others faced a longer walk north to encampments deep in the wooded hills. Many men, and some women, were being armed with spears and axes by serjeants of the city guard, and marched off down to the riverbank. Keren saw every kind of face in their number, every shade of fear and anger.

Ahead was the broad carriageway which sloped up on great piles, and led across the short bridges which linked a couple of rocky islets prior to entering the Bridges district itself. As the company trotted across, hoofs hammering on the heavy woodwork, Keren could see wharfs and jetties coming into view on either side. Then further off to the right, along the west bank, dozens of masts jutted from the waves near the main docks of Scallow, some trailing torn sails and rigging into the dark, choppy waters. One vessel, a long shore-lugger, lay upturned and mastless on the pebbly shore, its hull punched through with a multitude of dark holes. Some said they had seen corpses moving in the waters the previous day, during the terrible panic as the ships began to slip beneath the surface. A host of small craft had put out to rescue survivors, and one ghastly story told of a boatman who tried to haul a body into his skiff only for the sodden corpse to seize his neck and drag him under.

Night and the shifting currents had loosened much from the sunken ships and a line of flotsam had been washed up along the shore while a scattering of crates and wooden debris drifted and bobbed further out. Keren could see hooded figures in boats

scavenging with hooks and nets, then the sight was gone as the stilt
road they were on dipped between two buildings.

The southernmost roadways were busy with detachments of
archers and spearmen taking up positions, and more than once she
saw some bargee shouting in fury as his vessel was tied up and shack-
led. Then a well-fed officer on horseback rode up accompanied
by a standard bearer and a scribe, and haughtily demanded who
they were and what business they had in the Bridges district. Once
Redrigh told him, his manner changed from disdain to unpleasant
amusement.

'Ah, our friends from Besh-Darok. Your task is to patrol the main
wharfs along Wracktown – there are several squads of spearmen
there already, so you won't be lonely.' He laughed but Redrigh
and Keren remained impassive. 'The way down is over there behind
that warehouse, so be quick about it.'

With that he wheeled and trotted off. Keren stared at the device
on his banner, a torch and a bow, and committed it to memory.

The way down to Wracktown was a series of shallow ramps built
against the heavy timber shafts that supported the buildings, roads
and walkways of South Bridges. Beyond a dilapidated gate the first
of them sloped down between two warehouses to a dim landing
from where the next led off at an angle underneath a confusion of
joists and cross-beams. The damp air stank of rotting fish and there
were heaps of rubbish everywhere, some identifiable, others less
so. They had reached the third and final ramp when the sound
of trotting hoofs made Keren turn in her saddle to see who was
following. It was Medwin.

'What are you all doing here?' he asked. His hair was dishevelled
and his beard was straggly in a way that brought a smile to
Keren's lips.

Redrigh explained their encounter with the officer, and when
Keren told him what the man's blazon was Medwin snorted
in annoyance. 'Gaborig of Goldenbow, a self-important know-
nothing. Almost no one uses this road – too many footpads and
kidnappers, and the planks themselves are unsafe. Any accidents,
twisted hoofs?'

'None, ser Medwin.'

'Well, thank the Mother for small mercies.' He nudged his horse forward. 'I'll ride the rest of the way with you.'

'I came here last night,' Keren said. 'Road down a sloping road east of here, not far from one of the canal entrances.'

'That is really the only safe way in,' Medwin said. 'In fact, I spoke to someone who saw Gilly arrive there by carriage and walk in. Same person also saw a mastless ship sail away from the outer jetties listing badly.'

At last they came to the main quay of Wracktown, a long, low dock swamped in perpetual shadow. A dank chill crept through Keren's clothing and the breath of the riders and horses around her turned white. As they rode along the mostly-deserted quayside, Keren could see hoarfrost glittering on the black flanks of the great hulks, and icicles fringing their timber supports and webs of hawsers.

'Night's edge but it's cold!' said Redrigh.

'It may be less icy by the time the rebel ships arrive,' Medwin said. 'But not noticeably so.'

'What about reinforcements?' Keren said. 'I heard that message birds have been winging to and fro all night.'

'Yes, several companies of infantry are rushing from the northeast but they won't arrive until mid-afternoon. The invaders, though, will be here within the hour.' Medwin inhaled deeply, let out a great foggy plume and regarded Keren and Redrigh with frowning concern. 'I want both of you to exercise common sense and caution in this – no wild heroics, mind. There are plenty of ordinary militia and spearmen to hand, so if it comes to the enemy trying to gain a foothold here leave the hand-to-hand fighting to others. Look after your men and get back to shore safely afterwards—'

'Indeed Medwin, we shall,' Keren said with a smile, suddenly realising how worried he was. 'Only our skills shall guide us.'

'Which will mean worrying me into my next life, no doubt,' the mage said. 'Remember, no unnecessary risks.'

With that, he turned his horse and left at a light canter. Keren and Redrigh shared a smile as they watched him recede along the shadowy quay. Then they fell silent when a militia guard officer and two spearmen emerged from between a couple of the mouldering hulks. Seeing the group of riders they came over, identified Redrigh as the commander and saluted.

'Red-Serjeant Jirgo, ser. Are you the Beshdars we were told about?'

'That's us, serjeant. I'm Captain Redrigh and this is my second, Rider-Serjeant Asherol. How many men have you here?'

Keren almost grinned at this field promotion but managed to keep her face straight as the militia serjeant replied.

'Four hands of spearmen, two of axemen. All the bowmen are up on that road, or deck or whatever they call it.'

Three heads craned back to peer up at the balustraded edge where a line of figures was just visible. It was like gazing up a weathered, rain-stained cliff of massive wooden columns.

'Wracktown seems pretty quiet,' Keren said when they looked back down. 'Did you evacuate the locals overnight?'

Serjeant Jirgo gave a bemused look. 'There's been no evacuation, ser Asherol.'

'Isn't that dangerous?' she said.

'Mayhap,' Jirgo said, a smile twitching at the corners of his mouth. 'For the invaders. If you come with me, sers, I'll show you what I mean.'

Leaving one of the other senior riders in charge, Redrigh and Keren dismounted and followed Jirgo down half a dozen worn, wooden steps to a lower, narrower wharf. The slanted, cracked and decrepit hulls on either side turned it into a shadowy gulf, deserted and quiet but for the knock of their bootheels on the old planks. A good distance ahead Keren could make out a detachment of men with spears and axes lounging by a barricade of crates and ballast sacks – she also noticed a growing murmur of voices which drew her gaze upwards. In the sterns of the vessels on both sides figures stood along the bulwarks, mostly men armed with spears and slings, but there were women and children too, the latter cavorting as children do, without a care in the world.

As Redrigh went over to talk with the militia men, Keren looked at Jirgo. 'Aren't they taking stupid risks, these people? This is an invasion we're facing, not a day in the forest.'

The serjeant shrugged. 'No one can force them to do what they

don't want to. Besides, some of them are better armed than we
are. Trust me, ser Asherol, you'll be glad of them when those mad
Islesmen get here.'

Keren was not convinced but the more she saw of other end-
of-wharf defences, the more she realised that any force of invaders
would also face retaliation from the old hulks, which were effec-
tively small forts. The walkways between them would become
killing ditches and clearly Redrigh and his riders were meant to
come down hard on any invaders who made it through.

After seeing about half of the dozen or so defensive positions,
Keren made her way back to the higher quayside at the eastern end
of Wracktown, near the sloping ramp she had come by the previous
day. Redrigh had stationed half of his riders there, including her
own mount. She led her horse along the line of abandoned huts
and lean-tos, stopping by a shabby Earthmother shrine to feed the
creature a handful or two of grain. She was staring at the shrine's
weatered statue, pondering the red tears on its face, when shouts
went up from a number of places. Quickly she tied her horse to
one of the shrine's posts then hurried down to the nearest low wharf
and along to its end.

'Ware sails!'

By the time she reached the low wall of crates and barrels, the
rigged masts of the enemy ships were clearly visible, sailing in fast
on the chill breeze that was coming up from the Sea of Drakkilis.
Around her, the militia speculated excitedly on what the Islesmen's
tactics might be – would they try to establish a beachhead on the
east shore, aiming to seize the city? Or would they put troops
ashore on the other bank and capture the western half of the Dalbar
mainland?

As the moments passed, the invading fleet grew nearer and the
sheer size of some of the vessels became apparent. While most
were the long, narrow two-masters favoured by the Islesmen for
their speed and manoeuvrability, another six or seven were of a
different scale entirely and had two or three decks, three or four
masts, and a bank of oars. Still closer they came and Keren could
feel the mood about her become sombre, and heard lowered voices
pointing out the banners flying from the large ships, identifying the

clan each belonged to. Yet everyone agreed that these giants of the sea came from across the Bay of Horns to the north, from the Jefren Theocracy.

The fleet slowed, the greater vessels moving into a rough line parallel with the eastern shore while the smaller ones formed groups at either end with a sizeable cluster holding close formation nearer the centre of the wide channel. Frowning, Keren peered out at the nearest of the Jefren ships and noticed what appeared to be large outriggers attached to either side of its hull with heavy booms. It looked like nothing she had seen before on a ship that size and as she stared, trying to make out more details, fires bloomed on one of the upper decks, amid a jumble of large, upright supports. For a moment she was buoyed by hope that some mishap had occurred. Then a ball of fire shot up from the ship's deck in a long, high arc towards the city.

There was a collective gasp of horror, and the reason for the outriggers was suddenly clear. As the deck-mounted catapults hurled more missiles into the air, the great ship bucked visibly but the outriggers kept it from rolling back.

The soldiers around her, and the Wrackfolk watching from their decaying hulks, cried out in anger and fear as the first blazing knot fell like a comet into a cluster of buildings well within Scallow's perimeter wall. Burning chunks erupted from the point of impact and fire took hold on nearby roofs and walls. The missile was probably an oil-soaked bale of rags, hay and tinder bound around a keg of pitch.

Mother's name! Keren thought. *If they're using such weapons against the city, what are they going to do to us? Or are they just going to ignore us?*

The militia soldier next to her raised his axe, a long-hafted, double-bladed piece, tugged off its waxed canvas sheath and laid it flat on the crate before him, As he retied his long black hair into a warrior's knot, he glanced at Keren and offered a small, grim smile.

'I'd return to my horses, ser, if I were you.' He looked up at the sky. 'The koltreys are gathering.'

She followed his gaze and saw the dark, soaring carrion birds. 'On the north Cabringa coast,' she said, 'they're known as blackwings, but they mean the same thing. I think I'll wait a little longer, see what happens—'

A mass roar of defiance went up from everyone along the edge of Wracktown as several ships tacked their way out from the shore, the few ships remaining from last night's chaos. Keren knew little about sea warfare, but she could not see how half a dozen vessels might prevail against such a fleet as this. And sure enough, they had covered less than half the distance when a volley of boulders fell upon them, swamping two and smashing one into a floating wreckage of timbers and struggling figures. The other three veered round to bear west, as if trying to get behind the firing arc of those terrible catapults. But the enemy had other weapons and as the Scallow ships approached the nearest Jefren dromond a flock of long black spears leaped out from its forecastle. The effect was devastating – two of the ships sunk immediately and the third, listing badly, turned away and headed for the jetties of Wracktown.

Angry murmurs came from the onlookers at this terrible onslaught, then someone shouted, 'Look!'

All eyes gazed past the crippled vessel to the tight formation of Islesmen ships. Some had unfurled sails and were moving slowly west, opening the formation. From it emerged a larger, wider vessel, mastless and flying no banners, and even at that distance Keren could see that a sorcerous emerald nimbus hung about it. A dread chill trickled down her spine as the ship turned to move straight towards Wracktown.

'One ship?' snorted the axeman beside her. 'They'll have to do better than that.'

'They probably will,' she muttered under her breath. Then she glanced over at the continuing bombardment of Scallow and cursed – almost a quarter of the city seemed to be on fire and a great pall of smoke was drifting north on the breeze. For a moment she thought she could hear the screams of the trapped and the dying but knew that was impossible. *The wind*, she thought. *The sound of the waves*.

Looking back out at the attacking fleet, she saw that the mastless, eldritch ship was closer and on a course that would cross with the fleeing Scallow vessel. The crippled vessel's helmsman managed to turn it slightly to avoid a collision but then, to Keren's horror, the glowing ship altered course and sailed on relentlessly. Crewmen on the Scallow vessel gesticulated frantically at the oncoming ship, all to no avail. In the remaining seconds figures leaped into the cold waters and struck out to either side.

Then the sorcerous ship struck. The Scallow ship did not shift or roll over, for the attacker's prow crunched straight into the port side near the stern and carved right through all the timberwork of hull, deck and keel without pause. The attacking ship ground its way through, exiting the starboard just to the rear of the prow. Almost hacked in two, the wrecked craft sank. The glowing ship, its wake aswirl with wreckage and bodies, quickly veered to port, bringing it back on course for Wracktown. It was, Keren reckoned, more than a minute away.

Her feelings of peril and foreboding surged. She turned to the axeman and his companions. 'We can't stay here – that thing's coming straight for us!'

Some of them just laughed. 'Don't get afeared, girly. We'll protect you!'

'Fools!' she cried and ran back along the wharf, shouting at the people up on the hulls to either side, telling them to abandon their homes and flee along to the main quay. A few obscenities were the only replies, until someone back at the end of the dock shouted:

'Night's blood – she's right!'

Once glance over her shoulder told her volumes. The eldritch ship was mere seconds from ramming the old vessel on the right, and people were starting to stream out of its wharfside doors in hysterical panic, joining those already bolting away from the dock end.

She ran for dear life, boots hammering the planks, arms pumping. At the steps she took them three at a time, expecting at any moment to hear a massive impact. She reached the top, not daring to look back, and dashed over to her horse, wrenched the reins loose and vaulted into the saddle. Only then did she look behind her and what she saw froze her to the marrow.

More than a hundred people had fled the hulks and jetties to gather on the lower wharfside, thinking themselves safe from peril. But from her higher vantage Keren saw everything, in terrible detail.

There was a thunderous, tearing crash as the glowing vessel slammed into one of the decrepit, old ships. The half-rotten hull burst apart and the enemy ship carved an inexorable path through it, ripping open cabins and holds given over to homes and taverns and workshops, obliterating them all. For a moment Keren thought it would slow, lose momentum and stop, but on it came as if it were an iron blade thrusting through toys made of twigs.

The whole quayside shuddered and Keren's horse whinnied, jerking to the side in fear. With a tight grip on the reins and a warm hand to stroke the beast's neck, she calmed it. Then another deep wooden crunch sounded above the din of smashed timbers, and shrieking, terrified voices grew near as the hulk-folk came pouring up from the lower wharf. Beyond them, the unrelenting enemy vessel was grinding its way through another old ship on a course heading for the dockside near Keren. Unlike the lower wharfs, the main quay was massively built on ten-foot wide piles sunk deep into the riverbed. Keren wanted to believe that it would be solid enough to stop the marauding destroyer but certainty failed her and she yanked on her horse's reins, urging it up the long ramp that led out of Wracktown.

She got out ahead of an uncontrolled mob and up on to a wide stilt road which curved westwards through a dense district of warehouses. She wheeled her horse in time to see the glowing ship strike the edge of Wracktown's main quay. As if it was tinder it broke with a loud splintering crack and huge, shattered pieces of timber flew into the air as the vessel battered on through the long, heavy planking to plunge into the great framework of supports underpinning South Bridges itself.

She stared in shocked disbelief as the ship, surely driven by the power of the Wellsource, disappeared from view. Yet she could hear the destruction it was wreaking, and feel the tremors, and see the crowds of people abandoning their workshops and homes. Then a long swathe of densely packed buildings and walkways began to slump and fall inwards, opening up a jagged chasm. Tall timbered goods houses either collapsed fully into the rift or toppled in from both sides. Many of the undersupports anchoring the Bridges district had been interconnected down the years, joists resting on underframes that were braced against load-bearing walls or crossbeams which, when they failed, pulled all else down with them. A score-strong crowd some distance in front of Keren suddenly found themselves scrambling for safety as the wide walkway section they were watching from tilted forward and began to break apart.

Keren was too busy trying to control her horse to help. As she fought the panicking beast away from the widening rift the stilt road she was on gave forth a sickening groan and lurched sideways. *I can't stay here*, she thought. *I'll die like the rest!* Digging in her heels, she urged her mount into a gallop along the unsteady road to a nearby junction and down on to a lower thoroughfare which climbed and ran north, almost parallel with the chasm of destruction. Reaching the road's highest point she stared at the still-unfolding catastrophe. I'm watching hundreds upon hundreds of people die, she realised, the horror of it settling hollow in her stomach.

Then the glowing, Wellsource ship burst into view on the north side of the Bridges district, destroying a loading dock and marina as it did so. Wreckage was strewn in the waters as the ship surged out into the dark expanse of the Sarlekwater. Keren breathed in deeply, almost afraid to look back round at the scene of chaos, but forced herself.

A tangled forest of shattered timbers was mingled with collapsed walls and roofs, and twisted ironwork balustrades. Buildings had been torn open to expose bedrooms, kitchens, offices, workrooms, with water trickling from broken pipes while the scattered contents of hearths were starting dozens of small fires. Bodies lay on fallen floors, or were impaled on upthrusting spars, or wallowed lifelessly in the debris-choked waters, or . . .

She averted her eyes, gazing north to see the evil vessel turning in a leisurely curve, coming back round towards the eastern wards of Bridges, its speed undiminished, its course starkly evident. In her mind's eye she imagined the dread ship repeatedly smashing in and out of the Bridges district until all that was left was a wide stretch of devastation and death. For a wild moment, she thought of riding towards the ship, somehow leaping on board and confronting the one behind all this . . .

Who could probably kill me by just looking at me, she thought. *Medwin, I've got to find him.*

Which meant heading for the east bank before the enemy ship cut her off.

Hauling on the reins, she turned her horse's head and spurred it into a canter back down the stilt road. As she passed the junction with the now-collapsed roadway, a long crashing sound announced the enemy ship's return. Fleeing people crowded the roads and walkways leading east and Keren had to use her horse to force a way through. Soon she was riding up to the platform on one side of a bridge linking South Bridges to a rocky islet from which a larger bridge stretched to the shore. The bridge before her was a sliding structure that spanned one of the two main canals which snaked through this side of the Bridges district. People were crossing in a constant stream, most on foot, most carrying bundles of possessions or small chests, or pulling small carts piled with belongings.

Keren was just approaching the bridge, edgily aware of the rumble of destruction drawing near, when a knot of youths off to the side began shouting excitedly and pointing. She looked south to the invading fleet and was surprised to see a flotilla of low, narrow ships, each driven by a bank of oars and moving fast up the inlet. Each flew a banner from its stern, a slender pale blue standard whose details were lost at that distance. As she watched, the lead craft swept straight towards one of the outlying Islesmen longships and rammed it amidships. Everyone who saw this let out a massed shout of triumph . . .

Later on, Keren was not sure if it was that or what was about to happen that startled her horse. But the creature reared then plunged forward, bucked violently, hurling Keren out of the saddle, then bolted for the bridge, scattering people to left and right. Keren half-landed on top of a group of Bridges folk who helped her back to her feet. Cursing the horse for a jittery beast, she thanked her helpers then hurried after it, squeezing past people, trying to keep the horse in view.

The unending sound of destruction beneath the timber façade

was suddenly a close roar getting closer. The other side of the
sliding bridge dropped, throwing everyone on it forward. Terrified
people fell, scrabbled for handholds or were crushed. Keren dived
at the bridge's side frame, wrapped her arms around a solid wooden
beam. At the same time, the road and platform she had so recently
passed along split apart in a cascade of wrecked timbers as the long,
mastless shape of the Wellsource ship smashed its way out. All of
this happened in only a matter of seconds but Keren, hanging on
while people fell screaming past her, found herself staring down at
the vessel as it passed by.

Through a shifting green nimbus she saw a man in loose-fitting
garments standing at the prow, bare arms folded as he stared ahead;
she saw the decrepit state of the ship; she could see into the hold
and espy torrents of rushing water within; and she could see a figure
lashed to the stump of the main mast, kneeling on the deck with
head bowed.

Almost before recognising the light brown clothing, she knew
it was Gilly. She wanted to cry out to him but the vile ship was
past and gone before she could draw breath.

She swung her legs up to the beam to sit astride it, trying not to
look down for too long. Her side of the bridge was attached to
a solid set of piles cross-beamed to others which were part of the
still-standing canal wall. But as before, buildings and other structures
were collapsing into the gulf of destruction wrought by the sorcerous
ship. Soon, the spreading devastation would drag the bridge supports
down with it.

Then something flew past and thudded into the woodwork
nearby. It took her a moment to realise that it was a light cord
attached to a crossbow bolt. Quickly she reached out to grab it then
stared up at the other end to see Medwin and Golwyth feeding out
heavy rope which was tied to their end of the cord.

Feeling almost weak with relief, Keren let out a hoarse, dry laugh
and began winding in her lifeline.

Chapter Sixteen

Divine Mother!
All who live and breathe take from thee,
And all who sleep and die go to thee.

from *The Word Of The Fathertree*, 5th Cantation

As Golwyth's men hauled Keren up from the wrecked bridge, Medwin was appalled at the state of her but kept the anxiety from showing in his face. Her rider's jerkin was torn at the shoulder, there was mud spattered up her left side, scratches and bruises on her face, scratches on her hands and blood smearing from a cut on her temple which she seemed not to notice. Yet she still had that indomitable air of readiness, a slender-faced, wiry woman willing to rejoin the fray.

Not this time, my lady of swords, he thought. *I want you kept safe – we may yet find your affinity with the Daemonkind of use.*

He gazed across at the devastation gouged through the nearer part of the Bridges district. Crowds of people were scrambling down stairs, ladders and gantries to low jetties where small boats were ferrying survivors to the shore, a sight sure to be repeated all across this stricken place. Not that the shore was so safe from attack, although the catapulted fire bales had become infrequent since Yared Hevrin's ramships joined battle with the Jefren dromonds.

May the Earthmother grant you surcease of woe and pain, Yared, and a return to the flesh in a time of peace . . .

Wiping her face on her sleeve, Keren came over to Medwin, her eyes full of hard, contained anger.

'Medwin, I have to get back across,' she began. 'Redrigh's

still over there, so if Golwyth can lay hands on a boat, a raft, something—'

'Wait now – Captain Redrigh can take care of himself, and in any case we have to send someone up along the lakeside with a vital message . . .' He paused, looked closer at her and frowned. 'You seem close to exhaustion, Keren. We'll get you back to the compound . . . send someone else . . .'

'No, you . . . you can't send me back to the city!' She was dismayed and angry. 'Please, Medwin, I'm not even tired . . .'

He gave her a long, piercing stare. 'Have you the strength for a fast gallop up the lake?'

'I have, I swear it.'

Medwin made a great show of reluctant mind-changing, ending with a deep sigh. 'Very well. There are another seven of those ramships waiting in a cove north along the lakeside – one of Golwyth's men will lend you his horse so you can ride with all speed up the lake shore. Once you find the ships, tell the captains I sent you.' From an inner pocket he pulled a pale blue banneret and gave it to Keren. 'They'll know this is a token of proof from Yared's allies. When you have their attention, tell them to sail down the lake to the city and engage that accursed ship. They may not be able to sink it, but they might delay it and let more innocents escape from the Bridges.'

Keren stared out at the receding Wellsource ship with a hawkish hate in her eyes, then stuffed the banneret into her jerkin and nodded to Medwin.

'I shall not fail you,' she said, then turned to Golwyth who led her over to a group of his men, standing by their mounts. Moments later she was off at a spirited gallop, crossing the great span to the shore where she climbed the main way and turned south along the shore road.

'Her safety is of great concern to you,' Trader Golwyth observed. 'Do you have children of your own?'

'Hmm?' Medwin was momentarily puzzled. 'Ah, I see. No, no . . . though once I was almost married. A long time ago.'

Golwyth regarded him with an amused frown, but Medwin said no more.

'I think, ser Medwin, it would be wise for us to retreat to the relative safety of the shore,' the master trader said.

Medwin shook his head. 'I would stay here a little while longer to see if I can locate the valiant Captain Redrigh. And perhaps make another attempt to break that sorcerer's concentration.'

Golwyth gave a crooked smile. 'Well, 'tis said that three times is a charm.'

'More likely the cause of a headache,' Medwin said wryly. 'Return to your compound, Golwyth, and if the Marshals are looking for me inform them that I shall be along presently.'

The master trader nodded and left. As the sound of his men leaving on horseback faded, Medwin walked a few paces closer to the broken edge of the long, shattered canal entrance and the canyon of devastation. From somewhere way down in the wreckage came the moans of the trapped and the sobbing and the murmurs of rescuers. In his need for centred calm he tried to shut it all out, but failed. Death filled this place like a choking vapour. Behind him the fires were out of control and had engulfed nearly half of Scallow, while before him in the Bridges – who could tell how many had already died? Thousands, certainly. The blind, fanatical minds who could perpetuate such merciless slaughter on innocents were undeniably evil but on a scale he had not encountered before.

And in his private, most secret fears he had begun to wonder what it would take to defeat such an enemy, and even whether it could be achieved.

Out in the wide channel to his left, the great Jefren dromonds were on fire, dark shapes shadowed in smoke and sinking as other lesser clashes took place amidst the tangle of ships. Small boats had begun swarming out from the shore, bearing loads of soldiers towards savage, bloody boardings. The Islesmen looked to be defeated, and it was all Yared Hevrin's doing. It was he who had gone to Bardow a month and a half ago with his observations of the Islesmen's demands and secret dealings, and offered a bold plan to portage a fleet of fast, oar-driven ramships overland via the Red Way. After meetings with the High Conclave, it was decided that a third of the ships would be diverted along the valley of Gronanvel to the Bay of Horns and thence down the

sea channel to Sarlekwater as a precaution against attack from
the north.

Yet still the Wellsource vessel was out there, the sorcerer's
presence impressing itself on Medwin's undersenses like a force
of nature. Since just before the arrival of the enemy fleet, a
broodingly oppressive glamour had settled over the entire region,
stifling certain aspects of the Lesser Power. Most thought-cantos
were unaffected but mindspeech across any significant distance
proved almost impossible.

Ah, Bardow, my friend, he thought. *Your counsel and support would
be so welcome . . .*

Clasping hands tightly at his waist, he cleared his thoughts,
expunged fear and doubt, and prepared to pit himself against the
enemy again.

Deep below the High Spire, secret and known to only a few, was
a chamber. The chamber was rectangular, high-ceilinged but not
overly large, with six delicate pillars spaced along one of the walls,
decorative arches linking them and framing elaborate mosaics. The
opposite wall had the same number of pillars except that each
arch led into a small alcove where Earthmother priestesses used
to come to pray and meditate. The masonry was all of a dark
stone, dark grey and dark blue, and the two thick candles burning
on a shelf near the door were only able to spread their halo of
illumination as far as the plain, square table where Bardow sat in a
high-backed chair, thoughtfully regarding what lay before him. On
the worn, unvarnished tabletop was a good-sized book lying open
with a separate sheet of crabbed writing sitting atop the curved,
frayed-edged pages, while beside it were two small brass-bound
caskets, likewise open. One casket held the Crystal Eye, cradled
in a goldwire framework, its perfect surface reflecting soft yellow
pinpoints of candlelight. In the other was the Motherseed, its ridged,
dark brown shape resting amid folds of blue silk. The former was
a fount of subtle powers, ancient knowledge and never-sleeping
vigilance, sometimes seeming half-alive, whereas the latter was
both key and door to the Earthmother's realm, a secretive talisman
through which the Goddess had spoken with Tauric and Alael.

But for Bardow at the moment, the most fascinating of them all was the single sheet of parchment. Picking it up, he reread for the fourth time Onsivar's translation of the passages gleaned from the palimpsest page in Keren's book. The concise yet graceful directions for melding the Rootpower and the Wellsource power was breathtaking – it explained certain obscure references to Orosiada's 'heartsfire' blade. But it begged the question of how those mages of old came to have sufficient Wellsource power to work with . . .

Then to his mind came the thought he had not yet dared to frame. *With Nerek's bond to the Wellsource, and Alael's affinity with that intense form of the Lesser Power – Earthmother's Gift the priestesses call it – might it be possible to re-enact that melding and create a weapon capable of slaying the Shadowkings?*

He shook his head and laughed. How could any of them hope to get within an arm's reach of any of those dread warlocks when a sea of swords stood in the way? Then he thought of where he was and imagined a desperate last stand, with the enemy fighting corridor by room to reach this underground place. Perhaps one or some of the Shadowkings would be tempted to be in at the last, to savour the triumph and ensure the safety of Eye and Seed. Indeed, a warrior wielding a melded weapon and waiting here might accomplish what defenders and walls failed to do. Yes, as soon as Nerek returned from hunting this sorcerer-spy, he would gather her and Alael together and see what could be done.

Reaching forward, Bardow closed the book then stood and stretched, wincing at the aches in his shoulders. He stared at the pure sky blue of the Crystal Eye, problems crowding his thoughts. Then he sighed and shut and latched both caskets. He had not heard from Medwin for several hours now and all attempts at mindspeech had proved fruitless. His anxiety over the Scallow situation was a constant burden, exacerbated by the news of Yared Hevrin's death, and his confidence in the dead man's gambit was an uncertain thing. From what Medwin said early that morning, it seemed likely that the possessed Coireg Mazaret was deeply involved in both the merchant's death and Gilly's disappearance. Bardow recalled what Nerek had said months before about her encounter with the man in Trevada, after she and Suviel had been captured, and it seemed certain that Ikarno's unfortunate brother was host to the revenant spirit of some powerful sorcerer.

That was when the yearning came upon him, a yearning for the pure strength of the Rootpower. His body remembered how it felt to have the force of it coursing through him, and his senses remembered the greater world that it had opened for him, and worse, his very intellect retained a vestige of the mental reflexes from that time when his mind was anything but cramped and weary . . .

Bardow found that he was clenching his fists so hard that the fingernails were digging into his palms. The pain was almost refreshing and helped brush aside the aching loss. He smiled sadly – strange that while he was able to banish such savage longing from his dreams, they still lay in wait for him in the waking day.

Activity, that was the answer. Keeping busy. Although he was several flights of stairs below ground, he knew that it was still light with a few hours yet till sunset. And it was more hours than that since Azurech's deadline had elapsed with no apparent action on the enemy's part.

'They'll wait for the sun to go down before springing any nasty surprises on us,' he had told an anxious Yasgur earlier in the day. 'He has a taste for the dramatic, this Shadowking Byrnak. Nothing would please him more than to see our city in flames by night.'

Yasgur and the High Conclave were planning to have guards on every main street across the city by nightfall, and Bardow knew that, despite his weariness, work was what he needed now. Besides, it was imperative to get Alael and Nerek back to the High Spire with all speed so that the melding of powers could be studied, though that *could* wait until the morning.

He patted the back of the wooden chair then, with the door half-open, he blew out the temple candles and left, locking the door with a charm as he went.

Even with eyes closed, Keren felt sure she was lying on the back of a horse, a gigantic and graceful horse whose stately gallop rocked her back and forth without the slightest jolting, nothing to make the hurt in her head flare up. But the weather must be bad, for her limbs and her clothing felt wet, as was the wide hard saddle on which she lay. She tried to curl up but with the effort came a stab of pain like hot needles through her head and she opened her eyes.

The half-swamped broken deck of the ramship still wallowed in waters shrouded by a heavy sea mist. By the dim grey light it seemed that the day was moving into late afternoon so she had not been unconscious for too long. The effects of the concussion seemed to ebb and flow between this weakened, nauseous state and limp insensibility. She had been struck in the head during the final clash with the Wellsource ship, out here in the Bay of Horns, when . . .

Keren frowned, trying to remember what had happened, but it remained stubbornly beyond recall. It was important, too, something she had to remember . . .

She groaned quietly, unable to dredge it from her memory. Maybe if she retraced events it would jog something loose. Yes, that might work. She remembered Medwin's little performance to coerce her into staying away from the hazards of the Bridges, asking her instead to run an errand to some ramships anchored at a jetty further up the Sarlekwater. Once she had found them and passed on the mage's instructions to sail down and engage the sorcerer's vessel, one of the captains said, 'Will you be coming with us?'

She had not needed to be asked twice. Leaving her mount with a stable near the jetty, she had boarded the last craft as its crew were loosening the hawsers. The journey down Sarlekwater was unexpectedly brief – once the oarsmen had swung into the rhythm of rowing, the ships had flown across the waters. As they had drawn near the now-broken outline of the Bridges district, the glowing Wellsource vessel had emerged from the western side, shattered wreckage spreading in its wake. Keren remembered standing in the stern, icy gusts of wind tugging at her clothes, watching the enemy turn its prow towards them and come on.

But the memory frayed away and the harder she tried to grasp the fragments the slower her thoughts grew. An awful chill washed through her but she seemed unable to shiver as the stone-like coldness flooded into her mind . . .

Her feet were all she could see, shod in open-toed sandals, walking up a mountain track with tiny blue turilu flowers scattered either side. Then it became a riverside path, clumps of reeds left and right, and a small, low wooden bridge across a tributary stream. Then a trail through tall, slender trees, golden leaves carpeting the ground. A paved walkway in a town or city, buildings burning all around. A smooth-floored tunnel leading up through a mountain, through gateway after gateway of pain—

She reeled back from the vision and found herself on the floating wreck, breathing heavily, fearing those images of the Ordeal beneath Trevada. Then above the sound of her gasping she heard a thud, then a splash from the choppy waters at the edge of the broken deck. A hand lunged up out of the water and scrabbled on the planking for purchase. She stared in fright as a second hand gripped the edge and a sodden figure entwined in dripping rags and seaweed hauled himself up to sprawl panting on the soaked deck. Head bowed, he then pushed himself up on to his knees and looked up at Keren. It was Gilly, wet hair plastered to his head, face a sickly fishbelly white. His smile was horrible.

'I am so disappointed in you,' he said, spreading his arms. 'How could you forget?'

Behind him, more hands came up from the water to seek handholds on the woodwork, and she cried out—

This time Keren knew she was awake from the pain that made a torture chamber of her skull.

No more dreams, she vowed. She would fight to stay conscious as she went over the bits and pieces of the memories that were slowly coming back to her. She was determined to make sense of it.

The first encounter between the ramships and the Wellsource vessel had been disastrous. She had warned the captains of the ensorcelled vessel's ability to hew through entire buildings, but one of them thought that he knew better. An attempt to ram the enemy's bows left one ramship sundered in two and sinking, and another with smashed oars and a crippled rudder.

The next time, the ramships had tried to strike the enemy amidships but the glowing craft had turned at the last moment and smashed off the prow of another pursuer. But one ramship captain had timed his own change of course as well and his ship's iron ram struck home in the enemy's stern. With one side of his oarsmen pushing backwater, his vessel had slewed round, the hooked ram tearing a gaping hole in the enemy ship's hull.

Seeing this, Keren was exultant – the sorcery that made the front of the ship invulnerable did not seem to extend to the aft. In fact, as she watched the emerald nimbus around the ship faded away as it slowed and began to settle lower in the water. Fear for Gilly suddenly rose up in her and she begged the captain of her ship to approach and board the sinking vessel.

Wordlessly, the captain shook his head and pointed. When she looked the glow of power had returned and the Wellsource ship had risen a little and was under way once more. At its prow she could just make out two cloaked figures helping a third one to stand. The battle turned into pursuit, the three remaining ramships chasing the enemy vessel north, up the lake towards the sea channel.

A grim, hammer-grey sky sent sheets of cold rain lashing down and the ramship captains had canvas covers pulled up on slanted spars. Keren stayed out by the stern, watching the hunters and the hunted. By the time her ship entered the passage to the sea she was soaked to the skin and glad of the heavy skin cloak offered by the helmsman's attendant.

The Wellsource craft drew ahead of its pursuers and when Keren's ship at last slipped out into the Bay of Horns she could see it surging towards a wall of heavy mist that was rolling in from the sea beyond Cape Fury. All three captains agreed to give chase, deciding that whoever encountered the enemy first would blow their horns repeatedly. Then as one they veered round to the northwest and plunged on into the clammy grey veil.

But they had not reckoned with the enemy's cruel cunning. Keren's ship was on the left and it had been scarcely minutes since entering the mist when that dread shape, bathed in febrile green radiance, came scything through the waters towards their port side. Panicking, fearful cries went up and the helmsman threw his full weight on the tiller, forcing a turn to starboard, but it was too late. The enemy's dark and rearing prow smashing into the ramship's side and from the stern Keren saw the covers ripped aside and men crushed as the glowing ship actually rode up and across its victim.

And stopped. Amid the cries for help and the screams and groans and cracks of the dying ship, Keren was thinking only about Gilly. The Wellsource vessel no longer had that viridian glow so she waded along to where it was struck fast, grabbed hold of some heavy netting that hung down and climbed up the side of the hull. At the bulwark she heard someone shouting and peered over the top. A man she recognised as Coireg Mazaret was struggling between three men cloaked head to foot in pale grey.

'No, it's mine . . . this body is *mine* . . . you'll not have it, not . . . have it, for I will fly, you'll see . . . no . . . Nooooh!'

At the same time another pair of similarly garbed figures were untying the limp form of Gilly from the shattered mast. In a sudden burst of fury she swung herself on to the deck, drew her sword and said:

'Release him, you scum, or you'll feel my blade in your hearts – '

All five of the cloaked figures looked round at her as one, and her tongue froze in her mouth at the sight. Each and every one of them had Gilly's face, chalk-white features and blank grey eyes, but still his face . . .

'In the Mother's name,' she said falteringly. 'What is . . .'

Something struck the old Wracktown vessel with a mighty crash, knocking Keren off her feet. As she struggled upright by leaning on the bulwark there was another thunderous impact and a series of shudders. Then the deck began to fall in, and the remnants of the mast toppled, dragged down by its own weight, crashing through the planks. The entire ship seemed to be breaking open like a rotten fruit, as if some ghastly curse of age and decay had finally caught up with it.

Across from her the five men with Gilly's face held Coireg and Gilly up between them, and as she watched they leaped straight into the dark gaping chasm of the disintegrating vessel. She screamed in wordless horror as they did so. She edged over to look down but another shock threw her backwards. Sobbing, she clambered back over the bulwark, holding on to the rough, sodden netting, swaying in the swell of the sea. From that height she saw the two remaining ramships nearby, one pulling away, the other coming for another strike.

It was then that the net from which she hung tore away and sent her plunging into the icy sea where her head struck a floating timber. Near-blinded by pain but driven by desperation, she clung to the same plank, paddling weakly. A large section of decking came into view and she somehow swam over to it, dragging herself up on to the solid, wooden sanctuary where she promptly passed out . . .

The last light of day was fading above her, and night was spreading out its cold and furtive cloak, but she now remembered what had happened, the battles and the perils, and the horrors, all of it. And right now her eyes needed to close and she needed to sleep, if only that scrape, scrape, scrape noise would stop . . .

After a while, voices penetrated her drowse.

'By the Tree! That's her, ain't it? And right where they said she'd be.'

'O'course, laddie – when they say they know, you can take it as fact. But is she alive?'

Keren forced her eyes open, saw two blurred figures looking down, one taller as if he were sitting on something which twitched its ears and whickered . . .

'Ah, yes, y'see? – don't you worry, m'lady, soon 'ave yer safe and sound.'

'Better move her up to the wagon. Domas'll not be happy if she catches her death o' it out here . . .'

Domas. As she sank into grey sleep, she held the name close like a warming candle of hope.

Interlude of Dreams

Lost upon seas of sleep,
With tattered sails and failing hull,
We founder in the gloom and plunge,
Unresisting into the sepulchral abyss.

Eshen Caredu, *Storm Voyage*, Ch. 3

Alael finally returned to her chambers almost a day after the encounter with the spellcaster at the College of Hendred's Hall. The subsequent pursuit had led north then around the mound of the Chapel Fort, across the Bridge of Hawks and off into the heart of the city. Osper Traum's spell-imbued musical device helped track the man's taint up to the Highcliffe district and down again, eventually petering out near the abandoned buildings of the empty quarter. Weary and exhausted, Alael and Nerek had ridden back to the palace, escorted by Ghazrek and his men.

After changing into a nightshift, Alael ate from a cold platter sent up by the kitchen then dismissed her attendant, Nuri, and shuffled into her small, cold bedchamber. The embers of a fire smouldered in the grate and a single candle burned on a delicate tabouret. Next to the bronze candleholder, shaped like a seashell, was a small slip of parchment on which was a message from Bardow asking her to come and see him tomorrow on a most urgent matter. Could it be to do with the book and the translation that she had hurriedly left in his study the night before? It seemed likely.

Then she was caught by a fit of yawning that made such considerations less important than sleep. So she crawled beneath chilly blankets which her body soon began to warm. Thus cocooned, she surrendered to the slumbering drowse that stole through her mind . . .

She began to dream that she was walking through a ruined city swathed in thick but strangely bright fog, her bare feet warmed by time-rounded stones, her hands caressing eroded marble columns and statues. Through arches she glimpsed gardens, fountains and pools and several times she passed trees which had grown up through the stonework. The smooth curves and bulges of their trunks and roots gave the impression of a living wood that had flowed from between the blocks in its unstoppable pursuit of the sun.

Then she stepped through a doorway and the dream changed, sight and sound becoming noticeably sharper. She was standing in lush undergrowth near the edge of a forest, with the heady odours of earth and sap filling her head. Almost before she turned to see the Vale of Unburdening she knew she had come again to the Earthmother's realm.

The river was as she remembered it, a pale and silent torrent of struggling forms, as was the dense, tangled forest and the towering, rocky valley wall. With her eyes she followed the flow of spirits as it curved away behind the forest, then turned to look the other way . . . and almost jumped with surprise to see a woman standing only a couple of feet away.

'Who are you?' she said. 'Where did you come from?'

The woman was a little taller than Alael and wore the pale blue robe of a priestess, with a loose-knit woollen shawl over her shoulders. She had golden hair gone mostly grey and a kindly face. She offered a ghostly smile.

'I do not know who I am, Alael, but I know that I came from there.' She pointed to the river.

Alael looked uncertainly from the newcomer to the river and back. 'Have you been sent by the Earthmother? Are you a messenger?'

The woman had a serene emptiness about her. She gave an amused shrug. 'Again, I do not know, but we have to go this way.'

At once she strode off through the knee-high grasses and flowers,

and some compulsion led Alael on after her. All movement became
a frantic blur for an eyeblink, then suddenly they were deep in the
green forest, looking into a peaceful sheltering glade. Shafts and
spears of light slanted down from above, making mossy rocks glow
and dew-heavy leaves glitter. Reflected radiance sparkled in a small
pool and whenever insects wandered through the shafts of light
they became for a moment winged, flashing jewels.

At the centre of the glade, four pillar lamps stood at the corners
of a raised tomb of pure white stone. The lid was decorated with
a multitude of animals and people, as were the sides, while carven
figures sat at either end of the stone monument. One depicted a
burly, bearded man in simple garments giving a book, a sword and
a little ship into the upraised hands of a kneeling supplicant. The
other showed the same man sitting next to a beautiful yet unsmiling
woman in a gown of falling folds. Alael glanced at her guide but
quickly saw that the statue was not of her.

'Is this . . .' Alael hesitated a moment, '. . . the tomb of the
Fathertree?'

The woman seemed baffled by this and said, 'Why should it be
a tomb?' Then she held out her hand. 'We'll see that next.'

Alael took her hand and together they walked forward. Again,
there was the blur of surroundings that swept and turned past them
till, only a few steps on, Alael was standing near the cliff-like face of
the great valley wall. In the grass before her were five graves that
appeared freshly dug, the rich brown soil heaped next to each one.
Behind them was a flat, wide slab of rock that jutted from the foot
of the cliff itself, and cut into its surface was an open tomb. At its
head, leaning against the cliff, was a large, square-cut block of stone
clearly meant to cover the sepulchre.

The woman released Alael's hand and went over to stare down
into the open stone tomb for a long, intense moment.

'There can be no words between the living and the dead,' she
said, seemingly to no one. Then she raised her eyes and Alael saw
that tears ran down features wrenched with anguish. 'No words,'
she said, voice choked with emotion. 'Nothing . . .'

Troubled, Alael look away for an instant and when she glanced
back the woman was standing right next to her, staring at her.

'She says that you must help Bardow,' the woman said.

'Who . . . the Earthmother?'

'She says you will have her gift – use it wisely.'

Before Alael could answer, the woman calmly pushed her backwards. Off balance, she twisted as she toppled and saw that she was falling into one of the open graves and she screamed as the darkness rushed up at her—

—and in her night-darkened chamber she struggled awake as her attendant, Nuri, opened the door, lamp in hand.

'Did the commotion wake you, my lady?'

'What commotion?' Alael said. Then she began to hear faint shouts from outside. Nuri, clutching her nightgown fearfully, edged into the room.

'Oh, milady, one of the guards told me the news. The enemy's set fire to the city walls!'

Parts of Scallow were still ablaze by the time the night closed in, mostly dense rows of housing and shops down by the main walls, while other fires still raged all across the half-wrecked Bridges district. Medwin stood watching the burning buildings and the bucket chains of desperate citizens from the window of a small hillside villa overlooking the main dock where darkness masked the jutting masts of many sunken vessels. From recent accounts he knew that the remnants of the enemy fleet were fleeing out to sea while some surviving crews and shipboard troops had reached the western shore and were moving northwest in an attempt to join with allies in the hills. All of which he might have considered a hard-earned victory had he been able to say with certainty that Gilly and Keren were safe and well.

Feeling weary and cheerless, he leaned on the window frame. Just a short while ago he had ended a mostly fruitless search with the thought-canto Spiritwing, which had revealed nothing but the faintest and furthest hint of Keren's presence. Of Gilly he had found nothing. The Spiritwing, however, had drained the last of his stamina, forcing him to retire to this house, owned by a friend of Golwyth. A servant had been sent ahead, and a good fire was burning in the iron hearth so he decided that now was a good moment to

go within and lie down before he fell down. Medwin closed the
shutters, pulled the drapes and stumbled across to a fur-heaped bed
smelling of herbs and sweet forest scents. A lamp glowed on a shelf
overhead but the impulse to put it out faded as sleep pounced . . .

He dreamed that he was walking through a strange house with
only grey daylight coming in through the small windows. It seemed
oddly drab and colourless as he passed through a low, narrow
entryway, then a scullery and a cluttered room full of shelves
and finally a wide, dark passage ending in double doors sitting
ajar. Beyond was a large room full of golden light, tables heaped
with all manner of timber, racks where varnished pieces were hung
to dry, frames on which leather was stretched and shaped. Sawdust
and offcuts littered the floor and the air was full of the pungency
of wood sap.

Across the room a tall, dark-haired man was working on something at a bench and as Medwin made his way round a sense
of distant familiarity began to nag at him. Then he saw the
horse figurines and amulets sitting in wall niches just as the man
straightened, and his surprise was profound. It was his grandfather,
Jharlo Medwin, who had worked as a woodcrafter near Adnagaur for
many a year. When Medwin was quite young, Grandfather Jharlo
had apparently admitted to the rest of the family that he had been
a secret Skyhorse worshipper for most of his life. Medwin's mother
once remarked to his father, when both thought he was elsewhere,
that it was 'a waste of time praying to an animal, and a disgrace'.
Their visits to Grandfather's workshop had been rare after that.

As Medwin approached, his grandfather glanced up and smiled
but kept on working. His large, weathered hands were gripping and
sanding down a small statuette of a young boy on a horse carved in
a fine-grained, yellowy wood. Medwin stared at it, and at the other
carvings decorating the room.

'Is that an offering, Grandfather? Are you going to dedicate it to
the Skyhorse?'

The elderly man laughed quietly. 'Ah, laddie, it's only a carving,
this one. Sometimes, y'know, a horse is just a horse . . .'

Then the dream drifted apart as Medwin opened his eyes, blinked
uncomfortably in the now oddly-bright glow of the lamp above

him. He levered himself upright, opened the lamp's glass door, blew out the flame and settled back under the warm furs.

And sometimes a dream is just a dream, he thought to himself, though failing to convince.

In his well-heated chamber in the Keep of Day at the Imperial Palace, Tauric lay in his large, ornate bed, one hand holding the horse pendant as he slept. In his dream he was down in a crypt suffused with pearly light and walking among scores of worn pillars, seeking a way out. At regular intervals along the stone walls were large alcoves fabulously decorated in a profusion of trees and flowers and vines, all interweaving and beautifully detailed. The recesses held the slanted tombs of kings, queens, mages and priests, who were also depicted in tall paintings hung beside each alcove.

As he walked, the figures in the paintings smiled at him and climbed down to shake his hand, praise his deeds, remark wonderingly upon his metal arm, and accompany him on his progress through the crypt. Once or twice he thought he saw a black dog moving among the busy pillars, but dismissed it as shadows. Quite soon a sizeable crowd of monarchs, mages and priests were following him or rather, he realised, guiding him along in a particular direction.

Before long, the grand procession came to a halt before a very imposing painting of a magnificent white stallion, the very image of equestrian nobility, standing by a long placid lake amid wooded hills with a domed temple on the other side of the lake. For a moment Tauric stared, wondering why they had brought him here. Then a tall and regal man garbed in blued armour and a long red cloak and wearing a black crown made to resemble a turreted citadel, came forward and rapped his knuckles on the painting's hard, dried surface. He smiled wordlessly at Tauric who shrugged and did the same . . . and staggered forward a step as his hand passed into the painting without any resistance.

With a gasp, he snatched his arm away and backed off a little. His well-dressed audience, on the other hand, were chuckling at his alarm, sharing winks and nudging each other, then encouraging him to step into the picture, into that lush lakeside vision with its noble horse.

Such a marvellous beast, they seemed to be saying, *is fit for only the bravest, the most dedicated of leaders*.

Tauric nodded, putting determination in his stance, the set of his jaw and the temper of his gaze. Yes, he fully deserved such a creature as his mount, so he faced the painting, raised his left foot and quickly plunged forward.

The ground on the other side was higher than it looked, and his landing sent a shock up his legs. And it was colder and much darker than the picture had suggested, with a rushing wind gusting and shaking bushes and branches all around and hurling swirls of leaves across the clearing and on to the restless surface of the lake. The horse, too, was not what it had seemed, careering around the clearing in panic. Then it wheeled on sighting Tauric and trotted over to nudge and shove him with its great head, as if urging him to flee. Tauric tried to calm the creature, stroking its neck and shoulder and murmuring soothing nonsense words.

Just as it was becoming more subdued, an immense bestial roar sounded from some distance along the lakeside. At once, Tauric felt the horse begin to tremble and pull away from him, but he held on to the mane and flung his arm over its neck.

'No, wait, brother horse!' he cried. 'Stay with me . . .'

Quickly he jumped and swung a leg across the horse's back even as the unseen monster bellowed and smashed its way through the forest towards them. The white stallion whinnied its fear, trotted off to the side of the clearing but there was only impenetrable, tangled forest hemming them in.

'There is no escape, brother,' Tauric said to it. 'We must face this horror together . . .'

Then, with Tauric holding on tightly, the stallion reared in its terror and despair and spoke:

'Which path shall we take, sire, which path? Quick – you must choose!'

Confused, Tauric could only point at the oncoming menace. The horse reared again and charged across the clearing as something

vast, faceless, shapeless and black came crashing out of the trees
and reached for them—

Then Tauric was sitting bolt upright in bed, eyes wide, thinking
that he had been woken by the shock of that strange, hideous dream.
But there were voices outside his chamber, the thud of a fist on his
door and a couple of his White Companions come to tell him of
the living torches who were burning all along the city walls.

In a north-facing room in a small tower on the Silver Aggor, Atroc
made his preparations for the night ahead. He had thrown out the
few sticks of rotten furniture and swept it clear of bird feathers and
old crumbling leaves. He set no fire, but lit three small rush lights
and put a taper to two bundles of herbs, blowing out the flames to
let them smoulder and give off certain fumes. Soon the room was
grey and choking with scented smoke, giving strange halos to the
little rush lights.

'Time to peer into the Door of Dreams,' he whispered and opened
the room's shutters. Cold air flowed in and he breathed it in then sat
cross-legged before the window, letting the odours and the peace
flow through him.

Atroc's dream brought him to a ridge overlooking a city dominated by a slant-walled fortress with a huge drum keep. The fortress
sat atop a wide rocky outcrop and the city was blessed with a wide
harbour sheltered from the sea by a long, curved headland. He
immediately recognised the city as Rauthaz, capital of Yularia and
lair of the Shadowking Grazaan. This was the very stronghold that
Gunderlek and his unkempt army had somehow seized less than a
year ago, only for it to turn into their tomb when the Acolytes sent
in their vile beasts.

Now, as he watched, a massive wave rolled in from the sea, a
long wall of water whose curling, frothing leading edge took on
the form of a great, stampeding herd of horses. Each mount had a
rider, thus there were a myriad faces and most of those in the lead
were ones that he knew. He saw Byrnak, Yasgur, Welgarak, Alael
and Bardow, the boy-emperor Tauric, Grazaan and Thraelor, Kodel
and Ystregul, Mazaret and Gilly, Keren and her mirrorchild sister
Nerek, and many more. The great horse wave thundered across the

city of Rauthaz and over the low hills, and as it rushed on towards the Gorodar mountains, Atroc found himself flying through the air, keeping pace with those riders at the front.

He soared higher and was able to gaze down at the peaks of the Gorodars as the great wave slammed up against their northerly slopes and surged over them without the slightest pause. Those pale wave-riders fought with their watery chargers as they crashed down on to the dark forests of northern Khatris and swept on, steadily turning south. To Atroc, it all looked remarkably like one of the allegorical canvases he had seen brought out of hiding after the battle for Besh-Darok.

South drove the flood, drowning all in its path, and he noticed that certain faces began to vanish from those leading players, quite a few Mogaun slipped out of sight as did a large number of Southern soldiers and officers. A group of Acolytes stumbled and were overwhelmed by the torrent. Then others began to fall – Mazaret, Yarram and Ghazrek, then Nerek, all gone in an eyeblink, closely followed by all the Shadowkings bar one, Byrnak. Gilly foundered in the raging white waves, as did Yasgur. By now the thunderous flood stretched from the Gorodars across to the Rukangs as it poured south across central Khatris then turned west and poured through the Kings Gate pass. Bardow, Keren and Medwin fell within sight of Besh-Darok, as did the last surviving Mogaun chieftains. Through the pass of the Girdle Hills the diminishing deluge ran, across the fields and the woods with but three riders lurching onward in the spray – the Shadowking Byrnak and off to one side, Alael and Tauric. The very walls of the city were drawing near but before they could be reached the extravagant, nightmarish scene began to fade. Much to Atroc's frustration the Door of Dreams was closing, with that element of timing he had come to hate.

Opening rheumy eyes, he saw immediately the fires blazing down at the city wall, with the majority clustered near the Shield Gate. So Bardow had been right about Byrnak's love of night's drama, and while he watched more fires began to bloom in the dimness some distance off to the south. As his eyes took in the darkness he began to espy large bands of riders moving through the even, snowy gloom beyond the walls. That meant that Byrnak and the other Shadowkings remained wary of committing the fullness of their strength. Of course, the dream he had just experienced seemed to suggest their ultimate triumph . . . but the trouble with some dream visions was that their meanings were so obscure that only a genius or a madman could fathom them, and Atroc had only ever aspired to be half of either and neither at the same time.

He rose from his cramped position and blew out the rush lights one by one. Yasgur would undoubtedly be asking for him very soon . . .

There was a knock at the door.

'Master Atroc, I am sent by Lord Regent Yasgur to ask that you join him in the vantage chamber in the Keep of Night.'

He chuckled quietly to himself, then cleared his throat. 'I hear and obey,' he said loudly. 'Inform the Lord Regent that I shall do all of his bidding that my aged bones can manage.'

As the messenger's footsteps walked away, Atroc laughed darkly to himself while gathering up the herb bundles, now reduced to cold charred twigs, and flung them in the hearth. Perhaps it would be best to keep his dreams to himself, at least until he had a better idea of their meaning. For while Prince Yasgur certainly had motes of madness in his character, he seldom showed evidence of genius when it came to assaying enigmas.

In bewildering silence she drifted, with her memories and thoughts trailing, nagging, dragging, shaming. This was a place of timeless time, of no thought and no action and thus no pain, yet still she was followed by all the spectral rags of her life, persistent ghosts which steadfastly refused to dissolve into the flowing silence. And even though she had managed to banish their tormenting presences from her mind, they never gave up trying to return, coming forward to present themselves to her or arranging themselves into stories too frightening to contemplate.

When one of those old dogged memories, an image of herself, broke away from the rest and floated up and out of sight she felt a measure of satisfaction. Later, however, it reappeared, gliding up from below and bringing a long string of shadowy, ominous memories. The image of herself looked serene and slightly amused, and as it came towards her she tried to turn aside, avoid contact, but failed. That errant fragment of herself thrust the memory string at her and she plunged into a dark story.

In the beginning, the world moved in the darkness of the valleys of the Great Lake of Night. Then came the Fathertree and the Earthmother, although they had other names then, and brought daylight and seasons, sowings and harvests, that the beast herds would raise their faces to the light and become human. The humans divided themselves into the tribes of the People, learned well the lessons given by the Earthmother and the Fathertree, and worshipped as they prospered.

Then, from the well of the Void stepped the Prince of Dusk with nobility upon his brow, joy in his eyes, a smile on his lips and a gift in his hands for the Earthmother. This was the Motherseed, a wondrous object which was both key and door to a realm full of life and growth and all the green verdancy cherished so deeply by the Earthmother. The Prince of Dusk tried to persuade his fellow divinities to keep the human tribes low and untutored, saying that learning and knowledge would bring them only pain and suffering. The Earthmother listened and agreed, but the Fathertree refused and went to live among the tribes of the People.

While the Prince of Dusk and the Earthmother oversaw the building of great temples in their name and enjoyed the devotion of innumerable followers, the Fathertree found that pain and suffering could exist without knowledge and learning. So he created the Crystal Eye so that healers could heal, children would live and wisdom would spread. This angered the Prince of Dusk and the Earthmother who came to him with the intent of forcing him to unmake it, but he had already made a gift of it to the wisest man of the tribes. He in turn had used it to teach many willing pupils how to wield the Godriver, as the Lesser Power was then known.

This infuriated the Prince of Dusk who raised up an army from his followers, imprisoned the Fathertree, and pursued the wise man and his pupils into deep, elder forests. The Earthmother saw unarmed people dying on spears or by club blows and, now knowing that the Prince was wrong, went to the Fathertree and offered her help and

her love. Together they confronted the Prince of Dusk and when
the Earthmother openly denounced him and rejected his advances,
his anger turned to hate. But she had the Motherseed and the wise
men had the Crystal Eye so he was forced to release the Fathertree
and retreat to his great temple.

There he brooded and nursed and fed his hate for many a year
before coming to a fateful decision. There was no hesitation in
him as he delved into the abysses of the world to see where the
Great Lake of Night seeped through. In one vast underground
cavern where darkness lapped at far-flung shores, he found a proud
and savage race whom he raised from beasthood to become the
Daemonkind, first and deadliest of his servants. Next, he cast his
gaze over all his worshippers and selected a few of the most loyal
for a similar elevation, and they were the First Woken. After that, it
was easier to construct all the sinews of the war to come, the armies,
the weapons, the duty, the training, the fortifications and bastions
which were ultimately overshadowed by the immense citadel of
Jagreag.

The war itself was a convulsion of blood that darkened every
land and every life. Seas reared up to bury forests and mountains
while new peaks and fields were wrenched up from the bed of
the oceans. The vast struggle culminated in the year-long Battle
of Kogil which ended with the fall of Jagreag, brought about by
the Staff of the Void, made by the Earthmother's own hand.

The Prince of Dusk was banished to his newly-formed realm,
where he gave himself a new name, the Lord of Twilight. His
surviving servants were imprisoned, apart from the Daemonkind
who he had sent away at the battle's end. Yet this marked merely
the beginning of an ages-long struggle less cataclysmic than the first
but pursued with the same relentless purpose . . .

The story tailed away with a few of the turning points of history,
the rise and fall of empires both dark and light, the instigation of the
Wellsource followed by the seeding and growth of the Rootpower.
The founding of the Khatrimantine Empire and its defeat a thousand
years later, along with the destruction of the Rootpower . . .

As the string of memories came to an end, she could not help noticing the thread of her own story weaving in amongst it all, brought to an abrupt end by that fall from the top of the High Basilica in Trevada. Then the memory string was gone, falling away, back into the depths, but the memory image of herself was smiling at her now. It glided towards her, garments slowly rippling, arms spread wide to gather her in despite her fear and panic, to wrap itself around her—

A long, long instant passed and all her perceptions changed. She was aware of her body and its weight as she lay on her back, and the uneven ground beneath, and the damp grass she could feel with her fingertips. She sat up dizzily, looked down at herself and saw that she was wearing the shawl and blue robe of the memory image. She felt ready to weep or scream yet could do neither . . .

Your road has been long and hard, Suviel, daughter of my daughters, yet your fight is not yet done, your song is not yet sung.

'I do not understand,' she said, covering her face with her hands. 'Who am I?'

You will learn all that eventually, little by little. For now, I have a small task for you to perform. Look.

Opening her eyes she raised her hand in time to see a young, slender woman with long fair hair appear some distance away.

Go over to her. I will tell you what to do and say.

Suviel Hantika sighed and it was a sound as empty as her memory. Then she got to her feet and did the Earthmother's bidding.

Part Three

Chapter Seventeen

A word and a sign,
In the deep, desolate dark,
Where bones and broken banners,
Litter the ancient stones.

Calabos, *Beneath The Towers*, Act 4, 15

Snow was falling steadily. Outside the city walls the air stank of burnt earth and badly charred flesh. The acidic smell raked at Nerek's nose and throat as she rode out of the Shield Gate with Yarram's one hundred knights. The first thing she saw was a wide section of wall along from the gate where blackened blocks of stones were still smoking despite the barrels of water poured down from the parapet. Nerek had been dozing in her room in the palace when the attacks began, but it took her only moments to get dressed, armed and armoured and hurrying from her chamber. Then she had paused, remembering the note sent last night by Bardow which almost ordered her to be at his chambers by dawn. But she reasoned that this attack would be over before then, and resumed her dash through the palace.

By the time she had reached the city walls, sheets of flame were leaping up as high as the battlements. Although everyone on the wall worked frantically to douse the sorcerous fires, at no time did they seem to be a genuine threat. But when the bands of enemy riders emerged from the chill gloom, and other fires started to break out all along the riverdocks and waterfronts, the intent became clear – terror. Up on the wall Nerek had heard first-hand accounts of how lone figures had come stumbling out of the wintry night then, by the light of battlement torches, ran screaming towards the wall where they burst apart in hideous eruptions of crawling flame. The thought that this had started happening within the city put looks of dread on the faces of the men and women guarding the wall.

When word went round that Yarram was soon to take a cavalry company out to harry the enemy, Nerek descended from the walls and hastened to the Imperial Barracks. She had been accorded the status of a knight with the Protectorate Order, which was how she came to be riding forth now into the icy darkness. Yarram's knights were intended as a deterrent to the roving enemy bands reported in the vicinity. Less than a third of them were light cavalry, garbed in padded armour and carrying short bows. Five of them, Nerek noticed, were women who wore their hair short beneath soft grey cowls while the male bowmen wore the more usual leather caps or half-helms. They were all grown women and looked so sombre and unsmiling that Nerek felt an inexplicable kinship with them.

'Never seen them afore?'

A brown-robed rider had edged closer to her, a young fair-haired woman who seemed to be unarmed. She was also vaguely familiar.

'No,' Nerek admitted, then recognition came. 'You're the mage who rode with Mazaret's patrols . . .'

A nod. 'Terzis of Ornim,' the woman said.

' Nerek . . . just Nerek. So – who are they?'

Terzis leaned a little closer and lowered her voice.

'They're all women who have lost children or husbands to either the Mogaun or the Shadowkings' attacks. They're known as the Daughters of the Fathertree – some of them used to be with the Hunter's Children until they fell out among themselves, others fought with the Valemen in the northern Rukangs . . .'

Nerek was about to ask why they were called the Daughters of the Fathertree when Yarram halted the column and split it in two, which left Terzis and herself separated and the Daughters divided. One group would ride up around the northern part of the wall while the other, Nerek's, would patrol the southern part then, assuming no serious encounters, head south down the

Grainway in the hope of meeting reinforcements sent from Sejeend a day ago.

As they rode, Nerek could see that the majority of the fire blackenings marked the west-facing stretch of the wall which made her wonder if the enemy had hoped to burn out the gates. But it was the strange absence of enemy raiding bands which pricked her unease – they came across recent hoof tracks through the snow and the mud, all churned well as if by the passage of a great many horses. Nerek and her fellow riders seemed to be the only living things moving through the freezing, shadowy dark.

Trying to keep the city walls always in view, the column of knights followed by the light of their torches a drovers' track which led round to the east. At one point it climbed a long ridge between two copses and from the crest they could just see over Besh-Darok's wall to catch sight of the fires still burning over at the waterfront. Nerek saw the three bow-women in her column mutter among themselves, then pause when they noticed Nerek's regard. One of the Daughters, a tall, raven-haired woman with pale eyes, stared back with open dislike, spat to the side and rode on in silence with the others. Nerek shrugged and looked away.

The column reached the southeastern end of the wall without incident. The massive fortification, some forty paces thick at this point, came to the brink of the headland and turned north along the cliffside, its foundations laid solidly in the ancient rock. Strong breezes were blowing from the north, hurling flurries of snow down on the riders so they scarcely paused before turning their mounts southward. Their commander was Yarram's deputy, Chaugor, a burly, bearded no-nonsense Dalbari who let them know that they would head for the shelter of Crownhawks Wood, in case the weather worsened.

Once they left the field and farm trails for the straight and well-made Grainway, their progress became swifter, but even with torch-bearers riding ahead this was seldom more than a canter in the enveloping night. Once or twice, Nerek glimpsed lights far away to the west but these soon disappeared, obscured by the heights and dips of the landscape. Occasionally, the passage of their horses would stir a bird from its perch in bush or tree, but other than that the land seemed cold and dead.

By the time they reached the edge of Crownhawks Wood, it was snowing more steadily. There was also a yellow light visible through the leafless tree and the blur of the snow. Nerek had heard that the Grainway curved through these woods before coming to a gorge beyond which lay the plains and low hills of Eastern Khatris. The light grew larger as they rode and Nerek knew it had to be a fire of some size, as did Chaugor for he slowed the column and ordered his light riders forward to scout. They numbered eleven, six armed with bows, four with spears and shields, and Nerek who readied her buckler but kept her sabre sheathed. As they rode on ahead, the main body of the column followed at a distance, torches doused.

Nerek could not help but feel alarmed at this tactic, which seemed to make the scouting party a tempting target. Then the fire came into view and caught all her attention. A pair of open wagons sat burning on the road with motionless bodies scattered all around them. Further along was a box wagon lying smashed on its side, smouldering and stinking of death. Then suddenly they heard it, the clash of weapons mingled with cries coming from further on, where the road entered the gorge. Their officer, a serjeant who was one of the spearmen, ordered one of the bowmen to ride back to Chaugor with the news while the rest waited by the blazing wagons. But even as the messenger was cantering away, the serjeant changed his mind.

'Let's find out what be happening up there,' he said, and they continued along the road at the trot.

They had gone little more than a score of yards when the serjeant's folly became apparent. The rapid thud of hoofs came from their left and Nerek turned to see at least twenty masked riders, some with torches, charging out from a gap in the trees and straight towards them. Two men without masks led them and one of them she recognised immediately as Mazaret, and so pale and gaunt that it could only be one of the rivenshades. The sight of the other man was like a blow, wrenching at the pit of her stomach, almost causing her to drop her reins. It was Byrnak.

For an awful instant their gazes locked, then the dread peril they were in came upon her in a rush as the panicking serjeant roared to follow him. She dug in her heels and her horse leaped forward, along with five of the others. The rest were caught up in a brief, brutal fight which left two spearmen and bow-carriers cut down and slain. Nerek looked round to see that two Daughters of the Fathertree had reined in to a halt not far from the scene of slaughter. Calmly they readied their bows as the enemy riders turned their attention to them.

The sound of fighting from further along the road was louder and Nerek turned her horse about, wary of being caught between two groups of enemies. Then the masked riders began cantering towards the Daughters, all of them shadowy figures limned with the glow of the fires. In the next moment, however, the mass thunder of hoofs heralded the arrival of Chaugor and the rest of his knights, galloping hard, their furs and cloaks billowing behind them, their horses exhaling pale gouts of vapour.

Nerek saw all this despite the darkness, for a strange alteration was sweeping across her body, a tingle of power that raced through her from neck to loins, from fingertips to tongue and caressed her ears and eyes. Wellsource power, rich and alluring. She could see that Byrnak and the Mazaret rivenshade had slowed their riders, and that *he* was staring across the night-veiled distance at her, his lips smiling and moving . . .

Join us, Nerek . . . there is a special place for you at our master's side . . . can you feel the power of the Wellsource once more? Such is his regard for you that he has had certain barriers removed . . . Why not cast off those doomed ones and return to us? Return to us . . .

The bond faded a little and as the knights came riding on with swords bared, the masked horsemen turned aside and dashed into the woods. A cautious Chaugor resisted the temptation to follow, instead gathering his men together with torch-bearers outermost as he waited for the survivors of the scouts to rejoin them. Nerek urged her mount into a trot but her head was spinning with a confusion of thoughts as her very senses continued to quiver in the flow of that power.

It had not been Byrnak, after all, she realised but his pet warlord

Azurech, the one that Mazaret had been hunting. Bardow and Atroc
had mentioned him . . .

Suddenly, she realised that the bow-women were riding off the
road and into the trees. She called after them but the only response
was a contemptuous backward glance. The serjeant was drawing
near, as was Chaugor who rode up with a torch-bearer and an
angry face. Once he heard what had happened, he stabbed a finger
at the serjeant, Nerek and one of the spearmen.

'You three – go in there and tell those harridans that I'm ordering
them to return to the road immediately. Go!'

Wet undergrowth cracked under their mounts' hoofs and dislodged snow made quiet sounds. They were about fifty yards into
the trees when shouts and the clash of fighting came from behind.
She glanced at the serjeant, then twisted in her saddle to look back
at the torch-lit road but all she could see was flickering movements.
When she turned back the serjeant's horse was there but he was
gone. Her newly-enhanced awareness fed her instincts and she
ducked in her saddle while swinging to one side . . . as a spear
came flying silently out of the darkness, cutting the air where she
had been.

There was a thud from the shadows as it struck wood, startling
her horse which set off through the trees. She swung her other leg
over, then dealt the beast a sharp slap on the withers and dropped
off, rolling to a crouch while the horse crashed off through the
brittle, snow-laden undergrowth. Her eyes showed her more with
the Wellsource now at her beck and call. She could see other
hoof tracks leading deeper into the woods, evidence of the two
Daughters, and just smell their taint on the air. She could also
hear those who hunted her, three in number, creeping carefully
but not, to her hearing, soundlessly in the dark. It was the work
of a moment to cloak herself in silence before setting out after the
Daughters' mounts. Her pursuers, meanwhile, chased hers which
was heading northeast, back to the road.

Nerek felt warmer, as if some quiet fire was spreading through
her limbs. She almost felt clothed in the power of the Wellsource,
such was its ubiquity, but she also sensed its ceaseless eagerness, its
unrelenting need to be *used*.

Snow crunched underfoot but made no sound. Black leafless branches rattled together as she pushed by in unbroken silence. Emerging into a clearing on a slope, she saw the signs of a struggle, dark swathes of disturbed snow and a moment later she found several bodies, two horses, one of the enemy mask riders and one of the Daughters. They had been dead a very short time, and the surviving Daughter had left tracks and a definite taint of blood in the air, proof of a wound.

The tracks led up the slope and along to a large tree that hung at an angle over a gully and a frozen stream. With sharp eyes she could see the Daughter sitting at the foot of the tree bole with the stump of a spear jutting from one thigh while both hands held a readied bow as she stared out at the darkness. Nerek decided to circle around to the other side of the tree rather than risk becoming a target.

She was halfway round when the darkness shivered and a tall shape lunged at her with a long blade. She spun away from the attack, swinging out her own sword in a savage mid-torso cut . . . just as an arrow whirred past her head. She heard her assailant grunt, then a light snapping sound. Under her focused gaze the shadows seemed to dissolve a little and the face of Azurech-as-Byrnak came into view. He was smiling as she backed off several paces, seeking cover from the bow-woman.

'So you do remember how to use the power.' He laughed, a glamour of silence masking his voice so that only she could hear him. 'Once tasted, never forgotten, eh? Our master has faith in you, Nerek, and the certainty that you will return to his side as the mirrrorchild of his power . . . He *knows* you.'

'He knows what he wants to know,' she answered. 'I am not who I once was.'

Azurech shook his head. 'How could a father not know the thing he made? Come back with me, Nerek – you know that the mages and the rebels cannot last much longer.'

That unspoken dread she already knew, but worse by far was the insistent voice which wanted more than anything to go back to him, and which was growing stronger all the time.

She steeled herself, then called on the Wellsource and filled her free hand with dazzling Sourcefire. Without looking away from

Azurech she brought up her sabre and ran its edge through her cupped palm. The sword burned in the darkness.

'I will never go willingly,' she said.

Before Azurech could answer, a strange ululating cry came from up in the sky. Something flapped down to perch among the topmost branches, sending laid snow sprinkling down. It gave voice to that shivering sound again then took flight on great wing beats, heading west. Azurech glanced up, then back at Nerek, bearded face alive with a malign smile.

'Till the next time, farewell.' Then he turned away into the shadows and was gone, leaving Nerek full of self-doubt as she turned her attention to the wounded archeress.

Bardow paced the floor of his inner chamber, torn by anger and worry.

'What was she thinking?' he said to Alael, who sat on a high chair next to a cluttered workbench. 'I left her explicit instructions to meet with us here at first light. Instead, I hear that she went riding off with Yarram down the Grainway, narrowly avoided fighting with Azurech and took an arrow in the shoulder, from one of our own archers no less.' He paused by the slender, mullioned window and saw that the morning was bright. 'This weapon of melded powers . . . will be a difficult undertaking, not least because the necessary powers may themselves be hard to bring forth . . .'

'Perhaps not, ser Bardow,' said Alael behind him.

'Hm, your optimism does you great credit . . .' As he turned his gaze to the young woman, his words failed when he saw the pure white flames dancing on her upturned palm. Elation bubbled up within him.

'The Mother's Gift,' he whispered, sinking into a nearby chair. 'Why didn't you tell me?'

Alael's eyes widened. 'I have tried to broach the matter several times, but you would not let me get a word in edgeways!'

'Ah, yes – I do apologise, Alael. I've been running myself ragged since the fires began in the night, and this business with Nerek caught me unprepared . . .'

The night had been one crisis after another. First were the

tortured unfortunates who came screaming out of the night to
destroy themselves horribly in bursts of tenacious flame. Then
there were the roving bands of enemy riders led by the rivenshades
of Mazaret and Suviel — Suviel was unknown to the people of
Besh-Darok, but Mazaret had been a public figure and panicky
sightings of him were not confined to the snowfields outside the
walls. Some claimed they saw him climbing over the wall to the
north of the Old Town near the Gallaro Gate; others said they saw
him stealing through the burnt trees of Lords Glade or clambering
wetly out of the Olodar near Five Kings Dock. One sighting near
Kulberisti Longmarket turned out to be a group of pale-robed
Tobrosans walking in mourning for one of their number, but
rumour of this led to a drunken mob taking out their fears on
a guardpost manned by Yasgur's now mainly Mogaun militia.

After that had come more of these vile flame sacrificers, only now
inside the city. It was while riding with Yasgur and his men through
the waterfront streets from fire to fire that he heard of Yarram's
expeditionary force, though not of Nerek's part in it. Since then
he had been trying to speak with all of his unruly mages, especially
the Nightrook, Blind Rina and the Anghatani twins, Rilu and
Luri, who were all searching for the mysterious spellcaster who
had survived the fall from Hendred's College window.

But now there was this evidence of the Mother's Gift, usually
displayed by the Earthmother priestesses and then erratically. He
gave a weary but happy smile, and Alael smiled too.

'Now,' he said. 'How did this come about?'

She told him about her dream, about finding herself in the Vale
of Unburdening and meeting a woman who took her to see a
monument then a group of open graves. Bardow felt a chill
when he recognised Suviel in Alael's description of her guide,
and was troubled when the account ended with the understanding
that Alael's power really was a gift. But to what end?

Bardow's mood dimmed and as if in sympathy Alael closed her
hand, snuffing out the flames.

'She does such things for a reason, doesn't she?'

'Usually.' Then annoyance at his own gloom took hold and he
slapped his hands on his knees. 'But we also have reasons for the

actions we take, and we must trust in our judgement for we know our cause is just.'

Alael was silent a moment, then said, 'On my way back from the college, I looked at that translation of the revealed lettering, but I hardly understood its meaning.'

'That is to be expected,' Bardow said. 'The rhythm and cast of writing was very different a thousand years ago. Scholars of the time used allegory and symbology as a matter of course – they would find our treatises and studies quite flat and lifeless. Was there anything in particular that puzzled you?'

She frowned. 'There was mention of "the Culvert", and later the inscription went on about "the Kindred" and their "quiddity".'

Bardow, however, was only half listening as a strange, insistent sense of foreboding began interrupting his thoughts. After a moment of confusion he realised that it was a warning from the Crystal Eye, one that he had been dreading and anticipating for days. Someone with the Wellsource at their fingertips had just entered the city.

He silenced Alael with an upraised hand then stood as a flood of alarmed thoughts and emotions streamed into his mind from the other mages across the city. Firmly, he persuaded them to rein in their anxieties and await developments, apart from Amral, Cruadin and Zanser with whom he strove to pinpoint the intruder's whereabouts.

Where is it? came the irritable Amral.

I've heard no sound of commotion, said Cruadin.

'I've perceived something of this person's course,' Bardow said. 'I think they came by the Shield Gate . . .'

Is that likely? Cruadin.

Bardow did not answer. Instead, aided by the others, he focused his perceptions through the Crystal Eye. He could almost see the streets and buildings near the Shield Gate, with the pale, blurred forms of many people going about their business while through the bustling scene walked a figure that was no more than a shadowy outline. As if it were a barrier that the Crystal Eye could not penetrate.

'I cannot see their face,' Bardow said. 'But it seems quite open about its intentions – now it's heading up to the Palace.'

Seal the gates!

Turn out the guards, all the knights . . .

Have the Emperor moved . . .

Bardow—

Someone new slipped through the mingling of panicky mindspeech, someone that he knew was level-headed.

'Yes, Terzis?'

It's Nerek, she said. *She's the one you're all sensing.*

'Aah . . . Then I imagine that there is quite a story behind this.'

She insisted that you would be the first to hear of it.

'Is she a threat to us here?'

No, I really don't think so.

Bardow frowned, not knowing whether to be pleased or wary, but decided that a little caution would still be wise.

'Thank you, Terzis . . . Almar, would you be so good as to join me in my chamber? Cruadin, alert the Emperor's bodyguard and have them seal off his floor – Zanser, I would be obliged if you could make sure that the sanctuary room is secure . . .'

Several minutes passed before the door opened and the crippled mage Amral hobbled in.

Bardow watched the older man sit in a wicker chair which creaked slightly under his weight. Bardow could feel Nerek's approach, by his own senses as well as his attunement to the Crystal Eye. The door opened and she entered. She stood there in silence for a moment, looking about her. Bardow could see the change in her immediately, an alteration that was visible in the confident tilt of her head and the straightness of her stance, a regained power which showed itself in the hue of her skin, the glint of her eyes. Bardow cleared his throat to speak, but before he could begin . . .

'Hello, Nerek,' said Alael brightly. 'We heard that you were hit by an arrow but you don't look hurt – have you been having adventures?'

Nerek gave her a grateful smile whose openness and warmth took Bardow by surprise.

'Greetings, Alael,' she said. 'And yes . . . I have had a strange and unsettling adventure which I shall speak of.' She turned to Bardow.

'But first I must apologise for failing to be here when you asked, Archmage.'

Bardow nodded. 'Apology accepted, Nerek, but it seems that events may have turned to our advantage. Now, tell your tale.'

He listened as Nerek, Byrnak's mirrorchild, told of the ambush on the Grainway, and how Nerek and others were ordered into the dark wood after the errant archers. When it came to her encounter with Azurech, her voice grew expressionless but relaxed again afterwards.

'. . . and when I went to help her, she put an arrow into my arm.' Nerek fingered a tear in the upper arm of her jerkin. 'I don't think she was very pleased when I took away her bow and broke it in half.'

'And how does it feel?' said Bardow. 'The return of the Wellsource.'

'I'm not sure,' she said. 'At times, it feels like a missing limb has come back to me and I'm not crippled anymore. However, once or twice this morning I've sensed its ebb and flow within me – I had forgotten that the Wellsource almost has—'

'A mind of its own?' said Amral who had listened in silence. 'Or shouldn't that be the mind of its creator?' He looked to Bardow. 'Archmage, this woman encounters a high servant of the enemy who does not attack her, while she regains her use of the Wellsource. She is clearly a danger to us all – who knows what dread beings might come to work through her?'

Nerek seemed to acknowledge his words and stood with a bowed head, while Alael was clearly upset.

'She is not the only one who has a burden to shoulder, ser,' she said angrily, holding up one hand ablaze with white fire.

Amral froze and stared at this, speechless, and Bardow seized the moment.

'Nerek, would you do the same?'

She frowned, then nodded and raised her right hand which silently burst into lurid green flame.

'Amral, you see before you two very courageous women, both willing to put their lives in utmost peril for the sake of a slim chance of defeating the Shadowkings.' Bardow stood, beckoned Nerek over to him then laid one hand on her shoulder and the other on Alael's. 'With these powers, we shall attempt to forge a weapon fit to slay our dark enemies.'

The elderly mage pushed himself upright and leaned on his gnarled stick. 'I understand how desperate the situation is, Bardow, but I truly believe that this is a course of folly.'

'Had we sufficient time and resources, we might be able to study and consider all the available courses of action,' Bardow said. 'But we don't have that luxury, Amral. We cannot afford to let any opportunity slip past.'

The crippled mage opened the door and paused on the threshold. 'This reeks of the enemy's snares, Archmage, and I confess that I am glad not to be in your shoes. If I can be of assistance, you need only send for me.'

'Master Amral,' Nerek said. 'I vow that I shall not betray any of you.'

'You may not, lady,' Amral said bluntly. 'But the power you carry most assuredly will.'

Bardow sighed as the door closed with a soft thud. 'He is by nature a cautious and bitter man, but his heart is good. Now—' He looked at the two young women and they looked at him. 'I have some complex explanations of what we must do and little enough time for them, so attend me well . . .'

After speaking with the dockside captain, Atroc walked along the deserted Squiresgold wharf, shivering in the cold, eyeing the pale and hesitant dawn. Snow masked the broad timbers all the way along, its whiteness heavily trampled around just two of the dozen or so piers that jutted out into the bay. A few fishing vessels sat tied up at one smaller jetty, their decks white, the crosstrees of their masts adorned with lines of dagger-like icicles, while overhead a few seabirds wheeled and cried out mournfully.

The ageing seer's breath steamed as he nodded to a pair of militia spearmen, both Mogaun, who were guarding a broken door in the high wooden fence which divided off one end of the wharf. They let him pass and on the other side was the rough planking of a long building with a set of steps leading up to a walkway. Going by the dockside captain's directions, he climbed up to the gantry and straight away caught a whiff of burnt wood and furs shot through with something nauseous and by now familiar. On his way to the waterfront he had passed by a handful of places gutted or damaged by the enemy's firebringers. Here a house, or there a workshop, or the outside of a building, and all had the taint of scorched blood and sorcery.

The walkway had a railing, for which he was thankful as he followed it round to the other side where it widened to a platform sitting on supports. Yasgur was there, standing hunched in furs and a heavy cloak as he stared moodily down at the fire raging in the private landing dock. He glanced round as Atroc approached.

'Finally,' he grunted, then looked back down at the blaze.

'Ah, my prince, I would have been at your side before now had I the wit to foresee your movements this morning . . .'

'Curb that tongue of yours, old man,' Yasgur said darkly. 'I've not the patience for it.'

Atroc smiled to himself and tramped over to join his master. Below, some guards and labourers were struggling to move blocks of marble and slate away from the fire using wooden rollers. The fire itself raged across a large pile of bricks and several heaps of loose ore. Iron, Atroc thought, or perhaps copper. And across the bricks was sprawled a skeleton.

Yasgur pointed to a long sea barge which was tied up at the other side of the private dock. 'Guards think that he was making for the ship when he started to burn.' He shook his head. 'Whatever is within them, it burns without smoke until it meets something made of wood or cloth – all the bricks and ore are sitting on flagstones but the heat is starting to make the wharf planking steam.'

'Does not water extinguish it?' said Atroc.

'Water only spreads it wider, then is boiled off.' Yasgur gave a dry throaty laugh. 'Sand puts it out, we found too late – we're waiting for barrows of it to arrive from the riverbank.'

'A cruel weapon, my prince.'

'A weapon of terror, and effective.' Yasgur turned to look at him. 'And the least of their eldritch horrors, I'll wager. I was only fourteen during the exodus but I remember what the Acolytes' nighthunters and firehawks did to the Imperial army at Pillar Moor. Picture that here.'

Atroc heard the bleakness in Yasgur's voice, the doubt, the weakening resolve, and he frowned.

'Truly, it would be a scene of devastation, my prince,' he said. 'Yet all here have seen such before, and Bardow and the Conclave are prepared.'

'Prepared for an onslaught of armies, of hordes?' Yasgur seemed to gather his determination as he faced Atroc. 'See now, I need to know that your loyalty holds true and keen as a blade before I speak further.'

Atroc let his shock show. 'I am the oath-made seer! As I served your father, so I shall serve you with all the wisdom and cunning given to me by the Dreaming Void. My bonds to you cannot be broken by man or god!'

This seemed to please the Mogaun Lord Regent who gave a grim smile. 'Then hear this – last night, after I had returned to the keep, a man claiming to be from the Four Guilds asked to see me in private. When my guards were sure that he had no weapons about him, I allowed him into the antechamber. Once we were face to face he handed me this . . .'

From within his furs he produced a folded slip of coarse parchment which he gave to Atroc. The seer opened it and began to read. In a plain hand it said:

From Welgarak, chieftain of the Black Moon clan, and Gordag, chieftain of the Redclaw clan, to Yasgur, son of Hegroun, chieftain of the Firespear clan and Prince of Besh-Darok—

Greetings, brother. Know that at the behest of the Shadowkings we have brought the Host of Clans south and are camped north of the hills that encircle your city. We send this message in the hope that you will meet with us, that we may speak on all that has come to pass. We would also put to you a proposal that would be of mutual benefit.

Will you agree to such a meeting? If so, send your response with the one who brings this to you. Decide upon a location and a time, pass it to him and it shall safely reach us. But decide swiftly, brother, for time is short.

At the foot of the ragged-edged square of parchment were the words, 'Signed in the name of honour' followed by a crudely-monogrammed 'W' and a 'G'. Atroc re-read it, and frowned – it seemed to be a veiled invitation for Yasgur to abandon Besh-Darok and the allies and rejoin the rest of the Mogaun host. Yet something in the tone of it did not seem right, somehow . . .

He sighed, handed the note back then met Yasgur's stern gaze with a lazy smile. 'Are you planning to betray your allies, my prince?'

'You have a knack for serving up unpalatable questions, old man.'

'Nothing can sweeten this particular dish, lord.'

Yasgur snorted and replaced the note within his cloak, then glanced back down at the sorcerous fire. Two barrows of sand had arrived and were being shovelled into the flames. The sand melted into small glassy pools, but the fire was dying.

'One of our guard posts was attacked by a mob of drunken louts in the midst of the fire attacks,' Yasgur said. 'I've now lost count of the number of warriors asking to leave the city militia, all of whom I've had to refuse. It is never spoken but many feel that I am betraying our people and our ancestors by taking the southerners' side in this.'

Atroc nodded. 'I fear that is so.'

'I gave no response to the man who brought the letter,' Yasgur said. 'He has taken a room at an inn near the Bridge of Hawks, says he'll wait until dawn tomorrow for my reply. But I find it hard to come to a decision.'

'Caught between betrayals, my prince,' Atroc said. 'Not the most comfortable place to be.'

'In the end I must put the survival of the clan above all else,' Yasgur said bitterly. 'I must decide where the safest place to stand is.'

To that Atroc said nothing, since the answer seemed quite obvious.

Below, the hungry flames crackled and hissed as they went out.

Chapter Eighteen

If you create a thing, its opposite is also created.

Mogaun saying

The portal of the Wellgate opened a door into the antechamber of
the throne room of the Red Tower in Casall. It was dim in there.
Byrnak glanced around him at the otherwise empty Chart Chamber
of the Drum Keep at Rauthaz, then stepped through. A thick gloom
filled the antechamber, broken only by a single oil lamp in a wall
niche. He glanced at the dusty, waist-high wolf statues sitting in the
corners, then looked round as a second portal appeared and Kodel
emerged. Even in the poor light, Byrnak could see that Kodel had
chosen to dress opulently in a high-collared long doublet in rich
green velvet patterned with gold thread embroidery, blood-red
breeches, high boots, leather gauntlets covered in small articulate
silver plates, and a jewelled duelling sword.

Byrnak, though, had opted for variations on black: boots, leggings
and plain leather jerkin, ebony-hilted broadsword in a battered
sheath. A grey wolf-fur collar on his black cloak was the only
digression.

'Is it prepared?' Kodel said.

Byrnak knew he was referring to the casket. Forged in the fiery
workshops of Rauthaz and inscribed with runes by Byrnak's own
flock of soul-bound Acolytes, it was a casket twin to Ystregul's
but designed to restrain Thraelor, Shadowking of Casall, should that
become necessary.

'Yes, it's ready.'

'And Grazaan?'

'Should be joining us shortly.'

Byrnak looked back at the wolf statues, and the huge tapestries whose details were scarcely visible in the low light. It was very quiet.

'I've not been here for a time,' he murmured. 'All this is different . . .'

Kodel nodded and smiled oddly. 'There have been quite a few changes. Shall we announce ourselves? Grazaan can follow in his own time.'

He gestured for Byrnak to lead the way but even as he reached for the double doors they swung open and the two Shadowkings were met by the face of Thraelor—

—on the body of a young woman dressed as a priestess and standing in front of heavy black and ochre curtains. With those familiar amber, expressive lips she was smiling widely and unceasingly as her gaze drifted from Kodel to Byrnak and back.

'The great lord Thraelor is seeing no one today and has decreed that all visitors will lose a limb chosen at random by . . .'

Kodel shook his head and put his hand on her waist, then drew her to him and silenced her with a kiss. 'Nay, fair mistress of the doors – your master will see us, I promise you.' He cast a mischievous grin at Byrnak then pushed through the heavy drapes. The woman, still grinning, approached Byrnak and slipped her arms about his neck with her face uplifted.

'I think not,' he said, disentangling himself from her arms, and stepped through after Kodel.

The great throne room of the Red Tower was long and high, with inward curving walls decorated at regular intervals by yard-wide bands of stained glass which rose up into the shadowy heights. They were clearly meant to be lit from behind by a string of lamps but very few were and then only by one, glowing near floor level.

Across the near-empty tiled floor, a scattered crowd of people milled or wandered around. There were mutterings, sobs and bleak laughter. All were dressed poorly or even raggedly and a few even stank of filth and ale, but each and every one bore the same face, Thraelor's face. At the far end, there were others clustered near the throne on which a huddled, indistinct figure sat. But it was the huge statue towering behind the throne which drew Byrnak's attention and prompted his first real sense of unease. Reaching up to three quarters of the room's height, it depicted Thraelor caparisoned in ornate full armour, with a slender crown on his head rather than a helm. One hand gripped the top of a concave, squid-emblazoned shield whose point rested on the plinth, while the other held a short spear couched under the arm. But the figure's shoulders were hunched while the head sat on a noticeably elongated neck and was turned to stare directly at whoever might be standing before the throne, its features twisted with undisguised and delighted malice.

By contrast, the occupant of the throne looked thin and emaciated. His long outer coat was rich and silky, shades of brown worked into the shapes of fin-serpents, octopedori and other sea creatures. But his face was gaunt and the wrists and hands were bony and shrunken.

'Brothers, greetings. It is an honour to welcome you to my court, but your visit is something of a surprise. Why do you come unannounced?'

'Concern has been voiced regarding your well-being, brother,' Kodel said smoothly. 'We decided to see you for ourselves.'

Thraelor smiled and shook his head. 'Ah, Grazaan's concern, you mean. Why isn't he here, too?'

'We are expecting him to join us shortly,' Byrnak said, stepping up to one side of the throne and leaning on the arm. 'But for the moment, I'm curious about these people who all have your face.'

'We could not help but notice that your physical state is not at its best,' Kodel said.

Thraelor glanced from one to the other, clearly amused. 'Why have I bestowed my face on the dregs of Casall, you ask? Well, before I answer, allow me to ask a question or two of my own. Byrnak, I understand you gave your own face to one of your underlings – why was that?'

Byrnak frowned and turned aside in irritation. 'It occurred to me that such a servant would be of great use in conveying my commands. My own features would lend them force, making it seem as if they came directly from my own mouth.'

'In other words, it was a mysterious inner whim for which you have a well-thought-out justification, much like that boy you remade as a mirrorchild—'

'That is not so!'

Unruffled by Byrnak's anger, Thraelor smiled. 'And you, brother Kodel – how are your nights? Troubled, I would guess.'

'Every night makes its own pattern of dreams, brother,' Kodel said tightly.

'Hmm, yes,' Thraelor said. 'I would also guess that both of you have blank moments you dread to even consider, much less try and explain.'

There was a moment of silence between them as Byrnak waited for Kodel to utter a denial. None came.

'Very well,' said Byrnak. 'It is clear that we are all suffering from the presence of our predecessor, yet it would appear that you, brother, suffer the most.'

'Appearances can be deceptive,' Thraelor said. 'You see, dear brothers, rather than undergo the nightmares sent by our holy predecessor, I have chosen to forgo sleep altogether. The strain has been considerable, as you can see. As for giving all these people my face . . .' He smiled. 'I like my features and I enjoy seeing them on others' bodies. Periodically I despatch several back on to the streets, that Casall may be beautified by my likeness, but sadly they do not live very long.'

Kodel rounded on him. 'But you cannot deny that you've been afflicted by blank and unaccountable periods of time.'

'I do certainly deny that,' Thraelor said. 'When those moments of weakness come over me, I remain aware while my fragment of our predecessor comes to the fore . . .'

'You remain aware?' Kodel said, frowning.

'His ramblings and rantings are incomprehensible to me and utterly pointless . . .'

Byrnak turned away, feeling the insistent pressure of another's voice trying to penetrate his thoughts. Realising that it was coming from outwith his own mind, he lowered his defences sufficiently for the voice to become clear.

Ah, great lord Byrnak . . .'tis your servant, Crevalcor.

'Crevalcor,' he said inwardly. 'What news have you?'

Little that is good, my lord. The invasion fleet was attacked by fast ramships sent secretly overland from Sejeend – the Jefren dromonds are all sunk and the Islemen have retreated to their island strongholds.

Burnak gritted his teeth. 'How?'

I'm sure that Bardow was behind it, Great Lord. Perhaps he put the plan's execution in the hands of a cabal not linked to the High Conclave in Besh-Darok. However, the undertaking was not a complete failure – we inflicted great destruction on Scallow itself and sank most of their fleet. Should we wish to attack the rebel hinterlands from the Sea of Drakkilis, there would be none able to stop us.

'I see. And where are you now?'

I am ashore on the southeast coast of Jefren, lord.

'I must meet with you soon – our strategies at Besh–Darok are coming to fruition. I could have the Acolytes send a nighthunter from Trevada to carry you to Casall. The Great Aisle would then bring you to me.'

I had thought to continue north to Bidolo, my lord, to consult with the high priests of the Jefren Theocracy. The heretics and bandits in the Druandag Mountains have grown more numerous and dangerous of late and now pose a genuine threat to south Anghatan.

Byrnak frowned. 'A few days ago they were little more than a minor annoyance. Why is the Theocracy finding it so difficult to deal with these brigands?'

They are well organised, Great Lord, and have rebuffed several forays into the mountain ravines. There is also a new element of the situation to be considered.

'And that is?'

A woman called Keren Asherol, former Imperial cavalry officer and once a rider in your warband. She played a decisive role during the struggle for Scallow—

'Keren,' he whispered.

She took part in a sea battle in the Bay of Horns and was washed up on the Honjiran coast a few miles west of Choraya. I have since determined that she was found by two horsemen who immediately took her north through a little-known high pass in the Nagira Mountains. They entered a narrow gully leading into the Druandags a few hours ago and should have reached their refuge by now. Her fate is a knot that will not yield, yet it is clearly one that is dangerous to us.

'I understand and agree,' Byrnak said, his thoughts dwelling on Keren and the mirrorchild, Nerek. With his senses he stretched out to perceive the fullness of the Wellsource then focused on certain currents within it. Satisfied, he withdrew and returned his attention to the sorceror, Crevalcor.

'Continue on your course,' he said. 'I shall speak to you later and hear your assessment of the circumstances.'

As you will it, Great Lord, so shall it be.

As Crevalcor's presence faded he turned back to Kodel and the seated Thraelor.

'Brothers,' he said with a broad smile. 'There are many pressing matters at Keshada which demand my immediate and personal involvement, thus I shall take my leave.' With a thought and an easy gesture, he opened in the air beside him a slender, misty-edged door of swimming darkness. 'This visit, though brief, has left me reassured and confident, brother Thraelor.'

'I concur,' said Kodel. 'I see no need to further impose on your hospitality and valuable time. I shall likewise return to my work at Rauthaz, and see what has detained our brother, Grazaan.' Quickly, he moved to join Byrnak.

'Ah, Grazaan, Grazaan,' Thraelor said, shaking his head. 'I'm worried about him, you know . . .'

Through the black door Byrnak, then Kodel, stepped, emerging on the shadow-patterned floor of the throne room in Keshada.

'He is mad, of course,' Kodel said.

'Undoubtedly,' Byrnak said. 'Uncomfortably so.'

Laughing, Kodel opened a portal door to Rauthaz. 'Till later, brother,' he said and passed out of sight. The door shrank to a black line then vanished. Byrnak watched his departure then sent forth a thought to summon one he knew was in the citadel. A short while later, the audience room's tall doors parted and Azurech strode in.

'Great Lord,' he said, kneeling before Byrnak.

'Developments, Azurech,' Byrnak said. 'What have you to say?'

His general looked up with his own face, devotion in every line. 'The armies are ready, Great Lord, and the tinemasters assure me

that the eaterbeast swarm is rapacious and blood-hungry. Also, the
Mogaun Host has completed its encampment north of the Girdle
Hills, and awaits your orders.'

'The nighthunters?'

Azurech frowned. 'The Acolytes seem scarcely capable of delivering
any kind of direct answer. All I am certain of is that we will have very
few available to us come the assault. However, the great war-wagon
has finished its trials without any difficulties.'

Byrnak nodded, knowing that the problem of the Acolytes would
have to be faced very soon. 'And Nerek – you encountered her? Is
she joined with the Wellsource once more?'

'I saw the fire of it in her eyes, my lord,' Azurech said. 'I could feel
the heat of it rushing through her, and almost hear her body exulting
in its glory.'

'Yet still she remains opposed to us?'

'Sadly this is so, lord. She has returned to Besh-Darok.'

'As I thought she would. And now that she's back in the city,
the stage is set for the next misfortune.' He glanced out of the tall,
arched window, past the shielding barrier at the snow-smothered,
abandoned lands. It was past mid-afternoon but under that pale grey
light it could be any time from morning to early evening. 'Did the
attack of the warblood sacrifices have the desired effect?'

'Dread and hysteria reigned, my lord,' Azurech said with a smile.
'Some of Yasgur's warriors were even attacked by a drunken mob.'

'Good. Nerek's presence in Besh-Darok will now loom large
to those of power in the city, thus no one will notice if we send
a Source-bound messenger bird to Kodel's spy.' Byrnak grinned
widely. 'It is time for the boy-Emperor Tauric to face his destiny
in Khatris. When word of his disappearance becomes known among
the city's rabble, panic will spread like wildfire. Go and prepare my
officers for the soul-binding.'

'As you command, Great Lord.'

It was a hard task, this secret departure, and it was hard to keep
himself convinced that he was doing the right thing. Tauric knew
that Bardow would be both furious and beside himself with worry
when he discovered what had happened, yet hoped that the letter

he had left in his chambers might put minds at rest. He knew that this task, this quest, was vital to all their survival and if they could make their way to the temple at Nimas undetected he would at last call on the spirit of the Skyhorse.

He was sitting crosswise in the back of their small supply cart as it jolted and rattled through the streets of the Old Town. The cold, grey gloom of dusk was drawing down across Besh-Darok. On his head was a wide-brimmed drover's hat and he wore a long, grubby smock over his breastplate and mailed leather, along with thick woollen gloves and disguising rags wrapped around his boots. But the deepening chill still bit at the tips of toes, and at his nose and fingers.

His standard-bearer, Aygil, and three others rode along with the cart, two behind, two ahead, and all cloaked and muffled against the cold and recognition. Four were all of his Companions that the priestly Armourer would allow, so Tauric had made sure that they were well armed.

The Armourer was driving the cart with its one mule, his hooded, hunched figure swaying as they progressed across the uneven, cobbled street. It had been late afternoon, perhaps three hours ago, when one of the Companions had sought him out with an urgent message from the Armourer. Tauric had been in the palace library, making notes on old Skyhorse rituals, so he had stuffed the scrawled-on parchments inside his doublet and made for the Keep of Night. As he rode in the back of the cart, the Armourer's words came back to him.

'Majesty – the time of destiny is upon us. We must depart for Nimas as soon as possible.'

In the priest's small chamber, in the gloomy glow of the solitary candle, Tauric had felt trepidation clutch at him as the blood began to beat in his skull. 'Why now? What has happened?'

'I had a vision, majesty. In the midst of my meditation, my senses were seized in a whirl of motion, as if wings were carrying me up into the sky, and when all came to rest I was standing on the highest pinnacle of a towering, star-gathering mountain. From there I could gaze across the entirety of Toluveraz from shore to shore and beyond while birds wheeled far below me and the very clouds brushed against my brow. Then through the terrible grandeur of the upper air a great pale horse as tall as a palace came galloping up to rear over me before regarding me with eyes full of time's reflection.

'"*He must come to Nimas,*" it said in a thundering voice. "*To the temple there before sunset tomorrow.*" And an instant later the vision fled like leaves in the grip of a gale, and left me here in my dim room . . .'

He must come to Nimas . . . The words still echoed in his mind as he sat in the back of the cart making its way through the darkening streets of Darok Old Town. Their route led past the tall house on whose roof Tauric and the Armourer and others had taken refuge during the early stages of the struggle for the city. He glanced up quickly, then away as the cart turned a corner into dark, puddled side streets. The Armourer kept to the back alleys as much as possible as they wound their way through the Old Town to the fishers' quarter. A variety of ketches and small netting boats ranged forth from two coves in the cliff-ringed northern curve of Andaru Bay. The southernmost one was where they were headed, and the smells of the curing shops and rendering yards grew strong in the air.

The fishers' quarter was a cramped district of small, close-built houses and narrow, badly cobbled streets, but there were many lamps aglow above doorways and many folk out and about. Tauric knew, from an earlier study of city maps, that the only direct route from the fishing community to the cove with its two piers was a sloping track hewn into the cliff face. So when the cart passed under a heavy gate lintel and turned sharply downward he realised where they were and looked round over his shoulder to see the abyssal darkness of the bay, the black, battlement-surmounted mass of the promontory and the utter, night-drowned expanse of the sea beyond. Then, as the cart rumbled down the track, he heard the Armourer whisper to him:

'Our ship awaits us down at the pier, majesty, but so does a lading official and a pair of harbour guards. I may have to employ a certain amount of mummery so I apologise now in case it appears that I am being disrespectful or insulting to you.'

'I understand, ser,' he whispered back.

In the event, there was no need for playacting. The lading officer was a sallow-faced, shivering man keen to get the inspection and

approval over so that he and his men could return to their warm
cabin up on the cliff edge. The Armourer presented himself as a
chandler from north Cabringa, then passed off the four Companions
as youths travelling to Sejeend to begin apprenticeships, the horses
as bound for a Roharkan breeding stable, the Companions' bundled
equipment as antiques and curios procured for wealthy clients, and
Tauric as his servant boy. The lading officer gave it all a cursory
glance, then shrugged and signed the Armourer's concocted mani-
fest. The Companions were down in the hold, seeing to their mounts
with a couple of the crew while Tauric watched the Armourer shake
hands with the lading officer then limp with his stick up the gantry.

Once on deck, he drew Tauric off to one side as the gantry was
hauled in. 'T'would be wise to maintain our roles whilst on board,
majesty, just until we put ashore further north.'

'I agree, ser. Perhaps I could wait on the deck, just for a short
while to see us leave.'

'As you wish, your majesty,' the Skyhorse priest said, amusement
in his voice. 'I mean to speak with the captain, so I shall attend
you after.'

Tauric nodded, but his excited attention was on the sailors as they
tugged on lines and exchanged shouts, making ready to depart. The
vessel was a small, two-masted cargo lugger with high prow and
stern, and this would be Tauric's first real sea voyage. Under his feet
he could feel the slow sway of the vessel as it rode in the swell, hear
the quiet lap of the waves and smell the salt of the wine-dark waters.
Then, more calls from the crew as they cast off. The deck lamps
swung, booms creaked and the sails made a great ruffling sound as
they caught the breeze and bore the ship away from the pier.

The young Emperor breathed in deeply and sighed, staring across
at the southern part of the bay, the Long Quays and the great bulk of
Five Kings Dock. Then the cliffs slipped aside and the palace and the
tall spindle of the High Spire came into view, and a spasm of guilt and
qualm went through him. Was it too late to turn back? He imagined
himself trying to tell the captain who he was and demanding that he
go about and make for the pier . . .

Then through his panicky imaginings he noticed something
happening ashore, at the mouth of the Olodar near the Earthmother

temple at Wybank. Knots of people with torches were coming along
the water's edge from upriver towards the area where the rocky shore
rose from the pebbly strand to become grey cliffs. He crossed to the
starboard side, gripped the wooden rail and stared out, wondering of
the torch-bearers were hunting for him. Then the Armourer's voice
came from the shadows to his right.

'Worry not, your majesty. It is not you that they are pursuing,
rather some cutpurse or the like.' He was silent for a moment. 'Tell
me, sire, are there uncertainties in your mind?'

Tauric laughed nervously. 'A host of them, good priest. A jostling
army of them!'

'And all begging you to give up this mad venture and return to
the palace, yes?' The Armourer nodded within his capacious cowl.
'Such are only the fears of past lives having their say, impossible to
silence yet possible to ignore.'

'Yes, ser priest,' Tauric said, gathering his resolve, 'You are right.
The Skyhorse temple at Nimas awaits – I shall not doubt or falter.'

The Armourer clapped him on the shoulder.

'My lord, you have grown this day and taken the first steps on the
path of fate. Now let us go below and see what we can find in the
way of a hot meal – when we disembark in a few hours, we shall be
lighting no fires to draw attention to ourselves . . .'

Nodding, he followed the priest down the open companionway
but his rising spirits were blunted by the cold chill of his metal arm
which fed the ache in his shoulder.

Bardow sat stony-faced at the great table in the steward's hall and
watched the twenty-two White Companions file out of the doors
under armed guard. Some fingered their horse pendants and all
looked disconcolate, having confessed all they knew in admirable
detail when confronted with the ire and steely gaze of an angry
Archmage. As the last of them left, Bardow leaned forward to rest
his elbows on the table and study the notes he had made on a long
strip of parchment. Then he glanced at Yasgur who had observed the
proceedings from a window seat at the side of the chamber, and was
now frowning silently to himself.

'At least now we know it all,' Bardow said.

'Pity we did not know five hours ago when they were still in the city,' Yasgur said gruffly.

Which Bardow took to mean, *Why didn't we know before all this that a servant of the Shadowking Kodel was ensconced in the Palace itself?*

He wished he had an answer. The Armourer was clearly a sorcerer of some ability to have devised Tauric's metal arm back before the uprising, and that was emphasised by the way in which he had remained undetected in Besh-Darok all this time. The question was whether he was solely a Wellsource adept or if he was able to employ the Lesser Power as well. Bardow had wondered about the timing of the secret departure, coming so soon after Nerek had returned with her powers restored. One thing he learned from the Night Keep guards was that some had seen a small bird flitting through the corridors in the early afternoon. Likewise, when one of the court servants entered Tauric's bedchamber later, he saw a similar bird, a slip of paper in his beak, spring up from a taboret and dash out the open window in a blur of wings.

Bardow smiled bleakly, certain that the bird had been sent by the Armourer's masters in Gorla and Keshada, signalling him to spirit the boy out. In his turn, the Armourer had used the creature to steal a note left by Tauric in his chambers ... Well, that was conjecture but he felt sure that Tauric would have left a letter, an explanation of some kind. Yes, a Wellsource-bound creature that small would have gone unnoticed in the confusion wrought by Nerek's own powers, which would draw the attention of the Crystal Eye as well.

'The immediate problem.' Bardow said heavily, 'is how to forestall any panic among the city's populace, or even how to keep the story from leaking out.'

'Cannot be done,' said Yasgur. 'Someone will talk, someone will realise that something is being concealed and rumours will breed like maggots in dead meat. I think that you are going to have to lie ...'

'Lie?'

'Skilfully and loudly, ser Bardow. Announce that the Emperor has been sent to a secret, safe location on the Cabringan coast, then later explain away our searching as pursuit of enemy spies.' He pointed at Bardow. 'And since we know the boy's destination, we could send someone after him.'

Bardow raised his eyebrows. 'Despite the five-hour advantage they have?'

'They are six, one of them is lame and they have only four horses. One man on horseback could catch them, and I know of one who could.'

As Yasgur got to his feet and pulled on his fur-trimmed cloak of black, the Archmage sighed. 'You're right, Lord Regent. I shall see to the announcements tonight, if you despatch one of your soldiers after our errant sovereign.'

'Good,' Yasgur said, opening the door, letting in a stream of chilly air. 'Till morn.'

The door slammed behind him, shutting off the cold. Bardow stared levelly at the place where Yasgur had stood, thoughts slowing from lack of sleep yet still harried by fears and doubts beneath which his own despair gaped like a waiting maw. A short time before the questioning of Tauric's Companions, he had conversed with Medwin through mindspeech and heard at last the full tale of the failed invasion attempt and the terrible destruction wrought on the city, Scallow. But he was most deeply struck by the disappearance of Gilly, captured by the enemy and now seemingly lost, perhaps dead, and Keren who, Medwin was sure, had yesterday reached the coast of Honjir alive but today could not be found or traced at all.

One by one we fall, he thought sombrely. *Even fate and chance seem to be against us. When will it be my turn, I wonder? Perhaps I should ride out to the old fort and await the end there, sword in hand . . .*

He smiled sadly as his responsibilities and burdens made a little procession through his mind. The last of them was the sword of melded powers, scarcely begun despite hopeful trials yet offering a faint glimmer of hope.

And after the loss of Keren, Gilly and now Tauric, he needed all the hope he could find.

Atroc was waiting in Yasgur's outer chamber, sipping a hot beaker of mulled wine and examining some of the tribal spears adorning one wall when the Mogaun prince entered, attended by a scribe and two pages. Seeing Atroc, Yasgur sent the servants away to an outer room then closed the door and crooked a finger at the old man. Atroc gulped the last of the wine, set the beaker on a low stand then followed him through drapes and on to the balcony.

This side of the Keep of Night looked south across a narrow jumble of low roofs to the wide, torch-lit battlements of the city wall. Beyond and above, the night was a solid darkness out of which snow came in gusts and swirls. But Atroc spared little attention for the surroundings, aware that Yasgur was full of grim determination.

'Can you guess why I wanted to see you here, old man?' the Lord Regent said.

'The Emperor's untimely disappearance, my prince?' he said.

'Yes.' Yasgur scowled out at the darkness. 'Insolent child allowed himself to be snared by a lackey of the Shadowkings promising him the power of some lost and forgotten god. When word gets out, the city will heave with rioting, whatever Bardow and the High Conclave do.' He leaned closer to Atroc. 'Defeat is in the air, old friend, and the time of severance is almost upon us.'

Atroc met his gaze. 'What would you have me do, my prince?'

'The man we spoke of before, the one who brought the message, has a room at an inn called the Three Dukes which is near the Bridge of Hawks, on the Old Town side. Find him and tell him that I agree to a meeting and as soon as possible. Tell him that I wish to meet out from the harbour, ship to ship.'

Atroc nodded, privately amazed at his own calmness at these cold preparations for betrayal. Part of him felt that Yasgur was wrong, that the die was not yet cast, the battle not yet lost, but he knew his duty and would not break his self-forged loyalty.

'Your will is my command, master,' he said. 'But to avoid recognition, perhaps I should wear something over these fine garments of mine!'

Yasgur laughed. 'I'll dig up something from the chests in my chamber. Also, on your way out find Ghazrek and tell him to attend me immediately. I have a task that only he can be trusted to fulfil.'

'Your commands are iron, great Firespear,' Atroc said, bowing his head.

Chapter Nineteen

When mask becomes face,
Sharpen your wits.
When face becomes mask,
Sharpen your sword.

Jefren proverb

Cold and weary, excited and fearful, exultant and prepared, Tauric
was all of these as he, his four Companions and the Skyhorse priest
once known as the Armourer entered the snow-covered ruins
of Nimas on near-spent horses. Morning mist veiled the white
surrounding countryside and made the gouged and burnt-out
buildings of the town seem pale grey. The roofless shell of the
Fathertree temple was visible as a wide, shadowy cleft in the rocky
outcrop at the market cross.

Tauric had visited Nimas once before, in his fourteenth year,
when the Duke of Patrein took him to the annual High Day of
Lights. This was a celebration to mark the end of the harvest and
the first day of winter – people came from all over Khatris and the
neighbouring lands, bringing lanterns of every kind, made from
parchment, cloth, leaves and bark, wood and metal. Suspended
on great, curved frameworks, they were kept alight throughout
the night and following day of the festival. His memory of that
time was golden, and he could never forget the fantastic multitude
of glowing shapes and forms, especially a well-guarded set of tiny
lamps from Tymora, each made from slivers of diamond, emerald
and riveril.

On that visit, Tauric had gained entrance to the temple as the Duke's son, but was kept from seeing the sacred sanctoral by a tall, richly embroidered screen that surrounded the chalern dais. Now he would enter it as Emperor, bringing the promise of new power, new beginnings and a new Empire. He thought of the small sheaf of notes he had brought with him from the palace library in Besh-Darok, and could only feel the folded shape of them beneath his cloak and armour and shirt, next to his skin. Late yesterday afternoon he had shown them to the Armourer who glanced at a couple, nodded and handed them back.

'Your pursuit of the Skyhorse creed's hallowed history is commendable and gratifying, your majesty,' he had said. 'It may be that some form of incantation will be required when we reach the sacred shrine, yet I believe that the ancient powers of the Skyhorse will recognise you as the rightful heir and confer their glories upon you.'

For all that this pronouncement was pleasing and reassuring, Tauric had wanted to ask the man's opinion on specific aspects of those scribbled chants and invocations, particularly one which mentioned 'the blood of the Skyborn' in the context of a sacrifice. In the event, he had decided to wait until they were actually facing the sanctoral itself.

As the Armourer led them through the ruins of Nimas, Tauric glanced round at his Companions, Herik, Rowlg, Drano and Aygil. All seemed alert and looked fresher than Tauric felt, yet he suspected that some if not all had dozed off in the saddle at some point in the long hard ride from the coast.

Tauric stifled a yawn as they approached the town's market cross. Once this would have been a thriving centre of activity, even in winter, with drovers and flocksmen haggling over cold-weather prices. Tauric knew that the blanketing snow concealed the chill, ashen evidence of pillage but in his mind's eye he imagined all the wreckage cleared away, the homes and marts rebuilt, the temple renewed and rededicated to the Skyhorse . . .

When they came to the foot of the wide, shallow steps curving up to the temple, Tauric expected the Armourer to have them all dismount and continue on foot. Instead the priest urged his horse up the steps, so Tauric and the others followed on, Aygil with his standard at last unfurled, the pale blue banner with its embroidered crown-and-tree device draped over his mount's hindquarters.

They came to the front of the gutted Fathertree temple where Tauric dismounted along with his Companions. Last to climb down, the Armourer limped with his cane up to the wide entrance, a doorless gap in the knee-high, broken brickwork which was all that remained of the temple's once great frontage.

'This is where you enter, majesty,' the Armourer said, peering out from beneath his cowl. 'And we will follow your lead.'

Tauric looked at the faces of his Companions and saw shining hope and the light of loyalty in every one. It humbled him and without hesitation he walked over to the entrance and stepped across the threshold.

From an ice-glazed notch up on the rocky outcrop, Ghazrek was able to look down into the ruined temple and out at the town. After a gruelling ride south to the gully near Crownhawks Wood then west by a little-known pass through the Rukangs, he had reached the outskirts of Nimas an hour or more ahead of the boy-Emperor's party. Leaving his exhausted horse tied up in a tumbledown stable, he had hurried to the temple and clambered up to find this suitably well-concealed spot.

And later when Tauric and his people came into view and rode steadily through the ruins, Ghazrek had watched them in utter silence, his breathing controlled, his movements kept slow and restricted. Such stealthy caution was due to the masked soldier who was watching the new arrivals from a similar notch just yards away, unaware of the Mogaun officer's presence.

Ghazrek had watched them arrive on foot from the south half an hour ago and scatter throughout the town, concealing themselves in the ravaged buildings. Studying their efficient, coordinated movements he knew that these were soldiers from one of the Shadowkings' citadels and wondered who they were, where they had come from and whether they were similar at all to the dog- and wolf-men the Acolytes used as guards. Then three of them stole round to the rear of the temple outcrop, and one of them climbed up its side to hide himself near Ghazrek, much to his disbelief.

Wedged in the narrow, uncomfortable gap with ice water dripping on him, Ghazrek shivered and in his mind went over Prince Yasgur's orders again.

'The boy is on his way to the town of Nimas with some of his followers and a servant of the Shadowkings. They're going to the wrecked temple to carry out some ritual that the boy thinks will give him powers . . . But all he's going to get is captured or even killed. You have to get there first, grab the boy and bring him back. If that proves impossible, do what you can to protect him even if that means revealing yourself to whoever they send to take him. Above all, keep him alive.'

If there had been room, Ghazrek would have shrugged. Instead he grinned and watched the six newcomers leave tracks in the snow as they entered the temple.

When he climbed the few, snow-choked steps up on to the chalern dais, Tauric could see that the sanctoral's position at the very back of the temple had sheltered it from the worst of the weather. As his companions ventured down the stairs into the open chamber to start clearing out debris, Tauric turned to the Armourer.

'Will you come down with me, ser priest?'

'Nay, my lord,' he said. 'Such a moment should be yours alone.'

Tauric smiled and took out his sheaf of notes. 'Then I shall recite some of these old incantations to show my devotion to the Skyhorse.'

For a moment the priest's face was unreadable then he smiled thinly. 'An appropriate and worthy decision, majesty.'

Exhilarated, Tauric laughed and descended the steep steps into the dank, dim sanctoral. His Companions had thrown out broken, rotten timbers and rubble light enough to be hefted, then pushed aside some larger pieces of masonry. Even in the poor morning light he could make out a few hints and details of the rich paintings that had once adorned these walls. Against the rear wall of the sanctoral, part of the temple's rear wall, were two square plinths set a yard apart, both having once supported a chest-high semicircular altar. Between them, rising no higher than Tauric's chest, was the hacked, moss-patched and blackened stump of a tree. Several fires had been set against or near it down the years, but as he looked closer Tauric could see bumps and irregularities that he recognised as chopped-off sproutings.

This tree never died, he thought. *Truly, the roots go deep.*

'We will wait and watch from above, majesty,' said Aygil, taking up his banner which he had leaned against a wall.

Before Tauric could object, the Companions bowed then filed up out of the sanctoral. When they were back up on the chalern dais, spaced around the sunken chamber, Tauric approached the tree remnant, went down on one knee in the black, muddy grime and in a low, steady voice began to read from his notes.

At once a strange languor settled through his mind and a heaviness pulled at his eyelids, but he strove to keep his eyes focused on the parchments he held. When he finished the first his senses felt befuddled, his vision blurred, and his balance uncertain as if the floor were about to tip him forward. But he turned over his parchment, determined to press on and especially now that the chamber was noticeably brighter than before. Then the Armourer's voice came from off to one side, just as Tauric was about begin another invocation.

'You can stop now, Tauric. Come up from there . . .'

There was an intake of breath from one of the Companions.

'But ser priest – look!'

Part of Tauric wanted to look round as the Armourer's limping footsteps hastened over, but all his thoughts were caught in an invisible web, somehow running between the words on the parchment, the words in his mouth and the treestump from which a pearly radiance was emerging in patches between the lichen and the charred bark. As he resumed, an angry voice spoke out:

'What are you doing? Stop it this instant!'

'But is this not what we came here for, ser priest—'

'If you will not stop him, stand aside, for I will!'

'Have you taken leave of your senses, priest?'

Through the web of words and unknown meanings, Tauric heard

the fearful determination in Aygil's voice then the hiss of swords being drawn.

'Step back!'

'Indeed I shall, foolish youth!' There was the sound of Armourer's footsteps and the tap of his stick receding, then his voice shouting; 'Come forth now – take them!'

There were gasps of disbelief from the Companions, then Tauric heard Aygil say, 'Majesty, we are betrayed. What must we do?'

The awful truth of it all, the Armourer's perfidy and his own willing part, sank in, yet it seemed to lack importance next to the ritual which had him completely in its grip. But out of the swirl of words and syllables and the heaviness of his limbs, he found the will to say to Aygil, 'Stand fast, Companion!'

Almost at once there was the thud of someone landing on their feet from some height, then the clash of weapons. Shouts, the scuffling of feet, a grunt of pain, all the sound of a brief but desperate struggle. Tauric's panic was only a single black thread in the great weave of mystery and power that surrounded him. He could hear it all but was powerless to move. Then the Armourer spoke out.

'They are only boys – kill them or capture them, and leave the leader to me.'

'Here they come,' Aygil said. 'Herik – can you stand?'

There was a gasp and a dry laugh. 'Aye, for a while, Aygil. For a while . . .'

'My brothers and my Emperor,' Aygil then said. 'It has been an honour beyond telling to have served you. May the Mother light your way . . .'

Others repeated the blessing and Tauric knew that if he could he would have wept. *Oh, poor poor fools – it is my folly that's led you to your deaths.*

'Mark your man!' was the last thing he heard Aygil cry before the cacophony of battle erupted above and around him. Tauric's full awareness was fixed on the harsh, argent glow that was pouring up from the tree stump like a confined column of feathery white flames. Events around him appeared to slow as the manifestation of power, the Skyhorse's power, drew him closer. It seemed to want to open up and pull him through but something was missing from the ritual . . .

There was movement to his left, a figure dropping down into the sanctoral. Still he felt transfixed but at the edge of his vision he saw a cloaked, hooded form that he knew. A glittering hand came up and a wave of raw emerald power lashed out. When it washed harmlessly over Tauric, the Armourer reached into his cloak and brought out a curved dagger.

'Iron never fails,' he said, then stepped in close and laid the blade's edge against Tauric's undefended throat.

In the next instant the Armourer jerked forward as a sword tip sprang out from the middle of his chest. The dagger fell from his hand. As the killing sword withdrew he coughed blood and fell to his knees before the shining, rushing pillar of power. Staring at the blood on the man's face, chest and hands, a realisation struck Tauric with the force of revelation. Then a hand grasped his shoulder.

'Come with me,' said a burly, bearded Mogaun, his face drawn with fear of the radiant force. 'If you take up a blade, we might be able to fight our way out.'

'The blood of the Skyborn is the key,' Tauric said as his metal hand reached out and pushed the dying Armourer up against the the bright, flaring pillar.

Dazzling light burst forth as if a door had been thrown open. Wind and forces dragged at Tauric, and he surrendered himself to them. As he flew forward into the raging brightness he glanced back to catch a final glimpse of his Companions. He saw the banner streaked with blood and still being held by Aygil, the last still standing and fighting, surrounded by the masked soldiers of the Shadowkings.

But closer than them all were the terrified features of the Mogaun warrior who had slain the Armourer, his mouth gaping in a soundless cry as he rushed after Tauric.

Yasgur's lieutenant . . . Ghazrek, that's his name, were Tauric's thoughts as the shape of a massive horse emerged from the engulfing light and reared over them both.

Earlier that day, a mile or more out to sea from Besh-Darok, a two-masted lugger lay at anchor with no lights but a hooded lamp, its aperture pointing north. The vessel had a long sternhouse with two cargo chambers, jack ladder hatches leading down to crew quarters, and a small upper deckhouse for the captain's cabin and some extra storage.

The wide doors of the forward-facing chamber had been wedged open so that Yasgur could look north into the pre-dawn darkness while warming himself beside a glowing, floor-bolted brazier. Sitting on a three-legged stool with his greatcloak hung open and trailing on the deck, he alternated between looking out the doors and staring into the hot yellow embers. There was an interesting mixture of odours in the air, cut wood overlaying a briny fish smell. Must have been the ship's last cargoes, he thought . . .

The creak of ropes and scrape of feet on wooden slats announced Atroc's ascent from below as he climbed up out of a hatch in the corner. He heard the old man puffing and cursing from the effort and smiled to himself.

'Your wine, my prince.'

Yasgur turned to accept a hot wooden beaker half full of steaming, mulled wine. As Atroc slumped gratefully down on a box stool on the other side of the brazier, Yasgur blew across the beaker, sipped and thought.

It had been more than a day since Tauric's disappearance, much of which he had contrived to spend apart from Bardow and the lords of the High Conclave. A bitter knot of guilt was gnawing him over his decision to abandon the allies' cause, and he decided that suffering it alone was more bearable. When they found out, it would be seen as a deadly betrayal, except that he intended to keep his clan and the remnants of the Mogaun Host out of the coming conflict and play no part in the destruction of Besh-Darok. His mouth would feel full of stones and his mouth might taste of ash but his clan and his people would survive. In the end, that was where his loyalty lay.

Of course, there was no telling if there would be any conditions to such a mass defection but he was sure he could renegotiate them from strength.

Raising his head to look out the doors he realised that Atroc was watching him thoughtfully. The old seer glanced away and Yasgur was about to ask why when a shout came from the deckhouse above.

'Light ahead and closing!'

'At last,' muttered Atroc who got to his feet and went over to lean against the door post and gaze out.

'Something on your mind, old man?' Yasgur said. 'Any final doubts?'

'Would it anger you to hear me say yes, lord?'

'No, but I would wish to hear them.'

Atroc half-turned and gave Yasgur a sidelong glance. 'It would be . . . difficult to explain. The Door of Dreams never opens wide enough.'

Troubled by this, Yasgur picked up a wood-handled poker from the floor and stabbed at the embers in the brazier. Bright orange flared in the coals, tiny sparks swirled upwards and hot ash fell hissing into the water scuttle below.

'Did you see the future?' he said.

A sigh. 'I glimpse only the dreams that the Void dreams, my lord master. Perhaps we too are but a dream of the Void, striving to know why the Void is dreaming us in this particular fashion . . .' The old Mogaun laughed suddenly. 'But know only this, my prince – I am your oath-made seer, my loyalty is to you while I trust in the Void.'

Yasgur looked up in surprise. 'You trust in the Void?'

'Aye, lord, just as I trust that one day you will take one of the clan's daughters as wife to give you an heir!'

They both laughed at this, and Yasgur shook his head. 'Find me one who doesn't have her mother looking out of her eyes,' he said. 'Then I'll serve the clan, as best as I am able . . .'

Out of the grey darkness of morning came a small ship with a single square sail, riding easily the choppy seas. It had rudimentary decking, a slope-peaked canopy at the stern and a hull bearing the pale-wood signs of recently repaired holes. As Yasgur stepped out for a better view, the ship was slipping alongside their lugger, its crew frantically hauling in sail while lines were thrown across to tether the vessels together. Yasgur's ship was one of a handful he

had retained for use by the city militia as well as by himself, and
its wholly Mogaun crew were sworn and loyal to him.

The other crew was also Mogaun, going by the calls flying to
and fro, and there seemed to be overly many of them for the size
of their ship. A handful more lamps were being lit on either vessel
and Yasgur frowned to see quite a few crew members armed with
clubs and spears. He beckoned over his own captain, a grey-maned,
black-toothed Mogaun called Uskog, and outlined the situation.

'You want I should break out the bows, lord?' said Uskog with
a hopefully malicious look in his eye.

'Not yet,' Yasgur said. 'Arm some of your deckers with hatchets
and post them by the mooring lines. Any trouble – cut them.'

Uskog nodded and turned to give orders while overseeing the
lowering of the gantry to the other ship, which sat a little lower
in the water. With both vessels in continual motion, pitching and
rolling, it took some effort to hold it steady for lashing down but
at last it was made fast at both ends. A tall figure emerged from the
other ship's covered stern, a bare-headed man robed in wolfskins
who Yasgur recognised immediately as Welgarak. As the chieftain
of the Black Moon clan strode over to the gantry, four of the
armed sailors came forward as if to follow but Welgarak halted
them with a gesture. Words were exchanged, then he turned and
started up the gantry, making use of the crude side rail. Before long
he set foot on the lugger's deck and faced Yasgur with a sharp,
flint-eyed nod.

'Greetings, son of Hegroun,' he said. 'Your blood is hot and your
bones are iron.' He glanced about him at the ship and its crew, and
seemed to relax a little.

'Iron bones and hot blood,' Yasgur said, smiling slightly at the
old tribal welcome. 'Is Gordag with you?'

'Yah, he is,' Welgarak said impatiently. 'He was hard to rouse
from his sleep . . . Ah, here's the laggard now.'

A short, stocky figure rushed out of the covered stern and tramped
up the gantry. Gordag was thinner than Yasgur remembered but he
still wore a horned helm over long pale hair tied back in a long tail.
He was also garbed in black, ring-mailed leather and a red-patterned
kirtle, and over it all a rough-woven woollen cape marked with the

red hook sigil. He also held the crumbling remains of an oatcake which he hastily devoured before coming aboard.

'Cousin,' he said to Yasgur, appearing tense as he turned to Welgarak. 'Have you . . .'

'Not yet,' Welgarak snapped.

Yasgur watched the exchange in bemusement. This was not how he imagined this encounter would begin.

'Cousins,' he said. 'Shall we move into the warmth of this deck shelter?'

Both chieftains agreed and followed him into the chamber where the brazier had been refreshed and a couple of lamps lit and hung from ceiling beams. More box stools had been produced and, as Atroc closed the chamber doors, the three chieftains sat around the brazier. An uneasy silence took hold and stretched into minutes until Yasgur became convinced that they were waiting for him to give the first ground. He gritted his teeth, took a deep breath and began.

'Events have taken an ill turn for us here,' he said. 'The boy-Emperor, Tauric, and a few others absconded from the city a day ago—'

'We know,' said Welgarak. 'Some of our scouts saw them riding west this time yesterday.'

Yasgur leaned a little closer. 'So you have him?'

Gordag snorted, and shook his head. 'There were orders to let them pass. Some of those fortress soldiers were tracking them.'

'The ones with masks?' Yasgur said. 'Why do they wear such things?'

Welgarak stared sombrely at him. 'Have you ever seen one of them up close, Yasgur?'

'No, I have not.'

'They wear two masks, not one,' the chieftain went on. 'Beneath that elaborate black leather one is another of black cloth, close-fitting and tied in several places, which they never take off.'

His face and words were grim, and Yasgur frowned. 'But why? Is it a badge of some kind, each with their own markings?'

'No, they all look the same, plain black cloth, all meant to hide their faces from themselves and from each other.'

The seriousness of Welgarak's demeanour provoked a quiver of unease in Yasgur and he knew that the discussion was moving towards something of importance, but he was at a loss to see how it might involve his own concerns. He was about to pose another question when Gordag cut in, angry impatience in his face.

'We can gabble over this in a while, curse it! There're just two things we have to know—'

'Storm take you, Gordag!' Welgarak cried. 'We agreed that I'd do the talking.'

'Huh – didn't realise you'd be so boring . . .' He looked at Welgarak. 'We'll have to talk about the "how" and "why" of it anyway.'

The other chieftain remained tight-lipped. 'Say your piece,' he said.

During this exchange Yasgur glanced past the arguing chieftains at Atroc who shrugged, clearly as puzzled as himself.

Gordag cleared his throat. 'Now, cousin Yasgur, we need to know if your mages have got hold of the third talisman.'

'A third . . .' Yasgur frowned. 'They recovered the Motherseed after the battle three months ago, and the Crystal Eye was spirited out of Trevada at the same time. I know nothing of another, but that does not mean that Bardow and his mages do not secretly have possession of something else.'

Gordag's disappointment was clear to see. 'Well, the Shadowking Byrnak seems to think that the third talisman is in their hands, or might be. He is hesitating, even though he has enough troops to take the city—'

'How many troops?' Yasgur said suddenly.

'More than sixty thousand,' Gordag said, 'and growing by the hour.'

Night's blood, he thought. *So many . . .*

'Where is he getting them all?' he said. 'Forced conscription?'

The two chieftains shared a look.

'You might call it that,' Welgarak said.

'So cousins, what was the second thing you wanted to know?' said Yasgur.

Gordag fixed him with a dark, intense stare. 'Will the rulers of Besh-Darok accept the Host of the Tribes of the Mogaun as allies?'

Yasgur sat back on his stool in wordless amazement, and as the grave-faced chieftains regarded him he had to strive to keep from grinning at the black irony of the situation. While Yasgur tried to digest this unexpected plea, the chieftains began to outline the events which had driven them to this.

The battle for Besh-Darok had pitched several of the great tribes against each other as well as the city's defenders. Many chieftains died and some of the smaller clans had been all but obliterated. In the aftermath, the ties of loyalty to the Shadowkings were forgotten as vengeance-driven raids degenerated into bloody slaughter. The Shadowkings had withdrawn to their strongholds to contemplate their strategy and the Acolytes were preoccupied with the emergence of the Jefren Theocracy, which absorbed several warlord domains to the south and east. By the time the Mogaun pattern of reprisal and counter-raid began to abate, the clans were then faced with entire towns and villages rebelling against their now-weakened rule.

Welgarak, whose domain covered a large part of northern Yularia, was with his warriors in the foothills of the Gorodars when two Nighthunters flew down from the sky to alight in the middle of his camp. Four slender, white-eyed Acolyte priests were their passengers, their leader bearing a personal invitation from Byrnak for Welgarak to return with them to the great keep at Rauthaz so that differences could be settled and new bonds forged. It was clear that this was a command couched in diplomatic terms but, reckoning that two nighthunters could quite easily rout the three hundred warriors stationed at his camp, Welgarak decided to accept the invitation.

The flight to Rauthaz was brief but uncomfortable ('Like riding a horse with eight shoulders,' said Welgarak), and on arrival atop the great keep he found that Gordag had received a similar summons ('Except I didn't waste time being polite,' Gordag said. 'Knew they'd kill half my family and drag me off anyway, and I said so. Then I went with them.') Deprived of their weapons, they were hurried down to a long, luxuriously adorned corridor where the Shadowking Byrnak awaited them.

On reflection, neither could recall very much of the encounter, beyond Byrnak blaming all their difficulties on Ystregul, the Black Priest, now incarcerated in Trevada. Both were certain that some kind of glamour had been cast on them since they came away from the meeting with the unshakeable intention of gathering the surviving clans together in northern Khatris, in advance of a new campaign against the enemy upstarts.

Also, both had promised to immediately despatch five hundred riders to Rauthaz. For use, they were told, as advance scouts and patrols between Rauthaz and eastern Khatris.

The warriors were duly sent, and the next few weeks became a ceaseless round of cajoling and persuasion as both chieftains went from domain to domain and sent messages to other chiefs and warlords further afield. A new gathering of the Host was proclaimed in the Forest of Gulmaegorn in northern Khatris and the Black Moon and Redclaw clans were first to arrive, soon to be followed by others. Then one evening, at the end of the first week, two nighthunters arrived from Rauthaz bearing five masked swordsmen and a single Acolyte priest. The priest delivered a letter from Byrnak which expressed his deepest respect and gratitude, and requested a further thousand warriors to aid 'the widening strategy of the war'. But there was uncertainty this time – the glamour cast by Byrnak had worn away and it was only after a long discussion among all the chiefs and warlords that it was agreed that eight hundred riders would be drawn from the tribes present to serve the Shadowkings' strategy.

They left the next morning, a long column waving to families as they rode northwest out of the forest, headed for a pass through the Gorodar mountains. Later that same day, some clan scouts reported seeing squads of black-masked horsemen patrolling the fringes of the forest. Welgarak and Gordag were troubled by this, uncertain of its meaning but resolved to seek answers the next day.

That night, however, all certainty was shattered. Gordag and his inner family of wives and children were settling down to slumber in the chieftain's great tent when shouts and wails came from one of its chambers. Quickly alert, Gordag snatched up a dagger and dashed through the flapping opening to see his women and children crowded into the corners, holding out sticks and weave poles to

fend off one of the masked soldiers who staggered around the
cushion-scattered chamber, mumbling alternately in the Mogaun
tongue and another rough language. The man had used a curved
sword to cut his way into the tent but had dropped it and was clearly
weaponless as well as deranged.

'Then he sees me, comes over and falls to his knees before me,'
said Gordag. 'My guards have come running in with spears and
blades at the ready, but all this one does is slip off that leather mask
then tear away the cloth one . . .' The burly chieftain breathed in
deeply and sighed. 'His head was hairless and there were scars on
his scalp but I still recognised him.'

All were silent as they listened to him and a sense of dread took
hold of Yasgur's thoughts.

'Who was it?' he asked.

'My sister-son, Galzar,' Gordag said evenly. 'I saw him off from
our camp in Mantinor after the return from Rauthaz, one of the
five hundred sons of the tribe that I sent to their doom—'

'We were not ourselves,' Welgarak said to him. 'There is little
sense in taking all the blame for the evil that Byrnak planted in us,
or in our warriors.'

'So what had been done to your sister-son?' Yasgur said.

'I do not know, but what was left of him was insane.' Gordag's
face was a mixture of anger and horror. 'A tormented spirit.' He
looked up at Yasgur with burning eyes. 'You see, there was another
spirit in his head, that is what he said over and over and over. And
when he saw that we understood, all he would say after that was
"Kill me, kill me!" My old seer, Nopa, was there and when he
heard this he only nodded.'

There was an appalled silence between them for a moment or
two, filled by the creaks and knocks of the ship and muffled crew
conversations from below decks. And Yasgur was remembering
how the hungry spirit of his father had possessed him for a time,
and recalled the ghastly black nightmare of it.

'So I took my dagger, one thrust to his heart and he was dead,'
Gordag said, eyes gazing into the hot embers. Then he shook
his head, as if trying to discard those dark memories. 'I can tell
no more.'

He rose, walked heavily to the door and stepped outside. When the door closed behind him, Welgarak spoke.

'He has not yet grieved – none of us have. We don't know if we should.' He looked at Yasgur. 'Do you understand what we have told you, cousin? Can you see what it means to us? You of all people should.'

Yasgur nodded as the full horror revealed itself. 'The Shadowkings are using those Mogaun warriors as hosts for the spirits of the dead,' he said, scarcely believing it as he said it.

'But not just hosts, eh?' Atroc said to Welgarak. 'Somehow they flense the victim's mind from his body, leaving it empty and ready for a new rider. But with Galzar there must have been mistakes made and enough of him was left to drive him to seek out his tribe . . .'

'It must be a place of terror, where this is done,' Yasgur said.

'It is said that there are vast caverns and tunnels beneath Rauthaz,' Welgarak said. 'Nests where Byrnak breeds his armies.'

'You said earlier that their forces now number some sixty thousand,' Yasgur said. 'Where have they found such numbers?'

Then he paused as the obvious answer came to him, and Welgarak nodded grimly.

'I have heard many rumours of vacant towns and villages across Anghatan and most of Yularia,' the chieftain said. 'Entire slum districts in Casall and Rauthaz stand empty, and the beggars have vanished. A more recent rumour spoke of rebels and fugitives holding out in an old fortress in the Druandag Mountains, but in the end nowhere will be safe. Their evil will drown these lands in endless twilight and life shall be a wheel of slavery and agony – we know this will be true.

'So when we were ordered to ride south, we realised that we had little alternative – we cannot leave these doomed shores for there are not the ships to carry us through the savage winter storms back to Shalothgarn, thus here we must stand and fight.' He smiled bleakly. 'We are caught between the pit and the fire, Yasgur Firespear. Byrnak continues to stay his hand but sooner or later he will open the gates and hurl forth his armies. We do not know what he has in store for us, but when it is done many of our warriors shall walk through Death's valley, whether we fight for him or against him. Better that we sell our lives for the price of honour, which is why we are here, offering to make an alliance with the rulers of Besh-Darok. What is your answer?'

Sitting back, Yasgur noticed that Gordag had come back inside and was leaning against the wide doorframe, watching. Atroc, on the other hand, had produced several pieces of twine and was patiently knotting them together, smiling as he glanced up at Yasgur who smiled in understanding. He got up and stepped round the hot brazier to grasp first Welgarak's hand then Gordag's.

'Cousins, be welcome. It will not be easy to convince the High Conclave but they will have to agree in the end. Now, how do you propose to move the Host of the Mogaun south to Besh-Darok without alerting the masks? Those creeping fortifications of theirs are less than a mile from the sea, north and south.'

'It can be done,' Welgarak said. 'With guile and timing. Now listen . . .'

Chapter Twenty

Speak to me,
Of the remorseless ghosts of kings,
The beat of dark and ancient wings,
And the ceaseless war,
At the heart of all things.

Gundal, *The Siege Of Stones*, Ch. 2, xxi

A dense wall of white mist encircled them, two men and a large horse from whose forehead sprouted two small horns. Tauric and Ghazrek stared across the circle at the creature which stared silently back.

'It looks like a witchhorse,' Tauric muttered to the Mogaun officer.

'Thought they all died out . . . after the invasion.'

'Or it could be a manifestation of the Skyhorse,' Tauric went on, 'or a sign . . .'

'I am not the portent of a departed god, unversed one,' the creature said, surprising them. 'I am Shondareth of the Dremnaharik, whom you call witchhorses.'

Tauric was disappointed but did not show it. 'Have you been sent to greet us?'

'*Sent?*' The word rang with umbrage. 'No, graceless one. I am trapped in this threshold place, like you: trapped by the foolishness of an old woman. Now, I have made myself known to you, thus you will respond in kind.'

'Ah yes . . .' Tauric felt a growing irritation at the witchhorse's haughtiness so decided to employ a little himself. 'Forgive me, good Shondareth – the method of our journeying had me quite discomposed for a moment. I am Tauric tor-Galantai, Emperor of Besh-Darok and the lands of Khatris, bearer of the Crown Renewed and . . . and protector of the Free Nations.' He bowed very slightly. 'It pleases me greatly to make your acquaintance.'

The witchhorse said nothing but dipped his great head gravely then turned to Ghazrek. The Mogaun officer glanced wide-eyed at Tauric who nodded encouragingly.

Ghazrek cleared his throat. 'I am Ghazrek, son of Naldok, two-spear hunter of the Firespear clan, banner captain to Yasgur, Chieftain of the Firespears and Lord Regent of Besh-Darok.' He bowed low.

The witchhorse gave another dip of the head then turned back to Tauric. 'You mentioned the Skyhorse earlier, Emperor of Besh-Darok – are you aware that he is long since gone from these realms?'

'His worshippers may be no more,' Tauric replied. 'But I believe that the powers of the Skyhorse are merely dormant and waiting for an awakening prayer.'

The witchhorse Shondareth shook its head dolefully. 'I fear that whoever told you this has cruelly misled you. The distinct powers and presence of the Skyhorse faded away a millennium ago when he transformed himself.'

'Transformed himself?' Tauric said in dismay. 'Into what?'

'Into the Fathertree.'

Tauric felt his legs go weak and a sick, hollowness bloomed in his stomach – he could feel that the witchhorse's words were true. The Armourer's deceit had been thorough, he realised, a ruthless fabrication made to ensnare and delude him. He had been a naive, gullible boy . . . a child, food for wolves . . .

He suddenly felt weary and lowered himself to sit on the hard, gritty ground, aware of Ghazrek's regard but not caring.

'I have known several Emperors,' the witchhorse went on. 'But unlike them, there is not the slightest glimmer of power about you. Could it be that you are not an Emperor at all?'

'Be assured, wise Shondareth,' said a hoarse voice. 'Tauric is indeed what he claims to be.'

The witchhorse moved to one side, revealing a night-black creature sitting on its haunches, watching them with golden eyes. Despite having no ears and no tail, it looked very much like a dog and, to Tauric, resembled exactly the dog he had caught sight of around the palace several times. He got to his feet.

'Greetings,' he said warily. 'Have I seen you before, in Besh-Darok?'

'Only when I wanted you to, majesty. And greetings to you, son of Korregan, and to you, son of Naldok.' Ghazrek, looking puzzled, gave a minimal bow. 'And to you Shondareth, son of Vindosarr. Did your sire find refuge in the Void also?'

'No – he died defending Kizar, seared by fire, torn by talons . . .' The witchhorse gave the dog-thing a long hard look. 'I do not know you but there is a power in you that I feel I should—'

'Not power, ser witchhorse, but the dregs of it, the tattered rags of former glory,' the creature said sadly as it turned to Tauric. 'I sympathise with your plight, more than you know.'

Tauric sighed deeply and closed his eyes. 'I appreciate your kind words but . . . I need to find something to fight with!'

He opened his eyes, looked down at his hands, one flesh, one metal. 'There is no Skyhorse to call upon, nor ancient powers, so a sword would suffice . . .'

'Or a tribe of witchhorses,' the dog-creature said.

'They would never agree,' Shondareth said abruptly. 'All the Dremnaharik suffered agonies in pointless battles sixteen years ago and only we few survived, by the blessed will of the Void.'

Ignoring the witchhorse, the dog-thing stood on all fours and walked over to Tauric. 'It is by the will of the Void that we are all here,' it said to him. 'But with witchhorses at your side in the coming battle you would at least stand a chance.'

Tauric glanced at Shondareth. 'This one is scarcely eager to fight a war.'

'There will be much persuasion needed, and they will be hard to convince,' said the dog-creature.

'But how could this be done?' Tauric said. 'We are trapped here . . .'

'It is possible to create a bridge from this threshold to elsewhere in the Void,' the dog said. 'I have the knowledge by which such a bridge can be made, but I am not permitted to use it. You or your companions would have to be the bridge makers.'

'Not I,' said Ghazrek.

Tauric felt a faint foreboding. 'How would any one of us gain this knowledge that you have?'

'You would have to carry my essence within your mind, thus providing all that you will need for building the bridge. I know much about you, Tauric, and I know how you felt when Alael used you to focus her talent, and then later when the Earthmother tried to use you for her pitiless ends.'

He felt strangely calm while hearing this, despite those very memories parading themselves past his mind's eye. He knew what had to be done.

'Will you try to enslave or deceive me, or make me do harm to myself or those I love?'

'None of those dark deeds will be part of my purpose,' the dog-thing said. 'I shall give you advice, knowledge and the benefits of my own experience, and if you choose your own path then so be it.'

'And who are you?'

'I am who you seek.'

'Be wary of such a compact, Emperor of Besh-Darok,' the witchhorse said. 'Especially in pursuit of a hopeless goal.'

Ghazrek only shook his head.

'If I must put myself in peril for even the slimmest chance of success, then I shall.' He looked at the dog-thing. 'Do what you must, but be swift!'

Barely had he finished the sentence when the dog-thing leaped straight up at him. Tauric staggered back, expecting some kind of collision but instead he was momentarily enveloped in a dark, shadowy haze. Then it melted and faded away, leaving him standing there, breathing heavily and looking from his hands to Ghazrek and the witchhorse Shondareth.

'It just . . .' The Mogaun was wide-eyed. 'It went at you then sank into you, like a ghost!'

That would be a fair comparison.

The voice was that of the dog-creature, yet now it was warmer and rounder. This was like the experience with the Motherseed except that this presence did not try to fill his skull and shatter his thoughts. There was stillness, too, and a great sadness.

Have you not yet guessed who I am, son of my sons?

I cannot say, he thought with a black suspicion growing in his mind. *Are you one of the—*

Shadowkings? No, I am both more than those poor half-gods and less. I have been a worm on the fisherman's line and the fish who took the bait. I have been a mouse burrowing in summer hay and the cat who pounced and the dog who chased. I have been the rootlet questing in the dark earth and the leaf which drank from the sun. I have been the thorn and the bloom. I have been the mother and the new-born babe. I have been the hunter and his horse and the boar he speared. I have been a proud and glittering army and the cook who filled their bellies. Once my vision and presence spanned the kingdoms from coast to coast and valley to mountain top. Once I clasped this mighty land as close as a lover holds his beloved and now I weep for all the pain and the loss I could not prevent . . .

'Mother's name!' he said aloud. 'You're . . . the Fathertree?'

There was an intake of breath from Ghazrek, and Shondareth took a couple of steps backwards.

I am all that remains, an echo of an echo, a fragment of a fragment of what once was.

Tauric's heart leaped. *If you open a way back to Besh-Darok we could rally the city and take the fight to the enemy's own gates . . .*

Ah, brave bold youth – such a course of action would avail you nothing. The great and dazzling power which once made the ground shake is now little more than a frail but stubborn candle flame amid the raging twilight. I would counsel you to approach the witchhorses in their sanctuary – persuade them to return with you and they will make powerful allies on the battlefield. Much more powerful than I.

Doubt assailed him. *But will we have time for talk and debate and persuasion?*

he asked. *The situation was on a knife edge when we left . . .'*

**That is not such a pressing concern for now – time has a
different meaning here in the Void.**

Very well, he thought, accepting finally all that had been argued.
How shall this bridge be made?

Simply face the wall of mist and look straight ahead.

Should I hold out my hand, or hold it up, or make some gesture?

If it will make you feel better, then certainly do so!

In spite of himself, Tauric laughed out loud, much to Ghazrek's
surprise.

'Are you well, majesty?' he said.

Smiling, Tauric nodded. 'It's time that we were leaving this place,
Ghazrek. Behold!'

He flung out one arm towards the mist which immediately rolled
away to reveal the glittering dark of the Void, and a strange bridge
of roseate stone began emerging block by block from the black
nothingness.

'To the witchhorse sanctuary,' Tauric said, stepping on to the
bridge, closely followed by Ghazrek and a subdued Shondareth.

Bardow sat at the head of the long scored table he had had moved
into his workshop early that morning. To his right sat Nerek,
to his left Alael, and between them power boiled in the air, a
writhing knot of green and white energies. Directly below it lay
the culvert, a narrow mould made from a single piece of agathon
wood according to the descriptions in the ancient text uncovered
by Hendred's Master of Parlance. Formed by the Palace's master
carpenter, it had been hollowed out in the form of a flat, straight
broadsword which stretched more than halfway down the table.
After that he had gone to the Imperial forge and persuaded the
weaponsmith to provide him with shavings and slivers of metal
from a variety of old blades, axes and daggers that were due to be
either melted down or reforged. Back in his workshop he produced
an old sword hilt which had been part of a hoard of items hidden by
palace servants in the last days of the old Empire; this he placed in
the culvert mould before scattering the fragments along its length
then laying the upper half in place. Then both halves were bound

together with bronze banding before the culvert itself was lashed to the table with leather straps.

Bardow sat with his hands flat on the table, staring at a bevelled slot which gaped beneath the radiant, roiling knot of powers. But his mind was consumed with maintaining the cantos Tract and Constrict to create a funnelling effect that would draw the melded powers down into the culvert.

With eyes closed and a frown on her face, Nerek had both her hands clasped tightly before her. Across the table Alael's posture was relaxed, almost slumped, her hands resting palms up on her dress-garbed thighs as she stared at the mingling glows with glazed eyes. Bardow hoped that both of them were remembering his directions, that each was focusing her power on the other and keeping them in balance until the coalescence took place. His use of the Lesser Power to guide these raging energies depended on such a contained harmony. Any unchecked imbalance could lead to a tremendous backlash and his own demise.

The colours of each power swirled around and through each other, shining silver, harsh emerald, rippling, flowing, coiling. Several minutes dragged by with no discernible change and Bardow began to wonder how long the ritual would take when swathes of hazy grey suddenly swept around the restless orb like a smoky veil unfurling. A moment later dark patches flickered across the surface and grew darker. When Bardow glanced at Nerek, he saw that her eyes were open and staring at the veiled orb without any apparent anxiety. The same was true for Alael.

'Do either of you know what is happening?' he muttered through gritted teeth.

'I was concentrating very hard on the Sourcefire,' Nerek said, 'and what you told us. And some part of my thoughts seemed to relax somehow, and I found myself thinking about . . .'

'So did I,' said Alael. 'I miss her.'

The darkness deepened upon the misty sphere, took on definite lines and shapes, colour, shade, and texture. With a start, Bardow realised that he was looking down into some kind of pillared chamber, half-lit by small golden lamps, its walls covered with exotic carvings, niches, figurines, and dramatic story friezes. The lone figure of a woman was bathing her face in a bowl on a marble plinth and once she had dried her face on a square of linen she looked up and gasped. It was Keren.

'Bardow! And Nerek and Alael . . . how . . . ?'

'We were thinking about you,' Alael said.

Keren glanced behind her then looked up, smiling. 'It is so good to see you and Bardow – and you, sister.'

A hesitant smile crossed Nerek's face. 'It gladdens me to see you well.'

'Thank the Mother you're alive,' Bardow said. 'What happened after the attack on Scallow? And where are you?'

'There was a sea battle out in the Bay of Horns and I was in the middle of it,' Keren said. 'I later made it to the Honjir coast where rebel outriders found me . . . They brought me north to the fortress of Untollan high in the Druandag Mountains.'

'I know of it,' Bardow said. 'Who leads these rebels?'

Keren gave a sardonic smile. 'An old friend, Domas, is in charge yet he also takes counsel from two mysterious advisers whom I've not seen. I know little else, apart from the fact that the Jefren Theocracy is bent on seizing this stronghold – they've moved large numbers of troops into the foothills nearby.'

'How many—' Bardow began.

'Bardow, you're beginning to fade and there's something I have to tell you while I can. Gilly was captured by Coireg Mazaret, or rather whatever is possessing him . . . I don't understand what happened but I know what I saw—' Keren's face was full of anguish and a remembered horror. 'Bardow, I saw five Gillys . . . they were carrying Gilly between them . . . and Coireg . . . into the water . . .'

Grey tendrils were emerging and spreading around the orb of powers. Bardow and the two women said goodbye to a fading cloudy figure before it was obscured. Bardow struggled to stay in control of the two thought-cantos as Keren's news sank in – the sorcerer possessing Coireg Mazaret had used Gilly to create five rivenshades!

Yet another of us turned into instruments of the enemy, he thought despairingly. *To have to fight such a pitiless enemy is one thing, but to have to fight enemies wearing the faces of our friends . . .*

A bright flicker of light came from the ashen-grey sphere, then another, then there were a dozen shifting spikes of light, a score or more. The grey shroud tore to rags that dissolved away to reveal an orb of perfect wonder, its silvery green surface reflecting their faces in undulations as slow concentric ripples radiated out here and there. Nerek and Alael sat back, eyes wide in delighted surprise. Bardow let the Tract and Constrict cantos exert their influence and the mirroring sphere began to elongate, drawing downwards in a smooth taper to the culvert, pouring gradually in through the bevelled slot.

Before long the gleaming last of it slipped into the mould and Bardow quickly closed it off with a small wood plug then fitted a bronze cover which he bolted into the mould itself. Standing, he went to the nearby windows and pushed them open to admit the coldness of the day, then moved away from the table and beckoned the women to do so as well. As they watched, pale wisps of vapour began to seep out of the culvert's rough outer surface, curling and dissipating.

'What happens now?' Alael said.

'The mingled powers are now transforming,' he said. 'Becoming a blade which is between power and iron. The transformation gives off a lot of heat which is why we are standing over here.'

Vapour was now rising from the mould in white rivulets as the moisture and juice in the wood began to boil. The air in the chamber grew heavy with the pungent odour of sap, despite the open windows. Then through it came a more acrid taint as dark tendrils of smoke started jetting from between the mould's two halves. The smoke's caress marked the pale wood with grey swirls even as the line that divided the halves of the mould grew black and scorched.

Charred smoking patches emerged on the mould surface, then spread. The heat from within was such that parts of the charred wood became glowing embers then collapsed inwards. The leather straps smouldered and parted, while the brass bands warped and buckled. The sword's blade was now visible, glowing silver-green as it settled down amid the ashen debris of the culvert. Bardow opened a nearby tall cabinet and from a shelf of dusty clutter took a bulky armoured gauntlet which he pulled on to his right hand. Then from behind the cabinet he dragged a cooling rack borrowed from the forge, an upright triangular box open down its long sloping side.

With his gauntleted hand he fumbled among the crumbling fragments of char and ember and lifted the melded sword out by its hilt. When he tapped it lightly on the table to dislodge cinders and ash, it rang with a pure double voice. He then turned to the triangular cooling rack and began fitting the sword's hilt into the metal hooks that would hold it safely clear of any surface. When it was done, he straightened to find Nerek looking at him.

'Am I done here, Archmage?' she said.

'You have urgent business elsewhere?' he said.

'Blind Rina and her coterie claim to have tracked our spell-caster down to the storehouses and livestock barns near the Long Quays. I hope to be the one to capture him.'

'Then go with them,' he said with a smile. 'If I need you I will send a message.'

As Nerek left, Alael came over and peered at the shining sword.

'I can almost feel its . . . its *swordness*,' she said. 'As if it knows what it is.' She frowned. 'Who will wield it?'

'I'm not sure,' Bardow said, pulling off the dusty and now slightly scorched gauntlet. 'I'll have to give it some thought.'

Yet somehow I think that any choice I make will matter little to the sword itself.

In the warmth of an afternoon sun, all was idyllic at the lake's shore. Children played in the shallows, small boats fished out on the placid waters, people walked or rode along the coastal track going to or coming from the graceful, white-towered town less than a mile away. Peace, smiles, and witchhorses. Everywhere, witchhorses in tribal families and lesser groups, most with foals and yearlings, and all looked so wise and noble with shining coats and long, lustrous manes . . .

Tauric sighed and sat on a wooden wayfarer's stool by the hill path which he and Shondareth had just descended. At the top of the hill was a sprawling, elaborate collection of interconnected tents and awnings, all brightly, luxuriously decorated, all busy with scores of witchhorses and ordinary people. This was the court of the great witchhorse chieftain who resided at its centre, receiving visitors, dispensing wisdom, listening to sagasongs composed in his honour.

And all of it, all the people and witchhorses, lake, shore and sun, every last bit of it was a fabulous illusion woven by just one witchhorse with the mysterious connivance and powers of the Void.

'As you can see,' Shondareth said, 'Like the others, Aegomarl is quite happy with his innerland.'

'I cannot believe that all of you are so uncaring and cold-hearted towards our plight,' Tauric said acidly.

'We are neither of those,' the witchhorse said. 'We merely know that the enemy is too strong. There are another hundred and eighty-six of us who feel the same – do you wish to speak to them, too?'

Tell him 'yes', said the spirit of the Fathertree in his head.

Tauric smiled. 'Why, certainly.'

Shondareth shook his head slowly and glanced to one side. A footpath appeared, branching off the hilltrack and winding down into a dense copse on the hillside. Following it, they entered the small wood and soon found themselves emerging into a clearing near a pool shaded by an ancient, wide-girthed agathon. Tall, pale trees reached up on all sides. As before, Ghazrek sat on a stone bench by the pool, eating from a gold platter of sweetmeats and baked delicacies. He looked up as they approached.

'How long?' he asked.

'A day and a half, perhaps,' Tauric said.

Ghazrek spat out a fruit pip and chortled. 'You've not been gone more than ten minutes!'

Tauric grinned. 'I wish it was me sitting there.'

'Room from another, your majesty,' the Mogaun officer said, indicating the bench.

Not yet, said the Fathertree. **I still have to see more of them**.

What are you looking for? he thought.

A little thing called guilt.

The next two innerlands were much like those they had already seen, grand explorations of vainglory, neither of whose creators would consent even to meet Tauric much less discuss the calamities engulfing Besh-Darok. Yet while Tauric was downhearted, the spirit of the Fathertree seemed to grow more optimistic and prompted Tauric to continue.

With an air of weary resignation Shondareth took him away from the pool (and Ghazrek with his food) and along another of the many narrow paths leading through the surrounding forest. The trees soon thinned and the sky grew grey and overcast. The air was warm and humid, though, and as they approached the edge of the forest Tauric heard a far-off rumble of thunder.

They emerged on a grassy slope which stretched down to join a wide expanse of patchwork farmland with copses and orchards, lined in cart tracks and hedgerows, all receding into the pale grey onset of early evening mist. A slumbering peace held sway over this landscape, disturbed only by herders calling to each other in the distance.

'This way, young explorer,' said Shondareth.

When he turned he was stunned by a majestic sight. The hills behind the forest merged with bushy, bouldery slopes which turned jagged and bare as they grew steep, while further up ridges and spines of rock sprouted from the towering flanks of mountains which stretched like a gigantic wall across the land. As he followed the witchhorse the nearer mountains ahead were a little lower and behind them reared a sheer promontory upon whose highest point Tauric could just make out a domed building and a cluster of slender towers.

It was Trevada on the Oshang Dakhal, which meant that this land was northwest Anghatan, a far more specific location than the other more fanciful innerlands he had seen so far.

Perhaps the creator of this will be open to persuasion, he thought.

Too soon to tell.

Shondareth led him down into a tree-sheltered vale where a few cottages were gathered on one side of a river, beside a watermill. Smoke drifted from some of the chimneys but a quiet serenity held sway. No one was in sight. Near the mill was a large barn and as they approached Tauric could hear a woman reciting some kind of verse. Pausing at the door, he gestured at Shondareth to wait as the woman finished to the polite applause of a few hands and a male voice spoke.

'A rendition that bordered on the pit of melodrama without quite falling in! Well done, Pel. Now, Suvi – what have you brought for me to hear?'

'A burial lament from Ebro' Heth,' said another woman.

'Good, good – proceed.'

The unseen woman called Suvi began. While the poem was full of sadness and regret, the woman's voice was strong and resonant. Near the end, though, her tone softened:

'Beneath the secrets of the sun,
Beyond the sorrow of eternity,
Lies the sweet heart of all things.
There shall I find rest,
Entwined in songs and stars,
And the joyful, dissolving flame.'

'Nicely expressed, especially in the final verses,' said the male voice. 'We may have time for more delights, but first we must greet our visitors.'

Tauric gave Shondareth a look of surprise but the witchhorse tilted his head at the barn and together they entered. Within, the walls were hung with paintings and tapestries and a selection of musical instruments, while gauzy lengths of pale blue and yellow material were draped between the overhead beams. Two large, bronze lamps shed soft light on three cowled figures sitting on a bench with their backs to the door. Before them a large, elderly witchhorse was reclining amid a heap of straw sprinkled with tiny red flowers.

'Joyful greetings to you Shondareth – I had heard that you were lost to us, that some cantrip out of the wastelands had snatched you away.'

'That was indeed my unhappy quandary, O noble Thoumyrax,

until a strange agency and this young man provided a means of return.'

The recumbent witchhorse gave Tauric an assessing look. 'Please accept my heartfelt thanks, both you and your enigmatic passenger, for bringing back my friend. From your dress and your careworn demeanour it would seem that you hail from the wastelands. Are you a slave there, or a fugitive?'

For a moment Tauric was wordless and confused.

How do I answer? he thought.

Tell him who you are, said the Fathertree, **and what you want. Speak plainly, directly**.

'Honoured Thoumyrax,' he began. 'I am Tauric tor-Galantai, Emperor of Besh-Darok, and I have come to ask if you will come back to the Realm Between and aid us in our direst need.'

There was an uncomfortable silence during which the witchhorse Thoumyrax just stared at Tauric for a long moment. Even the three women made no sound. Then Shondareth spoke.

'Well, Thoumyrax? Would you be prepared to walk away from this, your innerland, and plunge back into the dark struggle?'

The older witchhorse looked at Shondareth. 'Ah, I fear not, my friend. The cause was lost when we and the Empire were strong – what is being played out back there is but the long-delayed final scene of the final act. Partaking of such a struggle would be a futile deed of sacrifice, so I must respectfully decline your request, Emperor of Besh-Darok.

'But I grow weary so I must retire for the evening.' He looked at the three cowled women. 'Thank you all for reading such illuminating verses to me, thank you Pel, you Cava, and you Suvi, thank you for your beautiful voices . . .'

As the women stood to make their farewells, Tauric gained a better view of them – the one called Pel had long dark hair and a calm manner, Cava had black curly hair, a darker complexion and mischievous eyes, and Suvi had shoulder-length golden hair and an open smile. Tauric and Shondareth quickly bade the older witchhorse farewell and as they left the barn with the three women Tauric contrived to be walking beside Suvi. There was something about her that kindled his curiosity and a suspicion.

'Do you live near here?' he asked as they emerged. Outside, evening was drawing in with its veils of mist and shadow.

She gave him an amused look. 'In a manner of speaking,' she said, pointing up at the mountains, at the raised promontory of the Oshang Dakhal where the lights of Trevada now glowed. '*That* is where I work, live, eat, pray and study, which I should really only tell you *after* we've been introduced.'

What . . . ?

Thoumyrax will have kept her from hearing you earlier.

'I . . . see . . .' He cleared his throat. 'Very well – I am Tauric dor–Barleth.'

'Barleth?' Suvi said with a small frown. 'Isn't that part of the ducal lands in Patrein?'

'I have the honour of being the son of his grace, the Duke,' he said, giving a slight bow.

'And I am Suviel Hantika of the town of Kessio in Cabringa.' She laughed and curtseyed, then turned when her friends called from the open doors of a stable a little way upstream. 'I must go or I'll be late,' she said. 'Safe journey, Tauric dor–Barleth.'

He watched her run off through the knee-high grass, young and energetic, and remembered the kindly but weary woman who had helped Keren get him to Krusivel then tended him after he lost his arm.

Why is she here? he thought.

Thoumyrax must have known her in her youth, said the Fathertree spirit. **And in his intense need to create a comforting innerland illusion, he's revived a portion of north Anghatan with great accuracy of detail and atmosphere. However, I suspect that every day here is the same day in late summer** . . .

As Tauric watched the three women ride north through the trees he felt a sharp yearning for peace, happiness and no more struggle.

That you could have very easily – peace and happiness, success and accomplishment, the love and devoted regard of admirers. All that and more, a castle, a domain or even a kingdom of your own. You could be king, emperor, anything that you could want or dream about could be yours – just ask Shondareth.

He paused, his thoughts arrested by the possibilities laid out by the Fathertree spirit, all his desires made real and solid. He reached out to touch the rough bark of a nearby tree and tugged a handful of leaves from a low branch, imagining creating such things from his own memories . . . then he looked up at the clouded sky and wondered how real such a place could be.

It would be real for you.

And unreal for everyone else, he thought, letting the leaves fall. *While I surrounded myself with my desires, all else would fall into chaos. No, it would be a lie and I am too much my father's son to forgo my duty – I know that now.*

Yes, the Fathertree said as the witchhorse Shondareth came walking through the grass. **Whatever the lineage of your blood, you were always the son of the Duke**.

In the coolness of the glade, where shafts of sunlight fell upon a small pool and a white stone monument, she waited patiently, just as the goddess had instructed. There was a large round rock jutting from the ground near the pool so on it she sat, staring down into the waters at the tiny fish and the tinier insects darting across the surface. After a time she looked up and let her wandering gaze come to rest on the monument and she was peering closely at the detailed carvings along its side when the densely intertwined screen of foliage rustled slightly. Then it bulged, sprig and tendrils writhing, and the tall figure of a woman garbed in a long cloak of leaves stepped forth. As the foliage closed behind her, the goddess walked barefoot and unhurried across the soft, mossy ground to pause by the monument and regard the waiting woman. A feeling of tense expectancy filled the air, and a gem-like light seemed to shift around her.

'Suviel,' the goddess said. 'Come here.'

The woman felt a muffled stab of panic on hearing that name, her own name, which seemed to want to own her rather than her owning it. But she had to obey so she rose and went over, eyes downcast.

'Look up.'

Suviel did so. The Earthmother towered over her, long dark hair interwoven with blue flowers, her face strongly featured, her eyes a pale, copper green that shone into Suviel's thoughts. For a moment the goddess regarded her with that numinous regard, then crossed to the impenetrable wall of vine and leaves on the other side of the glade. Suviel could only follow.

'I have several tasks for you,' the goddess said. 'Firstly, it would be advantageous to restore a few of your memories and abilities . . .'

One moment she was empty as a shell with only a name rattling around inside of her. The next, the knowledge and history of the lands of the Empire that was came cramming into her thoughts, names, places, meanings, all those things that Suviel had shrugged off in the Vale of Unburdening. She almost wanted to weep.

'Now, watch.'

The Earthmother made a small gesture, and power rippled all around her as the wall of vines parted to form a dark, oval opening as tall as the goddess herself. Glittering ripples raced across the dimness within then dissolved away to reveal a view of a gloomy chamber lit by two large candles. On a table were several items, a book and two caskets which suddenly became transparent and glasslike, revealing their contents. Suviel made a small sound in recognition.

'The Crystal Eye and the Motherseed.'

'The prizes which the Shadowkings, especially Byrnak, desire above almost everything else,' the Earthmother answered. 'Possession of these talismans would give them the power to deal with the Lord of Twilight once and for all, but I shall not permit that for I will have my revenge!'

The goddess' anger shivered through the moist air and the surroundings seemed to become subdued and dimmer. She made another powerful yet tiny movement of her hand, and the scene changed. The chamber shivered into a gleaming swirl which then coalesced into a view of a paved courtyard with an open gateway looking out at a wide expanse of water beneath a cloudy sky. In the foreground was a stocky, bald man in the brown robes of a monk and two others in military garb, red cloaks, identical silvered breastplates and elaborate gold masks. Familiarity was fitful – the masked men were officers of the Jefren Theocracy, but was that not the Sea of Birrdaelin in the distance? Had the Theocracy come so far, then? The bald man, though, was Coireg Mazaret. From the memories available to her, she knew the name and little else, yet it seemed to imply something more, something which remained elusive.

A few yards away from Mazaret stood a line of five figures, five hooded men dressed like riders or scouts. The first approached Mazaret, went down on one knee and pushed back his hood . . . Suviel felt a surge of recognition and shock which she firmly quelled. It was Gilly Cordale.

The features, however, were chalk-white and the eyes pale. A suspicion formed in her mind as Mazaret exchanged a few words with him then presented a bone-handled dagger in a curved sheath. The man took the weapon, stood and without a backward glance walked to the open gateway and stepped out of sight. The next man came up to Mazaret, knelt and bared his head, which was identical to the first.

They were rivenshades, sorcerous doubles depending on part of someone else's spiritual essence for a kind of half-life. From her memories Suviel knew that this had been done to her, robbing her of all that she had been. The Crystal Eye had restored most of it, before she died . . .

'Even the enemy's own servants unknowingly further my purpose,' the Earthmother said as the dagger bestowal was repeated for the rest of the rivenshades who followed the first out of the gate.

'What are they going to do?' Suviel said.

'They are being sent forth as assassins,' the goddess said. 'Deadly blades in whose hilts are wells of poison baneful enough to kill any living thing, however strong and vital – when the Shadowkings' bodies die, the fragments of the Lord of Twilight will be free. The Acolytes secretly allied themselves with the Jefren Theocracy when it became clear that Byrnak and the others wanted to keep the Lord of Twilight under lock and key, as it were, and this is the outcome of their pact. They may prove to be useful if other strategies fail . . .'

The Earthmother's fingers twitched. Once more the scene rippled and swirled, reforming to show a dark, stone chamber. Small lamps burned on chest-high stands in all four corners, illuminating the large iron casket that hung on chains from the shadowed ceiling. Below it, emerald radiance burned in the patterns chiselled into the dungeon's flagstones, intricate symbols whose every curve and hook spoke of an ancient power. Yellow lamplight and green iridescence swam across the glyph-crowded surface of the long canister and tinged the grimacing bearded face staring out from the opening at the top of canister.

'Ystregul,' the Earthmother said. 'The first of the Shadowkings to be driven mad by his fragment of the Lord of Twilight. As you can see, he is constrained and guarded by a plethora of spells and traps. Although I could step into that room this very instant, my mere presence would set every alarum in Trevada shrieking.

'Therefore, Suviel, I shall send you to a less sensitive area in Trevada from whence you will find a way into the passage beneath the Basilica, enter that chamber and release him.'

Thus making it easier for an assassin to reach him? Suviel wondered. *Certainly, it would make it easier for him to attack me . . .*

But she bowed her head before the goddess, hoping only for an early return to the tranquility of nothingness.

'Divine Mother, I am yours to command. When shall I begin this task?'

'Soon, Suviel. Very soon.'

With his feet planted on ice-free projections and his good hand gripping a crack in the rock, Tavo paused for breath. He was getting close to the top of the cliff face now, he was certain. It had been a long and tortuous climb during which he had fallen twice, endured wind-driven rain, hail and snow, and was almost discovered by that turncoat bitch, Nerek. That was several hours ago when she and a couple of those dog-mages had appeared on the stone bridge that linked the mainland city battlements to the two sheer rock islets whose fortified watchtowers guarded the approach to the harbour. As they gazed down from either side of the bridge, Tavo had lain flat and utterly still while driving all vestiges of the Wellsource from his being. After a time he had peered out to see the bridge empty once more. With a prayer of thanks to the Prince of Dusk, he had continued upwards . . .

Feeling a little recovered, Tavo moved the fingers of his good hand up the narrow rock fissure to where it ran horizontally, then with one foot braced on a knee-high ridge he pushed himself higher. His other hand was all but useless, broken last night in a fall that had left him in stunned agony on a ledge two thirds of the way down. He had used the Wellsource then to fuse all the bones into a clenched fist so that he was free to use that lower arm or elbow as leverage. There was still a lot of pain from the wrenched and torn muscles, but it merged with the pain from all the other wounds he had suffered in the last few days, not least the burns he received in that cursed college. Then there were the slow distortions of skin and bone brought on by the combined use of Wellsource and Lesser Power. This had all left his body feeling like a sack of torment that he was slowly hauling up the sheer rock.

The cliff face was like a huge, insane pattern carved into the stone by the weather, a vertical maze of ledges, holes, jutting protrusions and cracks. In spring and summer it was also home to thousands of birds whose decaying nests and excrement still littered every shelf and hollow, thus as he climbed he acquired a stinking encrustation of filth. He cursed it with every upward step, every foot- and hand-hold that took his weight and did not crumble. The light was failing as the sun dipped towards the horizon, but he had been in bone-chilling shadow for most of the day and only the heat of the Wellsource in his veins kept the frostbite from eating his extremities.

Then, with the sky dark grey and turbulent, the vertical face turned into a steep slope dotted with hardy bloodspine bushes. Carefully he crawled up it, still using any holds he could find, progressing doggedly onward and upward as the incline grew steadily shallower till at last Tavo was lying on flat, snow-covered ground. To his right loomed the massive walls of Besh-Darok, its parapets and towers lit by watchfires. Part of him wanted to get up and dance and shriek his defiance, and mock them for letting him slip through their grasp. But he put aside the urge and crawled away from the walls to seek cover behind a snow-laden clump of hogthorn bushes. Now that he was concealed he could employ the Wellsource in a way that was impossible in the city. He opened himself to it, felt its ardour, the pushing force of its need to be used rushing through him . . . Its intensity almost overwhelmed him in his weakened state and his body trembled as he struggled to shape its power to his own needs. Finally he had what he needed, an eye that would let him see the nearest allies and servants of Gorla or Keshada. Sitting upright, he trained it to the southwest, peering through a curious mist made of the distance. Almost at once he spotted an outlying tower of the long growing wall, and a moment later a presence there became aware of his regard. Recognising him instantly as a servant of the Shadowkings it offered to send help, and he gratefully accepted.

As he quenched the Wellsource within him, he sat back, breathing heavily.

Soon, my masters, soon you will know the truth, that the third talisman lies not within Besh-Darok but at the bottom of the Wilderan Sea!

Chapter Twenty-one

Have little to gain more,
Be empty to receive,
Become broken to remain whole,
Be nowhere to be everywhere.

Shaman proverb

At the dark, mirror-calm pool near the clearing where every witchhorse's trail began, Tauric sat on a smooth rock by the water's edge, disconsolately tossing fragments of dry twig and watching the widening ripples. Behind him, Ghazrek was finishing off another tray of delicacies – for the Mogaun officer it had been less than half a day since their escape from the temple at Nimas, while Tauric had spent almost a week visiting many of the witchhorses in the cocooned illusions of their innerlands. But hardly any were inclined to hear his plea for help and not one showed the slightest shred of concern or understanding.

Strangely, the spirit of the Fathertree within him seemed quite satisfied and suggested that Tauric return to rest by the pool while it pondered on all that they had seen. Tauric felt that rest was the last thing he needed – he had experienced no tiredness at all – but agreed nevertheless. He had hoped that relaxing and clearing his thoughts would help him to think the situation through for himself, but instead he ended up brooding over the mistakes he had made, the naive trust he had placed in those who turned out to be enemies. Indeed, was it not possible that he was making the same mistake again?

You are entirely justified in posing such a question, said the Fathertree. **In my own defence, I can only point out that I have not and will not coerce you against your will – if I cannot persuade you, that will be an end to it**.

How could I know if you've tampered with my . . . judgement, making me favour your suggestions?

You could not, but I swear to you by the Sacred Void that your mind is your own, unchanged by my hand.

I see, he said, scattering his last few twig fragments across the pool. *Well, then – have you mulled over all that we've witnessed and reached any conclusions?*

Yes, and yes. First we have to go over to Shondareth and ask him how to create an innerland.

Tauric was startled. *Are you sure?*

All will become clear very soon, and there will be no danger or risk. I just need you to trust me.

He laughed quietly. *Very well*, he thought, then looked around and saw the witchhorse cropping berries back at the clearing. As he stood, Ghazrek glanced at him.

'That's it, majesty,' he said. 'Don't give up. Rub their noses in it if you have to . . .'

Tauric smiled and nodded, then strode across to Shondareth and asked the agreed question. The witchhorse gave him a piercing stare.

'So, you concede the futility of your quest. Are you seeking to join this community of inner peace?'

Tauric gave a shrug. 'I cannot be sure until I know what it entails, and what it demands of me.'

'The innerland is a quality of this sanctuary, provided by the Sacred Void,' Shondareth said. 'It will give to you all that you demand. To claim your own domain simply make a new path through the forest you see around this place. The foliage can be tough here and there but once you force your way through you'll reach a place full of shadows and mist – whatever you can imagine will be created there for you.'

With that, he turned and walked off into the trees along a nearby track and was soon lost to sight.

Tauric hunted along the edge of the tangled, enclosing wood and found a stretch of unbroken undergrowth with some bushes beyond. The spirit of the Fathertree approved so he strode forth through the high grass and weeds, pushing past the bushes which proved to be well armed with tiny thorns. After a substantial patch of this, which left him with a multitude of scratches, he emerged in an open area made dark by the encroaching cover of massive trees. In the shadows, mist drifted and forms were uncertain.

'This must be the place,' he muttered. A shiver passed through him and at once the hazy dark swirled and a tall figure took shape, its outline blurred but its features suddenly very clear. The face of Byrnak glared at him for a second before melting back into the spectral dimness. Tauric shivered.

It would seem that we need to exercise some care and attention, and be quite specific about our creations . . .

To his left the misty darkness suddenly rushed away and he was gazing across barren, sodden fields to the high walls of a city by the sea. Shanty towns clustered next to the walls or spread along the main roads in and out. As Tauric watched, gouts of smoke began to rise from the hovels crammed closest to the gates.

This is the city of Choraya in Honjir where the refugees were evicted on Byrnak's orders. Ten thousand died in the fires and another 90,000 fled along the road east into Roharka. Starvation and disease claimed many more.

Tauric stood watching in numb horror as scene after scene of wrecked civilisation was laid out around him, landscapes merging into one and other like a tapestry of destruction. Here was the burning city of Tobrosa, its vast outpouring of smoke spreading east to the Rukangs; close by was the Yularian capital of Rauthaz with Gunderlek's ragged banners fluttering from the keep as eaterbeasts hunted his men through the streets; there, the desolate, snow-deadened shell of Nimas, and further on a string of Anghatani villages going up in flames as their inhabitants were led away in chains.

The ancient ruins of Alvergost, a broken, winter-struck citadel full of refugees fearing the kidnap gangs who hunt by night.

Soldiers and sailors fighting madly, desperately, on the decks of great ships engulfed in smoke, while on the near shore a city is in flames.

In a coastal town in Yularia, a mass beheading of priests and nobles . . .

With tears running down his face, Tauric sat on a fallen tree and covered his eyes.

I am sorry for showing you such terrible sights, said the spirit of the Fathertree. **But this is the reality of what was and is still being done, and which we have to resist with all our might. For if the Shadowkings win, the Lord of Twilight will eventually return and all of this will be but a foretaste of the torment he will inflict upon all these lands. So . . . I am sorry, but it is necessary**.

'I think I understand,' Tauric said. 'But if the witchhorses wouldn't listen when we went to them, why would they come here?'

They do not need to come here, the Fathertree said. **All their little refuges are joined together thus we shall guide this dark evocation through them all, like a vessel with a cargo of suffering to provoke their pity and their shame. Your companion put it quite succinctly as we were leaving the pool . . .**

Tauric frowned, trying to recall, then he smiled. 'Rub their noses in it?'

Exactly.

The day of the second battle of Besh–Darok dawned grey, veiled in mist, the air made icily sharp by a savage night frost that showed no sign of loosening its grip. The city presented an impassive bulwark to any besieging force, high, sheer walls with well-designed battlements and towers, and wide ramparts. The walls were manned all along their considerable length and had innumerable standards and banners hanging from jutting poles or draped down the parapets. The impression was that of indomitable strength but Byrnak knew the truth: the city's garrison totalled little more than 13,000, taking into account the much-diminished forces still loyal to Yasgur, the new knight orders and the meagre reinforcements coming in by sea. By contrast, he had all but emptied Gorla and Keshada to bring with him over 75,000 black-armoured troops, each one carrying the spirit of a fanatically-loyal Wellsource warrior stolen from the Vale of Unburdening by his own soul-bound Acolytes.

And the most important truth of all was that delivered by one of Kodel's spies who had managed to escape Besh-Darok with the news that the mages did not after all possess the Staff of the Void and were conducting their own search for it. When the half-dead spy was brought before him after nightfall and had told all he knew, Byrnak laughed long and loud. But when Azurech then eagerly suggested that the attack on Besh-Darok begin immediately he dismissed the idea.

'This may be the last such great battle to take place in these lands,' he had said. 'Let it be fought in the cold light of day, that the full extent of our punishment be visible to all.'

The Shadowking Byrnak now sat on a black stallion charger, resplendent in a long black war cloak over dark silver chainmail, armoured gauntlets and an obsidian helm sculpted with an encircling crown of incurving tines. Around him were the two hundred longswords of his bodyguard, a full score of former Acolytes now soul-bound to his will, a gang of stewards and attendants and a number of standard-bearers carrying tall, dark banners. From the crest of the ridge, which had been utterly stripped of verdure, he could stare across the dark, serried ranks of his warriors to survey the entirety of the white, snow-blanketed flatness that surrounded the city.

He had drawn up his forces in a rough, semi-circle about half a mile distant from Besh-Darok. There were eight divisions of 5,000 men each, being mainly swordsmen and spearmen augmented by companies of riders and bowmen; six wings of cavalry of 2,000 men each; five echelons of bowmen, each numbering 1,000; and five rods of elite warriors, each 800 strong. The catapult and wall-scaling companies came to roughly 1,000, their smaller numbers belying their importance.

In addition there was a recently-completed war machine whose slower progress from Gorla had kept it from even coming into view until a short time ago, while the Mogaun host's desultory southward pace meant it would not take part in the initial assault. Eaterbeasts he had aplenty, but he had the use of a mere handful of nighthunters, being all that the Acolytes of Trevada claimed they were able to rouse from an unforeseen hibernation cycle. Byrnak had accepted this with all the equanimity he could muster while vowing privately that the Acolytes would be brought to heel once the war was over.

Across the spread-out formations no runners hastened, nor message birds flew – he had no need of them. Every commander and sub-commander was soul-bound to his perception and will, thus every part of the battlefield was within his grasp: even as he sat ahorse, gazing down from this ridge, he was able to see through the eyes of a bow echelon commander waiting with his men on the slopes of a bushy hill south of the city, or a cavalry sub-commander waiting in a gully to the north . . .

And all the time he was aware of the watcher in the high tower of the Palace behind those walls, the continual searching regard of the Archmage Bardow. He could also feel the presence of the Crystal Eye, guarding and warding, ever-vigilant and attuned to the Archmage, thus making of him a formidable opponent. But he was the only one – the rest of the city's mages were fools and weaklings of little importance.

Then Byrnak smiled, realising that he had left Nerek out of the assessment. She was of the Wellsource, shaped by his own fury to be a weapon yet without the use of soul-binding. Thus, being a free agent, she had turned against him and committed herself to his enemies' cause. Whatever her skill with the Wellsource, she would learn that it obeyed his dictates, not hers.

He breathed in the dry, ice-cold air and imagined that he was breathing in anticipation. It was almost time for the great drama to unfold but first there would be an instructive interlude. Half a mile north of his position was a long, low ridge with the fort in whose ruins Ystregul had revealed his treachery just a few months ago. Since then the fort had been partly rebuilt and regarrisoned by the enemy, and a flag now fluttered above it as smoke rose from a nearby cooking fire. His spies had told him that there were less than two hundred within its patchwork walls so on either side he had marshalled a wing of cavalry and a rod of his elite warriors. None would escape.

Focusing his thoughts along the soul-bound web, he began giving

orders and directions. Horsemen readied spears and longaxes while
the elite fighters bared longswords glittering with power. His vision
drifted among a score of perspectives till he came to that of the
commanders of the two bow echelons waiting just south of the fort
itself. Pausing for a moment, he savoured the feeling of standing amid
thousands of masked bowmen, all with arrows affixed, all waiting
silently for the word to draw and aim. He felt the keenness of
both commanders as he prepared them, heightened their tension
as if they too were bows being drawn, bent back by his own hands
and aimed high—

As one, they both said, 'Loose!'

Yasgur was hurrying along the rampart from the Gallaro Gate to
the Shield Gate when one of his staff captains suddenly cried out,
'They're attacking the old fort!'

Yasgur whirled in time to see arrows rise in a vast, dark flock, reach
the apex of their flight then fall towards the fort's incomplete walls.
Nothing could be heard at this distance but imagination supplied him
with the feathery, rushing sound, the sharp raps and clanks of impacts
on armour, the gasps, grunts and cries of the wounded and the dying.
Another cloud of arrows rose and fell, then a larger black missile flew
up from beyond the ridge and smashed into the fort. By now all of the
soldiers manning the city walls were standing at the notches, staring
out at the ruthless assault.

There was a moment or two when nothing seemed to be
happening, then Yasgur saw one of the large formations of foot
troops moving towards the ridge. Way off to the right a mass of
cavalry was climbing the shallower slopes of the ridge and as they
and others from behind the ridge converged on the fort they began
to resemble a swarm of black insects rather than an army of men.

And, he realised, he had heard no horns or drums signalling the
Shadowkings' army's movements or charges.

'Not a sound,' he muttered.

'They hear his comands in their minds, Lord Regent,' said a
woman's voice nearby.

It was Nerek, the woman who had once been the Shadowking
Byrnak's lover, or so it was said. She wore a dark blue cloak over

a plain corselet of banded leather, and had a long dagger and a curved sabre at her waist. Bare-headed, her face was impassive but her eyes seemed tired and sad. Yasgur also noticed a greenish tinge in their whites.

'What do you mean?' he said.

She faced him. 'Byrnak has soul-bound all his senior officers to himself. He can see what they see, and they can hear his every order.'

As the implications of this sank in, Yasgur had to strive against his own despair and anger. 'So . . . the army is the man, and the man is the army.' He stared at her. 'Then what are his weaknesses?'

She frowned. 'I don't think he has any – he is an accomplished strategist and tactician, yet . . .'

'Yet?'

Nerek shrugged. 'He has a predator's instincts, and sometime lunges in too soon for the kill.'

Yasgur took this in and wondered how he could ever turn this morsel to his advantage. Now that Byrnak had marshalled his forces around the city, there seemed no way for the Mogaun to come to their aid without laying themselves open to brutal attack. It would require a devastating and unexpected manoeuvre to throw Byrnak's assault on to the back foot. His racing thoughts halted suddenly when a cry went up along the battlements, and he looked round at the old fort.

The flagpole was gone and as he watched, hundreds of black-garbed troops formed into long gangs hauling on ropes. The walls of the fort were then methodically and swiftly torn down until not one block rested upon another. The message for Besh-Darok was stark, and when Yasgur glanced either way along the silent wall all he saw were grim, fearful faces. For a long, aching moment no one made a sound, as if the sight of the demolished fort had robbed every onlooker of the will to speak.

Then he heard someone start to clap rhythmically and sing out in a hoarse but strong voice. The song was in the Mogaun tongue but it took Yasgur a few lines before he recognised it as an old nonsense rhyme called 'Father Whisker Knocked Down His Hut' which told of an elder's attempts to stop ants invading his hut. A ripple of surprised laughter passed along the ramparts and others took up the refrain, a simple slow cantering verse that ended with the singer quickly stamping one foot then the other before the next verse began. The old song spread through the Mogaun warriors, the native Khatrisians joined in and the volume and tone of it grew and changed. Soon, thousands of voices were shouting out the words with a kind of crazed defiance, and the stamping of feet was like thunder. Yasgur was not given to dramatic gestures but as the song reached its bellowing crescendo he seized one of the flags set in iron holders along the parapet and leaped up on to the battlement itself.

Holding the flag aloft, he flung out his other hand to point at the far-off cluster of banners that signified Byrnak's presence. A mass roar greeted this and he had to wait for it to subside a little before shouting at the top of his voice, 'I can see you, old Father Whisker!' His outstretched, pointing hand he turned into a beckoning gesture, which raised another gleeful roar. 'Come to us – *we are waiting!*'

He descended to more cheers and stamping just as Atroc came striding jauntily along the ramparts from the south. Yasgur saw a certain satisfaction in those wrinkled features and the almost inevitable suspicion kindled in his mind.

'Did you have a hand in that, old man?' he said.

'Ah, my prince – songs are the secret voice of the soul, and when my soul spoke I could not stay silent!'

Yasgur grinned fiercely. 'It was a song well sung, old friend,' he said, clapping him on the shoulder, then muttering closely, 'and timely. The men were ready to break . . .'

'My lord,' said Nerek. 'I must take my leave – my mount is being reshod at the Ironhall Barracks and I wish to be sure that it is done well.'

'Be on your way, lady,' he said. 'Fight well.'

She sketched a bow and hurried away down the long stairs that were carved into the wall. Yasgur watched her leave then turned back to Atroc.

'Any news from the harbour?' he said.

'I've just come from there,' the seer said. 'Two sails spotted on the horizon away to the south, but no sign yet if they are friend or foe.'

Yasgur nodded, sombre once more. Most of the liberated towns and cities south of the Great Valley had promised to send troops for the defence of Besh-Darok, yet precious few had actually arrived. There had been messages from Adnagaur speaking of three ships of volunteers but it would be another hour or two before the approaching vessels could be identified. In the meantime, he would have to muster and deploy his men as best he could. He had sealed the Gallaro Gate and the Shield Gate by fixing additional iron bars across the insides then piling tons of rocks behind them. Thus the enemy would have to either climb over the city walls or knock them down.

He stared over the walls at the wide, still formations of Byrnak's army, the dense ranks startlingly black against the whiteness of the surrounding terrain. There were several smaller units spaced between the larger ones, ladder carriers and grapple-rope throwers, he was certain. There were so many of them, more than the eye could encompass.

And of the Mogaun there was no sign.

Then the sound that Yasgur had been dreading came sharp and sudden through the cold air, horns blaring from the northern and southern sections of the wall. From his position between the main gates he had a better view of the northern flank and saw three massive arrays of black-armoured soldiers flowing across the ground towards the city. Then the horns were replaced by the regular booming of great war drums, which he had positioned on flat rooftops near the main wall.

The orders had all been given and the rows of bowmen and axemen waited along the wall while the city's few catapults were being readied. Soon the terrible test of battle would begin.

Nerek had just reached the foot of the long stone stairway when she heard the blare of the horns. As the booming of the war-drums began reverberating across the city, she was running along a side street that led from the wall to the wide Shaska Road. From there it was a straight dash south to the crossroads and east along Captains' Way. The Ironhall Barracks was a high-walled compound whose broad entrance was flanked by two stone statues of armoured knights, each showing signs of recent restoration. As she approached, one of the duty officers recognised her from the previous day and let her in.

The stable was a long, low building on the west side of the parade ground and the smithy was at its far end. The forgeman took her to her horse's stall where she saw that the reshoeing had been done to her satisfaction, and minutes later she was riding out of the barrack gates.

The battle was now well-joined as the enemy fighters strove to reach the battlements on tall ladders or grappling ropes. From where Nerek was, she could look up and across the roofs of the artisan and college wards, across the treeless expanse of Lords Glade, to the long stretch of the south wall. Clusters of fighting men were visible all along it and reinforcements were rushing in from the guard towers. Northwest, looking past the twin hills of the Old Town, she could see a similar struggle taking place on the northern wall. Yet the defenders seemed to be holding out, using every advantage to the full . . .

There was a bright flash from somewhere behind her and as she jerked round she caught sight of a large flighted creature tumbling out of the sky over the palace uttering a jagged shriek as it fell. Two of the half-dozen small figures clinging to its back were shaken loose before it dipped its snout downwards and spread its wings. Swooping low over the outer walls, it wheeled and came down out of sight behind the buildings south of the Imperial Barracks.

It was one of Byrnak's nighthunters, she knew, sent with the purpose of landing warriors on one of the High Spire's great balconies. Only there was someone with vigilant eyes watching from the tower and ready to strike, someone that could only be Bardow. But she had seen the other figures on the creature's back and knew that any warriors nearby could never stand against such peril. She had been on her way to the Imperial Barracks anyway, but now here was the kind of unforeseen peril that she was well suited to confronting. Wheeling her horse, she urged it into a spirited gallop up towards the Palace.

Bardow felt at once exhilarated and uneasy in the moments following his attack on the nighthunter. When the wall assaults began, he had prepared in his mind a few Lesser Power thought-cantos in case the enemy looked like breaking through, among them Sunlance. Usually, unleashing such a spell would have cost him so dearly as to leave him insensible for hours yet here he was, leaning on the balcony and feeling only a little dizzy.

The Crystal Eye, he thought. *Being attuned to it has advantages – I wonder what the disadvantages are . . .*

'Archmage! Are you wounded?' said the captain of the Protector knights set to guard the wide, many-windowed chamber that Bardow had chosen as his vantage point.

'I am well,' he said, waving the man away. 'But the creature has come down in a street near the Imperial Barracks. Despatch messengers to the garrison commanders of the Palace and the barracks, and send a couple of your own men along the south-facing aggors to observe for me . . .'

The knight-captain nodded and turned away to issue orders. Bardow breathed in deep as vitality flowed through him. Indeed, the better he felt, the more worries seemed to take root at the back of his mind, but what was the point of such worries when Byrnak's army was closing on them like the jaws of a savage beast? Wrapping his cloak tighter, he turned to look back inside the large chamber. Seeing one of the senior stairsmen over by the door, he beckoned him over.

'Good ser,' he began. 'Inform the High Steward that I must have as many attendants out on the Spire's balconies as possible – he can use potboys from the kitchen if necessary, but I have to have the skies around the Spire watched.'

'I'll see it done immediately, my lord,' the stairsman said and dashed out of the room.

Then Bardow frowned as the Crystal Eye sent a quiver of warning through his thoughts. He ducked back out on to the balcony and gazed down, letting the Eye guide his vision and enlarge the details far below without the need for a though-canto. The sweeping, blurring view came to rest on an armoured woman riding on horseback up from Ironhall Barracks and kept pace with her past obscuring buildings as she headed towards the area where the nighthunter had landed.

It was Nerek. She must have seen it come down and was intent on investigating. The sight filled Bardow with anxiety and irritation. *She should know better than to put herself in that kind of danger, when she should be conserving her energies . . .*

Bardow called the knight-captain out on to the balcony and explained the situation. 'Thus I need you to send another of your men down to find her and tell her that I wish her to return here with him. That it is my command.'

'It shall be done, my lord,' the captain said and hurried off.

Alone once more, Bardow gazed out at the panoply of Byrnak's army, the dark swathes through the snow that marked the marching courses of warriors in their thousands. But the city's drums were maintaining their same regular beat – if the enemy did gain a foothold, the beat of the drums nearby would double. For the moment, Yasgur's men were managing to hold them off and Bardow's attention was drawn to the Mogaun Host, now emerging from the mist-grey low hills north of the city. Yasgur had told the Archmage of his meeting at sea with Welgarak and Gordag, and what had been agreed there, but in the light of Byrnak's swift mustering of his forces, what else could the Mogaun leaders do but throw in their lot with the Shadowkings once more? An attack on the rear of Byrnak's northern formations might help the city for a while but would invite terrible reprisals.

Besides that, another more unsettling element was about to enter the battlefield, a huge, horse-drawn war-wagon which was slowly moving closer to Byrnak's westerly flank. Aided by the Crystal Eye, Bardow could make out that it was a massively built vehicle rolling along on eight great wheels. There seemed to be some kind of long arm beneath a wide draping of stitched skins and hides, and a strong feeling that the Wellsource was part of its construction and purpose . . .

Was it a ram meant for bludgeoning through fortifications? But what kind of ram would it have to be to breach Besh-Darok's mighty wall? Or could it be a catapult with a fearsome throwing capacity and range enough to reach anywhere in the city?

Suddenly, events on the northern battlements caught his eye, the defenders cheering and waving flags as the enemy retreated with its wounded and its remaining ladders. Bardow smiled bleakly, knowing that this was only the first of many assaults and certainly the least. The main body of Byrnak's vast horde still waited, facing the west wall with that mysterious war-wagon crawling ever nearer. He called over an attendant and told him to seek out Alael in one of the lower level libraries and ask her to join him here. Then he looked back out at the ominous wain, studying its unfaltering progress.

Like all of Byrnak's warriors, he wore a shaped, leather mask, but his was larger and more elaborate with a ribbed ruff which curved up and over the back of his head then flared out with a trailing edge of feathery tails. The leather was a rich, dark brown and had a dull polished gleam to it, much like the full chest corselet that he wore. He had been waiting just inside the entrance to the Imperial Barracks when Nerek arrived, standing with a red-edged black cloak draped over his shoulders and a bared longsword held before him, its blade dripping blood on the broad flagstones.

Now, cloak discarded, he circled as slowly as Nerek, watching her every move as she watched his. She had already glimpsed the hacked and lifeless bodies scattered along the corridor beyond the entrance hall and knew that this one's companions were almost certainly in the High Spire by now. The thought of Bardow or Alael in danger sent a ripple of anger through her.

Then the masked warrior attacked with a whirling barrage of blows that struck sparks from Nerek's own sword and forced her back. Snarling, she unleashed a stream of Sourcefire, formed it into a long gauntlet around her left hand with which she grabbed the man's longsword high along the blade. Wrenching it out of his grasp, she swung it swiftly and took his head from his shoulders. As the corpse fell twitching to the ground, spilling dark ichor across and between the flagstones, a familiar mocking voice spoke in her thoughts:

And still you deny and defy me, dearest Nerek, said Byrnak. *For as long as the Wellsource flows in your flesh, part of you will always belong to me. I would offer you shelter and redemption again, except that I know you have made your choice. Such glorious futility! But worry not, for soon I shall bring it to an end . . .*

She thrust the poisonous voice from her mind and strove to block

Byrnak's presence altogether. Then she threw the longsword aside
with a sharp clatter, crossed the entrance hall and stood on the
threshold of the double doors to the barrack concourse. The dead
bodies of some dozen knights were lying all around the doorway,
a carnage of severed limbs and exposed innards. A few had deep
wounds that smouldered, proving the presence of at least one
Wellsource adept up ahead.

A deep bestial shriek from outside made her look round. Through
one of the hall's open windows she saw that snow was falling again,
but more important was the dark hulking shape of a nighthunter
that was now perched on the peaked roof of a building next to
the barracks. It made any notion of leaving by this route somewhat risky.

For Nerek, however, the only way was in.

Yasgur's heart leaped when the grey veils of snowfall swept down
from the north and across the city. He had teams prepared and
waiting at the seaward towers of the wall, both north and south,
and now disguised with masks and uniforms taken from the enemy
dead. His original task for them had been to climb down and go forth
to wreak general havoc and destruction, but now another target had
come to the fore.

The Lord Regent and his staff were currently ensconced in a
round, covered tower that was part of a spur wall jutting inwards
from the Gallaro Gate fortification. From here he had an excellent
view of both northern and western walls, as well as all the enemy
forces ranged against them. It was the long, low war machine
slowly trundling its way towards the city that had occupied his
thoughts increasingly for the last half hour. The thing was surrounded
by hundreds of guarding swordsmen so it would be pointless to
send his disguised warriors against them. No, instead they would
capture one of the enemy's catapults, which were far heavier
than those within the city, and use it against that huge wagon.

The most likely catapult was the one still stationed beyond the
smugglers' ridge. It was the most isolated one, but there were still
risks aplenty from the cavalry and foot formations that were in direct

line of sight of it. Hopefully, the weather would conceal his men as they went about their task.

Yasgur had his flag-officer send the order and as the man clambered up into the tower's cupola, he shivered and poured himself a beaker of hot wine from a bronze kettle sitting on the hot bricks of a brazier. More runners brought messages and reports as he sipped and he replied with more commands. The Shadowkings' army seemed to have paused, perhaps for a period of realignment.

'My lord,' said a woman's voice behind him. 'I have urgent news.'

Steeling himself, he turned to meet the cool, dark gaze of the female mage who called herself the Nightrook. She was a tall, slender woman in a long, azure coat and her pale, precise and unsmiling features gave away nothing but a lofty composure. Yasgur still felt nervous in the presence of sorcerous abilities but forced himself to be courteous.

'Who is it from, lady?' he said.

'Your seer, Atroc. He speaks through my colleague, Zanser, and wishes to tell you that three ships, each bearing a hundred and fifty troops, are now docking at the Long Quay.'

'Good!' Yasgur suddenly felt the dangerous glimmer of hope. 'Tell Atroc that I want them marched quickly up to the old Lords Glade where they will wait for my next orders. And he is to have this passed on through the duty officer at the quay.'

'He understands your commands, my lord, and assures you that—'

'Wait,' he said, frowning. There was cheering and whoops coming from the north wall, men leaning on the battlements and pointing out. Yasgur stared north through the shifting greyness of snow and began to make out movements among the enemy ranks. Then he saw a wedge of horsemen sweep in to attack them from the shoreward flank, and understood.

The Mogaun Host had moved against Byrnak's unprotected and unsuspecting troops! Whatever the Shadowking's response, right now his forces were being torn apart.

Welgarak felt full of a burning exhilaration as he led the Mogaun charge on into the disorganised rabble of Byrnak's soldiers. On a hillside back the way they had come, the Host's second wave was hacking that leaderless mob of horsemen to pieces while Welgarak aimed to take his own riders on a broad sweep through the nearer block of infantry.

Like a honed edge, the Mogaun horsemen pushed on relentlessly. Welgarak's axe rose and fell in a bloody arc, every blow an act of revenge for the lies and foulness inflicted upon the Mogaun tribes by the Shadowkings. All around him other chiefs and warriors fought with the same grim resolve, fully aware that any of those masked soldiers might once have been proud members of their own clans.

Through the dissolving ranks of black masks, the bloodied horsemen rode. To those troops on the ground, caught in the jostling, shrieking, gory chaos, the advancing riders were like a wave of death against which none could stand. Suddenly, the breaking lines turned into a rout but Welgarak ignored the fleeing men, instead signalling with a raised totem of fur and ribbons and a drawn-out call that took his hurtling riders in a tight wheel towards the next mass of infantry.

From a lifetime of combat on foot and in the saddle, Welgarak knew that timing was everything. The commander of the other infantry formation had seen what happened and had swiftly rearranged his lines to meet the new threat with spearmen ranked along the front. Unfortunately his rear and flanks were now vulnerable and as Welgarak slowed his own charge, Gordag came racing up from a snow-hidden gully to the north, at the head of 1,000 riders which slammed into the enemy's left flank. A second wedge numbering 500 came thundering out of a dark, icy wood to the west and struck them in the rear.

Yet still they held, that compact array of infantry, until a bolt from one of Welgarak's crossbowmen found the commander amid his guards, punched through the heavy leather mask just above his ear, through the skull and into his brain. Welgarak could see the spears of the front line waver as word of their commander's death spread panic and he knew that it was time. With a whispered prayer to the ancient storm gods of the Mogaun, he raised his totem and called the charge. When the infantry saw that line of horsemen approaching at the gallop, with groups of Mogaun swordsmen rushing in as well, the lines broke. A few stood and fought in stubborn knots but most fled away into the snowfields west of the city.

Still on horseback, Welgarak and Gordag met on a hillock beyond the carnage. Both bore wounds but to Welgarak it seemed that Gordag was worse off. Blood from a gash on his jowly cheek had matted the fur collar of his heavy jerkin.

'You let those beetles get too close with their pig-stickers,' he said, irritation masking his concern.

'Ach, looks worse than it is,' Gordag said. 'But what about you? Where did you earn that scratch?'

Welgarak followed his pointing finger down to his right leg where the leather greave had been torn away and a half-clotted gouge in his calf wept a long red smear. Surprised, he began to feel it through the numb cold that was sinking into his flesh.

'Seems like we both have to see the binder, brother,' he said. 'Before our former master makes his move.'

'Don't know as we have time f'r it.'

Hearing the grim note in Gordag's voice he quickly looked up and southwards. It was snowing more heavily now and the far side of the city and the countryside beyond were frost pale and blurred. Nearer, however, were those units of the Shadowkings' army which were the most immediate threat to the Mogaun, yet there was no sign of them heading this way.

'You'll see 'em in a moment,' said Gordag.

But he heard them first, harsh rasping cries carried by a swirl in the winds overhead. It was a sound that took him back to the siege of Rauthaz over a year ago when the Acolytes of Twilight had released a swarm of eaterbeasts into the city's streets. Their cries were the sound of a bottomless hunger for blood and they struck fear into his heart, but he crushed it with his anger and need for revenge.

'We cannot fight them here,' he said.

'Agreed,' said Gordag.

'We shall have to ride swiftly and find a place . . .'

So saying, they rode back, bellowing orders to their men to mount up and ride north for their lives.

Chapter Twenty-two

Dire storms woven of stars and blood,
Rage forth from the ghastly dark,
To tear at our walls,
And test our valour.

Keldon Ghant, *Orosiada: A Masque*, Act 1, Sc. 2

Atroc was labouring his way up the recessed stairs on the southern wall, glancing out over Lords Glade, when he heard a deep, reverberating thud followed a moment later by a shudder that passed through the solid stone of the wall itself. Instantly, he knew what had happened and fear put vigour into his legs as he ran up the rest of the stairs. He had been on his way to find one of Bardow's mages, so that he could inform Yasgur that the 300 Cabringan swords were now in Lord's Glade awaiting his command. Now, he also needed to know what was happening.

Bardow was out on his balcony, shivering despite his heavy cloak, closely watching the great wagon's slow approach to a point on the wall along from the Shield Gate and closest to the Imperial Palace. Even as it drew near he could feel the Wellsource energies building within it yet he still knew nothing of its construction due to the enormous patchwork hide which lay draped across most of its length.

Fifty yards away it halted and, as the horses were unharnessed, a long boom was attached to the rear. Two dozen heavily-armoured and helmed troops quickly took their places, lifted the boom and began pushing and forcing the wagon into motion again. Only when it was nearly at the wall itself and attracting a barrage of rocks and arrows did a few of its toiling attendants dash forward and tug lashings free and drag the snow-caked sheet away. Bardow saw a long wooden arm as thick as a man and as long as three draught horses put nose to tail. It was hinged at the front, its axle protected by a bronze-banded wooden carapace which extended the wagon's full length. Affixed to the end of the arm was a strange element, a squat stone cylinder with a six-foot iron spike jutting from its centre. As a green nimbus began to flicker and leap around the puzzling war machine, it moved still closer until obscured by the wall despite the height of his balcony.

The next moment, there was a loud thudding noise like a huge hammer blow. Bardow saw soldiers on the ramparts thrown off their feet as a glowing green web of jagged cracks suddenly appeared halfway up the inside of the city wall. The glowing lines faded to dark and down on the streets people were running in panic while Bardow could only stare in dread, his remaining hope resting with the shining sword which sat in its case in his chamber.

Alael was in the High Spire's fourth-floor library, seated under lamplight at the great horseshoe-shaped table, poring over books of legendary tales, when she heard the impact. It was like a far-off, muffled boom, followed by a tremor that came up through the tiled floor. Suddenly she had to find a window to look out of but there were none in the library, whose many delicate documents had to be protected from dampness and sunlight. But she knew that a door on one of the library's upper floors led to an outer passage with arches that opened on to a sheltered balcony.

Quickly, Alael rose, crossed to a spiral staircase, hurried up two flights to a dark and musty-smelling floor whose shelves were crammed with leather volumes. A door at the far end led through to a bright corridor and moments later she was leaning over the balcony rail to see what was happening. The balcony was a little higher than the Palace's Silver Aggor and afforded a good view of the city wall. It was snowing quite steadily now and soldiers were running away from a section of the ramparts directly before the Palace while shouts came from below. Alael had noticed the dark fracture lines on the inner face of the wall and was wondering what they were when there was a thunderous crash from the other side. Dazzling light flared along the dark lines and chunks of stone fell along with great shattered sheets of mortared facing. She cried out in shock, scarcely believing that such destruction was possible. She would have to find Bardow, but she knew he was in the Vantage Chamber a full five floors up. First she would return for her notes and pens, then go and seek him out.

She dashed back along to the library door, stepped back into the quiet gloom and began to descend the stairs. Only when she reached the intermediate floor did her gaze chance to alight upon her place at the great table where all her books and neatly-piled notes now lay scattered across it and the floor. Alael halted, staring, her momentary confusion displaced by a deepening unease. Then she heard a footstep.

From the floor above.

And from below came a voice, casual and mocking.

'Ah, lady Alael, at last we can renew our acquaintance.'

A tall figure cased in brown-black mask and armour, his shoulders draped with a night-black cloak, stepped out from behind two of the shelf stacks. A mailed hand came up and tugged off the mask, revealing the colourless, pale-eyed visage of Ikarno Mazaret. Except that she knew this was one of the rivenshades, on whose armoured hands and chest she could now make out splatters of blood.

She met that chilling empty gaze and for a moment or two listened to the slow footsteps heading towards the staircase. Then she whirled and dashed over to the door which led out of the library, though where it went she knew not.

Nerek was standing on the threshold of a room full of dead guards when she heard the first impact, a deep muffled boom that reverberated throughout the immensity of the High Spire. The sound faded away and through the quiet came a susurrus of hurrying feet and lowered voices as people sought windows to look out of. On the floor of the second floor guardroom, however, the blood of eight men lay in smears and darkening pools. No alarm had been raised and Nerek knew that she had reached the room only moments after the killers had left.

Then she heard the crash of weapons and a scream from beyond an archway where a narrow side-stair led up to the third floor. As she ducked through the arch and ran up the steps, she reflected on the many passages and stairs that honeycombed the great tower, and the ease with which the enemy intruders had gained entry. But then, if the tower had not been stripped of most of its garrison to man the city wall, cornering them would been straightforward.

The stairs came up in a servants' dining room where two armoured knights lay sprawled in their own blood while a third was on the floor by the long table, propped against a chair and gasping his last. She went over to him but quickly saw from the blood he was losing that there was no helping.

'Up . . .' he whispered. Blood was weeping from between the fingers he had clamped to his throat. His other hand tremblingly pointed across the room to a plain arched doorway. She nodded, strode to the archway and another flight of stone steps which she took two at a time. She was halfway up when the boom of the second impact reached her ears, along with a tremor that she could feel underfoot. But she did not pause at all.

Yasgur's hopes had gone from ashen grimness to sudden elation when the Mogaun Host charged in from the north and scattered Byrnak's careful formations across the snowbound fields. Then the elation collapsed back into ashes when a strange darkness poured out from behind a wooded rise almost half a mile to the west and seemed to race across the ground. His suspicions were too terrible to put into words but the Nightrook had no such reservations.

'Ah – eaterbeasts,' she said casually. 'Such a savage weapon, effective and terrifying but also a little . . . unpredictable.'

Eaterbeasts were bred from the twisted, malformed seed of predators long-since extinct from these lands. No two were completely alike, yet they all had a lust for pursuit and slaughter which the tinemasters played upon with confinement and starvation. As Yasgur watched, the great mass of creatures swarmed across fields and hillocks, darkening the whiteness, guided by a few riders on the edges. The Mogaun horsemen had seen the onrushing menace and were already galloping away from the scene of their surprise attack, heading northwest. Some eaterbeasts on the easterly edge of their horde must have caught a whiff of the blood from the carnage there for a long limb of them split away and raced off to glut their bottomless hunger. The rest followed the Mogaun.

Then the first hammerblow fell, a deep resonant crash that Yasgur felt in the pit of his stomach. He whirled round and grabbed hold of one of the tower roof supports as he leaned out and stared along the outside of the western section of the city wall. Byrnak's war machine had reached the wall and its massive arm with its spiked stone head was being wound back on taut hawsers by some unseen means hidden beneath a long wooden shell.

He felt a hand on his shoulder. The Nightrook.

'Zanser says that the enemy is charging to attack the south wall once more.'

As expected, he thought. 'He is to tell the wall captain that reinforcements will be sent but he must hold the rampart.'

She only nodded and turned away, just as a group of panicky runners arrived with messages. Yasgur swiftly despatched them with orders moving units from the seaward defences along the wall to take the place of others being sent round to the southern stretch. And all the time he was trying to keep an eye on the war machine while wondering if his disguised team had survived the fleeing infantry and the swarming eaterbeasts. But ultimately the wall, twenty paces thick and built from huge blocks of Arengian granite, was impregnable in the face of a solitary sledgehammer, even one as prodigious as this . . .

The spiked arm swung up and struck for the second time, and this time Yasgur was watching. This time he saw the flash of dazzling green an instant before the deep crack sound reached his ears. He saw dust and fragments spraying from the point of impact, and pieces of stone and mortar tumbling from the inner face of the wall and down into the street below.

Suddenly the impossible seemed possible and utter ruin loomed closer, like an onrushing threshold of darkness.

*   *   *

Byrnak's fury at the treachery of the Mogaun, followed by the rout of his leaderless infantry, demolished his composure and left him ranting and raging for long, incomprehensible moments. Then fearful self-awareness reasserted itself as he felt a long-dormant darkness stir within.

Fool. That inner voice was quieter and calmer than before but no less menacing. **You seek to control too many** . . .

Angry at himself for losing control, Byrnak drew on the Wellsource to shut the presence away behind a barrier in his mind. Then he extended his being along the web of soul-binding to the tinemasters who were tending the vast eaterbeast herd in a dale to the west. Into the mind of the chief tinemaster he placed a brief but specific set of orders then quickly returned to his own senses in time to see the Shadowclaw, as he had named it, hammer into the wall of Besh-Darok for the first time. He also saw it with the eyes of the commander who had steered the war-wagon through the snow, and laughed out loud, feeling a thrill of pleasure as the strengthened flare-iron spike, drenched in Sourcefire, buried the first third of its length in the wall, splitting one of the granite blocks. Byrnak's exultation spread to those around him as well as the soul-bound who were scattered across the field of battle.

'Let us approach this instrument of my will,' he told those about him. 'And watch it carry out my judgement.'

So saying he led his entourage of followers, adepts, standard-bearers and bodyguards down from the high ridge, an intricate panoply in shades of grey, black and funereal bronze. At a trot they crossed snow-laden fields which lay between two great phalanxes of infantry who were preparing themselves for the next assault on the walls. They were less than a hundred yards away when Shadowclaw struck its second blow. Byrnak could almost taste the fear and unease of the men on the wall, and grinned.

Now you know that destruction is at hand, he thought. *At last you recognise that this is your final day, from which a new world will be born* . . .

The arm of the Shadowclaw machine was being slowly winched back down against a retaining force provided by the huge mus-culature that was hidden by the long wooden carapace. It was a singular device concocted a few months ago by one of Byrnak's Wellsource adepts in alliance with one of the tinemasters. With a little encouragement from their master, they had arrived at the idea of an irresistible siege machine and work had commenced.

And now, as the mighty arm gradually came down, the four Wellsource adepts crammed into an armoured compartment at the wagon's rear began drawing together a knot of Sourcefire to be poured into the spike and its keystone just prior to the next unleashing. Simultaneously, the scaling squads were charging towards the south wall in advance of the infantry, while the bow companies sent a withering hail of arrows up at the ramparts . . .

Alarmed warnings flickered along the web of the soul-bound. He quickly looked round and saw a large boulder come flying in to strike the ground a score of yards away. The falling snow swirled in its hurtling wake as it gouged a dark wound in the earth. Rocky soil sprayed out as it bounced onwards, spinning from the impact but now diverted from the course that would have sent it into the Shadowclaw device. Instead it landed amid a cluster of panicking spearmen and crushed half a dozen of them. Before it had come to a rest, Byrnak's angry presence was already spreading itself along the web of his soul-bound servants, searching for the origin of the missile, staring from the eyes of—

A commander of the ladder crews, scanning the snow-veiled western fields from halfway up the city wall;

A blade-captain of the 3rd Talon Warriors, who had seen the boulder's descent;

A captain of bows near the now-demolished ridge fort, whose keen vision had tracked the trajectory back to the other end of the ridge;

A cavalry officer up on the ridge who, looking east, could see one of the catapults out on its own, its crew working frantically at the winch . . .

Ride forth! Byrnak ordered. Slay them!

Yet even as the galvanised horsemen thundered down from the ridge, the catapult crew were wrestling another boulder into the big cup at the end of the arm . . .

Then finally, with his own eyes, he saw the Shadowclaw leap

upwards, the glowing iron spike swinging along its inexorable curve to smash into the fractured face of the wall. Sourcefire burst outwards and into the granite blocks, fatally weakening them along hundreds of cracks and fissures. Driven by the weight of the keystone, the great spike clove through, breaking the wall. A huge, oval section simply shattered and collapsed in a roaring torrent of rubble which spilled out to either side of the wall and sent up roiling clouds of dust.

All fighting stopped for a moment of shocked silence. The deserted stretch of wall above the gaping hole had suddenly become a bridge, but the builders had never planned for such an eventuality. The long spanning section slumped at the centre, dust and fragments rained from the ragged underside then it gave way and came down in two pieces.

Byrnak could see that the falling debris had half-buried the Shadowclaw machine, but he was unconcerned since it had fulfilled its task. Fighting had resumed along the south wall and it appeared that his men were finally gaining the upper hand. Next would come his personal entry into the city to take possession of the palace and those two fascinating gewgaws, the Motherseed and the Crystal Eye. A silent command to several unit commanders brought several squads forward bearing many lengths of broad hooked ladders designed to provide a traverse across just such a mass of rubble.

The snow was getting heavier, falling already upon the broken blocks and slabs, a slow accumulation of whiteness.

So shall all this be buried, he thought with a savage delight. *Soon, twilight itself shall fall.*

In the witchhorse sanctuary, time stood still. The 'innerland' that the spirit of the Fathertree was building was a strange, grim patchwork, utterly different to the comforting illusions which the witchhorses had created for themselves. In depicting the ruin and agony endured by the peoples and their land, the Fathertree spirit had devised scenes so full of horror and tormenting grief that Tauric was unable to look at them for very long. And once it was done, the spirit of the Fathertree showed that it was able to move the entire composite illusion through the witchhorse sanctuary, steering it from innerland to innerland like a vessel leaking its cargo of suffering.

Bright summer days and sweet, eternal sunsets darkened and grew cold. The smoke of burning towns swept over lush hillsides, and grass and leaves withered at its touch. Forests were hacked down, lakes and rivers became poisoned by the corpses that had been left to rot in them. In the blink of an eye farmhouses went from sturdy, thatched buildings to wide patches of charred, smoking debris. Illusory crowds of smiling people succumbed to war and butchery, becoming the dead and the grief-ridden, and everywhere the children, ragged, hollow-cheeked, vacant-eyed . . .

When at last it was done and the vision of destruction was spread to every corner of every witchhorse's innerland, Tauris returned to the pool at the Fathertree's behest. Ghazrek, now tossing fruit seeds into the silvery waters, looked up.

'That was quick, m'lord,' he said. 'Were you successful?'

'I'm not sure,' Tauric said.

It will have had an effect, said the Fathertree in his thoughts. **Hopefully, the correct one**.

Some moments later, witchhorses began to emerge from the pale, tangled forest in ones and twos, gathering slowly and sombrely at the pool. Tauric could not tell if all were present but Shondareth eventually came forward to stand loomingly over him.

'All our innerlands are no more,' he said. 'You have filled our hearts with suffering, and we sicken with sorrow.' The witchhorse paused. 'We were wrong to abandon the Empire and its people – we would do what you ask and return to join in battle but we have to know the name of the spirit that you carry . . .'

All were silent for a moment, even within Tauric's mind and he thought that the Fathertree had slipped away. Then that voice spoke in his thoughts and, very clearly, the thoughts of everyone else, including Ghazrek.

You know my name, Shondareth.

The great witchhorse bowed his head, as did all of his companions. Ghazrek stared at Tauric, open-mouthed.

'We thought you scattered and lost to us, lord Fathertree.'

I have been all of that and more. Indeed, a name is almost

all that is left to me and that spoken in whispers. But it gladdens me to see you willing to pit yourselves against our ancient enemy – I know that it is a hard choice for you.

'We are ready, oh lord.'

Then it is time for us to leave this place. Tauric will lead the way.

Startled, Tauric got to his feet. *How do I lead the way when I don't know the way—*

Turn right to walk around the pool. The Fathertree's voice was once more confined to his own thoughts. **When you reach a sizeable path heading through the trees, follow it** . . .

He nodded and walked on, Ghazrek at his back and the great herd of witchhorses coming after. Just as the Fathertree spirit had said, a broad track curved away from the pool and on through the pale, misty woods. Before they had gone very far, the track split into three. Tauric paused.

Which one do we follow?

It matters little – choose one.

He thought a moment then walked towards the right hand path.

Will we reach Besh-Darok in time to help? he asked. *Or are we going arrive days after the battle?*

Time as you understand it works differently in the Void, and especially so in the witchhorses' sanctuary. Be assured, however, that we shall have much to do on our return . . .

The first indications that they had crossed back into the real world were the deepening cold and the large flakes of snow that began fluttering down. At length the trees thinned and they emerged at the edge of a wooded hillside swept by a cold wind. The land was locked in winter's grip, its every dip and rise, every bush and stream masked in whiteness and a soft, muffling silence.

'The world sleeps,' said Shondareth.

'But a battle also rages,' Tauric said, pointing to plumes of smoke rising from far beyond a line of low hills and ridges in the middle distance, knowing that Besh-Darok had to lie in that direction.

Then Shondareth bent his forelegs and knelt before Tauric. 'In

ages long past, the kings of Khatris rode into battle on witchhorses
– perhaps, majesty, it is time to revive the custom.'

With tears brimming in his eyes, Tauric smiled. 'I am deeply
honoured.' He stepped in close to the kneeling creature and found
that he had to climb up on its neck first then edge back to behind
the shoulders. Another witchhorse extended the same courtesy to
Ghazrek, and then the entire herd set off at a canter down the
hillside towards the smoke trails.

At the foot of the hill they crossed a brittle, frozen brook and
were climbing a bare, white slope when eerie howls came floating
through the air. There were screeches, ululating wails and the
growing thunder of hoofs. Suddenly, beyond the next dip and
rise, horsemen came galloping madly over the wide, uneven brow
of a hill, from between two copses there. Then more appeared to
either side in a widening wave of fur-clad riders, first hundreds then
thousands, which poured down the hill into a bushy dale then up,
heading straight for the witchhorses.

Tauric stared fearfully at the oncoming horde of Mogaun, thinking that his end had come.

Not yet, said the Fathertree. **Watch**.

The leading Mogaun saw the witchhorse herd massing on the
slope above them and swerved to avoid them, as did the rest, some
veering left, some right. The others followed their lead, a torrent
of tough, grim-faced riders which flowed around the eight score
or more witchhorses, their eyes widening at the sight. Ghazrek
shouted a question in a tribal tongue at one of them as his horse
laboured up the snowy incline, and got a brief response. Ghazrek
then looked at Tauric with an anxious expression.

'Eaterbeasts, majesty,' he said. 'They are fleeing eaterbeasts.'

Suddenly a muttering went around the witchhorse herd and
Tauric caught a single word, *krondemari*. Then the great majority
began to move out across the top of the slope in a broad curved
formation which forced the Mogaun to make a wider detour.

'Why are they doing this?' Tauric asked Shondareth.

'These eaterbeasts are the krondemari, a twisted race born of an
old and corrupted seed,' the witchhorse said gravely. 'They must
die – we are sworn to this.'

No wiser, Tauric could only sit back and watch. The great Host of the Mogaun began thinning to stragglers and the wounded. Then what looked like a solid blackness poured over the higher hill, led by a few tapering columns of the fastest. They caught three limping horses and their riders who all went down, their screams of agony almost lost in the swarm's surging roar of yelps and howls. Tauric felt a rising sense of horror as the vast numbers kept growing while the front edge of the swarm reached the dale, tore through the bushes and came charging up towards the waiting witchhorses.

There was a moment of stillness, then the entire line of witchhorses lowered their heads and as one breathed out long plumes of foggy whiteness again and again until there was an unbroken bank of dense, pale vapour rolling down the slope. When the first snarling, slavering eaterbeasts encountered it they plunged straight into it, not seeing any danger. Tauric stared closely as the creatures careered on through the mist, having never seen one before. From the dark furry pelts he at first took them to be large predators, like Rukang wolves or Nagira bluefangs, then he saw the flat heads, sinuous necks and bodies, and wondered.

They were a stampeding carpet of creatures, packed tightly together so that they half-clambered over each other even as they dashed up the hill. But when they emerged from the mists their coats were encrusted with rime frost, their movements were slower and jerky, and their voices were weak. Some got as far as a few yards from the witchhorses before they crept to a halt and froze on the spot, all colour leaching from their forms as the icy sorcerous death seeped through them.

As the deadly white mist flowed out and along the dale, so did it choke off the eaterbeasts' rasping screeches and lock up their limbs with ice, to an accompanying chorus of snaps and cracks. Brought to a halt, they were transformed into a landscape of immobile, opaque forms, gaping jaws and sightless, glassy eyes. The weight of those which had climbed atop others crushed them into chunks and splinters of grey ice and black bones before succumbing themselves.

Some of them, little more than a couple of hundred, had evaded the spreading fog, but groups of witchhorses were hunting them down. Grey, motionless statues soon came to dot the facing hillsides in knots and scattered clusters. But why had they been chasing the Mogaun? he wondered, feeling a thread of bleak sorrow as he watched the last of them die the death of ice.

Mourn them not – they are savage, the krondemari, bred only to kill, said the spirit of the Fathertree.

The witchhorses seem to loath them greatly – why?

Both races share a common ancestry, but one branch of that ancient root race was corrupted and degraded by the Lord of Twilight. The witchhorses see this as putting tortured souls out of their misery . . .

Shivering, Tauric wondered at the kind of retribution that could survive down through so many ages. Then, hearing Ghazrek calling him, he turned on Shondareth's broad back to see a small group of Mogaun horsemen drawing near. A couple carried tribal standards, one with stylised bloody claws, the other bearing a black sickle moon, while yet others held small grey flags aloft on their spears. Shondareth himself turned to regard the newcomers approach through the snow which had eased off to a few flakes falling in the still air.

Leading them, and carrying no banners, were two older men, one tall, the other barrel-chested, whom Tauric took to be chieftains. With the Fathertree spirit making their speech intelligible, Tauric listened to Ghazrek making greetings and introductions and when they heard who Tauric was, they stiffened and stared at him for a long, hard moment before exchanging hurried murmurs. Then they urged their mounts into a walk and came over to halt before Tauric while a puzzled Ghazrek followed.

'Greetings, Tauric King,' said the taller of the two. 'I am Welgarak, chief and father of the families of the Black Moon clan, and this is Gordag, chief of the Red Claws. In the name of our tribes and clans we give thanks to you and your—' He regarded the assembled witchhorses. '—friends from the witchhorse nation.'

'You accord us more courtesy now than ever your people did during the invasion,' Shondareth said sharply.

'Different chieftains led the clans then,' Welgarak said. 'Other voices gave orders, other hands held the spears. But much has changed of late.'

'Everything has changed,' Gordag cut in. 'The past is an empty lie and the present is full of butchery and hungry spirits. We must ask you this, Tauric King – do we ride together against the Shadowkings in accord with the secret alliance we sealed with Yasgur, chief and prince? Or will you say nay and let all our lands become death's dining board?'

Stunned at the man's offer, Tauric forced his face to remain composed. Yasgur had concluded a treaty with the Mogaun? But when, and why? And did Bardow know?

Then a sense of reproach came over him – if he had not been so obsessed and deluded by the Skyhorse sham, perhaps the Archmage might have told him more.

Some things are learned too late, said the Fathertree. *But the experience is never wasted. Now you must decide . . .*

With inward agreement, Tauric straightened and looked the leaders in the eye.

'Chieftains of the Mogaun – I call on you to ride with me against the Shadowkings, and fill their lands with harm and despair!'

Chapter Twenty-three

They have eaten out the vitals of the world,
And left standing a gaunt mockery,
Of broken walls and scorched beams,
Fit only for the dead and the condemned.

Ralgar Morth, *The Empire Of Night*, Canto xxiii

There was only silence on the crowded balcony as everyone stared
down at the breached wall with its flanking slopes of broken
stonework. The dust was settling with the snow, churned in dark
mud on the outside by the thousands of enemy troops gathering
there, waiting for the order to move into the city. Bardow could see
scarcely any defenders attacking from the wall on either side of the
gap but he knew from the Nightrook that Yasgur had pulled most of
his men off the western and northern walls and was rushing troops
to the south ramparts. There was also a rumour that remnants of the
Hunter's Children had raised a civilian militia over in the Old Town
and were busily provisioning and refortifying the Chapel Fort.

For Bardow, however, these seemed like the last desperate acts
of a doomed civilisation. All the struggles, the negotiations, the
sacrifices, Mazaret's pursuit of Azurech, the defence of Scallow,
all of it seemed to have led them to this confrontation with
the Shadowking Byrnak, a demigod glorying in his talent for
destruction. The only hope left was that the melded sword would
be capable of killing him. Nerek was the only person who might
get close to Byrnak, therefore she was Bardow's choice to wield
the weapon. From his attunement with the Crystal Eye he knew

that she was in the High Spire on one of the lower floors, but it also showed him the presence of another two Wellsource adepts close by.

Fearful suddenly, he glanced back into the Vantage Chamber. It was now quite crowded with attendants, servants and scribes, all of whom had sought refuge here in the last quarter-hour due to rumours of killers stalking the bottom floors. Who could only be the two intruders. A handful of knights had accompanied them yet they were not safe here, for when Byrnak forced his way into the palace he would come searching for Bardow. And Bardow wanted as few innocents as possible to suffer when that dread encounter finally took place.

Below, he could see Byrnak's black-armoured troops swarming across the rubble unopposed, so he ducked back inside through one of the archways and went over to stand in the middle of the chamber.

'Friends,' he said. 'Pray listen to my words. I have something of great importance to say and time is against us . . .'

The various muttered conversations died down but before he could go on, a pain bloomed in his head, a dire warning from the Crystal Eye. Enemies had already reached this floor and were closing in. Then a loud hammering began at a door in a side alcove, beyond which was a narrow servants' passage and stairway. Bardow had locked and barred it earlier but it was never meant to withstand the furious assault it was now receiving. Even as frightened people were moving away, the door burst inward in a scattering of broken planks and splinters.

A tall, black-cloaked and armoured figure stepped through, firmly grasping the struggling form of a young woman clad in a blue gown. It was Alael, and she wept openly as she strained weakly to escape. Her captor turned to face Bardow who felt a jolt of amazement at the sight of the face of his old friend Ikarno Mazaret, quickly turning to anger and grief when he saw the silver-pale hair and bone-white complexion of a rivenshade. After him came a shorter, slighter figure, likewise garbed in dark armour but highlighted with silver adornments. The woman had Suviel's features and, like her companion, wore a permanent expression of mocking amusement, except that a dark grey ichor was dribbling from the corner of her mouth and she looked unsteady on her feet.

'Is she still . . .' the Mazaret rivenshade said but before the other could answer, someone else appeared in the wrecked doorway and stared at the two in black. It was Nerek. Bardow regarded her with uncertainty, taking in the burning gaze, the blueish tint of the skin, and the emerald power that held her in a dangerous, gleaming aura.

Nerek was aware of all the other people in the high chamber, the frightened servants, the handful of knights standing before them with blades bared, the two rivenshades with their captive, Alael, and Bardow who stood next to a rack in which the melded sword hung. But all were like shadows cast on a cave wall by the raging fire of the Wellsource as it rushed through her senses. After the Suviel rivenshade had ambushed her in the library, Nerek had ignored the wound in her side and gone in pursuit. There had been two searing encounters on the floor below, but now it seemed to her that this would be the final clash.

The Suviel rivenshade was still dangerous. As Nerek advanced, the 'shade opened her mouth wide and expelled into the air a long serpent of Sourcefire adorned with several eyes and a mouth full of whiplike tendrils. Nerek held up one hand wreathed in green fire so shaped that each finger was lengthened into wickedly serrated talons. As the sickly green serpent writhed through the air towards her, she slashed at it repeatedly until it fell apart in dazzled shreds that drifted down to burn smoking marks into the tiled floor.

Without hesitation she lunged forward, taloned hand outstretched. She grabbed the rivenshade round the throat and bore her backwards. Two burning hands came up to Nerek's neck, one scrabbling at the collar of her leather corselet, the other inching up to her face. But she tightened her scorching grip and forced the woman down on to her knees. The Wellsource thundered in her mind like a rejoicing, pitiless chorus of spirits as she choked the life out of the rivenshade, squeezed, ripped, crushed . . .

Then the Wellsource, its full, ferocious, sonorous strength fell away from her, dwindling, fading and finally extinguished. Dizzy and breathing heavily, she straightened and staggered back from the still, lifeless body. Over to one side she saw that Bardow had unlimbered the melded sword and was pointing it at the Mazaret 'shade, who still held on to Alael. Then she realised that there were newcomers in the chamber and she turned to look.

The main door was wide open and Byrnak stood just inside the room with a dozen black-armoured and masked swordsmen at his back. Every breath seemed held for an instant, every eye fixed on him. Byrnak's bearded face was flushed with triumph, his gaze bright and eager, his mouth smiling cruelly as his stare took in the room's occupants and came to rest on Nerek. Nerek felt pinned to the spot by that regard and knew that he would revel in his victory before exacting measures of pain. He seemed to radiate power and dominance, his presence exerting a palpable pressure on the thoughts. He grinned with open lust, but before he could speak, one of the knights abandoned his self-control and with raised sword and a battle cry charged at him.

Without looking away from Nerek, Byrnak snatched a dagger from his waist and casually tossed it at the oncoming attacker. The dagger flew unerringly towards the knight and punched into his throat. As he staggered to a halt and fell choking to his knees, one of Byrnak's men stepped forward with a glittering broadsword and took off his head with a single blow. The body slumped to the floor, blood spreading across the tiles.

There were sobs and whispers from around the chamber and Nerek, her side burning from the rivenshade's earlier attack, felt powerless, helpless and empty. No, not empty, for the hot core of her anger had never left her and the sight of Byrnak only fanned it brighter, hotter.

'This is the end of their pitiful rebellion, Nerek,' he said. 'After all that they have done, they have all come to the same place, this arena of futility where only I can prevail. And so may you, Nerek – if you renounce them and their cause, I will allow you to stand by my side once more. Decide!'

Nerek needed no time to consider her response. She drew her sword. Byrnak smiled. The Shadowking was about three paces away and, as she advanced, Keren Asherol came unbidden to her mind.

Were you here, sister, she thought, *you would either do this properly or not at all. But we have come to the bitterest end, and all we have left is to try and die well.*

Behind her, Bardow shouted, 'No, Nerek – leave him to me!'

But she ignored him and leaped forward to strike, crying out, 'For Keren and Falin!'

Her words caught Byrnak by surprise, and her swordpoint slipped in past his imperfect parry, lanced through cloth and leather and pierced his upper arm. He had meant to toy with her for a while before having her taken away, but she had insulted him with names out of the past and violated his very flesh. The Wellsource surged in time with his sudden fury, and he swiftly healed the wound before surrounding himself in radiant inviolability.

She came at him again with a series of blows that he beat aside as if she were wielding a stick. With the last he stepped in close with a shoulder charge that knocked her backwards. As she lay sprawling and struggling to regain her feet, his awareness flickered around the soul-bound web, observing his warriors as they poured through the wall breach and spread along the streets. There was stiff resistance coming from the northern districts between the city wall and the river, a few thousand troops commanded by Yasgur, while savage fighting had erupted around the western part of the palace involving several hundred sword and axemen who were trying to seize the breach and throw his men back. But they were too few and his masked soldiers were pushing them back step by fiercely contested step . . .

Byrnak smiled – he could almost smell the mingled taints of blood, iron and snow – then focused his attention on Nerek again as she readied her sword and planted her feet apart, an unbending resolve in her eyes.

'How foolish,' he said. 'What will this serve?'

'I will have fought you to the end,' she said. 'Then I'll be dead and finally beyond your reach.'

He simply laughed.

Then he attacked, rage-filled blow after blow cutting and slashing with devastating speed. Somehow she managed to dodge and parry

every one with a steely grace that reminded him of Keren. That
stoked his fury higher still and with an insensate bellow he lashed
out with a swing that shattered her sword and knocked her to the
floor again.

She lay at the foot of a long, curved flight of steps that led up
to a series of arches and thence to the balcony. Byrnak turned his
back contemptuously and looked straight up at Bardow who was
still pointing that Sourcefire blade at the Mazaret rivenshade. The
rivenshade had released the girl, Alael, and she was cowering behind
the Archmage whose face betrayed his despair. Curling his lip in
scorn, Byrnak sneered then turned to face Nerek again. He took
a second sword from his waist and threw it down to clatter on the
floor next to her.

'Pick it up.'

'Leave her alone,' said Bardow. 'Face me instead, if you dare!'

Byrnak burst out laughing. 'A mighty challenge from a little man!
Have patience – I will face you soon enough and wrench the Crystal
Eye's whereabouts from you . . .'

A dazzling flash of ice-blue struck him full in the chest, forcing
him to stagger back a step. But he was uninjured, protected by the
coursing currents of the Wellsource as they shaped and sheathed
themselves to his will. Bardow on the other hand looked drained
and weary – it seemed the attack had used the last of his strength.
But then the Archmage reversed his grip on the Sourcefire sword,
bent down and half-tossed it down the steps. It landed very close
to Nerek who reached out for its hilt as she lurched upright.

Again Byrnak laughed. 'How sorrowful, Nerek. That little
Sourcefire skewer cannot harm me – you cannot use a weapon
against its owner. You would be as well trying to make an axe out
of water, or a spear out of mist . . .'

But she appeared not to be listening as she lunged at him with
the weapon, a straight-arm thrust aimed directly at his chest. Out of
reflex he brought his own heavy sword across to parry the blow . . .
and events seemed to slow as he watched his own flare-forged,
razor-honed blade break apart as it met hers. Then he saw strange,
silver-white patterns rippling and coiling along the Sourcefire sword
as it rushed inexorably towards him, cutting straight through his

radiant barrier. Something like genuine fear began shrieking in him, urging him to turn aside—

Too late.

The Sourcefire blade sliced through mailed leather and underpadding and entered his chest without sound or resistance, running him through with the first foot of it jutting from his back. Nerek let go of the hilt and stepped back. At the same time he heard a thousand soul-bound voices cry out in agony while a dark exulting presence bellowed:

... **yes** ... **Yes** ... **YES!** ...

Strength fled his limbs. As he fell to his knees he strove to reach the minds of his guards, aware that there was uproar behind him. But he could feel them all, together with the Wellsource, slipping away from him. He could hear that fragment of the Lord of Twilight laughing madly, feel him raging across his thoughts, testing its limits, crooning **die**, **die**, **die** over and over. It felt like he was splitting in two.

Through greying vision he could see Nerek reach down to the sword's hilt, perhaps to pull it out. And from within, the Lord of Twilight's presence surged up like a black wave, triumphant, voracious, and unstoppable;

... **at last** ... **At Last** ... **FREE!**

He felt the dark spirit tear loose from him, like a myriad tiny rootlets ripping up, carrying whole layers of himself away—

He felt the Sourcefire sword being drawn forth, ice-edged fire, sliding smooth, clean and numb—

He heard Nerek suddenly screaming somewhere but could see little through the soft greyness of oblivion that swirled and lapped around him. Then the grey softness retreated, parted to admit a pale blue light which shone down into him from an eye. Perfect and pupilless, it seemed to stare into the very core of what was left of him, scrutinising every depth and height, every veil and hidden place. Then the blue regard pulled away for a moment then returned with the one thing absent from his inner self.

Pain.

The pain of others.

*   *   *

Scoured of vitality yet compelled to resist the leaden burden of exhaustion, Bardow lay half-sprawled at the top of the curved steps, watching the terrifying drama unfold. When Nerek impaled Byrnak with the melded sword, the black-masked, dark-brown armoured guards behind him groaned as one and reeled back, some staggering back out of the open door. Wellsource energies flailed and wavered aimlessly around the kneeling Shadowking like a convulsing web of emerald lightning.

The few remaining knights had seized their opportunity and were busily slaughtering those unresisting guards who had not fled. While this was happening Nerek had leaned closer to the immobile Byrnak who knelt at the centre of the juddering web of Wellsource power, staring down at the impaling blade and trembling visibly. A foreboding of dread struck Bardow's thoughts but before he could say anything, Nerek had grasped the hilt and was pulling the sword out of Byrnak's chest.

Byrnak spasmed, his head thrown back, arms thrown wide. A dark haze seeped out of his armoured body, coalesced into a wraithlike figure which writhed horribly around him until it finally tore itself free. As it rose into the air, an eldritch obsidian radiance poured from it, drenching everything and everyone in deathly grey for a moment. Then a soundless snarl appeared on its nightmarish countenance before it swept straight at Nerek and vanished into her.

Nerek let out an agonised scream and fell limply to the floor, sword clattering from insensible fingers. Aghast, Bardow levered himself up, gasping with the effort, cursing his weakness. *I must sleep soon*, he thought as he descended the steps.

'Archmage,' said one of the knights who was standing over Byrnak's prone form with a dagger. 'This one yet lives – shall I finish him?'

Suddenly all eyes were on Bardow. He wanted to fall down and sleep, right there on the cold stone floor, even as his mind was still trying to take in all that had happened. There were shouts and sounds of fighting from out in the main passageway, all fainter than before and he had no idea of how events outside had been affected by what had happened in this room. But he had to make a decision.

'Keep him alive . . . for now,' he said wearily. 'But bind and gag him . . . and do the same with Nerek.'

His heart felt heavy as two of the knights approached Nerek with long cords stripped from one of the window drapes. But the moment one of them pulled her arms straight, she jerked violently into motion, scrambled away from them and, muttering and sobbing, leaped to her feet. She grabbed a long dagger from a sheath at her waist and stared wildly about her.

'. . . away, take him, he is . . . is inside . . .' She stretched out her empty hand to Bardow, imploring him, 'Help me, Bardow, help . . .' Then her face twisted, a grimace of pain and rage, and her voice became guttural. '**Kill you all, water these stones with your blood . . . your** . . .' Now one side of Nerek's face seemed distorted while the other was slack. 'No, I will not allow this . . . **you I will kill you then kill them** . . .'

Then Nerek whirled and dashed across the chamber to the broken door, shrieking and slashing at the terrified servants as they dived out of her path. Bardow watched her plunge through out of sight, knowing that she was fighting for her life and soul against a brutal and pitiless foe. He gestured one of the knights to follow her.

'Keep her in view,' he said, 'but do not attempt to get in her way – it could mean your life.'

Even as the knight hurried out, another of his men yelled and pointed at something behind Bardow. He turned to see the Mazaret rivenshade carrying an unconscious Alael out on to the balcony. Seized by fear and anger, Bardow struggled up the steps.

'No!' he cried. 'Wait . . .'

Then a great dark shape flew up to alight on the balcony. The rivenshade slung Alael over his shoulder and climbed on to the back of the nighthunter which stared at all the people within with rapacious, jewelled eyes. It spread its leathery wings and launched away from the balcony, massive wingbeats carrying it up.

I should have protected you better, Alael, Bardow thought as he watched the creature fly off in the direction of Gorla. *Once the sword was made, I should have sent you away by ship . . .*

He staggered over to the balcony rail. The snow was easing off and Bardow could see that chaos reigned in the streets below while fire tore through building after building. He was so exhausted, so utterly bereft of stamina and hope that even the Crystal Eye could not help him. He could still feel its watchful presence, so it was still safe in the hidden chamber, and he could just sense that it was trying to tell him something but his poor battered mind could not take it in.

Then voices were raised by those who had ventured out on to the balcony, and hands pointed northwest, the direction of Keshada. In a kind of stoic despair, Bardow turned that way to peer out at the far-off, snow-blurred fields, expecting to see another black-armoured phalanx moving towards Besh-Darok. Instead, riders began emerging from the veil of falling snow, fur-clad and skin-wrapped, some bearing rough banners daubed with tribal emblems, lashing their mounts into a frantic charge across the rolling, white-shrouded landscape . . .

Bardow found he just had strength enough to cast his vision forward a little, and the sight that met his eyes sent a wave of hope through him. For there, galloping among the sturdy mountain horses of the Mogaun and towering over them, were creatures he thought he would never see again – witchhorses!

Nearer the city, the Shadowkings' army had dissolved into a leaderless, strung-out and scattered horde with several skirmishes and brawls taking place among them here and there. But they still presented a great danger – how would these new allies fare against them?

Tauric felt as dwarfed as a child riding on Shondareth's back, clinging to his thick white mane. Hurtling along amid the thundering, thousands-strong host of Mogaun warriors, he could see bandaged wounds aplenty but no lack of vigour and eager determination. The flanks of many horses and a few witchhorses bore scratches and cuts from the earlier confrontations with the eaterbeasts. But that blood-maddened swarm of creatures was no more.

Half a mile distant lay the city of Besh-Darok. From several places within the walls smoke roiled up into the snow-heavy air, and as they rode nearer he could see crowds of black-armoured troops milling around a large dark shadow on the western wall. As he realised what it was, a sickening fear struck home.

'Name of the Mother!' he said. 'They've breached the wall . . .'

'But something is amiss,' said Ghazrek. 'Those troops are not moving into the city in any numbers, and those over there—' He pointed to a long, disorganised phalanx less than a quarter of a mile west of the city '—have not sent riders out to challenge us even though we must be in full view.'

By unvoiced consensus, the advance of the Mogaun and the witchhorses had slowed, and the two chieftains were cantering beside Tauric and Ghazrek.

'You see well, cousin,' Welgarak said to Ghazrek. 'Now we must take advantage of this confusion while it lasts.'

'What has happened?' Tauric said. 'Is it possible that Byrnak has fallen?'

'That is scarcely believable,' Welgarak said, stroking his grey moustache. 'Yet it would explain all this.'

'Shall we attack from here and from the north?' Tauric asked.

'That would be too perilous, O king,' Welgarak said. 'There are still a few of Byrnak's underlings who may try and direct matters if he has indeed come to grief, Azurech and others. And even if they fail, these masks' numbers are so formidable that we must use our strengths – speed, surprise and witchhorse sorcery.'

'And have you a plan, chieftain of the Mogaun?' Shondareth said.

'I do,' the elderly chieftain said with a hungry grin. 'Listen . . .'

A short while later Tauric and Shondareth were riding towards the Gallaro Gate, Besh-Darok's northern gate, accompanied by a score of witchhorses. The rest were galloping straight towards the huge crowd of soldiers struggling among themselves by the gap in the wall. Welgarak and Gordag had positioned the Mogaun host in sloping fields midway between the city and the old smugglers' ridge but north of the main disorganised mass of the enemy and concealed by long, dense hedges.

The witchhorses, arrayed in a broad wedge, slowed as they neared the wall breach and the enemy soldiers looked up, noticing their approach. Then Tauric saw an astonishing thing – as the witchhorses slackened their pace, some thirty or forty of them at the front suddenly dashed towards a low, bare ridge directly ahead. At the

crest they all jumped in a tremendous leap that carried them through
the air above the many hundreds of masked troops. As they soared
overhead the witchhorses breathed out the foggy vapours of death.
Meanwhile the remainder of the witchhorse wedge were sending a
similar misty cloud pouring down into that teeming mass of soldiers.
An agonising, frozen extinction began to spread.

The leaping witchhorses came to ground at the other side
of the besiegers and found themselves beset by a company of
swordsmen. But they engaged the enemy with fury, lashing hooves
and white breath.

Shondareth turned to Tauric. 'We are nearing the city. You must
hold on tight.'

Tauric laughed nervously. Welgarak's plan had included sending
a group of witchhorses into the city, but Tauric could now see that
their way in would not be at ground level. He tightened his grip
on Shondareth's mane, clamped his legs to the creature's flanks, and
tried not to be frightened.

No need for fear, said the Fathertree spirit in his thoughts. **In
times long past the witchhorses held high-leaping tourneys
among themselves – hardly any were hurt** . . .

That is . . . reassuring, he thought.

'Are you ready?' Shondareth said.

'I am.'

Then the witchhorse reared back, plunged forward a few paces
and leaped up at the city wall. Tauric felt forces dragging at him,
icy wind blasting in his face, but he kept his eyes open to watch
the ground fall away and the battlements of the wall loom straight
towards him. He let out a wordless cry, then the crenellations were
passing by right below his feet as Shondareth landed easily on the
snowy flagstones of the rampart. As they trotted to a halt, the rest
of the witchhorses were nimbly alighting nearby.

Breathing heavily, exhilarated, Tauric gazed out at his city under
the low, leaden sky, its roofs and dense-packed buildings looking
grey and pale the further away he looked. Smoke was pouring out
of large storehouses by the river and he could hear fighting in the
streets below.

'Shall we now go to the Palace?' Shondareth said.

'Yes,' Tauric said, suddenly sombre. 'To the Palace.'

Atroc splashed his way along an alleyway between tall tenement houses, trying to get to the barricaded streets north of Captains Way where Yasgur and 2,000 warriors were holding back the enemy. The alleyway was a dark, stinking, muddy gully but it was also narrow and easily missed by strangers, like the Shadowking Byrnak's soldiery. It also ran parallel to the main street that led past the Imperial Barracks and, with any luck, he would be able to reach the Queens Bridge and the towpath there without running too much risk.

Ah, but risk comes from just living, Atroc reminded himself, stepping over a soldier's motionless corpse. *If the Void had wanted us to have a safe life, we would all be living in shells at the bottom of the river . . .*

A street loomed at the end of the alley, tall, grey and swept by gust-driven snow. Another alley opening was visible at the other side of the street but a glimpse along it revealed a patrol of masked and armoured soldiers drawing near. Carefully he edged out on to the street and ran at a half-crouch across to a doorway, then made his way west. The next corner he knew led round to a terrace of merchant houses that faced the Square of Swords, but if it was deserted he could still find another back street down to the river.

Where I shall wish for a nice, safe shell . . .

But when he turned the corner, he found himself beholding a chilling sight. From the city wall north of the Shield Gate, great white horses were taking long, graceful leaps from roof to roof and approaching the square. Atroc stared in fear and fascination then scurried over to squat between two bushes and watch. It was as if his dream-vision of the wave of horses was coming true before his eyes. Then he noticed the small horns on the horses' head, and saw that only one of them had a rider . . .

Shouts and an agonised shriek came from the guardhouse of the massive Keep of Day which faced on to the Square of Swords. Then the main gate opened a few feet and a lone figure came running and stumbling out, one hand grasping a long dagger. It took him a moment to recognise the person as Nerek, but wandering and seemingly deranged. Most of the white horses had landed in streets north of the palace but the one with the rider had come down near the square and was cantering over to the distraught Nerek. The rider was Tauric, and Atroc felt such elation that he leaped up and began hurrying over to meet them both.

Then Nerek caught sight of Tauric on his steed, let out a cry and fell sprawling in the snow. Tauric was quick to reach Nerek, dismounted and crouched by her. What happened next took Atroc completely by surprise. In the space of a brief moment Nerek had jerked to life and was writhing on the ground, and in the next she had run Tauric through with her dagger. Tauric cried out as she got to her feet and pushed him to the ground. The great horse roared and lunged, breathing out a plume of white fog which left Nerek wrapped in grey, jagged ice.

But only for a moment. The ice burst apart and Nerek swung at the horse's neck, hacking through its throat. Steaming dark ichor gushed forth and the massive creature bellowed once before crashing to the ground.

Atroc had fallen to lie on his stomach from where he watched the terrible slaughter in fear and horror. Nerek then screamed 'No!', dropped the bloody dagger and sank to her knees, head wrapped in her arms. Then she threw back her head and in a strange, inhuman voice shrieked '*Yes!*'

There was a dazzling, white flash of light and when Atroc's sight returned he saw Nerek on the other side of the square, staggering away towards the gap in the wall. But when Atroc finally reached the spot where Tauric and the white horse had been slain there were only fading wisps of water vapour and a large, misshapen scorch mark on the flat stones of the square.

Part Four

Chapter Twenty-four

In the haunted earth below,
Beyond underground battlements,
Behind the weltering darkness,
Lies an ancient, sleeping prize.

Gundal, *The Siege of Stones*, Ch. 8, ii

In the glade of the monument, standing alone in the moist, green light, Suviel watched the fierce drama of the siege unfold in the oval, mist-edged window which the Earthmother had formed in the screen of foliage. With a cool equanimity she observed the assault on the walls and the desperate hand-to-hand struggle which sprawled across the ramparts, and when the Host of the Mogaun came charging south to scatter Byrnak's troops across the snows, she only observed, nothing more.

But when Bynark's war machine struck the wall and on the third impact broke it, she felt a distant ache. Events tumbled after one another in terrible succession – the ashen wraith of the Lord of Twilight tearing away from the insensible Byrnak to sweep down on Nerek, the abduction of Alael, the arrival of the witchhorses and Tauric's death at Nerek's hands. She almost gasped at that final sight, Tauric falling to the ground, blood from his chest and mouth darkening the snow, while the possessed Nerek then slew the witchhorse—

'Suviel.'

The goddess's presence flooded the glade, and all her confusion suddenly drained away. In the window a dazzling burst of light blotted out the bloody spectacle, then faded to show a purposeful Nerek now outside the city, approaching a riderless horse and moments later galloping westwards . . .

With a small gesture of the Earthmother's pale hand, the window dissolved back into the lush green tangle of leaves, tendrils and tiny red and black flowers. She had adopted another form which had the perfect likeness of the monument's carving of the seated woman — her skin, hands and eyes were like white marble made flesh, and the stone-milk of her gown hung and flowed like cloth.

'Suviel.'

Again, her name, and all that she had been stood forth in her mind, all her memories and experience waiting to be called upon like a legion of helpers and all rooted in an unquestioning faith and obedience to the Earthmother.

'A fragment of the Lord of Twilight has finally been uncaged,' the goddess said. 'All he will want to do is hunt down the other fragments of himself, thus you shall smooth the way for him.'

The blank, white eyes regarded her. 'Release Ystregul from the chamber beneath the High Basilica in Trevada. I have taught you how to deal with the constraining spells, but know that once you have done so every denizen of those ancient halls shall be bent upon your destruction.'

'What will the next task be?' Suviel dared to ask.

A cold smile curved the polished lips. 'If you succeed in this undertaking and survive the aftermath, find a safe place and wait — I shall come to you. Have you faith in me?'

'I have.'

'And are you obedient to my will?'

'I am.'

'Then accept my blessing and my gift and go . . .'

With the goddess's last word, a sudden blur of darkness and half-glimpsed shapes whirled around and past her, as if she were stationary amid a rushing abyss. Just as suddenly all sense of motion died away to leave her standing in the dank darkness of a high windowless chamber. Behind her in the corner a faint, pearly radiance was fading from a shiny vine tendril which climbed up the wall less than a yard from a gap in the cobbled floor. By such meagre means had the Earthmother opened a door for her. Once that numinous power had faded, there was only the weak glimmer of torchlight filtering in through the small, barred window of a door set high on one wall, at the head of a flight of steep stone stairs.

But with her magesight Suviel had no difficulty in finding her way up the steps, and with her enhanced undersenses she could easily perceive the whereabouts of Ystregul's prison. Wrapped in a multitude of spells it stood out like a flaring beacon surrounded by misty outlines of other corridors and rooms. The chamber she had appeared in was actually a dozen yards or more deeper in the rock of the Oshang Dakhal than the Shadowking's prison, but she would have to climb to a higher floor in order to gain access to that part of the Basilica's vaults.

The door at the top of the steps was unlocked and, cloaked in an eye-beguiling glamour, she stole along the corridors in search of a way up. These many underground passages and rooms had been burrowed into the rock over two hundred years ago by Zothelis, the Archmage of that time whose ambition it was to create an entire town within the Oshang Dakhal. Left unfinished after his death, the many rooms were employed by successive stewards of the High Basilica as storerooms and dormitories. The Acolytes of Twilight, however, had found a new use for them.

Suviel could almost feel the pain of the prisoners they held as she climbed stairwells and stalked along corridors. Pain in many shades, contrasting with the banal cruelty of the captors and torturers who had become mere instruments in the service of an inhuman power. She could almost feel their pain but only because those assembled elements of her old self were feeling it instead, and she caught flickers of anguish as she proceeded along a torch-lit passageway which led to a particular downward spiral stair.

The passages were not deserted and twice she had to make a detour to avoid senior Acolytes accompanied by parties of novitiates. For the rest her glamour was sufficient to fool the guards and turnkeys as they did their rounds, and soon she was descending to that level where the Shadowking was held. Several spiral turns of steps brought her to a small, dim antechamber full of a curious blue-green radiance which emanated from the strange, hooked emblems fixed on the walls above arched doorways. Without pause she stepped through the arch to the right then had to duck into an alcove to allow a guard pass in the narrow corridor.

Moments later she was standing before the door to Ystregul's prison. It was riddled with alarm spells binding it to the massive doorframe but fortunately there were none linking the frame to the stone wall. She knew which thought-cantos to use and after a few careful, tense moments she reached out to push the heavy wood frame. Cradled in a web of Lesser Power, it swung noiselessly inwards. She stepped over the threshold and swiftly put an illusion of the undisturbed doorway in place behind her, then turned to regard the prisoner.

Great ancient glyphs of power burned bright emerald in the floor beneath him, while to Suviel's eyes the Shadowking's casket hung at the centre of innumerable interlinked skeins of sorcery. Standing in that chamber felt like waiting between huge jaws eager to grind any intruder to nothing. But the Earthmother had told her how to unlock those faltering energies in such a way as to make their unleashing work for her. Recalling those instructions, she was able to employ the Earthmother's power in the creation of two spells, one to break the chains holding up the casket, the other to reflect the backlash energies against the spells binding the casket itself.

When they were ready, Suviel added one last refinement to the chain-breaker which would delay its unfurlment for a few seconds, long enough for her to find another chamber to hide in.

She stood back to survey her handiwork. The chain-breaker hung in the air above the casket, a small, opaque orb with misty tendrils stretching out towards the four heaving chains. The reflective spell clung to the high ceiling, a rough, pearly oval from which a pale web spread across the stone.

It was time. With a single thought she kindled the first spell into life and hurried from the chamber, intending to head back to the stairs. But a trio of Acolytes was standing along at the antechamber, deep in discussion, so she hastened down the corridor before her. She had gone perhaps a dozen paces when she felt the chain-breaker fulfil itself in a spasm of Lesser Power that jolted through her senses. An instant later there was a mighty crash, and the outfall of

shattered spells sent vibrations through the stonework and a wave
of disorientation through Suviel's mind.

Shouts came from behind and in front as doors were thrown
open. In panic she dived along an empty, unlit side passage and
turned its corner only to find that it ended abruptly in a solid door.
The lock was a complex mechanism that she was able to defeat in a
matter of seconds. Once open, she slipped inside and then shut and
locked the door behind her. Within, the chamber was sunk in utter
darkness but her magesight revealed bare outlines – debris piled in
one corner, a few trestle tables littered with broken pottery, candle
stubs, torn and mouldering parchment. And near the centre were
four iron pillars, two of which each had a man bound to it and seated
on a half barrel. Both were blindfolded and had leather strapping
across their shoulders, waists, thighs and lower legs. Both seemed
insensible until one raised his head and said weakly:

'Is . . . someone there?'

Suviel felt frozen by a nameless fear as her dislocated memory
began to recall fragments of a confinement in blackness, suggestions
that she had been in a place very like this before her death . . .

She turned to the door and her soft boot scraped on the floor.

'Who's there?' said the man.

Clearer and stronger this time, the man's voice set off a new surge
of emotion, desperate hope warring with dread.

The other man stirred. 'Wha . . . What're you sayin'?'

'There's someone in here with us,' said the first. 'but they won't
say anything.'

'Really, now? Must be some twisted fiend come to gloat over
the prisoners . . .'

Suviel moved towards the door, then froze, realising that something was sitting in the way, a creature of some kind, its form
as black as the room, its large, ungainly head coming up to her
shoulders.

Suviel Hantika, it said in harsh whispers that she heard only in
her head. **Do you recognise those two men?**

No. I . . . Yes, a part of me does, she replied in her thoughts. *Who
are you? What are you?'*

A friend who would see you well and whole again.

A feeling of terror gripped her mind and a longing for the Vale of Unburdening swept through her, prompting a prickling of tears in her eyes.

Wholeness . . . is of no interest to me, she said. *I have no need of it.*

How would you know what you want or need? the creature countered. **It suits the Earthmother for you to be this poor, disconnected thing that stands before me. Your ignorance and fear serves her purpose!**

Purity is purity, she replied doggedly. *Purity demands pure sight.*

'In that case I think there may be something wrong with your eyes, it said sardonically. **'Let me help you . . .'**

Before she could say or do anything, a hot charge sprang through her like a storm of coalescence. Emotion and memory and will embraced one another, joining empathy and intuition in a festival of the senses that lasted for a long, glorious instant. Tears came freely and silently in the darkness now as she understood what had been done to her and others by this struggle between gods. Now that she was whole, she was able to view the entirety of the cruel conflict and see how the Earthmother's meddling had piled deceit upon injustice in the pursuit of her vengeance. Through her machinations, one part of the Lord of Twilight was in possession of the mirrorchild Nerek and heading for the citadel Gorla, while the most dangerous of the five Shadowkings was now free by Suviel's own hand.

I was dead, she said in her thoughts, *but now I am alive.*

Conundrums proliferate in times such as these, the creature said wryly.

Smiling in the darkness she regarded the hazy outline. *Conundrums like yourself?* she said. *You remind me greatly of the hound-like beasts I saw in the desolation which the Realm of the Fathertree has become. Which power do you serve, I wonder?*

I serve no power the creature said. **I am but a shadow of what once was, a memory of a memory, the faintest echo of a departed glory. No, I serve no power and have only the meagrest vestiges of a vanished night left to me**.

Suviel was stunned by realisation. *High Father,* she said. *Forgive my disrespectful—*

No, no, no, said the spirit of the Fathertree. **No formality**

or stiffness — we have no time for such indulgence. Our angry Shadowking is just emerging in the main hall of the Basilica, having slain six Acolytes on the way, just out of displeasure, you understand. The whole place is in uproar and almost all the guards and Acolytes have left the underlevels, so now would be a good time to release those two friends of yours and find a way out. Agreed?

Yes, but . . . how can we possibly stand against the hunger and wrath of gods?

By striking at where they are strongest the spirit said. The citadels Gorla and Keshada may exist in our world, squatting upon the Girdle Hills, but they also continue to exist in the Realm of Dusk. Through one of them we may reach the very heart of the Lord of Twilight's power but we will need to muster whatever strength remains of the defenders of Besh-Darok, which will include the Crystal Eye and the Motherseed—

And attack those citadels? Suviel was aghast.

One of them — Keshada. It's only as strong and invulnerable as those who command it. After Byrnak's fall, his army's loyalty split between those who serve his general, Azurech, who now rules Gorla, and those that follow the gang of rivenshades, who hold sway over Keshada. You can see how one of these two— The Fathertree spirit nodded at the captives who had lapsed back into silence. —would prove useful in that place.

You would have me lead him back into peril, she said. *After all that he's been through . . .*

All of the world is in peril, Suviel. Uncountable lives, good, bad and indifferent, are balanced on a knife edge and those who can fight, must. There is much more to tell you but time grows short — attend to your friends and we shall speak again later.

And before her magesight the strange, hound-like form faded away, glimmering outlines of its head and suggestions of eyes and a mouth melting into the leaden gloom. With a mixture of sadness and anticipation, she turned and walked back to the pillars and their seated prisoners. The taller of the two raised his head at her approach.

'Ah, our visitor returns.'

'Have they brought anything to drink?' said the other. 'A good wine would be most welcome.'

'Hush,' she whispered. 'There are enemies about.'

'A visitor who speaks,' murmured the first. 'And a woman, to boot.'

'Hmm, you noticed that too, eh?'

Suviel shook her head, then broke off a scrap of thread from within her gown and used it to make a wordlight, a tiny speck of radiance which she floated in the air above her head. She then reached out to the taller man sitting before her, and tugged his blindfold up and off. Blinking and wincing at even that meagre glow, Ikarno Mazaret gazed up at her with a wary smile.

'Greetings, lady. Whoever you are, you have my deepest thanks.'

Emotions surged and clashed within her as their gazes met. There was a sense of loving triumph in being her beloved's rescuer, and there was sorrow and heartbreak in realising that she was a stranger to him.

'My duty and pleasure, sir,' she said, quickly freeing his hands then turning to the other captive. She surreptitiously wiped tears from her eyes before lifting the other's blindfold and cutting his bonds. Flinching from the tiny hovering wordlight for a moment, Gilly Cordale peered up at her and smiled. His face was gaunt, there was a good deal more silver in his hair and beard than before, but despite losing most of his memory and essence to the rivenshades, something unquenchable in his character remained.

'A fair sight,' he said. 'I am in your debt, m'lady.' Then he looked round at Mazaret who was leaning on his pillar.

The two men regarded each other for a long moment.

'You're somewhat shorter than I expected,' Mazaret said.

'Well, you're certainly uglier than I imagined,' Gilly replied.

Both men laughed quietly as Suviel looked on in delight. Then Gilly faced her, as did Mazaret.

'Lady,' said Gilly. 'I have no knowledge of my name or anything that has happened to me, beyond my awakening here a day ago. Such holds true for my friend here also—'

'Except that I have been held prisoner in this stone pit for several days that I know of.' Mazaret regarded her levelly. 'Tell us honestly, lady – do you know of us, and do you know our names?'

'Yes, I do,' she said to them. 'You are Ikarno Mazaret, and you are Gilly Cordale.' As both men began to speak at once, she held up her hands. 'Please, sirs, we have no time for questions – we are deep inside a stronghold of deadly foes and if we are to escape we must act now while all is in commotion . . .'

A familiar presence brushed against her undersense, making her pause.

Act quickly if you can – Ystregul just left Trevada on the back of a nighthunter, heading east.

Then the spirit of the Fathertree was gone again, leaving her in the gloom with her charges.

'Weapons,' said Gilly. 'We need weapons and disguises.'

Suviel shook her head as she coaxed the Mother's Gift into life about her fingers and began assembling illusion cantos in her mind.

'No, disguises first, then weapons.'

It was two days after her sorcerous talk with Bardow, Alael and Nerek (and three since her arrival in Untollan) that the commander of the ruined mountain stronghold paid Keren a visit.

She was lying on her decrepit, skin-covered pallet in the strange pillared and windowless chamber that was her prison, reading from a children's book of fanciful tales when approaching footsteps outside the door made her look up. She had already had her evening meal of thin stew and hard bread, so knew that this was out of the ordinary. Closing the book she got to her feet, blew out the floating oil lamp on the shelf near her bed which left one lamp burning in a niche opposite the door. Then she waited in the shadows as a key rattled in the lock and the door swung open.

'Domas! So I wasn't dreaming that I'd heard your name.' Then relief turned to irritation. 'But why have you kept me prisoner? You must have known who I was . . .'

'Yes, Keren, I have known it was you, since before my men brought you here, in fact. And I'm sorry for this captivity but I've had to agree to certain conditions to gain the help we've needed this past week . . .'

The former rider captain looked at once weary and on edge. He trudged past her, hunkered down to sit on her pallet and beckoned for her to join him. By the door, a pair of leather-clad guards waited impassively, each holding a torch and a spear.

'So . . .' She sat down beside him. 'Who are these allies of yours? More to the point, can I be of use to you here? And have you had any news from Besh–Darok?'

Domas gave a slight shake of his head. 'They have asked me not to talk of them with you, but as for news . . .'

He paused, reluctance in his face, and Keren feared the worst.

'This morning white ravens brought messages from one of my eyes in eastern Khatris, saying that the Shadowking Byrnak had ridden forth with all his might and surrounded Besh–Darok. This afternoon another message came with news that a dread device had breached the city's main wall, and that the Shadowking's horde was pouring in . . .' He looked away. 'I'm sorry.'

'There's been no more messages?'

'None . . . yet.'

She felt stunned to numbness by this, almost too stunned to move. *Bardow, Alael and Nerek*, she thought. *I spoke to them just two days ago* . . .

'Then, that's it,' she murmured. 'The Shadowkings have won . . .'

'Not according to the . . . to my allies,' Domas said. 'They insist that the Crystal Eye and the Motherseed have not yet fallen into the hands of the enemy, which means that the Shadowkings are still vulnerable.'

Keren laughed bitterly. 'To what? Talismans that only a mage could wield?' Then she frowned. 'But if they haven't been seized by Byrnak, where are they? I'd wager that your allies know more than they're telling you, Domas—'

'That would not surprise me,' Domas said, getting to his feet. 'But who are they?'

Domas went over to the door where he paused and looked at

her. 'You're about to meet them – they asked to meet you once we'd finished talking.'

'But we haven't finished . . .' Keren said as he opened the door and gave a slight bow to someone outside.

'My lords . . .' he said and stepped back.

A tall man, in a long, dark red coat entered the chamber. He was young with high cheekbones and short golden hair, and Keren had never seen him before. After him came a similarly tall, similarly dressed man, except that his coat was darkest green, his face was narrow and his eyes were dark and powerful and cold . . .

She gasped, scrambled to her feet and retreated to the opposite corner of the room. When she had first encountered the second man, months before, in the refugee camp at Alvergost, he had called himself Raal Haidar. Only later, in that desolate otherworld Kekrahan, did he reveal his true form and name, Orgraaleshenoth, prince of the Daemonkind, first and mightiest of the Lord of Twilight's servants.

'Damn you for a fool, Domas!' she cried. 'What have you done?'

'Keren, you must listen to them,' Domas said. 'This is not what you think . . .'

But all that was going through her mind were memories of the torments she had endured at Orgraaleshenoth's hands as they climbed the deadly tunnels of the Ordeal below the High Basilica in Trevada. Fear racked her spirit, hate fired her blood, and her senses quailed at the thought of being in the Daemonkind's power once more . . .

'Keren Asherol.'

It was Orgraaleshenoth's companion who spoke, the handsome, younger man. Yet even as she regarded them in the wavering yellow glow of the torches, her fearful mind imagined the outlines of their true shapes, muscular bodies and limbs, rough pebbled hide, narrow reptilian heads, and great hooked wings. And through such spectral imagining came the merest whisper of betraying recollections that she had briefly coveted that mighty frame and had hoped to become a Daemonkind herself.

'Keren Asherol,' he said again. 'My name is Rakrotherangisal and, like my oath-cousin, I am of the Israganthir whom you call Daemonkind. Unlike him, however, I am no bloodline prince, being no more than a mere vassal in our flokkar . . . Or I was until heresy led me into this exile . . .'

At this, Orgraaleshenoth stepped forward and stared across the chamber at her with dark, penetrating eyes. Inwardly she quailed, outwardly she stood straight and made herself meet his gaze. *Show no weakness*, she thought. *Survive*.

'Do you remember,' he said, 'during our journey up through the Oshang Dakhal, you asked if you would ever be rid of me?'

'You answered "never",' she said.

A wintry smile passed over those sharp features. 'I should have reversed the question, for the answer would have been the same, except that I would have neither known nor understood it until well after my banishment by the mage Suviel.' The Daemonkind prince looked around her chamber for a silent moment. 'When I bound your essence to me, to strengthen and protect you as we passed through the wards of the Ordeal, there was an irrevocable co-mingling of our essences. After returning empty handed to the Realm of Ruin, I began to see that nothing was as it had been before and I felt a restlessness utterly new to me.

'I began to argue with the flokkar wisdoms over our unyielding loyalty to the Lord of Twilight, pointing out how little reward we have earned for long ages of devotion. I was threatened with the Pinion and other punishments so I took myself away to the fringes of the realm where the thinning weft sometimes permits glimpses of this world, the Realm Between. There I met my cousin, Rakrotherangisal, and a strange spirit who claimed to be the last remnant of the Fathertree . . .'

As Keren listened in astonishment, the young Daemonkind spoke again. 'The Fathertree spirit showed us many things but the most terrible was a vision of what will happen should the Lord of Twilight triumph . . .' A haunted look came over him. 'All the Realms would be broken and the wreckage would sink into the Void, merge with it into a single, sunless domain. He would become the Lord of Life and Death, all who survived would be slaves to his desires, and there would be no other power capable of restraining him. We cannot allow this to happen.'

Keren looked from the Daemonkind to Domas who nodded gravely at her. But suspicion was a stubborn companion.

'How are we going to stop it? After all, Byrnak has broken Besh-Darok's wall or so I've been told—'

'That is so,' said Rakrotherangisal.

'And yet the Crystal Eye and the Motherseed are not in his possession? How? Why?'

'The Shadowking Byrnak,' Orgraaleshenoth said, 'is no more. He was struck by a weapon whose like has not been seen for millennia, a blade which did not harm his physical form but severed certain bonds within him. Byrnak is now naught but an ordinary, mortal man while the god fragment that he carried has seized the mirrorchild Nerek and ridden off in search of the other fragments. Leaderless and under attack, the Shadowkings' great army has retreated to Gorla and Keshada, and for now two of the Three Gifts remain safe.' He gazed at her and it felt like an iron weight on her spirit, already burdened with the news about Nerek. 'With the third Gift, we may be able to prevent the Lord of Twilight from coalescing . . . with all three it might be possible to banish him to his own realm.'

'The Staff of the Void,' Keren said. 'Is that why you're here? Is that why you had me brought here?'

'Under this very fortress, Keren,' Domas said, 'a vast tunnel slopes down more than a mile into the bones of the world. At the bottom is a chamber containing the Staff of the Void, but the tunnel is full of traps, barriers and guardians . . .' There was a rapt tone in his voice. 'I've been down to the tunnel entrance, I've witnessed it—'

Keren glared at Orgraaleshenoth. 'And you want me to go down there with you, don't you? Go through that torment again . . . No, never, may the night curse you! And curse you, Domas, for dragging me here . . .'

But Rakrotherangisal was shaking his head. 'Any one of the tunnel's defences could destroy you in the blink of an eye. We may be able to withstand and defeat them, but in all likelihood we shall meet our doom at the foot of that great shaft. Therefore, we need someone who will carry the Staff back up to the surface, someone who can be trusted to see that it is not misused.'

'This is why we had you brought here,' Orgraaleshenoth said, his dark eyes looking sombre. 'You have unique qualities that would be of great value to this task, but the choice is yours – if you decide not to go with us, we shall invite volunteers from among Domas' defenders, then winnow them . . .'

Domas spoke up. 'If your doubts prevent you, Keren, I would be the one to go in your place, then you could command the defence of Untollan for me – you'd be a strong hand.'

The choice is yours . . . In her mind's eye she remembered her sword lying broken and smoking on a tunnel floor, remembered the blinding crash and the razor fire that tore and roared through her body time after time. With the memory came a faint trembling which she could feel in her hands.

'Lady, I understand what you endured in the Ordeal,' said the younger Daemonkind. 'But if you accompany us below you will not be subject to any such suffering, I swear.'

'What vow will *you* make?' Keren said to Orgraaleshenoth.

He faced her, but she saw no arrogance or angry resentment in his features, only a kind of proud sadness.

'By wing and talon, by ward and blood, I swear that I shall do to you, Keren Asherol, no malice by will or action.'

Still, she was unsure. 'Tell me more about this great tunnel,' she said. 'I've heard about Untollan before, heard that it was an ancient stronghold from before the Long Winter, that it later became a Nightbear monastery, then the seat of the Brigand Kings, then . . .' She shrugged. 'I never heard tell of any tunnel.'

'Because it has been covered and sealed in the heart of these mountains for untold centuries,' said Rakrotherangisal. 'To your eyes the Untollan seems to be an impressive, near-invulnerable fortress high up on a mountainside. Yet there are other ancient, ruined fortifications all around the Druandags, mostly among the outer mountains.'

'He speaks truly,' Domas said eagerly. 'I've *seen* them – they all have the same architecture, and where carved decorations remain they too are of identical design.'

'So what does that mean?' she said. 'That they were all built by the same people . . .' *As if to guard the inner valleys of the Druandags,* she thought, *But there's naught but a wasteland in there, stagnant pools and rocky soil where nothing healthy grows . . .*

Domas opened his mouth to speak but the younger Daemonkind was first. 'Simply put, they were all part of the same structure, the same citadel, built by the same power.'

'In ancient Othazi,' said Orgraaleshenoth, 'it was known as Kol Galeltuntollan but its original name was a Yulatsi word meaning "sky might" and that is the name which has survived in the myths and legends of the First Times . . .'

Domas smiled sardonically. 'Welcome to Jagreag.'

Ystregul sat in a padded saddle strapped to the back of a nighthunter, hands tight on the goads as he guided the creature down through darkness, wind and snow. But as the wide, round roof of the citadel Gorla emerged through the snow, there seemed to be nowhere for a nighthunter to land. He snarled, then spotted a curved platform jutting from one of the upper floors and a high, open archway spilling golden light into the night. A few moments later, his nighthunter was arresting its descent with powerful, rushing wingbeats that swept fallen snow up off the platform in great swirls and clouds. Growling irritably at the cold and the snow, the beast came down on its rearmost legs first before lurching forward on to all fours. As handlers in long, hooded cloaks hurried up to take charge of the hulking creature, Ystregul slipped from its saddle and landed lightly on his feet. His dark hair and the blackness of his rich garments were dry and unmarked by snow, and his eyes held a pent-up fury as he strode into the warmth and pungent smells of the nighhunter stabling.

A clutch of green-robed Acolytes came forward and knelt, their shiny shaven pates reflecting the torchlight. They stood and parted as another garbed as a common warrior walked up to him and, grinning, bowed. He looked like the Shadowking Byrnak, but was too tall . . .

'Greetings to you, Great Lord Ystregul,' said the man. 'I am Azurech. Welcome to fierce Gorla. Its garrison will shout your name in celebration—'

'Where is he?' Ystregul said, his teeth bared in anger. 'You have his face but you're not him – where is he?'

The man called Azurech bowed his head. 'Lord, he knows of your approach and awaits you in the great banqueting hall. Come – I will take you to him.'

At the rear of the stables, heavy wooden doors led into a long, blue-lit room full of jewelled saddles and goads and at its far end was a dark, glittering doorway. Azurech stepped through first and vanished, and Ystragul quickly followed.

They emerged on a curved walkway at one end of a long oval room with a shadowy, curved ceiling supported by huge beams. Torches and lamps shed plentiful light on the dark woodwork of the place and on the shields and banners adorning the walls. Two long tables filled most of the floor space, while at the other end was a heavy dais set up on wide pillars. A solitary figure in brown rider's garments sat hunched at a table with his back to the room and facing the half open drapes of a balcony arch.

'Leave us, Azurech,' the figure said in a hoarse voice.

The tall warrior bowed and vanished through the door.

Ystregul frowned, as if not expecting this lack of response, then descended to the floor of the banqueting hall and strode around the side, walking towards a flight of steps which led up to the dais.

'I am here for retribution, Byrnak,' he said, every word seething with hate. 'You will pay for the imprisonment you placed me in – every second of my captivity shall become a year of suffering for you . . .'

'What would *you* know of captivity?' came the other's voice, clearer now, higher.

Ystregul stopped in his tracks. 'That is not Byrnak's voice,' he said. 'Stand up! Face me . . .'

The figure pushed back the chair, stood and turned.

It was a young woman, slender, fair-haired and plain.

'A wench,' Ystregul said with contempt. 'Where is he? I know he's near. I can almost smell him—'

'You need look no further,' said the woman who grinned with a mouth suddenly gone red and eyes blazing black. She sprang into the air and swept down on him. Ystregul spat an oath and seemed about to unleash his power when he froze. The woman slowed her dive to hover just before and above him, and reached out her hands to cup his face. His head went limp and lolled back, and his eyes gazed up into hers.

'I feel him within you,' she said, still hanging in the air. 'That part of myself trapped in your flesh and bone for all these mortal years. Ah, you feel him too, don't you? His anger, his hunger, his longing for escape and union, and you can feel him eating your thoughts, can you not?'

Ystregul uttered a wordless, choking sound and one of his hands shot up to grab the woman by the throat. She just smiled.

'Such strength, such relentless purpose,' she said. 'And none of it yours. Very well – then let us embrace, you and I—'

Without any sign of exertion, she lifted him struggling weakly into the air then rose higher with her own form pressed against him. A dark green nimbus began to enfold them, a shifting veil shot through with black glitterings. Strange gusts of wind battered around the banqueting hall, blowing out torches, causing banners to flutter and drapes to billow and flap. Chairs fell over, unlit table candles toppled over and rolled, and a sole goblet tipped sideways, spilling an ochre wine across the table.

At the centre of the sorcerous maelstrom, what had been two forms now appeared to be one but blurred by the green aura with its glittering black motes which swirled like snowflakes. Moments later, the commotion began to die away as the lone figure, cloaked in green radiance, drifted down to the floor. Another moment and the green had shivered into first the semblance of then the solid appearance of garments, a long cloak of black bear fur over gleaming red mail and black leather harness.

Azurech appeared at the glittering doorway, came over and knelt down before him.

'Rise.'

He did so and looked up, for tall as he was, the other overtopped him by head and shoulders. Awe and devotion shone in Azurech's face and for an instant he seemed unable to speak.

'Great Lord,' he said at last. 'Are you a god?'

The face that smiled down at him had Ystregul's heavy features
and savage smile, but it was tempered by a calmness in the eyes and
an air of deliberation.

'No, Azurech, I am not a god. Not yet.'

Chapter Twenty-five

Bells toll with rusty throats,
And the whispers of the world,
Stir the tattered night,
While blind heroes stalk their prey.

The Black Saga of Culri Moal, vi, 7

Overnight, in the hours following the siege and the breaking of the wall, the prevailing winds had swung around to the east, sending waves of sleet across the city. By early morning the winds had changed again and as the cloud cover rolled away the temperature plummeted. When Bardow left the palace in the mid-morning for a meeting with the Trade Guild, the surrounding city streets were littered with the bodies of horses and men, frozen near solid and caked in snow and ice. However, he had seen from his carriage window that there was no shortage of volunteers – labourers, woodworkers, apprentice boys from the yard shops, even entire families – hacking and heaving at the frost-bound corpses, slinging them into carts brought up from the quays.

When he returned, nearly two hours later, their numbers had swollen and much of the carnage had been cleared. And when Bardow saw smiles on a good number of faces, his heart sank, for he had met with similar feelings among the city's senior merchants. Although there was the expected regrets over the deaths of Tauric and the witchhorse herd (and promises to erect a suitable memorial), their mood was one of triumph. Almost. A second attempted assault on Besh-Darok had failed, and now that the Shadowking Byrnak was in chains in the palace dungeons the worst danger was past and everyone could get back to business.

Bardow had been sorely tempted to wreck this happy illusion by pointing out that they still had another four Shadowkings to face, but knew this would not help when it came to presenting the Crown's list of badly needed supplies. Instead, he praised their efforts, side-stepped questions about the succession, and was inwardly pleased when they agreed to more than half of the quantities on the Crown's list. Now, as his carriage rattled and jolted up towards the Square of Swords and the long gate that led through the Keep of Day, he could see thin trails of smoke still rising from burnt-out buildings north of the Palace. Even after Byrnak's capture and the loss of his commanders, the fighting had raged on house-to-house with the masked troops putting buildings to the torch as they retreated back to the breach in the wall. Where the mounted Mogaun were waiting.

What occupied Bardow's mind, however, was the state of Yasgur's city militia as well as the knightly orders. The street chantries and healing halls were full to overflowing with the wounded and dying, and the bulk of Ironhall Barracks was a charred ruin. And he was on his way to a meeting of the High Conclave, with the Mogaun chieftains, where he intended to propose launching an immediate attack on either Gorla or Keshada with every able-bodied fighter they had.

Madness, they'll say, he thought. *Until I tell them what I learned from Byrnak last night, about the Lord of Twilight and Nerek. Even then, they may not believe me . . .*

As the carriage turned into the snow-covered Square of Swords near the Keep of Day, he could see a group of solemn children laying flowers at the spot where Tauric and his witchhorse were slain by the mirrorchild Nerek.

Poor Nerek, he thought. *And Tauric – you so wanted to fight for your people, and when you came back here to fight, you also came back to die. But where, pray tell, are the bodies of you and the witchhorse? Is the hand of the Earthmother at work in this?*

Then the carriage turned again, leftward into the Keep of Day's dim tunnel and past its three gates and inclined drawbridge. When he disembarked under the covered north west entrance to the High Spire, his personal guards Antor and Rafe climbed down from atop the carriage and followed him inside. People bowed or nodded their greetings as he made his way through the bustling, circular main hall to the square-built hub staircase.

Two attendants emerged from an alcove in the hub itself, with a stair sedan in which Bardow sat. Moments later he was being carried up the steps. The steward of Five Kings Dock had sent a few of these stair sedans up to the palace last week and all of them had survived the enemy invasion of the palace, much to Bardow's relief since the High Conclave was being held in the restored throne room.

Before long the sedan carriers, breathing heavily, set the chair down near the tall double doors of the throne room. Thanking them, he stepped out, shook the folds of his heavy brown and purple robe (which was making him perspire) and faced the entrance. Four guards in mail and white surcoats flanked it and the imperial standard hung above, bordered with black. Bardow ordered Antor and Rafe to wait here, then approached the door which two of the guards opened for him.

Inside, a broad oval table sat at the centre of the polished grey marble floor which shone with the reflected glows of many lamps. The lords of the High Conclave were there, most of them seated, apart from Yarram who stood staring off to the left. Atroc was standing behind Yasgur, his wrinkled, stubbly features creased in amusement while his master sat grim-faced at the table.

Eyes looked round when Bardow entered, and as he made his way across the glittering floor he noticed behind the pillars on the left a couple of his fellow mages Cruadin and the Nightrook standing near the balcony archway. Then he also saw the two Mogaun chieftains, Welgarak and Gordag, their swords bared.

'Cruadin!' he said. 'Nightrook — what's wrong? What are you looking—'

The tall, fur-clad Welgarak glanced round at Bardow's approach, as did the others, and stepped back to reveal someone standing in the archway, with the outer shutters and the drapes closed behind them. When he saw who it was, he stumbled to a halt, a sudden scouring fear filling his mind.

'Who are you?' he said.

'She claims to be the mage Suviel,' growled Welgarak. 'But I have seen her pale sisters riding with the masks so who can tell who *or* what she truly is?'

The Nightrook turned to Bardow. 'I sense no Wellsource taint in her.'

'The Armourer lived in our midst for several weeks,' Cruadin pointed out. 'Undetected.'

'She appeared a short while since, Archmage,' Yarram explained. 'As we were gathering. Said we had no time for talking, that we should be attacking the enemy citadels . . .'

'And claims the masks have a sorcerous tunnel under their towers,' said barrel-chested Gordag. 'Leads straight to Rauthaz. Says that's how their troops get here so quick . . .'

'We are keen to know the truth, my lord Archmage,' Yasgur said brusquely. 'Can you provide it?'

Bardow gathered his composure. 'I believe so, my Lord Regent,' he said, then made himself turn and face the woman in the doorway. 'You have the semblance of Suviel Hantika,' he said. 'But she died in Trevada three months ago. How does a dead woman come to be standing before me now?'

She smiled sadly and gave a little shrug. 'Only the Earthmother can answer you, Bardow.'

Is it really her? he wondered, noting everything from the relaxed stance and crossed arms to the look of wry amusement in the eyes, and seeing familiarity everywhere. Her face and hair and eyes seemed to be that of a healthy person, but there was also a faint luminous quality to her that made him wary. Knowing there was only one way to be sure, he turned to the lords of the High Conclave.

'Honourable lords,' he said. 'With your permission, I would like to have the Crystal Eye brought up from its sanctuary so that I may determine the nature of our visitor.'

All gave their assent, and with mindspeech Bardow asked the mage Zanser to bring the Eye up to the throne room. None spoke as they waited, tension slowly mounting. After a tense wait, the portly mage entered and crossed the polished floor, heavy-footed and out of breath but carrying a banded casket under his arm. He passed it to Bardow then with wordless relief sank into an empty chair.

Bardow set the casket on the table, unlocked it with a touch and opened it. Nestling in blue silk, the Crystal Eye. Gently, he laid his right hand evenly and well spread upon its clear and shining surface. He was already attuned to the song of its powers but physical contact significantly heightened his abilities and made them more immediate.

He looked round at the woman who stood in the archway, her hand now clasped at her midriff. Tracks of the Wellsource were his quarry, hints of hidden purpose, seeds of malice . . .

'I am ready,' she said.

'It is done,' said Bardow, taking his hand from the Eye and surveying all those around the table. 'There is no taint in her, my lords, thus she may be who she says she is.'

'Are you sure?' muttered Welgarak.

'Could she be an impostor?' said Atroc.

Bardow beckoned the woman over and said, 'Place your hand on the Crystal Eye as I do and say "I am Suviel Hantika".'

As she crossed the room, Cruadin and the Nightrook unwaveringly watched her while Welgarak and Gordog kept their blades at the ready.

Bardow touched the Eye again and as she followed suit he saw the first signs of anxiety, trembling in her fingers. She breathed in deeply, as if steadying her nerves, then spoke.

'I am Suviel Hantika.'

Bardow momentarily felt dizzy as a cluster of images rushed through his mind. At the same time, the woman gave a sharp intake of breath as if in pain, but her hand remained on the Eye.

'What was it?' the Nightrook demanded of her. 'What happened? Did the Eye reject you?'

'No – it showed me how I died.'

Bardow nodded in agreement, seeing again the desperate struggle in the tiny, pillared fane atop the High Basilica, the Daemonkind's attempt to snatch the Eye, and how Suviel had used it to banish the creature to its own realm. But in the moment of her triumph, the fane – damaged by all that had gone before – had broken apart, casting her down to die on jagged crags.

'Suviel,' was all he could say past the emotion in his throat. He took her cool hands in his, and there were tears in her eyes too.

'Oh, Bardow, my mentor and friend,' she said. 'How I have longed for your advice . . .'

'Seems I might be taking it from you, this time,' he said.

'That may be so,' she said, turning sombre. 'There is much to say and much to be done—'

'Like riding out to attack those citadels?' said a slender, hawkish man called Tylo Nokram, Lord Commander of the Knights Protector. His words were full of scepticism.

'And don't forget that big tunnel what runs all the way to Rauthaz,' said Gordag.

'There *is* such a tunnel,' said Yasgur.

Suddenly there was silence as everyone looked at the Lord Regent. Behind him, the old seer Atroc was grinning widely, almost as if in pride. Yasgur got to his feet, black fur cloak hanging heavily from his shoulders, and regarded Bardow.

'You are certain of this woman?' he said.

'She is Suviel Hantika – I am sure of it,' Bardow replied, glancing at her. 'What tunnel is this?'

'They call it the Great Aisle,' she said. 'It's an immense corridor passing underground from the two citadels of Rauthaz in the north, with a branching off to Casall and Trevada. The Wellsource made it and is part of its very substance.'

Yasgur shrugged. 'I learned less than that, lady. At the height of the battle, when Byrnak's troops lost their heads and began to break, I had six of my men don the enemy's livery, masks, armour and all, and sent them over the wall to join the enemy's retreat. Five of them reached Gorla to the west and found their way in during the confusion – two escaped and returned this morning with tales of a gaping, misty tunnel that stretched off into the distance. They learned little else, except that one of the Shadowkings arrived on a nighthunter in the middle of the night then left a few hours later by this Great Aisle.'

Suviel nodded. 'He is returning north to unite with his brothers, and if that happens they will become unstoppable. That is why we must act now.'

'But there are tens of thousands of masks in each of those citadels,' Welgarak said darkly. 'How can this be done?'

'By taking the Crystal Eye with us,' she said. 'And we need only attack one of the strongholds. Keshada is held by the rivenshades and they are divided amongst themselves. Also, there are allies within who may be able to help us.'

'The Crystal Eye?' Bardow said.

'Aye, Bardow,' she said with a rueful smile. 'The Motherseed, too.'

'And once we are within the citadel Keshada?' Yasgur said. 'What then?'

'When we enter Keshada, we shall be crossing the threshold between this world and the Realm of Ruin for that is where both citadels have their true foundations. From there, certain ways lead further on.' She paused and looked around at the engrossed faces, and Bardow felt a touch of pride. *She has them,* he thought.

'Sirs,' she went on. 'If fate is kind, we shall be leading an army into the realm of the Lord of Twilight himself!'

The meeting had taken place at a long, narrow stone table before a tall, open window, but was now coming to an end. Mazaret had seen and heard it all from where he lay on the floor of a high gallery, as had Gilly. But Gilly had left a short while ago when they overheard one of the women mention where they had imprisoned this Alael.

'Once I have her,' he had whispered, 'I'll get her up to these entrances Suviel mentioned, and wait nearby for you . . .' He had given a muffled chuckle. ''Course, your own task might take a while but we'll be patient.'

Then he had crept off into the shadows, garbed perfectly in a mask-soldier's armour and livery which Suviel had provided. Mazaret had been less than enthusiastic about his own disguise but when she explained what he had to do, the need was obvious. Thus his hair was now utterly white, his skin was the colour of bleached bone, and his eyes were pale ash grey, and when he peered down he saw another five men who looked exactly the same. Suviel had explained that they were rivenshades, that their creation had taken away all his memories, and how he would have to kill them to regain what had been stolen.

He shivered as he watched them, and the three strange, identical women who sat talking and harshly jesting with them. They all looked like Suviel and although she had also explained about them, she said that it was not necessary to slay them for her sake.

But did he want to kill them, any of them? She had given him a long, straight sword with a small, hooked rune high on the blade, but was he capable of wielding it? He had wanted to know more of the life that was lost to him, who his friends and enemies were and which Suviel was, for if she truly was his friend would she have sent him into such peril? Admittedly, she had tried to explain the battles and struggles of the past which had led to the present, but his mind had become lost among the mazy trail of Shadowkings and chieftains, rivenshades and realms. Yet it was Suviel who kept returning to his thoughts, her bright, steady eyes, her kind smile, her patience . . .

Raised voices from below caught his attention.

'. . . not going to sit in their city while we have their little queen,' one of his own rivenshades was saying to another. 'They will come for her, so *you* should make sure that *your* warriors are ready. No one else will . . .'

The other laughed derisively, as did two of the women. The speaker shrugged and walked diagonally across the room, out of Mazaret's sight. For a moment, he continued to hear footsteps then realised in panic that the rivenshade was climbing steps up to the gallery where he lay prostrate. As quietly as possible he crawled along to a darkened doorway which led off, rose to a crouch and hurried along to where the passage met a high, wide lamplit corridor. The floor consisted of interlocking green tiles which resembled letters while the walls were of a pale, roseate stone across which huge figures strode in a long, continuous, intricate relief carving.

Mazaret paused uncertainly for a moment, then decided that he would ambush this rivenshade, render him insensible . . . then decide what to do. But even as he drew his sword, a voice spoke from behind him:

'Planning a little treachery, brother? Isn't that somewhat rash?'

Surprised, some instinct made him draw his sword as he quickly turned to face another of the rivenshades who stood leaning against the wall. He wore a white, high-collared doublet, an extravagantly embroidered crimson shirt, and rested one hand on the pommel of a slender sword whose point sat on the tiles. Mazaret said nothing and hurriedly backed away before the one following him emerged from the passageway, halted and frowned at them both.

'We do not have time to indulge in this foolishness,' he said.

The one in white smiled lazily. 'Trust me, we do.' He brought his blade up, levelling the point at Mazaret. 'I thought at first that this was one of our brothers, but I realised that it was not . . .'

The grey rivenshade stared at Mazaret for a moment, then a thin smile crept across his face. 'It's him, the original!'

'The seed of us all, brother,' said the one in white. 'But now just a shrivelled husk, empty of all meaning and purpose, and long past the time of his final death. Come – ' he said to Mazaret, 'I shall be happy to bring you the mercy of the grave.'

'The only mercy of any worth,' Mazaret said, 'would be to silence that gibbering tongue of yours.'

'Ah, so a sliver of spirit yet remains,' said the white rivenshade as he straightened and took a step or two along the corridor. 'If the Acolytes had been more attentive, I'm sure they could have got another of us out of you, eh?'

Before Mazaret knew it, the white rivenshade made a straight arm lunge with his sword at Mazaret's heart. Pure reflex caused him to turn and lean away simultaneously, and sweep his own blade up across his body to block the swift side cut that came next. The strike of steel rang sharply between the stone walls of the corridor.

After that, it became for Mazaret a desperate balancing act between trying to learn from his body's battle instincts and trying to stay alive. Several times the rivenshade's sword tip slipped past his defences to inflict minor wounds, each less minor than the last. The sword that Suviel had given him was slightly shorter than his enemy's but heavier, and on the few occasions that he was able to strike back the rivenshade almost wavered.

But not for long. Reeling back from the rivenshade's darting, weaving blade, Mazaret retreated a few steps, trying to ignore the rawness of the wounds in his ear and cheek, neck, arm and hand. *At this rate I'll soon be dead!* he thought in panic. *I've got to stop him somehow . . .*

The rivenshade came closer, smiling a smile that was half a sneer. Mazaret feinted weakly at his face, then seemed to leave himself open. The rivenshade swung at his undefended side but Mazaret turned that side away and shoulder-charged his foe. But the rivenshade leaped back, leaving Mazaret to dive forward on to his leading foot . . . and instead of carrying onward he went into a crouch and spun with a wild slash at his enemy's midriff. The rivenshade seemed to have anticipated it all except Mazaret's swinging blade which caromed off the flat of his own sword, nicked the knuckles of his hand and raked his bare lower arm.

Panting, Mazaret saw the minor cuts and cursed his luck, expecting the pale foe to be at him again in a moment. Instead, the rivenshade shrieked in agony, dropped his sword and fell to his knees.

'The Void sign!' he cried as pale wisps of vapour began to leak from his mouth. White fumes were pouring from the wounds on hands and arms, wounds that were widening. Mazaret was engrossed by the grotesque sight for a moment until the hiss of a sword sliding from its scabbard snatched him back, and he whirled to face the grey-clad rivenshade.

'You were sent by the Void, weren't you?' the rivenshade said, pale, hating eyes tempered with wariness. 'Sent with an inscribed blade . . .'

The Void? Mazaret thought. *But isn't that just a great emptiness, a sea of nothing? Bardow would know . . .*

Then realisation struck him – some of his memories had returned and some of the names and places Suviel had mentioned suddenly had meaning. *By the Mother!* he thought. *I'm inside Keshada!*

Then suddenly the rivenshade was on him with a flurry of savage, hacking blows. But Mazaret had some knowledge of swordplay in his mind now, in addition to a lifetime of visceral reflexes. Swiftly, he backed away down the corridor while shrugging off the short green, patterned coat given to him by Suviel. The rivenshade

followed, leaving behind the remains of the other, which was by
now reduced to a few limp articles of clothing draped over lumpy
objects oozing white vapour.

When the grey-garbed rivenshade came within reach he attacked
with arm extended, using his sword's length to best effect. Mazaret,
though, was ready and with his free hand swaddled in layers of coat
he grabbed the other's sword by the blade, then leaped forward and
drove his own weapon into his foe's chest, running him through.

The rivenshade let out an ear-shattering wail of torment, released
his sword and staggered back. Mazaret pulled his own back out of
the enemy's chest, saw pale wisps drifting off the long, tapered blade
then noticed something glowing near the hilt, the small hooked
rune . . .

The rivenshade's breathing rattled and wheezed, then with a
white, misty sigh, he sank to his knees by the wall, keeled over
and began to dissolve.

'So you are Ikarno Mazaret,' said a silky, mocking voice.

It was one of the Suviel rivenshades, garbed like one of the
mask soldiers except that silver glyphs adorned every item of her
clothing. She regarded the collapsing rivenshade with amusement
as she walked up to Mazaret.

'I would expect nothing less than complete victory from the real
Mazaret,' she said, laying a hand on his arm. 'If you come with me,
I'll help you kill the others, then we can rule Keshada together. And
you can love me as you loved her . . .'

Mazaret felt as transfixed by her as he was by his returning
memories. And Suviel's words came back to him through his
confused thoughts – *It is not necessary to slay them for my sake.*

He shook off her hand and stepped back from the sudden rage
in her features.

'No!' he cried and turned to run.

But her screamed words came after him as he fled.

'The Prince of Dusk is coming, Ikarno Mazaret, and when he
triumphs you will be mine!'

It had taken Keren several hours and a night of sleep before
reluctantly agreeing to accompany the two Daemonkind renegades

down into the depths of Jagreag. But by the time they and Domas appeared at her chamber door with armour and weapons for her, the Jefren forces down in the rocky valleys were mounting a determined assault. Her chamber was one of several that honeycombed a tall crag high up the mountainside, and she saw several family quarters, a nursery and a scullery as she was taken along to a square, curtained doorway leading outside. Beyond was a walled shelf open to the skies and whipped by winds so cold Keren almost cried out.

From there a long stairway of cracked and worn steps snaked down the mountainside. Most of the steps had been brushed clear of snow but some had ice patches that made Keren careful with her footing as she followed Domas. On the way down they passed landings where children played on the threshold of open doors and others where no doors were visible to the eye. Keren's attention was drawn more to the conflict going on below – from this height she could look down into the gorges and ravines that gashed the Druandags' scree and boulder foothills. Troops, horses, cart and lines of bound prisoners swarmed through them and over the hills in their thousands.

'They're not sparing any effort,' she said to Domas through chattering teeth.

'What you should say is that they don't mind wasting lives,' Domas said. 'You'll see soon.'

Several minutes of downward trudging brought her nearer to the focus of the siege and she began to understand. The main battlements of Untollan were hewn all along the southwestern face of Mount Harang, which was less a mountain and more a series of sheer, slope ramparts surmounted by a snow-blasted fist of rock. The battlements were unassailable except for one place where a broad ridge shouldered out from Harang's flank and sloped down into the rocky vale. Past owners of the citadel had reinforced that point with walls and towers and it was against them that the Jefren generals threw their might. But at a terrible cost – corpses and their blood darkened the ground all around the jutting fortification, and yet more bodies lay scattered all down the side of the mountain's shoulder along with broken weapons and shattered scaling ladders.

The long staircase ended at the entrance to a long, open gallery cut into the face of Mount Harang about a hundred feet above the main battlements. The gallery's inner wall, crowded with chipped, weather-ravaged carvings, was broken by several heavily draped doors which Domas off-handedly referred to as 'quarters and training rooms'. Before long he brought them to a halt at a part of the gallery which projected from the rock face, a tapering shelf sitting atop a natural outcropping which ran like a narrow tower right down into the roots of the mountain. When Keren joined Domas out on the small balcony the icy wind cut like a knife through her leather armour and trews, adding to the chill in her flesh. But nothing could detract from the magnificent, panoramic view, the grey and white foothills, the shadowy ravines, with the uneven, snow-streaked lands of southwest Anghatan stretching away towards the Sea of Birrdaelin. Keren took it all in, the wide vastness, the rushing broken clouds, the birds wheeling overhead, the paleness of distant uplands, even this sharp, biting cold. She wanted to fix it for ever in her mind for she knew she was about to vanish into the darkness below ground and face an unknowable fate.

A small bird fluttered down to land on the shelf's low wall, a greenwing which eyed her and her companions for an instant or two then sprang away on blurred wings, uttering a piercing cluster of notes as it did so. Keren watched it dart away up into the air above Untollan and wished she could do the same.

'Keren Asherol,' came the voice of Rakrotherangisal. 'The time is at hand.'

She turned and nodded. Domas put a hand on her shoulder.

'I wish I were the one,' he said with a rueful smile. 'Even if only to get away from the Jefren and their slaves.' He bowed formally to her and the Daemonkind. 'May you walk in the way of the Light.'

The Daemonkind both gravely returned his bow. 'May your wings never fail,' said Orgraaleshenoth.

Keren following the two Daemonkind a few paces along to a draped entrance through which they ducked. She paused on the threshold to glance back at Domas, who raised his hand in farewell. She did the same and slipped past the heavy curtains.

It was warm and dark inside, a narrow corridor stuffy with the odours of hot candle tallow, leather and a certain aged mustiness.

She had just realised that it smelled like an old library when they turned a corner and emerged in . . . an old library. A one-armed man in battered rider's leathers looked up from an open book, gave a single, unsmiling nod and went back to the page he was on. By the few wavering candles, the library seemed small and cramped but as she followed the Daemonkind across to a large door, she saw that a shadowy gap between shelves in the diagonally opposite corner was actually a passageway through to more shelves stacked with a jumble of books and scrolls.

Beyond the large door was a walkway which ran as a shelf along and above a torchlit main corridor busy with archers and spearmen hurrying out to the ramparts, and stretcher parties bearing the wounded into the healers. At the end of the walkway were stairs leading downwards, a feature that Keren was to become more than familiar with over the next hour or so as the Daemonkind took her down into the dark, decayed labyrinth of Jagreag.

They were passing through lightless areas now, and the Daemonkind produced a pale, illuminating glow from the crystals atop their staffs. It was bright enough to see where they were going, and for Keren to catch glimpses on either side of the irresistible devastation of time. Corridors so old that they were like bent and rounded tunnels, muddy underfoot and bearded with ash-grey mosses populated by tiny, white spiders. Chambers that were decrepit caves where unseen things scurried. Stairways worn by running water into slippery, uneven slopes, and everywhere the smell of stagnant dankness.

Once, their route took them out on to a narrow ledge passing across the vertical face of a crack in the mountain itself. Halfway along Keren looked up to see a long, pale jagged shard of sky and a few bright droplets of ice-melt falling from above. It was gloomy where they carefully walked while an icy, swallowing blackness gaped below.

In fitful silence they travelled, with one or other of the Daemonkind warning her of unstable walls or dangerous areas of floor, and the deeper they went the quieter their voices. When they came to a long, wide stairway, the Daemonkind dimmed their staff-mounted crystals to a glimmer, just enough to see by.

'We must make as little noise as possible,' said Rakrotherangisal. 'There are creatures at this depth who should not be disturbed.'

Chilled by his words, Keren followed him down the crumbling, debris-strewn steps. After several minutes the wall on the left became marred by large jagged gaps beyond which was a black emptiness. It both intrigued and unnerved her, like a looming, faceless presence. Then, a short while later, she was negotiating a section of steps worn near smooth by water trickling from a crack further up when her foot slipped and she lurched towards one of the open gaps. Her hand shot out to stop her fall and struck a layer of dust and rock fragments, which cascaded out into the black. For a long moment there was silence . . . then the faint clatter of the fragments hitting the bottom. The Daemonkind stared at her.

'I'm sorry . . .' she began to say in a strangled whisper but stopped when a light flared in the blackness, far off in the blackness. She glimpsed the merest outlines of an immense chamber with an upward curving ceiling broken by several giant shards of rock thrusting down.

Orgraaleshenoth grabbed her by the arm and in a moment all three of them were rushing down the rotting stairs. After much slipping and stumbling they reached a landing where without hesitation Rakrotherangisal turned right, and as they hurried along Keren could hear an eerie, high-pitched piping far behind.

'Who are they?' Keren said, gasping.

'The *Issusk*,' Rakrotherangisal said shortly, then glanced at Orgraaleshenoth. 'We should make for the sundered bridge.'

The elder Daemonkind nodded. 'They know we are here now, so the longer route is pointless.'

From the landing they dashed through a circular room half-choked with strange spiral vines to a corridor that sloped down-wards. At its end it curved to the right and Keren was the first to run out and find herself staring across a massive, chain supported bridge. The high piping sounds were louder and a faint radiance was coming from below, but what held her attention was the large empty gap near the middle of the bridge. Gauging it by eye, she guessed that nearly twenty feet separated the sagging, ragged edges.

'We may have to take that longer route,' she said over her shoulder. 'This is . . . *Hey, what are you*—'

The Daemonkind were suddenly on either side of her, lifting her by her arms as they rushed out on to the bridge. Fear choked her throat and for a long, terrifying moment she believed that it was an elaborate trap until they reached the gap in the bridge at a hurtling sprint and, still carrying her, jumped.

Her own legs and body were trailing as they soared through the air, and she was able to stare down into a long, sheer-sided canyon. A huge mob of creatures, some upright on two feet, some carrying blazing brands, were surging along it and some pointed upwards at the Daemonkind and Keren. Hooting voices rose in anger above the morass of wails, clicks and barks.

Then they landed on the other side, Keren held higher until her bearers slowed enough for her to be set down safely. She wanted to be angry at them for throwing such a scare into her, but realised that there was no time for such tantrums.

Further downward they went, another stairwell, and another wrecked, muddy corridor at the end of which was a wall of compact rubble worn into solidity by time, water and millennia of lichen and questing vines. It was a heavy curtain of these that Rakrotherangisal pulled aside to reveal a low, dark tunnel through the ancient debris. Squeezing and scrambling through it left them streaked with black mud but Keren forgot that as she got to her feet and saw the huge, sloping door which filled most of a high, enclosed chamber. By the glow of the Daemonkind staffs, it seemed to have been made of a single, imposing slab of striated grey granite, its surface covered in spiralling panels of carved men and beasts.

Keren felt a wave of weary hunger pass through her, so she sat on a mossy boulder and dug into her harness pouches for pieces of dried meat. She had just started on her second mouthful when Orgraaleshenoth said 'Here' and rapped the tip of his staff on one of the carven panels. There was a responding knock, then a deep grinding sound as the upper edge of the carved door began to tilt inwards. Pivoting on a central horizontal axis the bottom half slowly swung out and up. Seeing this, Keren swiftly uncapped her leather water bottle and downed half the contents, then stood and hurried after the Daemonkind who were already striding through. She had just joined them when the door began to swing slowly back and she paused to watch it close with a solid, reverberating thud, followed by a series of quiet muffled taps from within.

When she looked round she almost cursed in surprise – the two Daemonkind had shrugged off human form to return to their own. Orgraaleshenoth was as she remembered, nearly twice her height, his head hairless and reptilian, his torso broad and muscular while his hide was rough and pebbled, black and emerald, and folded wings jutted above his shoulders. Rakrotherangisal was shorter by a head and his hide was black and red but his amber eyes were as steady and unfathomable as Orgraaleshenoth's.

He turned to the older Daemonkind. 'Nighthunters have arrived to fight for the Jefren Theocracy. Untollan will soon fall.'

Orgraaleshenoth nodded. 'With Byrnak gone, the Acolytes know that the remaining Shadowkings are incapable of regaining control. Grazaan is paralysed by his own fragment of the Lord of Twilight and Kodel has gone into hiding—'

'Ystregul is no more and Thraelor has stirred himself . . .'

Their words were tinged with a wry amusement, but Keren was appalled. 'But what will happen to Domas and his people, his families . . .'

'There are many hiding places, and several escape tunnels have been prepared,' said Rakrotherangisal. 'But not, unfortunately, for us. Come, the Processional awaits.'

Together they strode along the plain stone passageway. Both the Daemonkind still had their glowing staffs but they seemed oddly shrunken in those big, taloned hands. Up ahead Keren could see a pale, misty radiance which gradually diffused as they drew near. Through the haze she began to make out the details on a sloping wall beyond the end of the passage, intricate patterns that snared the eye. But it was the scale of the stonework which came to dominate her field of view and when at last the passage opened out, Keren found her footsteps slowing as she stared about her.

Rakrotherangisal had referred to it as the Processional while Domas called it 'a vast, sloping tunnel', yet such words could not begin to describe its gaping immensity. By eye alone, she guessed it to be perhaps 200 yards wide and some 300 high. Every surface was burdened with carven images, the sheer walls reaching up to the massive, sloping ceiling, all covered in depictions of semi-naked figures struggling or fighting or marching in triumph. All of it was in a leaden grey stone cracked and streaked by yawning gulfs of time, lit by a strange, sourceless radiance as pallid as light cast through tainted ice.

Beyond the passage a flat shelf extended for several yards to the head of a rack of stairs wide enough to accommodate an army. Although the steps looked freshly cut and unworn, they were littered with chips and fragments of masonry no larger than her hand. Ahead of her, the Daemonkind were already descending with their hulking yet lithe gait and as she hastened to join them she noticed another feature of the colossal shaft. Towering alcoves, dark and empty, were hewn into the walls at regular intervals on either side, twin rows of shadowy openings marching down into the hazy, faintly glowing depths. She also noticed that each one had a platform jutting from its base, a wide slab of stone as thick as one of the Daemonkind was tall.

'Once, every one of these alcoves had an enormous statue of the Lord of Twilight standing before it,' Orgraaleshenoth said. 'But when Jagreag fell, they were all hauled up to the surface and destroyed, then the fragments were taken out on to the Sea of Birrdaelin and thrown into the waters.'

'He was known to imbue some likenesses of himself with a kind of life,' Rakrotherangisal said. 'So the victors made sure that none were left standing.'

Keren nodded in silent understanding. As she walked down the steps, she stared at the empty alcoves and found herself imagining a fifty-yard high statue of Byrnak standing in one of them, grinning, watching her . . .

She shivered. *This is a place of ghosts.*

Even the air smelled deathly, cold and harsh with the odour of the fine stone dust that their feet disturbed. There was also a musty staleness, the faintest hint of immemorial corruption which Keren tried not to be too conscious of as she carried on beside the two Daemonkind.

'What manner of guardians or wards shall we be facing?' she asked.

'That is not an easy question to answer,' said Rakrotherangisal. 'The ancient spells protecting this place seem to respond differently to each intrusion.'

She stared at him, surprised. 'So others have been here before us?'

'The records in Untollan's library speak of more than a score such attempts since the fortress was first occupied during the Othazreg clan migrations five thousand years ago. Most were groups of fortune hunters following local legends and mountain stories, or fugitives from pursuit, but one was a small army led by the chieftain who ruled Untollan a few generations after the Othazreg migration. Although not one member of that army returned, a few others did and each had a different story to tell.

'One claimed that they were attacked by wave after wave of glass-like spiders and insects which burrowed into the flesh and killed from within. Another said that grotesque, leathery white creatures had come flying out of the alcoves and snatched his companions up into the air before tearing them apart. Yet another emerged from the Processional broken in mind and spirit and would only talk of fog creatures that sucked blood from their victims.'

Keren stared ahead of her, down the long, receding rake of stairs to the pale, misty blur far below. In the wake of the Daemonkind's account, the great shaft took on the aspect of a tomb-like throat into which they were descending.

Then her gaze picked something out of the distance, something larger than the small shards of fallen masonry. As they drew nearer it began to resemble a prone, huddled form while further down other similar shapes were coming into view. When they gathered around it Keren could see that it was an ancient, desiccated corpse, its clothing gone to frail tatters, its skin reduced to stretched membrane over brown, pitted bones. A layer of fine, grey dust covered the sad remains, and clung to the few strands of spider web that draped it.

'I wonder how he died,' Keren muttered, crouching nearby.

'There's no visible evidence,' said Rakrotherangisal, dipping his great head for a closer look. 'No cuts or holes—'

'Someone comes,' Orgraaleshenoth said in a low, warning voice.

Standing straight with her companions, Keren instinctively looked down the stairs and felt the first chill touches of fear. A tall narrow shape had emerged from the misty depths and was ascending towards them. Its outlines were vague, its substance opaque and lacking detail but on it came, steadily, silently. Suddenly, Keren saw that it was a figure, pale as milk-clouded water, walking up the stairs yet its outlines shifted oddly . . . then she realised that it was two or more figures moving in single file.

Wordlessly, the Daemonkind positioned themselves on either side of her, staves aglow and at the ready as the sorcerous guardians drew closer and spread out across the steps. At last they were near enough for Keren to discern details and she gasped, seeing that she and the Daemonkind were facing themselves!

'Go back,' came their hideous, scraping whispers. 'Flee this place . . . death waits here for thee . . .'

Then the spectral images swept up the stairs and were upon them. There was no solidity to them but Keren could feel a cold caress across her hands and arms as she backed away. The one that was her counterpart had only a rudimentary likeness, with crude features and no distinction between skin and garments. But the eyes were white pits and the mouth moved incessantly as it glided around her before swooping in again. When it tugged at her hair and clothing a choking fear made her wrench out her sword and slash wildly at the harrying spectre. As her blade struck home, it seemed to open a blazing, amber gash in the opaque creature which uttered a thin shriek . . .

In the next moment, there were only three patches of smoking vapour dissolving into fading tendrils. Breathing heavily, Keren looked at the Daemonkind.

'They were a warning, Keren Asherol,' said Orgraaleshenoth as he planted his staff firmly on the step before him. 'The guardian spells only sent them forth because our presence was noticed. Therefore . . .'

He raised his staff and made a circular pass with it between the three of them. For a moment Keren saw nothing different, then noticed a faint nimbus around her two companions.

'I have laid a glamour upon each of us,' he went on,' one that will conceal us from strange eyes and some but not all sorcerous divination. The guardian spells will know that someone is passing through, but not who or where. Thus we must be utterly quiet. From here on we are in deadly peril.'

The descent continued, and the dusty, shrivelled cadavers grew more numerous. After a time they found themselves treading among a proliferation of scattered bones as if this had been the site of a terrible slaughter. The dried-up husks of bodies, most lacking head and limbs, lay everywhere, even upon the platforms that protruded at the foot of the great, dark alcoves. Keren recalled Rakrotherangisal's account of the army that had marched down into the depths and knew that these had to be their remains.

Then from an alcove above her came a sound which chilled her to the bone, a long, rasping breath that made her quail and glance fearfully over her shoulder. As she did so, several misty, shapeless forms came gliding out of the nearby alcoves. Others issued forth on the other side of the shaft while still more drifted slowly and silently down from the sloped ceiling.

A cry of terror bubbled at the back of her throat. Striving to keep from uttering even a whimper, she found herself halting and hunkering down into a crouch to avoid the pale guardians as they swooped to and fro across the bone-littered steps. But Orgraaleshenoth was gesturing for her to continue. So, trembling, she forced herself upright and resumed her careful downward path.

They encountered another two clusters of victims' bones, neither as numerous as the first. But their progress through those areas prompted further eruptions of formless, misty guardians and some were beginning to resemble the Daemonkind, having a vaguely similar outline and protrusions that were almost wing-like. But they were still blind to the three intruders who continued their descent while pale shapes danced and whirled in the air above.

They were passing through the third scattering of dusty cadavers when Keren realised that she could at last make out the foot of the long stairway. Somewhere down there was the Staff of the Void, and assuming they were able to locate it and seize it without difficulty, there was still the question of returning to the surface. *Perhaps the Staff could be used as a weapon in these circumstances*, she thought, hope rising in her.

But hope was dashed when a faint crunch came from across the steps, followed by the sharp rattle of bones. Rakrotherangisal was rising from where one of the ancient steps had crumbled under his weight, sending his foot slipping down to kick one of the desiccated corpses. It had burst apart in a cloud of dust and clattering bones towards which the pale guardians were now swooping. Petrified with fear, Keren could only watch as some began surrounding Rakrotherangisal, nudging him or trying to envelop him even though he was still veiled in the concealing glamour. Then he raised his staff, its crystal aglow, and struck out at them.

A high-pitched moan of alert anticipation went through the scores of guardians as they gathered around the young Daemonkind. Then Orgraaleshenoth turned to Keren and she heard in her thoughts just the one word:

Run.

In the next moment he had cast off his own cloaking glamour. All around him the misty guardians were taking on Daemonkind forms, and Keren saw him raise his blazing staff on high before she turned and fled down the steps. Moments later, a great flash of light from behind sent her own shadow flickering ahead of her but then it was gone as a mass of voices roared with pain and anger. The terrible cacophony reverberated up and down the shaft but Keren still hurried downwards, careful of her footing, determined not to pause or look back.

The cold air chilled her chest, and her legs and feet were aching and trembling when she reached the bottom. There were still sounds of fighting far above her, diminished by distance, but before her now was a huge, gloomy hall of pillars whose floor was the sole source of light, a meagre grey radiance like corroded silver. Not knowing what perils lurked here, she stole through the vast hall, flitting from column to column beneath impenetrable shadows.

The Staff of the Void sat upon a waist-high pillar of light atop a wide dais that lay at the focus of the great chamber. Curved, shallow steps led up to it and as she reached the uppermost of them, the sound of beating wings made her whirl, sword at the ready. Then she relaxed a little on seeing that it was Orgraaleshenoth who was carrying the bloody form of Rakrotherangisal in his arms.

The Daemonkind staggered when he landed near Keren, and fell to his knees as he made to place his companion on the steps. Keren rushed over and immediately saw the ghastly nature of Rakratherangisal's wounds, gashes welling with black blood, gouges exposing bones and organs.

'My death is upon me, Prince Orgraaleshenoth,' the younger Daemonkind said. 'Have we triumphed or failed?'

'You have done more for the Israganthir this day, brother,' Orgraaleshenoth said, 'than centuries of service to the Grey Lord.' He turned to Keren. 'Get me the Staff – quickly!'

She jumped to her feet, dashed up to the white pillar and lifted the Staff of the Void. Warm to the touch, it looked to be made of translucent marble shot through with blue veins, and was heeled with silver and gold bands while its head was a simple orb of some dull black stone. Swiftly she returned to Orgraaleshenoth with the Staff held out . . . But it was too late.

Orgraaleshenoth's great hulking form was still as he bowed his head. Keren then began to notice that he too was badly wounded but could say nothing.

'Enemies draw near,' the Daemonkind said. 'We cannot stay here.'

Even as he spoke, she heard sounds of battle coming from the far end of the hall.

'Is it the guardians?' she said. 'But who are they fighting?'

Then she knew.

'The Theocracy,' she said, suddenly filled with grief and despair. 'How can we get out? We're trapped . . .'

The Daemonkind took the Staff of the Void from her unresisting hands.

'There is one place we can escape to,' he said. 'But I am weak from combat, so I hope that this talisman will be of use to me . . .'

In his great taloned hands the Staff looked small and fragile, then a moment later soft glints of light seemed to swim through its marbled opacity. As Keren watched this transformation, she thought over what he had said and made a sudden, intuitive leap.

'You mean to flee back to the Daemonkind domain,' she said. 'The Realm of Ruin.'

'That is so,' Orgraaleshenoth said evenly. 'I would advise you to accompany me, given the situation.'

Shouts and bellowing came from the far end as the fighting finally spilled out of the Processional and into the hall, scores of red-cloaked, gold-masked warriors and several screeching nighthunters, all skirmishing with pale images of themselves.

'I would have to become Daemonkind,' she said, mouth suddenly dry. 'Wouldn't I?'

'To survive there, yes. It would not be permanent, however,' he said. 'You would be Daemon*like*, not Daemon*kind*.'

One of the nighthunters had destroyed its attackers and, with several figures clinging to its back, was now flying across the hall, heading straight for the dais. Keren stared at the glowing motes swirling in the Staff of the Void, then tightly clenched her fists.

'Do it,' she said.

A rushing brightness bloomed from the Staff and engulfed them both, like great hands of light lifting them up, hands that she felt beginning to change her.

Chapter Twenty-six

I have seen the Shadow raise cruel
legions from the earth. I have seen stars die
and standards burn in the withering night.
And I have seen a black dream give birth to
a ruined world . . .

Wujad's Vision, stanza 19

At a point nearly two thirds of the way along the Great Aisle, a man
stood waiting. He was tall and well-built and wore a long black robe,
open down the front over rich, dark green clothing. The robe was
sleeveless, showing off his muscular arms while his black bearded
features and calm, impassive eyes looked around him.

Here, the Great Aisle was a little narrower than it was further
south. The high, wide-curving wall was the same, unchanging
Wellsource-derived barrier, its shifting, grey-green-blueness casting
a dull gleam, as if the restless depths of an ocean were surging beyond
it rather than the earth and stone bones of the continent. It was cold
in the tunnel, and getting colder as the man who had once been
Nerek and Ystregul stood waiting.

Tiny glowing points emerged from the gloom far to the north
along the Great Aisle, the light of lamps that drew steadily nearer.
Before long, a column of cantering riders came into view, a
dozen mounts wide and stretching away back into the shadowy
distance. Lantern bearers flanked the column while a cluster of
heavily-robed men rode before it, some carrying silky, fluttering
bannerets. Those in the lead saw the lone man up ahead, standing

in the middle of the Aisle, arms at his sides as he calmly watched them approach.

When it became apparent that the man had no intention of removing himself to the side, hands went up and the order to halt echoed all the way back along the Aisle. In a great din of thudding hoofs, cries and rattling harnesses, the column came to a stop about a dozen paces short of the waiting man. One of the robed men came forth on a spirited horse, his narrow, elegant face contorted with fury.

'Out of the way, wretch! You are delaying the march of the great and mighty Shadowking Thraelor . . .'

The man who had once been Nerek and Ystregul gazed past the robed rider to his companions and saw that they, too, had the same face. He smiled wryly at this, which enraged the robed rider still further.

'Do you seek to mock us?' he bellowed. 'In my master's name, I swear I'll have your head . . .'

As he drew a sword from a saddle sheath, the other swung back at him with a hard, black look. In the next instant he was flying backwards off his horse, landing awkwardly on one shoulder. There was a commotion among his companions, all of whose free hands came alight with emerald flames of power. But before any retaliation could take place, their close grouping parted to allow another rider to come out. It was Thraelor himself.

'Hah, just one man, eh?' he said in a hoarse voice. 'If you're another of those assassins, know that I dealt with one of you before leaving Casall and my brother, Grazaan, is torturing another this day . . .' Thraelor, gaunt and skull-faced, peered at the silent man. 'Hmm, you don't look like one of them – have you anything to say for yourself, before we ride on over your carcass?'

A look passed between them and Thraelor's eyes widened.

'What kind of power are you?' he said sharply. 'One of those dog-mages, I'll wager, with some kind of relic in your pocket.' He turned to his robed followers. 'Destroy this upstart for me!'

Green flame-wreathed hands came up, brightening, but when the lone man made a casual, sweeping gesture their powers went out like snuffed candles. Then life drained from their faces and they toppled out of their saddles to lie dead on the floor of the Great Aisle. Then the man made a wider, more violent sweep of his arm and a force like the gust of a hundred storms roared along the tunnel. Horses were thrown onto their sides, riders were snatched from their saddles and hurled back over the heads of the others while masks, saddlebags, flags and garments were blown still further back. For seventy yards or more north along the Great Aisle, all was a heaving mass of havoc, panicking screaming horses and riders desperately trying to bring them under control.

Through all of it Thraelor had remained untouched, sitting immobile on his horse. His face was slack and dull-eyed, but another lay over it like a translucent mask, spectral and crimson. As the man who had been Nerek and Ystregul approached, the masked Thaelor climbed down from his horse.

'At last,' the crimson mask said. 'This one has fought me every step of the way, and I would be rid of him for good.'

'Then let us join,' said the other. 'Greatness awaits.'

Garments dissolved into ashy veils and features yielded and stretched as the two forms flowed together slowly. It took only moments for the coalescence to run its course and when it was over only one figure stood in the middle of the Great Aisle. He was noticeably taller than before, and was differently, more austerely garbed in a collarless, sleeveless robe of dull purple over plain black shirt and trews with open-toed sandals on his feet.

Some of the riders in the leading ranks had seen the transformation, and a few of their serjeants came to kneel before him in their awe and fear.

'My lord,' said one, swallowing hard behind his black leather mask. 'Is our master . . . dead?'

'No, for he is with me and part of me now.'

The serjeants glanced at one another for a second.

'Then our loyalty is to you, great one,' the spokesman went on. 'What name shall we know you by?'

'In time I shall take back my true name, but for now you may call me Shadowlord, nothing more.'

'What are your commands, O Shadowlord?'

'We shall ride north to Rauthaz,' the Shadowlord said, 'and pay my brother Grazaan a visit.'

'A noble spirit he was, once,' Alael said in the voice that made Gilly's skin crawl. 'But he let envy into his heart and became an enemy of life, a dark destroyer. Soon shall his long campaign of evil be brought to an end, when I take my vengeance . . .' There was a pause, and she drew a shuddering breath before speaking in her own voice. 'Oh, leave me alone, I beg you . . .'

As she wept quietly in the shadow of the draped storeroom, where they had taken temporary refuge, Gilly shook his head and tried to take stock of their situation.

Despite having overheard Alael's location in the meeting hall, it had taken him some time to locate the room then find his way in. Ever since parting company with Ikarno Mazaret, he had noticed a growing confusion taking hold throughout the citadel of Keshada, shouts, troops running hither and yon. Soldiers hurrying past his hiding places muttered rumours of a clash between the pale lords, running battles on the stairs and a distant army approaching from Besh-Darok. Indeed, he had to take a different route to avoid a bloody skirmish on the fourth floor.

Alael was held in a large chamber on the fifth floor, its doors watched by six guards. But Gilly had found a way in from the next room, through a cramped wooden screen high on the adjoining wall. Once inside, however, he had been aghast to find Alael lying full-length on the floor, her form cloaked in a tenuous golden nimbus, her eyes wide and sightless. Yet somehow he had managed to carry her up a stack of furniture to the high opening and through to the other room. There, the aura faded a little and she seemed to regain awareness sufficient to walk with Gilly's help, so he led her on to the next chamber by a short connecting passage. They had just emerged in what seemed to be a dining room when the golden aura brightened about her and she began speaking in a voice which felt like several voices in perfect unison. Yet there was no attempt to communicate with him, rather the words seemed part of a strange monologue, like ceaseless broodings over past wrongs

and anticipated retributions. The very sound of it made the hairs
on his neck rise.

Then the aura and the voice had faded and Alael, recognising
Gilly, had wept to see him. And Gilly likewise felt the sting of
tears and memory for, during his quest through the citadel, he had
been unexpectedly waylaid by a wave of knowledge which had
burst into the empty grooves of his mind, filling many gaps. He
knew who Alael and Ikarano Mazaret and Suviel were, but when
Alael mentioned the name Tauric it meant nothing to him.

Now, huddled in a storeroom across the corridor from the dining
chamber, he listened to Alael's explanation.

'It's the Earthmother,' she said tearfully. 'She wants to use
me, dominate me completely, so that she can attack the Lord
of Twilight.'

'But he is divided among the five Shadowkings,' Gilly said,
remembering what Suviel had told him.

'He was, but the part that was in Byrnak has escaped into another
host and has already joined with another two of the god's fragments.'
Alael closed her eyes tightly for a moment, then opened them to
show her fear.

'What can we do to stop the Lord of Twilight becoming whole?
I've been fighting the Earthmother with all my strength, but could
she be right? Should I just give in to her?'

Gilly got to his feet in the darkened storeroom then helped her
to stand.

'I don't know what the answer is,' he said. 'But Suviel may.
I overheard some of the masks here saying that an army from
Besh-Darok is heading for Keshada. Suviel said she was going to
return with help, and she said that we were to find you and wait
for her by the entrance to the Realm of Dusk . . .'

'But that's . . .' she said.

'The Lord of Twilight's domain,' he said. 'But that was what she
said, to go to the seventh floor where there are several doorways
to that place and hide nearby . . .' He laughed softly. 'Although I
cannot say where Mazaret has got to.'

With every step a stealthy tread, Gilly led her from the dining
chamber and along to a stairwell he had happened across earlier. Its

stairs spiralled around a massive stone pillar covered in niches and alcoves of every size and in each one stood a male figurine or statue. While the central pillar was constructed of a dusky, ochre stone, the statues were of a dark grey stone, well-polished to highlight the details of garments, features and motion. For each statue performed some small action in a repeating cycle, sharpening a sword, lighting a fire, pulling on armoured gauntlets, writing on a sheet of parchment, braiding a rope. There was even one that grinned while tossing and catching a spinning coin, over and over again. Gilly was not sure if they were all supposed to represent the Lord of Twilight, but something about them gave him a chill and he hurried Alael up to the next floor.

There, the corridors seemed deserted and finding stairs to the seventh floor was a straightforward matter. As they climbed, shouts and the crash of weapons came up from a few levels down, but whether this was from the masked soldiers resisting an incursion or fighting among themselves, he could not tell.

The doorways were where Suviel said they would be, in the outer wall. Gilly stood with Alael on the threshold of one, staring out at the strange, rocky waste, which lay perhaps five or six yards below, knowing that other windows on this floor looked across miles of snowbound fields from a far greater height.

'This is the place,' Gilly muttered.

'But how do we get down?' said Alael.

He shrugged, then stepped out on to the wide ledge that ran along the outside, spotted the battlement of a large, square keep round to the left and ducked back inside.

'What is it?' Alael said.

'Some kind of fortification next to the wall further round,' he said. 'I saw guards on its ramparts, so we can't go that way . . .'

'Perhaps there are stairs along the other way,' she said, dashing off along the corridor inside.

Shaking his head, Gilly went after her. *Strong-headed women or implacable goddesses,* he thought. *Is there that much difference?*

Ahead of him, Alael stepped through one of the tall openings, back out to the ledge, and was gone from sight. Gilly sighed and called out to her.

'Alael, this is a dangerous place – come back and wait . . .'

There was no response so he hurried through the nearest opening and saw her descending a wide ramp which led down the outside of the wall. Annoyed, he ran after her, catching up as she reached the foot of the ramp, and put out a hand to her shoulder, only noticing the faint golden nimbus in the last instant. She turned with hot amber eyes and made a back-handed strike at his face, not seeming to put any effort into the movement.

It was like being hit by a sack of vegetables swung by a fairground strongman. Pain lanced through his jaw and head as he was knocked flying to land on his back on a mound of pebbly sand. Gasping, head spinning, he struggled to sit up, probed his tender, throbbing jaw and blinked hard. Alael was now some yards away, heading into a dusty gully which, further down, looked dim and shadowy. Spitting out grit, he got achingly to his feet and glanced over his shoulder at the keep. It looked small and shabby next to the smooth, towering perfection of Keshada, but there was no sign of activity.

'Well, Suviel,' he muttered. 'You said naught about the possibility of the girl being possessed by the Earthmother, but I'm sure that if I lose her I'll *never* hear the end of it, eh?'

He chuckled to himself, tore off the black mask he had been wearing for hours, loosened his blade in its scabbard, and set off down the gully.

Byrnak rode through the ravaged fields of ice and snow with a host that was not his own at his back, with a scouring, inner emptiness, his thoughts clouded by fear. Ahead, the long dark walls and the tall gates of Keshada loomed ever nearer, bringing the need for subterfuge and his ability to bluff their way inside.

No, it's not bluffing, he told himself. *I am still Byrnak, and they will know my face . . .*

Hooded riders rode either side of him and the one on his right edged a little closer before raising the cowl to look straight at him. As he met Suviel Hantika's gaze, he could feel the enmity of Bardow's eyes boring into him from the other side.

'You know what you have to do?' she said. Her lips moved in a mutter which somehow reached his ears perfectly. Her voice, which had come to him in the cell where he had lain with his mind torn by shrieking tongues of pain; that voice, which had whispered soft, sorcerous syllables to block out the torment, then offered him a bargain which would safeguard that barrier.

He nodded. 'Get the turnkeys to open the gates, enter with Yasgur and his warriors, order the officers inside to confine their men to quarters . . .'

'And think of no other purpose, Byrnak,' came Bardow's mistrusting voice. 'No deviations and no deceit, and your thoughts will remained untroubled.'

'You must convince the men at the gate,' Suviel Hantika went on. 'You must play the part.'

'I know,' he said. 'I shall.'

Onward they rode and all too soon the dark, fluted immensity of the wall was blocking out all else. The ramparts, however, seemed deserted – a few grey banners and flags fluttered and a dusting of snow flew off the battlements in the chill breeze. Even when they reached the gates themselves, the air of abandonment was undiminished – high, sheltered balconies that should have been crowded with bowmen were empty while other armoured shutters hung open and unmanned.

When Byrnak and the two mages led the way into the low walled courtyard set out before the gates, a voice did at last ring out from one of the flanking towers.

'Who dares to approach the citadel Keshada?'

Byrnak glanced at the mage Hantika who gave a cowled nod of the head, then he urged his horse on ahead as the host slowed behind him. He clenched his reins tightly as he rode up to the high tower, then forced a sneer on to his features as he looked up.

'Do you have eyes in your head, fool? Can you not see who I am?'

There was some whispering for a moment, then:

'Lord, it was said that you fell in the city palace—'

'Wrong, fool – I have returned after securing my victory with those who stayed loyal in the forge of battle. Open these gates and I shall permit you to join them . . .'

'O great one, the pale lords told us to keep the gates shut fast—'

'Shall I make an example of you then, fool? Perhaps turn you into something fit only to be fed to the eaterbeasts . . . Or I might spare myself the effort and feed you to them as your are, since your brains are clearly naught but *offal*!'

'I hear and obey, Great Lord!'

He relaxed in his saddle, feeling himself tremble with the effort of playing the part that had once felt so real.

But was it ever real? he wondered. *Were we five hosts ever anything more than rivenshades animated by an ancient purpose . . .*

Muffled clanks from within the towers disturbed his brooding. As the host of Mogaun riders and the smaller column of knights (garbed in black masks and cloaks) drew near, the sounds of chains and turning ratchets came forth and the huge, iron gates of Keshada began to open inwards. As the phalanx of horsemen approached the gaping entrance, he noticed Yasgur riding beside the mage Hantika, head inclined towards her and talking quickly. But she shook her head and the Mogaun chieftain slipped back to be with Welgarak and Gordag. All three watched him with unforgiving eyes as he resumed his station between the cowled mages. The main gates were now fully open and the inner 'cullis gate was rising.

'And now?' he asked.

'And now we enter,' Suviel Hantika said. 'Remember – order all officers to confine their men to quarters. We have to reach the Realm of Dusk as soon as possible, so there must be no delays.'

He nodded wordlessly and stared off into the waiting gloom of the entrance. When that fragment of the Lord of Twilight had uprooted itself from his being to invade Nerek, it had also torn out every last shred of his affinity with the Wellsource. Sitting close, here at the threshold of Keshada, it was as if he had become a ghost to this vast temple of power.

And since the mages had refused him any kind of blade he was for the first time, truly, utterly defenceless.

'Time is not our ally, Byrnak,' muttered the mage Hantika. 'Lead the way.'

Gritting his teeth he urged his horse forward.

Suviel kept a close eye on Byrnak as she rode beside him through the gates of Keshada. Her undersenses told her that there were only a handful of soldiers in the gate towers, now hiding rather than risking what they imagined to be Byrnak's ire. Ahead, the high, dark entranceway became a wide ramp leading up into a huge, inner courtyard and she knew that it was empty. Only when they rode up from the ramp did she realise that it was only empty of the living. The dead were there, in abundance.

Black-clad bodies were scattered everywhere, hundreds upon hundreds of still forms lying in the contorted positions of death agony. An orgy of violence had been played out across the vast chamber, and blood drenched the flagstones and walls. A long platform jutted out into the courtyard from a semicircular walkway, and at its end some kind of last stand had been made, with bodies gathered in mounds.

The host rode slowly through the slaughter in horrified silence. Suviel thought at one point that she could no longer stomach the stench of blood and death but she mastered herself and rode on without pause. As she passed the dead soldiers she noticed that some had a torn-off strip of green cloth tied about the upper arm, and began to realise that the majority of the corpses wore no such badge. Thus it seemed likely that a green-badged force of mask soldiers had ambushed and massacred another faction, then had gone off to hunt through the rest of the citadel above them.

And as she rode she saw no bare heads among the slain, no unmasked faces that might belong to Ikarno or Gilly.

Where are you both in all of this? she wondered.

Byrnak seemed strangely composed amid this carnage, his bearded features bearing little more than faint puzzlement. Suviel recalled Yasgur's vigorous suggestion that the former warlord be bound hand and foot before they entered Keshada, in case he galloped away to rejoin his troops. She wondered what the Lord Regent was thinking now.

A wide ramp which curved up to the semicircular walkway had to be cleared of bodies before the small army of Mogaun and Besh-Darok knights could ride up to a wide, plain doorway. Suviel rode by Byrnak into a high, curved hall where hanging lamps sent amber light down among the shadows of pillars. There were still more bodies strewn on the floor, puddled with dark, viscid blood. The more she saw, the more she realised that a full-scale battle had taken place here. As the clearance teams got to work again, she looked at Byrnak.

'What could have caused such slaughter?' she asked.

'I know not,' he said darkly. 'Without soul-bound officers to guide them, they may have decided upon new loyalties . . .'

A moment later Byrnak led the way towards a tall archway which spanned the distance between two pillars, wide enough for two wagons or five riders travelling abreast. But what caught Suviel's attention was the glittering haze that swirled against the blue-blackness of the opening.

'Wait,' she said to Byrnak. 'Where does this lead to?'

'The drill yards on the third floor,' he said with a glare. 'From there, a smaller traversing door will take us to the seventh.'

'Perhaps we should send some scouts through first,' Bardow suggested.

'As you wish,' said Byrnak, shrugging.

A handful of Yasgur's men were sent through on foot, returning a short while later to report similar scenes of slaughter and no living in sight. Reassured, Suviel glanced at Bardow, nodded to Yasgur and his fellow chieftains, then gestured Byrnak to continue.

Passing through the archway's glittering darkness was like stepping through a thin veil of icy spiderwebs which caressed her face and hands. On the other side, it was brighter due to the plentiful lamps hanging from the numerous circular vaults which partitioned the great ceiling. Again, death's silent multitude were in attendance, sprawled in blood-spattered blade pits, slumped on target ranges with feathered shafts sprouting from chests, necks, heads, or lying in gory heaps, some hands still clutching practice weapons. All part of the same story of murderous conflict.

And still Suviel stared at all those within view, searching, searching, hoping not to see Ikarno's face. At first she had imagined that she would somehow know if he came to harm, but the streams of Wellsource power that poured through Keshada were blinding her to him. Even with the Crystal Eye's enhancement of her abilities with the Lesser Power, the Wellsource was ultimately the stronger.

She could only hope and pray that the Fathertree spirit had been right to insist that she bring the Eye and Motherseed with them.

When all the talismans are used together, it had told her, *even gods walk in fear.*

Riding on Byrnak's left, she went on surveying the faces of the dead while staying alert to the slightest perception or impression of Ikarno or Gilly from the outermost fringes of her undersenses.

A raised, columned walkway passed around the drill yards and following it they soon came to another glittering door, a smaller one wide enough for only two horses. Once again, scouts were sent through, and came back with tales of deserted passages and rooms full of butchery.

Suviel passed through with Bardow and Yarram, the Lord Commander of the Fathertree knights, closely followed by the knights of the order who had survived the battle at Besh-Darok. The doorway from which they emerged lay at a T-junction of three tall, wide corridors well lit by oil lamp cressets set into the walls. Some swift questioning of Byrnak revealed that they were on the other side of this floor from the gateways to the Lord of Twilight's realm. The leg of the T-junction lead inwards to a hub gallery encircling a stairwell: from the gallery, another corridor ran straight to the outer wall of Keshada and the waiting gates.

'I don't like it, m'lady,' said Yarram. 'I should like to spread out from here and secure every corridor on this floor before moving forward . . .'

'I understand your caution,' Suviel said. 'But we do not have the time to spare for such an approach, nor is there room in these corridors for our thousands of riders.'

'Then we will have to scout ahead in strength,' said Yasgur. 'And at speed – let me send riders of my men along the passages nearest our route even as the rest of our army is coming through and moving towards our destination.'

Suviel could think of no other swifter, more effective tactic so with Bardow's nod and Yarram's reluctant consent, she agreed to Yasgur's proposal. As it transpired, Yarram's fear of room and corner fighting was unnecessary since this level seemed as deathly and forsaken as the rest of the citadel. Suviel was at the front when the spearhead of riders, mostly heavily armoured knights, emerged from the radial corridor into the wide, spacious gallery that was the outermost passage. Its inner wall was an expanse of polished, fine grey marble into which a line of shoulder-high niches had been carved, each holding a metallic head muttering in some lost tongue. The outer wall, in blocks of rough-hewn, rust-brown stone, was broken by smooth-edged triangular openings which afforded a generous view of the Realm of Dusk.

With Yasgur's scouts visible further along the gallery and the rest of the army filing out of the corridor, Suviel dismounted and walked over to one of the triangular openings. Pausing on its threshold she stared out at the seared, rocky desert then left at the dust-hazed jumble of ramshackle fortifications, then right along the wide shelf which remained deserted along all of it that she could see. But of Gilly and Alael and Ikarno there was no sign, and her heart sank.

Had Gilly and Ikarno failed to find her and keep her safe, and perhaps turned their efforts towards fostering dissension among the rivenshades? That might explain the slaughterous scenes elsewhere in the citadel, but where were they? And where was Alael? If the Earthmother had taken full possession of her, she could be out there in the Lord of Twilight's realm this very moment in which case time was growing perilously short . . .

She was about to turn back to her horse and the milling crowds of riders when, through her undersenses, she felt another's presence nearby, beyond the shelf. She knew that there was a wide ramp there and as she stepped forward the full length of it came into view, as did a pale-haired, dark-cloaked figure who sat near the bottom. A few steps down the ramp and the man's profile and features became clear and familiar. Suviel smiled and almost laughed with a weak relief. The white hair, pale skin and grey eyes were all just as she had left him. Then he glanced round, smiled bleakly and nodded.

'Ah, Suviel, Suviel,' he said in a low, silky voice. 'How I've longed for this moment. Your face has haunted all my days and hours, even when I was out there in the desert, hunting down his men, one by one.'

He stood smoothly and easily and turned to stare up at her. When

she looked into his eyes she know with sudden, dark certainty that
it was not him.

'You can tell, can't you?' the rivenshade said, drawing out a
bright, slender sword as he started up the ramp. 'You *know* that
I am only his image, a reflection plucked from the mirror. Well,
who is to say that the image cannot be superior to the original?'

The smile grew voracious. 'After all, I killed him. Oh, he was
cunning, I'll grant you – the way he pitted us all against each other
showed an admirable capacity for duplicity and trickery. But in the
end it was me that cut him down with this very blade, then I left
him to bleed his life out into the sand and returned here . . .'

Suviel began to back away, up the slope, preparing in her mind a
thought-canto to dazzle the rivenshade, hoping that the surrounding
Wellsource ambience did not disrupt it. Then a hand snaked up over
the edge of the ramp, grabbed the rivenshade's ankle and yanked
it sideways. As he went down in a tangle of cloak and arms, a
lithe, brown-clad figure leaped up on to the ramp and dived on
him. A hand bearing a straight broadsword rose and fell once, and
the rivenshade cried out, convulsed violently for a moment, then
was still.

The brown-clad figure rose to stand over the corpse. Suviel felt
a jolt of fear and dread when she found she was looking into the
tear-stained features of . . . herself.

'I wanted to see you,' her rivenshade said, voice shaking. 'I had
to know why he could love you but not me – but now he can't
love either of us, since this dreg killed him. I saw it happen and
I picked up his sword afterwards.' She bent down and lifted the
sword that Suviel had inscribed with the Void sign for Ikarno. At
her feet, the rivenshade's body was dissolving into a dense, white
vapour which was pouring down the ramp in a slow, pale tide. 'I
knew he was dying. I saw such a lot of blood—'

'Takes more than a cut like that to kill me off,' came a hoarse
voice that made Suviel's heart leap.

Up from a hollow beyond the ramp a tall, pale figure in a flowing
grey robe came half-staggering into view, leaning on a broken spear.
Both women watched his slow, painful approach until he reached
the foot of the ramp where his legs failed him and he fell to his

knees. Suviel cried out and dashed past the rivenshade, running to crouch by his side.

'Though in truth I can feel my death upon me,' Mazaret gasped.

'No, I won't let death have you,' she said doggedly, tugging at his robe where one of his hands clasped a blood-dark wad of cloth to his side.

'It is you,' he said wonderingly. 'After all the grief, after seeing all those shadows of you . . . and at last, you're here. My beloved.'

Then he breathed in sharply and she saw the pain in his eyes. Without further pause she closed her eyes and focused on her attunement to the Crystal Eye, driven by love and desperation, calling on its strength, its powers and its enfolded knowledge. She delved down into the flow of his body, the flux and reflux of blood and sensation, and followed the waves of pain back to their source, a cruel sword puncture which passed through two lower ribs on the right and out the back. Suviel forced severed channels and nerves to rejoin, muscles to reknit, sealed the gashed walls of viscera, while numbing the hot, twisting pain.

Hesitant footsteps approached, and almost simultaneously came the creaking whisper of many bows being drawn taut.

'Hold, lady,' said Yasgur's voice. 'Throw down the sword and come back up the ramp . . .'

Suviel cracked open her eyes to see the rivenshade of herself standing a few feet away, silent tears running down her face, the inscribed sword blade held up in one hand. Behind her at the top of the ramp, and clustered along the shelf above, were dozens of Mogaun archers with readied bows trained on her.

'There is no path through this realm that I could walk,' she said. 'The Lord of this place is coming and I will not be an instrument for him to use.' So saying, she raised her empty hand and made a slash across it with the sword, then took the sword in that hand in order to slash her other palm. Then calmly she sat at the foot of the ramp with her back to the wall of Keshada and closed her eyes.

Suviel looked on with a sense of foreboding as she considered these final words. When the rivenshade's form began to dissolve into that thick vapour, she noticed that Mazaret was watching with sadness in his eyes. She reached out to stroke the whiteness of his hair, and he looked at her, took her hand and kissed the palm of it. Above them the archers had relaxed, and the growing noise of horses and men spoke of a busy corridor.

'It seems that you've brought an army,' Mazaret said. 'And were those Mogaun tribesmen I saw?'

'The story,' she said, 'is longer and more complicated than a Dalbari family tree and can wait. More importantly, how do you feel?'

'The pain is gone,' he said.

'Good – there is much to do,' she said. 'We must find Alael . . .'

'One of the men – when some of the masks still thought I was a rivenshade – spotted a woman and a man heading out into the desert down that gully,' he said, pointing.

'How long ago was this?' Suviel said.

'Perhaps two or three hours.'

She groaned. Mazaret carefully got to his feet and helped her up.

'They won't have got very far on foot,' he said.

But Suviel shook her head. 'This is the Lord of Twilight's realm – distance and direction are not quite what we are used to.'

'Then the sooner we despatch some scouts, the better, eh?'

Smiling, she nodded. It was the only thing that could be done, as well as pray to the Void that she could get the Motherseed and the Crystal Eye to the Wellsource before any clash took place between the Earthmother and the Lord of Twilight. If she could achieve that, and if the spirit of the Fathertree somehow managed to have the Staff of the Void brought here by his mysterious allies, then the burden of the final clash would fall to her.

And in all likelihood, it would result in her obliteration, her unequivocal, irrevocable death.

The Shadowlord's attack on the Drumkeep at Rauthaz was executed with immaculate timing and ruthless brutality. At the northern end of the Great Aisle, a short distance before it ended at the mustering halls beneath the fortress, he opened a multitude of side-portals, each one leading to a point of defensive strength. The thousands of mask troops Thraelor had brought from Casall would, with speed and precisely reckoned tactics, be able to overwhelm a garrison almost four times their number.

When all his troops were in position, many on foot, many still mounted, the Shadowlord gave the order. For a few minutes the Great Aisle was filled with the din of numerous charges, then the portals closed behind them, leaving him standing alone in the silent, slivered gloom. For a moment he stood motionless and smiling, ever smiling, as if thinking pleasant thoughts, then he turned and began to walk towards Rauthaz.

But well before reaching the fortress's underhalls, he made a doorway appear and with a leisurely gait passed thorough it to emerge on the snowy battlements of the curtainwall surrounding the Drumkeep. Fighting was going on down in one of the high walled inner yards while a riot tore through the city and smoke rose from pillaged warehouses. The Shadowlord brought another door into being and walked elsewhere.

A high roof retreat set above and back from the Keep's forge, a square paved area where devices of gears and wire sat upon ironwork tripods, pointing to the sky.

A walkway across an eaterbeast breeding pit, where the tinemasters fled at the sight of him and the beasts raised their snouts to wail in devotion as he passed.

A long corridor of polished black carvings, statues, reliefs, with frail hanging lamps spreading golden light everywhere. Every surface was crowded with gleaming, ebony forms, and one corner sported a tall ornate mirror. As the Shadowlord paused to gaze into it, the reflection changed to show an armoured figure sitting in a huge grandiose throne whose back merged with a wall that looked like an expanse of faces frozen in black ice. The entire scene was plunged in ashen blue light, and the Shadowlord gave a nod of approval before turning the corner and walking on.

The Shadowking Grazaan was standing in a wide doorway in the wall, where the tiled floor of the corridor changed into the seared brown sand and rock of the Realm of Dusk. Further along, the wall with its exquisite decorations was fading and retreating as the Realm asserted its supremacy.

Grazaan stood facing outward but a ghostly red face watched and grinned from the back of his head as the Shadowlord approached.

'I am casting an illusion into his mind,' said the face. 'He believes that he is running towards the Wellsource to use it against you.'

'Foolish,' said the Shadowlord who seized Grazaan and swallowed him whole, his face and jaw enormously distended to accommodate the physical form. Again, the blurring of forms, the striving for assimilation, amalgamation and eventually, union. Clad in blood-red armour covered with green, staring eyes, the Shadowlord rose and gazed out at the Realm of Dusk.

'Kodel,' he said. 'But first, our guests.'

Chapter Twenty-seven

What dread voice now calls forth,
To stir the seas to howling,
And plunge the world,
Into the deepest gloom.
What awful whisper!
What dire curse!

Calabos, *Beneath the Towers*, Act 3, iii, 35

The gully that led away from Keshada proved to be just one of several ravines and arid watercourses which criss-crossed each other for a mile or more before coming to a line of low hills. A handful of experienced Mogaun trackers had picked up the signs and traces of Gilly and Alael's trail which had headed straight for the hills before turning sharply right along a winding gorge. The Besh-Darok army, however, had now come to a halt at the mouth of the gorge while, on a ridge overlooking it, a small party were making last adjustments to their mounts and saying farewells.

From where he sat on his horse up on the ridge, Mazaret was able to survey a great swathe of this god's domain. The slope-sided gorge meandered through sandy rock striated in shades of rust and ochre, while to his left the low, broken-backed hills were worn leaden teeth beyond which lay a flat, ash-white plain. At its centre sat the truncated, shattered and jagged remains of a great peak, Hewn Mountain, at whose heart was the Wellsource. That, he knew dolefully, was where Suviel was going with the Crystal Eye and the Motherseed to carry out a task that would very likely kill her.

That was not how she depicted it but he could tell from her unwavering calm and iron resolve that she had come to terms with her own mortality and was ready for death. For Mazaret, though, it was almost unbearable to think that they had faced such unimaginable torments of body and spirit, only to reach this most bittersweet parting of the ways.

Suviel was tending to her horse and packhorse while Bardow tried fruitlessly to talk her out of it. As he made his case, she glanced over at Mazaret and their eyes met for a moment of painful longing then broke away. Mazaret forced his thoughts along less sorrowful paths by considering the travelling companions she had asked to go with her.

Atroc seemed to have become more wizened since Mazaret last saw him, his gaze darker, more sardonic. He could understand why Suviel might consider him a worthy ally, given his status as Yasgur's seer and his perception of the mysteries, but her other choice left him baffled and uneasy.

Byrnak sat upon his horse, a black-cloaked, bear-like figure hunched over his ornate high-fronted saddle, frowning as he stared out across the leaden hills to the splintered crags of Hewn Mountain. Mazaret had heard from Yasgur how Byrnak had created his massed armies of mask soldiers by first using Mogaun tribesmen as hosts for the resurrected spirits of old, then drawing on the menfolk of towns and villages throughout the north. This went some way towards explaining why the Mogaun Host had switched sides before the siege of Besh-Darok. There was also no doubting the cold hatred in the eyes of Welgarak and Gordag whenever they regarded the once-Shadowking. Atroc, on the other hand, now looked on him with a kind of grim affection, and had told Mazaret how Byrnak lost his fragment of the Lord of Twilight before relating his first-hand account of Tauric's death.

All in all, these accounts of the siege of Besh-Darok and its attendant tragedies left him with a burgeoning need for battle, despite the quivering ache he still felt in his side.

As Mazaret sat there studying him, Byrnak straightened in his saddle and glanced round at Suviel. But when he caught Mazaret watching him, he quickly looked away, fear in his eyes. Mazaret was jolted with surprise at this, then stirred by a rising anger but before he could urge his horse forward a soft touch on his arm made him turn. It was Suviel, her gaze full of warmth, humour and love. Mood softening, he dismounted and embraced her.

'Worry not about Byrnak,' she murmured in his ear. 'There is no danger left in him.'

'Yet I've seen fear in his eyes.'

'Everyone here is fearful, beloved.'

'Fear is the seed of hate,' he said, then relented, seeing that she was unyielding. 'Then why take him with you?'

'To act,' she said. 'To bluff. There is no telling who might be waiting at the Hewn Mountain, guarding the Wellsource, and if Byrnak could persuade them that he is still what he was, even for a short while, that may be all the advantage that we need.'

Arms about each other's waist and heedless of anyone else's regard, they walked a short distance along the ridge.

'The thought of you facing such dangers,' Mazaret said, as if about to say more. But he found it hard to express the combination of anger and powerlessness which held his thoughts in a deadly grasp. Suviel smiled sadly and nodded.

'When we're guiding our horses through those sombre hills, I'll be thinking the same of you,' she said. 'Pursuing the Earthmother through this realm of evil, fighting off whatever horrors the Grey Lord sends against you . . . I fear what you will have to face.'

'Are we going to die, then, you and I?' he said, turning to face her.

'I do not know, but it seems likely.' Then she shrugged. 'Yet the future is unwritten and much may happen in the time that is left to us. We are not alone in this struggle.'

Mazaret knew she was speaking of the spirit of the Fathertree, and heard the weary hope in her voice. Moved by the wish to give her some token of his devotion, he reached inside his mailed jerkin and took out the small ivory book leaf that he had found in Khatris months before. After Suviel had released Gilly and himself from the Acolyte's dungeon, he had rediscovered it in an inner pocket without realising its meaning. But as the rivenshades of himself were slain one by one, pieces of his memory returned and revealed what

had been lost. She seemed puzzled when he gave it to her but as
she read the inscription in a low voice between the two of them,
she smiled.

> 'Oft times in dreams, my love,
> It seems that you lie beside me.
> Yet with the waking day,
> My soul's desire becomes but a dream
> And it seems that the day will never end.'

There were tears in her eyes as she carefully put the ivory leaf away
in one of her cloak's pockets. Then she took both his hands in hers
and kissed them.

'One moment by your side, beloved, is timeless,' she said. 'You
will always be with me.'

'And you with me.'

They embraced one last time before Suviel broke away and
hurried over to her waiting horse. Minutes later, three mounted
figures and a packhorse were riding slowly down the ridge's scree
slope towards a grey, rocky vale which curved away in the hills.
As Mazaret watched them go, Bardow came over, leading his own
mount by its reins.

'This is a risky affair, old friend,' he said. 'She has the two talismans
with her, as well as the melded sword.'

'Will they help her to defend herself?' Mazaret said.

'Perhaps . . . Or they could make her more of a target.'

Mazaret nodded grimly.

'Then it is time we moved out,' he said, urging his steed round
to the downward path. Below, the host of Mogaun and Besh–Darok
riders waited in a long column that snaked back along the dusty
gully, with a few knots of scouts on the raised ground across from
the ridge.

Let us find the Lord of this place, he thought. *I'm sure we can do
something to get his attention!*

Gilly knew that this was a god's realm but when he followed the
possessed Alael around yet another rocky dune and saw that eerie

grey forest directly ahead, he at last began to believe it. From the moment they left Keshada, Alael had been striding along a perfectly straight course. For the last hour or more the forest of tall spindly trees had been some distance away on their left. Yet there it was, now spread right across Alael's path.

From which she was not deviating in the slightest.

Gilly toyed with the idea of trying to physically restrain her but only for the briefest moment — two previous attempts had ended with him tossed aside and nursing bruises.

What else can I do but stay on her trail? he thought. *And hope that Mazaret and Suviel catch up with us . . .*

Even from twenty yards behind, he could still see the golden nimbus that enfolded her and which grew brighter as she approached the fringe of the grey forest. But as he watched, she took a few steps inwards and was suddenly gone from sight. Alarmed, he rushed over to the spot where she had entered and even as he approached the spindly trees changed colour from silver-grey to darkening shades of green. Twigs and sprigs sprouted from roughening branches, bushes burst up out of the burgeoning ground, berries, buds and blooms swelled beneath lush arrays of leaves, and flowering vines wound up trunks and along boughs, dividing, spreading, entwining. It was an eruption of foliage which seemed to be confined to the vicinity of Alael's passage through the forest. Gilly stared at the dense greenery in amazement, then gathered his resolve and plunged in.

The forest rustled around him in slow writhings of its verdant profusion. The air was moist and heavy with odours of growth. Green shadows blurred the distance and added to the strangeness of these restless surroundings. Spurred by tense fears, his imagination provided the luxuriant, unfurling vegetation with eyes and ears and other features. Annoyed at himself, he tried to suppress such transient fancies yet even as he pushed past hanging loops of vine the combination of a dark berry and a few leaves in the gloom off to one side looked just like a face staring out at him . . .

Then the face became whole and startlingly familiar as a grey-cowled man stepped out of the foliage and lunged at him with an outstretched dagger. Gilly gasped and threw himself to one side, then backed off behind a few trees while drawing his sword.

Through the few branches he could see the hooded man straighten and stare back at him with his own face.

His attacker smiled, flipped the curved dagger and neatly caught it. 'The Lord of Twilight sends his greetings,' he said.

'And us,' came another voice from close by.

Instinctively, Gilly ducked and rolled, hearing something slash through the foliage where he had been standing a moment before. Again, the hasty retreat, desperately trying to get both his assailants in view, even as they came after him.

And there was another, identical to the first and thus to himself. He had been sceptical when Suviel told him of the sorcerous creatures called rivenshades, but here was the evidence.

'What a sad, feeble thing you are,' one of them said. 'Hard to believe that we are *copies* of you.'

'Mayhap we are better than him, brother,' said the other. 'Stronger, faster and deadlier, with all the weaknesses refined away. The Grey Lord undoubtedly saw this to be true and sent us after better prey.'

Still Gilly backed away through the forest, trying to follow their voices while searching for a tree with lower branches.

'Come now, fellows,' he said. 'It is ridiculous that we hunt each other like this. I mean, we're practically family – we should be sharing a bottle of wine and telling each other tall tales. In fact, I know of an excellent tavern in Sejeend, secluded, with a magnificent fire and a goodly choice of ales . . .'

'Your prattling wearies me,' said one of the rivenshades. 'It will be a pleasure to cut out your tongue.'

But Gilly made no reply. With careful quiet motions, he had climbed a particular tree and was crawling out on to a leafy branch as one of the cowled rivenshades crept towards it, stealthy and oblivious. He waited until the last moment them slammed him into the ground and savagely skewered him through the back twice.

But after the second blow, the rivenshade twisted under him as if unhurt, throwing him off to roll on to his back. There was not a spot or streak of blood on the rivenshade's clothing as he sprang to a crouch, dagger poised for the lunge, face bright with glee. Gilly struggled to bring his sword round but as the hooded man drew back for a slashing blow something large and dark came crashing out of the undergrowth up to the right. In a rushing blur it bore down on the rivenshade, snatched him off his feet and carried on into the forest. There was a shriek of agony cut short, and Gilly felt a little dizzy as he scrambled to his feet, alert to his surroundings.

Warily he followed the trail of broken vegetation left by the mystery benefactor. He had noticed few details, a black and green pebbled hide, a muscular torso and what might have been large, folded wings, none of which sparked any recollection. Then from up ahead came a gasp, a thud and a grunt . . . And a stream of memories poured into his mind. The dizziness struck again but passed as swiftly, leaving him with knowledge and the memory of the last time had seen such a muscular, winged creature. As Gilly stepped into the small clearing the Daemonkind was sitting on the leafy ground, leaning against a bare rock. One of the rivenshades was impaled by the neck to a nearby tree with his dagger, while the other lay full length and face up beside the Daemonkind, dagger jutting from his chest. The creature raised its great reptilian head and regarded Gilly with amber eyes.

'The man Cordale,' it said. 'I saw your memories seep out of these two when I slew them with their own blades. I trust you are now more yourself.'

'Enough to recognise your race, ser,' Gilly said as boldly as he could. 'How is it that you recognise me?'

'We were travelling companions once, for a short period,' said the Daemonkind. 'I am Orgraaleshenoth, prince of the Israganthir.'

Gilly tightened his grip on his sword, futile though he knew it would be against one such as this.

'Do you intend to send me flying across the lands again?' he said. 'If so, there are a few towns in west Cabringa that I have never seen—'

'Hear me, Cordale – my allegiance is not as it was, and I have suffered wounds at the hands of my people accordingly. And know this – your friend Keren Asherol is here in this realm and she has the Staff of the Void in her possession . . .' The Daemonkind paused and got slowly to his feet, uttering a groan as he did so. 'We must seek out the mage Bardow and inform him of this.

He is with an army from Besh-Darok which is following your trail . . .'

'But I'm supposed to be watching over the girl Alael,' Gilly said.

'The Earthmother vessel?' Orgraaleshenoth shook his head. 'Neither you nor I have the power to contain her – that is a task for others.'

'This is very true,' he said. 'So – shall we retrace my steps to meet the Besh-Darok army or wait here for them?'

'Waiting here would be to invite peril – once the Earthmother's influence has waned the forest will revert to its master's will.'

Gilly sheathed his blade and regarded the two dead rivenshades. 'Yes – I don't think I want to be around to see what he does with these.'

The hills were made of dust and the dust was fine, grey and cold. It rose in swirls and veils on the slightest breeze and puffed up from their horses' hoofs to cake their clothing and filter into weapon scabbards and mouths. Suviel made Byrnak and Atroc wind spare pieces of garments around their mounts' jaws and nostrils, since they were choking on the dust, and also wipe it away from their animals' eyes as often as possible.

Their passage through the hills lasted less than two hours but it felt far longer. Shaking and beating their cloaks and robes once they reached the other side dislodged some but not all of the dust. And Suviel insisted that they pressed on so garments were replaced and on they rode.

The ash-white plain was warm and dry and seemed to be composed of small bone fragments. Suviel had examined a handful of it and, frowning, wondered if this was real bone or just some kind of pulverised stone. When asked, Byrnak only shrugged and said:

'This is *his* domain – it has no meaning for me.'

Less than an hour later they drew close to the lower slopes of Hewn Mountain. It was a little warmer and there was a faint sound in the air, like a high continuous note, like a voice yet not quite like a voice. As they followed Byrnak around the foot of the mountain towards the entrance, past massive fallen shards of stone, the sound grew and became strangely pleasing to the ear.

At last the entrance to Hewn Mountain gaped jaggedly before them, the end point of a darkened road which ran arrow-straight out across the plain. Suviel brought them to a halt before it and turned to Byrnak.

'I can feel the power of the Wellsource beating against my mind,' she said. 'Most of my other-senses are closed to me and I cannot tell if any guardian waits within. Can you?'

Byrnak gave her a look of hollow dread. 'I can feel nothing. *Nothing.*'

Dismayed but not showing it, she turned to Atroc.

'What might a seer see?'

The old Mogaun set his lips in a line, frowned and closed his eyes. Then he cocked his head as if listening, opened his eyes and smiled.

'We are being watched,' he said. 'There are two of them.'

Suviel nodded grimly and turned back to Byrnak.

'We'll continue on foot,' she said. 'Lead the way.'

Resignedly, he did so, with Atroc at his side and Suviel following with the packhorse. The passageway had a floor of rough black marble and sloped down into the heart of the mountain. Its grey walls reared up not to a ceiling but to tall, fanglike towers and crags, open to the skies. The high sound was louder, the air warm and sharp with the taste of stone.

Then, when they were halfway down the corridor a stocky figure clad in dark green garments stepped out from concealment and crossed his arms before him. It was Coireg Mazaret. Suviel felt a rush of foreboding as she recalled how he had been possessed.

'Greetings, Crevalcor,' Byrnak said. 'Such an unexpected surprise to meet you in this place . . .'

Coireg, smiling sardonically, gave a little bow and further down another figure emerged, tall, hairless and garbed in long, grey robes.

'Ah, and the devoted Obax, too' Byrnak went on. 'What, I wonder, brings you both . . . ?'

The man Byrnak addressed as Crevalcor unfolded his arms. Silent emerald flame wreathed his hands. Byrnak stepped aside to cower against the wall, while Atroc moved to one side.

'A pleasing end to your charade, Byrnak,' Crevalcor said, shifting his gaze to Suviel as he started walking towards her. 'And more pleasing by far to meet an enemy of our master who also happens to be an adept, or what passes for one amongst these enfeebled adversaries.'

'And you are?' she said with as much disdain as she could muster while concentrating on a cluster of thought-cantos.

He laughed out loud. 'I am Crevalcor of the First-Woken, and the bringer of your death.'

Suviel unveiled her shielding thought-cantos even as his hands came up, each finger spilling forth a dazzling tendril of power. But even with the Crystal Eye's enhancement of her abilities she knew that she could only resist this assault of raw Wellsource fire for a short time. Ten incandescent tendrils probed and flared and burrowed into the barriers she had erected, while the grinning Crevalcor watched her with blazing eyes from a few feet away.

There was only one option left to her. She reached into one of the packhorse's bundles and dragged out the melded sword, still in its scabbard. Crevalcor laughed at the sight but when she cast aside the scabbard, revealing the glowing, silver-green blade, the smile froze on his lips and he turned as if to run. But Suviel was faster, lunging forward to strike him in the side . . .

Bellowing in agony and fear, he fell back against the passage wall, wrenching the sword's hilt from her grasp. Suviel could see the vague outlines of something spectral shifting around him as he sank to his knees. But then fury twisted his face and a gout of blazing green fire burst from his mouth and flew at her. The remains of her thought-canto barrier absorbed most of the attack but some still reached her.

A web of pain lashed through her body and she cried out as she fell to the marble floor. She could not feel her right leg and her right arm was weak and trembling. Despite her dizziness she could hear someone sobbing and muttering through tears, 'So sorry, Ikarno, I'm sorry . . . forgive me, please . . . so sorry, so sorry . . .'

The spirit of Crevalcor of the First-Woken was gone and Coireg Mazaret had finally returned to his own body.

Suddenly, Suviel was aware of footsteps approaching.

Struggling upright on her good arm she looked up to see the Acolyte Obax coming to a halt nearby. Pale eyes in a gaunt face surveyed them both.

'To overcome one of the First-Woken, and expel his spirit from a host . . .' The Acolyte gave a low, throaty laugh. 'That requires an unshakeable strength of purpose, not to mention cunning and an unusual weapon.' A booted toe nudged the hilt of the melded sword, pushing it aside, as his long-fingered hands took on an emerald aura. 'Your only mistake was in not bringing stronger servants—'

'Torturer!' shrieked a voice quivering with fury.

It was Coireg Mazaret, his wide, unblinking eyes fixed on the Acolyte, his entire form drenched in Wellsource radiance, its glaucous potency shining from every pore in his enraged face. At first, Suviel thought he was slowly getting to his feet then she realised that he was actually rising into the air.

'You were the one!' Coireg went on. '*You* and those Shadowkings, pouring pain into my thoughts then . . . then putting your servants in my head – *my head!*'

'Hold your tongue, *cur* – you are in the presence of a Lord of the Nightbrothers . . .'

Coireg's only response was an incoherent cry as he flew across the passageway. Obax unleashed a bolt of emerald power but it was absorbed by Coireg's bright aura. Then his hands were about Obax's neck and the pair swirled and wrestled and clawed at one another for a few moments before Coireg rose higher, dragging the Acolyte up off his feet.

Suviel watched the two struggling forms diminish into the heights and sweep away out of sight, and she wondered at a fate that could remove her enemies yet leave her crippled. Powerless, she could not do what had to be done . . .

'Atroc,' she said. 'Atroc . . .'

'My lady,' he said, crouching beside her.

'Atroc, is there anyone else?'

A pause. 'No – I can feel no one else.'

'Good,' she said, relieved. 'First, help me over to the wall so that I can lean against something.'

Once this was accomplished, Suviel could sit straighter and nurse her weakened arm in her left.

'I have a task for you,' she told Atroc.

The old Mogaun gave her a narrow look. 'Is there any hazard in this task?'

'It may cost you your life,' she said.

'Hmm, an interesting offer – what would my part of the bargain entail?'

'On the packhorse is a bag containing two small caskets,' Suviel said. 'Inside them are the Crystal Eye and the Motherseed, both of which have to be carried into the Wellsource itself. The bearer will probably not survive exposure to such raw power.'

'Then let me be the bearer,' said Byrnak.

'Why?' she said. 'Why would you want to do this?'

The big man's face was lined with fear and exhaustion yet a kind of sombre resolve lay in his gaze.

'If anyone's death should be the price for defeating the Lord of this place, that death should be mine.'

Suviel sighed, silently cursing her helpless frame, then glanced at Atroc who nodded.

'He speaks truthfully, lady.'

'Very well – take the talismans from their caskets and carry them in one of the saddlebags. Take the sword with you . . . and Atroc will accompany you . . .'

As the old Mogaun shrugged and Byrnak dug through the packhorse's bundles, she whispered a brief prayer to fate and the Void, seeking comfort if not intervention.

The sword felt right in his hand as he strode down the open passage with the heavy saddlebag slung over his shoulder. At his side Atroc, the Mogaun seer, had to scurry along to keep up with him while asking a series of irritating questions.

Before them the chamber at the heart of Hewn Mountain came into view and he slowed, hesitancy creeping through his thoughts once more. He could see pale reflections of that rich viridian glow in polished marble surfaces and the hesitancy turned into fear. What if he was seized and possessed again?

'Have you given your blade a name, ser Byrnak?' asked the old seer.

He looked round, his thoughts thrown into disarray.

'Why, no . . .'

'All swords should have a name,' Atroc said with a grin. 'Especially this one, heh?'

Byrnak looked down at the weapon, considering the heavy simplicity of its hilt and the shimmering silver-green surface of its yard-long blade.

This is what freed me from illusions and domination, he thought. *This brought me the reality of pain and suffering and made me see what I have wrought . . .*

'I will call it "Truth",' he said. 'For it cuts through lies.'

He set off again, fears gone. A dozen or more paces on he entered the chamber of the Wellsource. Huge vertical shards of rock encircled it, their looming darkness adding to the shadows, while the light of the Wellsource shone from the roughly carved fane that sat at the centre. Strange black pillars and slabs formed a square around it and as Byrnak approached one of the gaps, a voice rang out from beyond it.

'Ah, at last, brother! Not a moment too soon!'

Emerald radiance bathed all within the pillared square, the marble floor, the rough cone of the fane, and the Shadowking Kodel who stood next to a seated statue seemingly made from silver. As Byrnak went over he heard an intake of breath from Atroc, who was watching from the pillars.

'Tauric!'

Kodel gave a hawkish smile, and Byrnak noticed that the statue lacked an arm.

'My original intention was to merge my friend here and Tauric together and use him to explore the Void. But now that Besh-Darok and its allies have worked so hard to bring together the three Talismans – the three Gifts – there's no need.'

'I have two of them here.' Byrnak said. 'Where is the third?'

'Oh, it should arrive before long,' Kodel said casually. 'Now, if you carry those baubles up into the Wellsource, not only will you advance our cause, you may also recover some of your powers . . .'

Byrnak stared at him, hand still tightly gripping the hilt of the sword he had named Truth.

'Then I had best be about it,' he said, moving to the fane of the Wellsource and mounting its shallow steps, then pausing on the second. 'Ah, brother, would you look after my blade?'

'Gladly.'

Byrnak made to hand Truth to Kodel hilt first but as the Shadowking came within range he calmly, swiftly, drew back and ran him through with it. Kodel let out a shattering cry of agony and, as he staggered backwards, Byrnak pulled the sword out of him and saw that there was not a trace of blood on the blade. But Kodel was now on his back, writhing, convulsing as a ghostly, blood red wraith struggled and fought to tear itself free of him. Byrnak turned back to the flowing, swirling brightness of the Wellsource, took the Crystal Eye and the Motherseed from the bag which he laid on the top step beside the sword Truth. Then he stepped into the emerald roar—

His mind, his ruined mind, struggled to understand: a voice, a river, a fist, a fanged jaw, a hammer, a sea of desire, a storm of blood, an army of mountains, all howling, drowning, crushing, grinding and beating him on an anvil of fire—

Some linkage between mind and body failed.

Byrnak's legs went from under him and he toppled sideways on to the fane and rolled down its side. But his hands remained faithful, clutching the talismans to his chest as he fell . . . But he could only feel one of them as he came to rest, the Crystal Eye, round and smooth. Cracking open his eyes he looked down and saw the Motherseed, suspended within the Crystal Eye.

'You have it – *you*!'

Holding the combined talismans to his chest, he pushed himself up on his other hand. Off to one side, leaning against a pillar and breathing heavily, was one of the Daemonkind. Yet in size it was diminutive and its head was small, almost humanlike.

'Where's Suviel?' the Daemonkind said plaintively.

'Who are you?' he asked.

The Daemonkind gave him a dark look and staggered across to lean over him. In one hand he noticed that the creature carried a small wrapped bundle.

'Don't you know me, Byrnak?' it said dangerously. 'Don't you recognise your sweet Keren?'

Mazaret grasped Gilly's arm and clapped him on the shoulder, jubilant to see him.

'When you decide to go sight-seeing, you don't do things by halves!' he said.

Gilly laughed. 'When I find any sights worth seeing, I shall be quick to announce them!'

Then Gilly introduced his companion, a tall, gaunt man in long, dark robes. Mazaret's eyes widened when his friend told him that this Raal Haidar was actually a prince of the Daemonkind. He considered questioning the 'man' himself, then decided to leave that to Bardow. Instead he gave Gilly a summary of events since crossing into the Realm of Dusk.

'After leaving Suviel's party, we followed your trail along that gully for over an hour,' he said. 'Then some of my outriders reported a column of near a thousand horsemen riding to intercept us further along one of the gully paths leading up to the higher ground, and sent another thousand of the lighter cavalry, mostly Mogaun warriors, on ahead to catch them in a pincer.'

'Did it work?' Gilly said.

Mazaret rocked his head judiciously. 'We caught a lot of them in the trap, but a good number escaped. Turned out they were a spearhead force for an army led by an old friend of mine – Azurech.'

Gilly swore. 'And how far off is he?'

'Normally, I'd say that a spearhead rides no more than two hours ahead of the main force, but these aren't exactly normal circumstances . . . Hold, what's this?'

A scout came riding up to the two men and threw back his brown cowl. 'My lord – we've found her!'

'Where?' Mazaret said sharply.

'We followed the edge of the grey forest right to where it stops at the foot of a sheer scarp, and heard some muffled roaring from beyond it. We rode back, then up and along the scarp to where it joined a ridge. From there we looked down into a wide valley and there was . . . Well, it looked a bit like a woman, and she was fighting monsters that came out of the ground—'

'You'll lead us there,' Mazaret said, turning to beckon over his personal ostler and bawl out commands. 'And have horses brought for these two men.'

In a long column, the Besh–Darok army rode with a great thundering of hoofs along the scarp to the ridge and spread itself along it while Mazaret stared at the sight below. The valley was flat and wide and desolate and its other side was a line of uneven, rocky hills. But there, on the floor of the valley, a glowing golden figure contended with three huge, lizard-like creatures which had burst up out of the ground itself. Mazaret turned to Bardow who rode by his left side, but the archmage frowned.

'That is most certainly the Earthmother, my lord,' he said. 'She is using the Body of Light. But these creatures I do not know . . .'

'They are the stone fiends,' said Yasgar from Mazaret's right. 'Dread beasts from old tribal legends. I never imagined that I would see them.'

Below, the Earthmother sent a spear of golden energy into the side of one of the stone fiends. It bellowed and collapsed into a long mound of rubble and dust, but then the ground erupted as another thrust itself out of the earth to do battle. Then suddenly the Earthmother uttered a piercing shriek of rage and the golden radiance of her form vanished.

'She's done it!' Bardow said. 'Suviel's joined the Eye and the Seed . . .'

'And that's Alael down there, man!' Gilly cried. 'Those things'll kill her—'

But in the next moment, the three stone fiends froze in their tracks and crumbled back into the ground amid great clouds of dust. Then gigantic, cruel laughter echoed across the valley, across the sunless, grey-blue sky.

'*Give me the Staff!*' said the towering, grinding voice. '*I will have it!*'

As Mazaret despatched three of his scouts on fast horses to retrieve Alael, figures began to appear all along the crests and dips of the valley wall opposite, at first hundreds, then more and more spreading wider. Some yards to Mazaret's left there was movement as the gaunt Raal Haidar guided his horse to the front rank and held a translucent staff aloft.

'It is not yours to have!' he bellowed. 'You will have to take it – if you can!'

More laughter, like low menacing thunder.

'*As you wish . . .*'

Suddenly a group of winged figures appeared in the air above the opposite valley wall, hovering and wheeling. Behind Mazaret, gasps and fearful mutters rippled through the ranks of his army.

'Daemonkind . . .' Bardow whispered.

'How can we fight them?' Mazaret said, aghast at this turn of events.

'I don't . . .' Bardow began.

'We must try, Lord Mazaret,' said Raal Haidar, holding out the translucent staff. 'This is an imitation – the real Staff of the Void is being taken by Keren Asherol to the shrine at the heart of the Hewn Mountains. Combined with the Crystal Eye and the Motherseed, it may be able to destroy the Wellsource and the Lord of Twilight.'

Just then, a scout hurried up on foot.

'My lords, my lords – a mounted force some ten thousands strong is approaching our rearguard. They have already sent forth heralds calling for our surrender.'

'Azurech,' Mazaret said, massaging a sudden ache in his side. He saw that the scouts had returned with an unconscious Alael, while across the valley enemy forces were now spilling down into the valley. 'We cannot stay here – we have to use our strength . . .' He beckoned Yasgar, Yarram and his other captains closer. 'We'll have the knights in the centre with a wing either side, except that the right one will be a feint—'

He was interrupted by a strange bell-like sound which filled the valley for a moment and made everyone pause. Then a dazzling pinpoint of light appeared along the valley to his right, and widened, becoming almost unwatchable. Then it was abruptly gone, revealing what to Mazaret's eyes seemed to be a herd of pure white horses, but as his vision re-accustomed itself he was assailed by a sense of stunned recognition.

'Witchhorses!' he said.

'By my ancestors, it's impossible!' cried Yasgur. 'They are being led by Tauric . . .'

Mazaret looked round at Bardow. 'You told me he was dead!'

'Atroc said he saw him die,' Bardow said, ' but there was no body found . . .'

'They're coming!' someone cried nearby.

Like the breaking of a dam, the Lord of Twilight's horde was now pouring down into the valley, its bellicose mass roar sounding clear and terrible in the still air. Mazaret gave out the command for every flag and standard to be unfurled, then looked round at the ranks of horsemen with his sword raised above his head. For a moment, the eyes of thousands were on him, then he roared out, 'For our homelands!' and dug his heel to his mount's flanks. The horse leaped forward and the downhill charge began.

Chapter Twenty-eight

Lo! For a bloody dream unfolds,
Ancient, strong and cruel,
From the embers of razed forests,
From the desolate ruins of cities,
From the aching pit of time.

The Black Saga Of Culri Moal, xii, 2

From the poolside of the witchhorse sanctuary, a wide track curved away through the mist-pale woods.

Before they had gone far, the track split into three and Tauric paused. Ghazrek, Shandareth and the rest of the witchhorses likewise halted.

Which one do we follow? he asked the Fathertree spirit.

It matters little – choose one.

He gazed at all three, pondered the right hand for a moment then shrugged and veered off along the left.

Will we reach Besh-Darok in time to help? he said. *Or are we going to arrive days after the battle?*

Time as you understand it works differently in the Void and especially so in the Witchhorses' Sanctuary. It may be that the battle for Besh-Darok has already been resolved, but be assured that we shall have much to do on our return . . .

Tauric expected snow-covered fields and icy air but when they emerged from the hazy mist it was into a wide, arid valley. Two great armies faced each other across the flat cracked ground with winged creatures hovering above the larger of them.

'Where is this?' Ghazrek said. 'This is not Besh-Darok – it isn't even Khatris . . .'

'We know this place,' said the witchhorse Shandareth who faced Tauric and knelt before him. 'You had best climb upon my back, King of Besh-Darok. We are in the domain of the Lord of Twilight and a mighty battle looms.'

'I can see the banners of Yasgur,' Ghazrek cried. 'And Gordag and Welgarak—'

'And there is the standard of Besh-Darok,' Tauric said.

Then the Lord of Twilight's army began its chaotic charge with a thunderous roar that made the ground tremble. Moments later the allies careered down from their ridge in close held formations. Now sitting on Shandareth's back, Tauric uttered a wordless battle cry and the entire witchhorse herd surged forward.

Although some sensation and strength was returning to her limbs, Suviel still needed Atroc's help to traverse the remainder of the passageway. Leaning heavily on the Mogaun seer she at last entered the hollowed out chamber at the heart of the mountain, where fangs of rock rose like towers all around it, and pillars and vertical slabs formed a square at its centre. She saw the pulsating glow of the Wellsource and felt its hungry song through her flesh and bone. And heard a woman's voice ragged with weariness and distress, shouting, berating.

'. . . and Tauric is dead, and Nerek is dead and all because of you!'

With Atroc she limped between two pillars and tried to take in all she saw – the silvered statue sitting on a stool, the curled up whimpering figure of Kodel, the strange half-human, half-Daemonkind creature, who was reviling and ranting at Byrnak as he sat with the Crystal Eye in his hands . . .

'Keren . . .'

The Daemonkind paused and looked up at Suviel, then stumbled over, holding out a slender, cloth-wrapped object.

'Please, Suviel, make me human again,' Keren said. 'Orgraaleshenoth said the Staff could do this.'

'It may, Keren.' Then; 'Byrnak – are you . . . *aware*?'

He looked up with a sombre introspective gaze then stood, came over and handed her the Crystal Eye with the Motherseed held captive within it.

'I have become aware,' he said, 'of many things and many places.'

With that, he strode away through the pillars to the passageway leading out and was gone.

'Curious,' said Atroc. 'Neither of you tried to stop him.'

'There is no power in him now,' Suviel said. 'Only visions.'

Keren and Atroc helped her over to the fane of the Wellsource where she sat on the steps and considered the three talismans for a moment. With the ovoid Motherseed suspended within its substance, the Crystal Eye now looked very like an eye and while motes of light floated up and down the Staff of the Void its headstone remained a dull, black sphere. Suviel smiled and casually tapped the Crystal Eye with the Staff.

The Eye distorted and twisted and in an eyeblink was gone. Keren and Atroc cried out in shock . . . then Suviel held up the Staff of the Void for them to see that its headstone had been transformed into the Crystal Eye with the Motherseed at its centre. Suviel could feel how the powers of each interlocked with each and multiplied them all. She only needed to glance at Keren to see exactly how Orgraaleshenoth had used the powers of his realm to alter her form, and it took only a thought to unlock that sorcery and let the reversal begin.

Another thought wiped the pain and weakness from her own body and a further notion sent the catatonic Kodel into a deep healing slumber. Breathing deeply, she stood and smiled at Atroc and Keren.

'Now I must enter the Wellsource,' she said, 'and use the complete talisman to destroy it—'

But at that moment a voice boomed out: 'That cannot be.'

Into the Wellsource shrine stepped a large, dog-like creature, followed by a wide-eyed and fearful Tauric who grinned suddenly when he caught sight of Atroc and Suviel. But Atroc was astonished.

'Majesty – you are alive!'

'So it would seem,' Tauric said, then looked at the dog creature, who Suviel knew to be the spirit of the Fathertree. 'All I did was walk forward along the middle branch – where are the witchhorses?'

'Even now they are fighting for all their worth,' the Fathertree spirit said, gazing at Suviel.

'Yes,' she said. 'Battle has been joined – I can feel it. But why do you delay me? The Wellsource must be quenched, extinguished.'

'But not by you – your attunement to both the Lesser Power and the Crystal Eye will prevent you using the full potential of the talisman trinity.'

A shocked realisation struck her. 'And because Tauric is not attuned to any of the powers, he is the one who has to use the talisman Staff.'

The spirit of the Fathertree sat on his haunches and seemed to smile. 'Precisely.'

'But I know nothing of the Wellsource,' Tauric said. 'Or the Crystal Eye or . . . or the Staff. How could I use them to destroy the Wellsource?'

'That is not what the talisman trinity is for,' the dog-thing said. 'Gods are the living dreams of the Void, and only a dream can destroy a dream.'

Understanding at last, Suviel nodded sadly and held the talisman trinity out to Tauric who hesitantly accepted it.

'It will guide and protect you as you travel down the Wellsource,' the Fathertree spirit told him. 'It is a long journey into the depths of the Void and in its uttermost depths you will find, and know you've found, a place for the seeding of power and the beginning of a new dream.'

'I am ready,' Tauric said.

The spirit then looked at Suviel. 'There are unknown dangers at those depths – will you go with him?'

Suviel nodded. 'I shall.'

'Approach the Wellsource together.'

Suviel and Tauric walked side by side over to the roughly-carved, conical fane then climbed the steps.

'May Fate's hand be open,' Atroc said.

'Farewell,' said Keren.

On the rushing, dazzling brink of the Wellsource with its voice weaving and swirling around them, Tauric said, 'I'm so very scared.'

'Good,' said Suviel, tightly grasping his hand while her other hand was in her side pocket, holding Mazaret's ivory book leaf. 'I wouldn't want to be the only one.'

Together they stepped into the coruscating torrent of power.

In the thick of the battle, a gash in his forehead oozing blood into his left eye, and with half his armour torn away, Mazaret yet knew they were prevailing. Despite the shattering din of the fighting he could see how the huge undisciplined horde recoiled and panicked as the Besh-Darok knights and the Mogaun warriors charged them again and again. Many of their leaders lay in the carnage of the first onslaught, during which the witchhorses had wrought such deadly havoc.

And there, overhead, the great white horses were soaring above the main press of the enemy which had been hemmed in on three sides. Plumes of white freezing vapour drifted downwards . . . and the enemy ranks went wild with panic, their retreat quickly becoming a stampeding, shrieking rout. Pursuit became bloody slaughter, and Mazaret and Yasgur had to go after groups of their own battle-maddened men to get them to fall back to their rallying standards . . .

Yet even as they began obeying the repeated orders, bellowed at them by captains and serjeants, Mazaret felt a breeze pluck at his ripped cloak and his hair. Turning, he saw that a wall of mist had fallen across the far end of the valley during the battle.

Bardow came riding up, exhaustion in his face.

'Best rally everyone, Ikarno,' he said, nodding at the hazy, towering barrier. 'There's worse to come – I can feel it.'

Then the breeze picked up and the wall of mists began to fray and come apart. Tauric and the witchhorse Shondareth landed nearby and trotted over.

'What can we expect next?' he said.

The next moment answered his question as the rising wind tore aside the misty veil to reveal a direful, reason-defying sight – a gigantic, towering citadel which stretched up unbelievably high, floor after floor of battlements and parapets and turrets, some of which Mazaret thought he recognised.

'Impossible!' said Bardow. 'It should collapse under its own weight!'

Then he saw it – the vast edifice was composed of those towers that the Shadowkings had employed, Gorla, Keshada, the Drumkeep of Rauthaz, the Red Tower of Casall, and others piled one on another, a supreme demonstration of arrogant power. Horns began to blare from its high walls, gongs to sound and drums to pound as gates opened all along the foot of the colossal tower and the Army of Twilight rode forth in their tens of thousands.

From a pebbly hillock Mazaret saw blue-armoured warriors astride giant war-wolves while trident-wielding handlers guided ferocious looking dogs the size of horses. There were spearmen in spiked chariots, scythe warriors riding green, six-limbed reptiles, and fur-clad savages with great clubs balanced on their shoulders. Mazaret knew that to order his men to battle against this vast host was the maddest folly, but he looked round at his captains and allies and saw only a grim, unbending resolve.

Then another blast of horns caught his attention and he turned to see a huge figure emerging from the gates. Towering head and chest above his tallest warriors, the Lord of Twilight was garbed in barbaric splendour, long fur cloak over his chainmail, heavy hacking blade clasped in his hand, and a rude helm with downturned horns sat above brutal, gleeful features.

Mazaret snatched a banner from his bearers, bellowed a battle cry which was taken up by the riders rallying to him. Then, with Yasgur at his side, and the witchhorses soaring overhead, he led the charge.

They were hopelessly outnumbered. The enemy was a surging sea of blades and death that absorbed their every charge and probing attack. Acts of heroism were innumerable, some scarcely believable even to those who witnessed them, but deaths were final and unanswerable.

Yarram, Lord Commander of the Knights of the Fathertree, died before his men, throat torn out by a war-wolf as he speared its rider. Welgarak, chieftain of the Black Moon clan, died from a cluster of arrows, surrounded by dead foes. Yasgur died trying to get through the cordon of black knights that surrounded the Lord of Twilight, crushed by mace blows. Bardow died in a circle of scythe blades and when Tauric tried to get to him on Shondareth, three Daemonkind swooped upon him and snatched him from the witchhorse's back.

His bloody, lifeless body fell to the ground away from the battle but vanished soon after.

Bleeding from numerous wounds, Mazaret gathered the remaining few hundred of his men on a low hill near the valley wall, thinking to make a final stand. The ranks of the enemy were reforming some distance away and Mazaret was checking his weapons and trying to ignore the pain in his side. Off to one side, Alael sat leaning against a standing stone, face buried in her hands. Then someone cried:

'He's gone!'

Dashing sweat from his brow he turned to gaze out at the fiendish throng, searching for that huge, horn-helmed figure. But the lookout was right – the Lord of Twilight was no longer on the field of battle. And as he surveyed the enemy's endless numbers and noticed their growing disarray and confusion, the ground suddenly trembled underfoot. Out in the valley, a chorus of moans and wails went up from the Army of Twilight. The sky darkened and a chill wind sprang up. The ground shook again, a brief sharp movement that was still no preparation for the violent quake that struck moments later.

Men and horse were knocked over and in seconds the hillside was a scene of chaos, horses screaming and losing their footing, men shouting in fear or pain. Mazaret was trying to stand when he noticed that everyone around him was becoming pale and ghostlike. Out in the valley, the horde had become a sighing mass of spectral forms and the immense tower was fading from view. Another landscape filled one half of the sky, a place of white mountains and bleached ground, while an eerie, curved region of shattered masonry, like the ruins of some vast, cylindrical palace, loomed over the other half. The valley itself tilted and for a moment, it seemed that those two sky-borne tracts would descend and collide with the Realm of Dusk.

But they drew back and receded into the darkness, just as the valley began to grow thin and ethereal, as its outlines blurred and others emerged. In the blackening mantle of the sky, stars began to appear as the last fleeting hints of the Realm of Dusk dissolved and Mazaret gave himself up to oblivion.

When he woke it was to the sharp caress of a cold morning breeze. Sitting up to a chorus of aches, he found himself on a damp hillside in the shelter of an overhanging tree. Across from him was another hill. Snow streaked the steep slopes of both and made pure white the mountain peak which reared beyond. From the bushes and trees he knew that he was somewhere in northern Khatris. He knew also that he was utterly alone.

Hunger gripped him. With improvised sling and spear, he managed to hunt and kill for food as he started walking eastwards. Three days later he reached a small fishing village on the east coast and found that he was nearly two hundred miles north of Besh-Darok. The village elders told him of how several days ago the sky had been rent by portents, visions and scenes of terrible slaughter. When he asked if they had seen any other strangers since then, they dolefully shook their heads.

With the little silver in his belt, Mazaret bought a small bow and a heavy woollen cloak then set off south along the coast road. Four days of walking left his boots cracked and wearing through at the sole, and he was trying to line the insides with thin pieces of bark when a group of hooded horsemen slowed and approached him. At once he snatched up his spear and backed away.

'Hold there, old father, we mean no harm,' said the leader who doffed his cowl. 'We only wish to ask if you've seen any strangers or soldiers north of these parts.'

But Mazaret was staring at him, almost trembling with relief and recognition.

'Kance,' he said hoarsely, aware of his seven days of stubble. 'It's me, Mazaret.'

Captain Kance, Mazaret's former Captain of the March, regarded him with a frown. Then the eyes widened and he scrambled down off his horse to bend his knee.

'My lord, you're alive! Please, forgive me . . .'

'Come now, lad,' Mazaret said. 'On your feet.'

Kance straightened, gazing at Mazaret in awe that became sorrowful. 'My lord, do you know of the Emperor?'

Mazaret sighed. 'Keep no hope in your heart, Kance. I saw him die with my own eyes.'

'Aye, my lord. His body was found near the Kings Gate Pass. It still lies in state at a shrine nearby – we could take you there if you wish.'

Mazaret breathed in deeply, then exhaled long and wearily.

'Yes, I would see him.'

As they rode south and west, Mazaret learned much of what had transpired after that final cataclysmic battle. Weapons and pieces of armour fell from the air across wide tracts of land, along with the living and the dead (and their horses). The Shadowkings' citadels, Gorla and Keshada, had collapsed in on themselves as the ground beneath them caved in. The black, encircling walls also cracked apart and dropped into a lengthening chasm which, inevitably, reached the shore.

At the same time, another huge fissure more than a hundred yards across opened in the ground by the Girdle Hills, extending west from the wall-swallowing chasm, passing through the Kings Gate and north all the way across Khatris towards Rauthaz in Yularia. Water surged in from the Gulf of Brykon, surrounding Besh-Darok and its environs with a great moat. The waters also rushed northwards and met torrents hurtling southwards, resulting in floods throughout central Khatris. There were also rumours that Trevada and the city of Casall were no more.

Such news seemed scarcely credible, but when Kance insisted that he seen the aftermaths of these cataclysms with his own eyes Mazaret listened with sombre astonishment, grieving privately over this destruction of the world he had known.

Two days later they reached the shrine. It was a pillared, ivy-wound building nestling in the lee of two great agathons, its outer and inner entrances well guarded. Now shaven and attired in a fresh uniform, Mazaret followed Kance past gate and door to the inner chamber. On a flower-strewn bier Tauric's body lay, garbed in sky blue robes, the pale perfection of his features testament to some mortician's art, and the efficacy of whatever spell had been used to suspend the corruption of his flesh.

'I salute you, my Emperor,' he murmured. 'May your spirit find peace.'

As he bowed his head there were footsteps as someone entered behind him. Turning he saw it was Alael, dressed in a high-throated wine-dark gown over which a brown cloak was draped.

'My lord,' she said, smiling sadly. 'I am overjoyed to see you safely returned.'

'Lady, I live, yet my heart is burdened with grief and unresolved worry . . .' He sighed. 'Has there been any word of the mage, Suviel?'

'Atroc claims that he saw her and Tauric enter the Wellsource together . . .'

He frowned. 'But I saw Tauric die in battle, in the Realm of Dusk . . .'

'He also died during the battle for Besh-Darok,' Alael said. 'Atroc witnessed that too. He believes that some other power was involved.'

Perplexed, Mazaret glanced at the still form on the bier. 'And what of Byrnak? What does he have to say?'

'He claims that he left the Wellsource fane after Keren Asherol's arrival and thus saw nothing further.' Alael grew grave. 'Keren . . . did not survive. Her body was found lying in a brook quite near here yesterday.' Her eyes grew distant, brimming with tears. 'She looked so peaceful . . .'

'So there has been no sign of Suviel, alive or dead,' Mazaret said, unable to conceal his despair.

'I do not know if it has meaning for you,' Alael said as she reached into one of her cloak's pockets. 'But when Tauric's body was discovered, this was in his hand.'

And she held out to him the ivory book leaf which he had given to Suviel at their last parting. But Alael was holding it with its back uppermost, and as he took it he saw that the rough surface bore an inscription which had not been there before. It read:

'*There is a price.*'

Mazaret looked at the ivory leaf, then at Alael, then the leaf again, unable to decide between hope and despair.

Epilogue

While nations snarl,
Like dogs on a leash,
This wounding knowledge,
Burns in the night.

The Black Saga Of Culri Moal, vii, 8

Gilly Cordale was ennobled in the sight of the High Conclave and made Earl of Falador. After mourning the death of Keren and the others for some time, he settled into his new role with gusto and wed a Cabringan noble's daughter who, in due course, gave birth to twin boys. 'Clearly, life has been too full of ease and comfort of late,' he was heard to remark to friends soon after.

With Tauric deceased, the High Conclave were forced to offer the throne to Alael once more, which she accepted on condition that her title would be Queen of Besh–Darok and Khatris. This was agreed and, after a tumultuous and joyful Low Coronation, and a dignified yet unifying High Coronation, Alael became the first woman to ascend the throne of Besh–Darok for over two hundred years.

At Queen Alael's insistence, a new office of Lord High Minister was ordained, a post to be decided upon by a council of electors. The first holder of the office was the former Lord Regent, Ikarno Mazaret (who would be re-elected every three years until his death at the age of 79).

★   ★   ★

After all the business of the election was over, after the congratulations, the hand-shaking, the songs and versifying, and after accepting the amulet of his new office from a smiling Queen Alael, he had to get some fresh air and be alone with his thoughts for a while. Thus Ikarno Mazaret went wandering in the flower gardens of the palace, with late afternoon sunshine warming the blooms and filling the air with their heady sweetness. He was strolling along a path between low, neatly-clipped bushes when he came upon a figure lying curled up amid a bed of melodyleaf and cup-o'-sky. At first he felt mildly annoyed, thinking it to be one of the serving girls, but as he drew closer he noticed details about the woman's garments and the greyness in her hair that made his heart pound and his thoughts race . . .

And even though he was mere feet away he doubted, until his gaze fell upon some leaves of grass clustered on her cloak. Then he saw that the leaves were arranged in letters and words . . .

Then she rolled on to her back, scattering the leaves, yawned and saw him standing there.

'Ikarno!'

He fell to his knees and embraced her.

'Suviel! We thought you had died!' Tears in his eyes, he pulled back and looked searchingly into her eyes. 'What do you remember before now?'

'I remember entering the Wellsource with Tauric then . . . a long dream of darkness . . .' She frowned and shook her head. 'Then nothing until I woke here . . .' She sat straighter and looked around her. 'Why, I'm in the Palace! Are the Shadowkings no more? Did we succeed?'

'We did, my beloved,' he said, 'but at a great cost.'

And he told her the names of the dead, and she wept to hear of so many. And as he began to tell her about all that had happened, he decided that, for the time being, he would keep to himself the message of leaves he had seen on her cloak:

'The price has been paid.'

The news of Suviel's return was widely greeted as a gift from the gods, but when Atroc learned of it he felt a faint prickling of unease. A joyous meeting with the lady mage and Lord Mazaret later that evening laid some anxieties to rest, yet the unease remained. Such that midnight found him in the small tower on the Silver Aggor, sitting cross-legged on a wooden bench, engulfed in the fumes of smouldering herbs.

Into his mind came fragments of the seeing he had soon after the battle for Scallow, the great torrent of riders that rushed across central Khatris, ending with only three who reached the gates of Besh-Darok, Byrnak, Alael and Tauric. The earlier vision had faded away at that point, but now he watched as the three figures dismounted and entered the city under a bright sun.

Yet this Besh-Darok was a centuries-old ruin, its tumbled walls and pillars half-buried in vegetation which had erupted from gardens and parks and spread everywhere. The decrepit, vine-entwined remnants of taller buildings stood over the abandoned city like sorrowful sentinels.

But even as the three intruders picked their way along an overgrown main street, clouds covered the sun and a dark mist began to seep out of the ground. The mist grew dense and black, and swirled around the three as they struggled to reach high vantage. But to no avail – the blackness swallowed them and rose to swamp the entire city . . .

Atroc awoke to a morning chill and the smell of charred herbs. His head felt clear and last night's unease seemed to have lifted, even though the vision itself seemed to make little sense. Perhaps he should ride north to that cove fort where Byrnak was being held, and ask him a few questions.

Then he laughed, suddenly remembering that he was due to meet with Gordag and the other tribal fathers this morning to decide their future.

It would have been better if I had died and you had lived, Yasgur, my prince and master. Still, we must ride whatever steed we are given.

The seer Atroc and Gordag, chieftain of the Red Claw tribe, negotiated a treaty of settlement with Besh-Darok and the restored authority in Tymora. Thus the League and Marches of the Mogaun

Tribes was established to the south and east of Arengia. Atroc himself outlived Gordag and wrote several important works, including one entitled *The High History of the Families and Clans of the Mogaun.*

The fate of the Daemonkind was veiled in mystery. Strange tales came from Casall over subsequent months, spread by travelling merchants. They told of how a crowd several hundred strong descended on the city's waterfront less than a day after the Lord of Twilight's defeat, seized four large ships and immediately weighed anchor. The accounts described them as tall, stern-faced men and women and agreed that they were not of Mogaun stock. Acolytes, some said, or Jefren weaponforgers, claimed others. But a dockside potionwife swore that as those ships' sheets caught the breeze, her charm-sight gave her a glimpse of ghostly, winged figures hauling on lines or clustered on deck . . . Then the vessels set sail into the west and were never again seen on any human shore.

Byrnak, former Warlord of Honjir, once Shadowking and host to a dark and savage god, lived for another six months. His lifeless body was found on a clifftop overlooking the Gulf of Brykon, a poisoned dagger in his chest.

The End
(To be concluded in *Shadowmasque*)

Acknowledgments

To my editor, John Jarrold, and my agent, John Parker, both of whom have, I'm certain, received training in Jedi disciplines of patience. Om, guys! To Darren, Melissa, Jessicas M. & G., and everyone at Earthlight. And to artist Steve Stone who makes sense out of my semibaked ideas.

To Dave Wingrove, whose steadfast encouragement and sheer talent is an endless source of inspiration.

To Michelle 'Cuddles' Drayton-Harold, whose wizard typing saved me a lot of time and stress (!), and to Ian Murray who provided the laptop at Easter. Yir a gent!

To Eric Brown, Bill King, Keith Brooke and Ian McDonald, whose friendship and kind words have meant such a lot over the years.

To my fellow colleagues at Vertex – there are so many of you that if I mention a few I'll offend the rest, so I'll just say hey, guys! – we're moving forward, right?

To those brave souls who helped out on this year's Mike Cobley House Move (10th Anniversary Tour) – Craig, Dave, Martin, Derek, Anne, Elsie, and Mr Salvation Army Guy!

To El Sloano and Tom, masterminds behind the Freedom Collective. To Graeme Fleming, Paisley's Prince of Prog, and to Ronnie and Katie, Ian Smith, headbangers Adrian and Spencer, and the BOC UK Online guys, Steve, Eric, Phil, Trevor, all the Andrews, Simon, and Paul fra' Yorkshire, as well as our Yankee brothers and sisters (hey there, LD, Zibe, Alma et al!)

To Michael Moore and Mark Thomas, who are saying what needs to be said.

And to the bands whose music has provided the soundtrack for months of toil – the inimitable Blue Oyster Cult, the very wonderful

ARK, Pallas, Porcupine Tree, Parallel or 90 Degrees, the awesome Nevermore, Symphony X, Mostly Autumn, Queensryche, Nightwish, RATM, Mahler, Berlioz, Holst, Tomita, Prokofiev, Berg . . . and lots more, including those purveyors of prairie metal, Hippykiller, dudes each and every one.

And to all those who are wondering where the story can go from here – well, it ain't over till it's over!

For more info go to
www.shadowkings.co.uk or www.periurban.clara.net